"A captivating novel... A heartwarming, action-packed historical romance that brings the Old West and its sexy cowboys to life. Rugged cowboys, mail-order brides, vile villains, the Old West, action, danger, romance, and love combine to give readers an enthralling story that sweeps them into the days of old. A beautiful beginning to a promising series, *Texas Mail Order Bride* is a novel you do not want to miss."

—*Romance Junkies*

Praise for *Twice a Texas Bride*

"Broday crafts a richly atmospheric Western complete with the grittiness of the frontier as well as the tenderness of blossoming love. With a touching and gentle, yet rugged and real story, Broday captures the West—and readers' hearts."

—*RT Book Reviews*

"Linda Broday is spot-on with her setting, story lines, and superbly drawn characters. *Twice a Texas Bride* is pure enjoyment."

—*Fresh Fiction*

Forever
HIS TEXAS
Bride

WITHDRAWN

LINDA
BRODAY

sourcebooks
casablanca

Published by Sourcebooks Casablanca, an imprint of Sourcebooks, Inc.
P.O. Box 4410, Naperville, Illinois 60567-4410
(630) 961-3900
Fax: (630) 961-2168
www.sourcebooks.com

Printed and bound in Canada.
MBP 10 9 8 7 6 5 4 3 2 1

Acknowledgments

Home and family mean as much to me as they do to my three brothers and their ladies in this series. We all have a fierce need to belong to someone, people who give us our identities and who will be there during the good times and bad. When we don't have that family unit, we often create our own, which is what Cooper, Rand, and Brett do. Often the bond is deepest when you're *not* blood kin.

I'm so fortunate to have family. I dedicate this book to my children Kevin, Melinda, and Lori; brother Irvin; sisters Jean, Irene, and Jan; cousin Sarah; and stepdaughters Monica, Kim, and Laura. While I won't name the rest of my clan, I haven't forgotten you. You guys always have my back. You fill my life with immense joy and have helped fill the gaping hole that Clint's and Mom's passing left. You're amazing, and I love you all!

I also wish to thank David Rabson, my masseuse and friend, who straightens the kinks out of my back, enabling me to sit at my computer, writing these stories for you.

I hope you enjoy this final book in the Bachelors of Battle Creek series. I think you'll agree I've saved the best for last. I look forward to sharing a new, exciting series soon.

One

A plan? Definitely NOT DYING. BEYOND THAT, HE didn't have one.

High on a hill, Brett Liberty lay in the short, blood-stained grass, watching the farm below. With each breath, pain shot through him like the jagged edge of a hot knife. The bullet had slammed into his back, near the shoulder blade from the feel of it.

If a plan was coming, it had better hurry. The Texas springtime morning was heating up, and the men chasing him drew ever closer. Every second spent in indecision could cost him. He had two choices: try to seek help from the family in the little valley, or run as though chased by a devil dog.

The blood loss had weakened him though. He wouldn't get far on foot. About a half mile back, Brett's pursuers had shot his horse, a faithful mustang he'd loved more than his own life. Rage rippled through his chest and throbbed in his head. They could hurt him all they wanted, but messing with his beloved horses would buy them a spot in hell.

He forced his thoughts back to his current predicament.

Through a narrowed gaze, Brett surveyed the scene below. It seemed odd that no horses stood in the corral. The farmer who was chopping wood had a rifle within easy reach. The man's wife hung freshly washed clothes up on a line to dry under the golden sunshine, while a couple of small children played at her feet. It was a tranquil day as far as appearances went.

Appearances deceived.

Help was so near yet so far away.

Brett *couldn't* seek their aid. The farmer would have that rifle in his hands before Brett made it halfway down the hill. The fact that Indian blood flowed through Brett's veins and colored his features definitely complicated things. With the Indian uprisings a few years ago fresh in everyone's minds, approaching the stranger could mean certain death.

No, he couldn't go forward. Neither could he go back.

They'd trapped him.

Why a posse dogged his trail, Brett couldn't say. He'd done nothing except take a remuda of the horses he raised to Fort Concho to sell. He could probably clear things up in two minutes if they'd just give him the opportunity. Yet the group, led by a man wearing a sheriff's star, seemed to adhere to the motto: *shoot first and ask questions of the corpse.*

He was in a hell of a mess and wished he had his brothers, Cooper Thorne and Rand Sinclair, to stand with him.

Inside his head, he heard the ticking of a clock. Whatever he did, he'd better get to it.

The family below was his only chance. Brett straightened his bloodstained shirt as best he could and removed the long feather from his black hat. Except for his knee-high moccasins, the rest of his clothing was what any man on the frontier would wear.

At last he gathered his strength and struggled to his feet. He removed a bandanna, a red one, from around his neck. On wobbly legs, he picked his way down the hill.

When the farmer saw him and started for his rifle, Brett waved the bandanna over his head. "Help! I need help. Please don't shoot. I'm unarmed."

With the rifle firmly in hand, the farmer ordered his wife and children into the house, then cautiously advanced. Brett dropped to his knees in an effort to show he posed no threat. Or maybe it was that his legs simply gave out. Either way, it must've worked—he didn't hear the sound of a bullet exploding from the weapon.

The man's shadow fell across Brett. "Who are you, and what do you want?" the farmer asked.

"I'm shot. Name's Brett Liberty. I have a horse ranch seventy miles east of here." When he started to stand, the farmer jabbed the end of the rifle into his chest. Brett saw the wisdom in staying put.

"Who shot you?"

"Don't know. Never saw them before." A bee buzzed around Brett's face.

"How do I know you didn't hightail it off the reservation? Or maybe you're an outlaw. I've heard of Indian outlaws."

Brett sighed in frustration. "I've never seen a reservation, and I assure you, I don't step outside the law. I'm respected in Battle Creek. My brother is the sheriff. If I took up outlawing ways, he'd be the first to arrest me." Likely throw him *under* the jail instead of putting him in a cell. But he didn't add that.

He glanced longingly toward the house, but the rifle barrel poking from a window told him asking for safety inside was out of the question. So was running. Their guns would cut him down before he'd gone a yard.

Maybe if he stalled, made sure he looked as unthreatening as possible and kept the man nearby, he might just make it. With a witness to the posse's actions, the sheriff might let him live. It was his only shot.

The ticking clock in Brett's head was getting louder, blocking out the buzz of the persistent bee. His pursuers would be here in a minute. His dry mouth couldn't even form spit. "Please, mister, could you at least give me some water?"

It was a gamble, but one that looked like it might pay off. Silently, the farmer backed up a step and motioned Brett toward the well with his rifle barrel.

"Thank you." Brett got to his feet and stumbled toward the water. He lowered the bucket and pulled it up, then filled a metal cup that hung nearby and guzzled the water down. He was about to refill it when horses galloped into the yard and encircled him.

"Put up your hands, or I'll shoot," a man barked, sparing an obvious glance toward the farmer.

Brett glanced up at the speaker and the shiny tin star on his leather vest. He set his empty cup on the ledge circling the well. "Your warning comes a little late, Sheriff. I would've appreciated it much earlier. Would you be so kind as to tell me what I did to warrant this arrest?"

The bearded sheriff dismounted. Hate glittered in his dark eyes, reminding Brett of others who harbored resentment for his kind. Jerking Brett's hands behind his back, the middle-aged lawman secured them with rope. "You'll know soon enough."

Ignoring the sharp pain piercing his back, Brett tried to reason. "I can clear up this misunderstanding if you'll only tell me what you think I did wrong."

No one spoke.

Brett turned to the farmer. "I'll give you five of my best horses if you'll let my brothers know where I am. You can find them in Battle Creek. Cooper Thorne and Rand Sinclair."

The farmer stared straight ahead without even a flicker to indicate he'd heard. While the sheriff thanked the sodbuster for catching Brett, two of the other riders threw him onto a horse. With everyone mounted a few minutes later, the group made tracks toward Steele's Hollow.

Brett had passed through there before daybreak, anxious to get home to the Wild Horse Ranch. The town had been quieter than a blade of grass growing. He couldn't imagine what they thought he'd done. This was the first time he'd traveled through the community. Usually he took a more southerly tack returning home after driving a string of horses to Fort Concho, but this time he'd had to deliver a sorrel to a man on the Skipper Ranch near Chalk Mountain, so he'd decided to cut through.

He made a mental note to give Steele's Hollow a wide berth from now on.

Not that there would be a next time if things kept going the way they were.

The combination of blood loss and the hot sun made Brett see double. It was all he could do to stay in the saddle.

By the time they rode into the small town an hour later, Brett had doubled over and clung to the horse's mane with everything he had. The group halted in front of the jail, jerked him off the animal and into the rough wooden building.

"Please, I need a doctor," Brett murmured as they rifled through his pockets.

After taking his knife and the bank draft from the sale of the horses, they unlocked a door that led down a dark walkway. The smell of the earthen walls and the dim light told him the building had been dug into a hill. They unlocked a cell and threw him inside.

"A doctor," Brett repeated weakly as he huddled on the floor.

"Not sure he treats breeds." The sheriff slammed the iron door shut and locked it. "See what I can do, though. Reckon we don't want you to die before we hang you."

"That's awful considerate." Brett struggled to his feet and clung to the metal bars to keep from falling. "Once and for all, tell me…what did I do? What am I guilty of?"

"You were born," the sheriff snapped. Without more, he turned and walked to the front of the jail.

৵৵

Panic pounded in Brett's temples like a herd of stampeding mustangs long after the slamming of the two iron doors separating him from freedom. This proved that the sheriff had targeted him solely because of his Indian heritage; he had nothing to charge him with.

His crime was simply for being born?

Dizzy, Brett collapsed onto the bunk as his hat fell to the crude plank floor.

Movement in the next cell caught his attention. Willing the room to keep from spinning, Brett turned his head. He could make out a woman's form in the dimness. Surely his pain had conjured her up. They didn't put women in jail.

He couldn't tell what she looked like because she had two faces blurring together, distorting her features—but he could hear her pretty voice clear enough.

"You're in pitiful shape, mister."

Since his bunk butted up to the bars of her cell, she could easily reach through. He felt her cautiously touch one of his moccasins.

"Checking to see if I'm dead?" he murmured.

"Nope. Do you mind if I have your shoes after they hang you?"

Brett raised up on an elbow, then immediately regretted it when the cell whirled. He lay back down. "That's not a nice thing to ask a man."

"Well, you won't be needing them. I might as well get some good out of them."

"They aren't going to hang me."

"That's not what Sheriff Oldham said."

"He can't hang me, because I didn't do anything wrong." It was best to keep believing that. Maybe he could convince someone, even if only himself. "I think he was joking."

"Humor and Sheriff Oldham parted company long ago. He's serious all the time. And mean. You don't want to get on his bad side."

"Wish I'd known this sooner. You sure know how to make a man feel better," Brett said dryly, draping his arm across his eyes and willing his stomach to quit churning. "What is your name?"

"Rayna."

"Who stuck that on you? I've never heard it before."

"It's a made-up name. My father is Raymond, and my mother is Elna. My mama stuck 'em together and came up with Rayna. I've always hated it."

"Got a last name, or did they use it all on the first one?"

"Harper. Rayna Harper."

"Forgive me if I don't get up to shake hands, but I'm a little indisposed. I'm Brett Liberty."

With that, blessed silence filled the space, leaving him to fight waves of dizziness and a rebellious stomach. Keeping down the contents seemed all he could manage at present.

But Rayna wasn't quiet for long. "Where did you get those Indian shoes, Brett? I'd sure like to have them."

"My brother." His words came out sounding shorter than he intended.

"Sorry. I've been in here for a while by myself, and I guess I just have a lot of words stored up. Sometimes I feel they're just going to explode out the top of my head if I don't let some out. What are you in here for? I couldn't hear too well."

"For being born, I'm told." Brett was still trying to digest that.

"Me too." Rayna sounded astonished. "Isn't that amazing?"

Brett had a feeling that no matter what he'd said, she would say the same thing. He wished he could see her better so he could put a face to the voice. Even though the conversation taxed him, it was nice to know he wasn't alone. Maybe she'd even hold his hand if he died.

That is, if she wasn't too busy trying to get his moccasins off instead.

"Why do you think it's amazing?"

"Because it makes perfect sense. I figure if I hadn't been born, I wouldn't be in here for picking old Mr. Vickery's pockets."

"So you're a pickpocket?" Surprise rippled through him.

"Nope. I'm a spreader of good. I don't ever keep any of it. I take from those who have and give to the have-nots. Makes everyone happy. Except me when I get thrown in the calaboose."

"You're a Robin Hood." Brett had seen a copy of the book about the legendary figure at Fort Concho. He'd learned it so he could share the tale with Toby, Rand's adopted son. Brett had taken the six-year-old into his heart and loved spending time with the boy.

"I'm a what?"

"A person who goes around doing good things for the poor."

"Oh. I guess I am. It makes me so sad that some people have to do without things they need and no one helps them. This past winter, my friend Davy froze to death because the only place he had to sleep was under a porch. He was just a kid with no one except me to care."

Rayna's unexpectedly big heart touched Brett. She seemed to speak from a good bit of experience. "Do you have a place to sleep whenever you're not in here?"

"I get along. Don't need you to fret about me. Worrying about them putting a rope around your neck is all you can handle. Do you reckon it hurts a lot, Brett?"

"I wouldn't know." Hopefully, he wouldn't find out.

"I'll say a prayer for you."

"Appreciate that, Miss Rayna Harper." She was wrong about him only having to worry about getting his neck stretched, though. He could feel himself getting weaker.

He could also feel her eyeing his moccasins again.

Pressure on the bottom of his foot made him jump. He raised his head and saw that she'd stuck one bare foot through the bars and was measuring it to his.

"Stop that," he said with a painful huff of laughter. "Doc'll be along soon. I'm not going to be dead enough for you to get them."

The next sound to reach his ears was sawing and her soft, "Oh dear."

"Why did you say that? What's wrong?"

"The sawbones had best hurry, or you won't be needing him. They've started building the gallows."

That ticking clock in his head had taken on the sound of tolling bells.

Two

BRETT MUST'VE LOST CONSCIOUSNESS. PANIC gripped him when he came to. For a moment, he couldn't remember where he was or why he was behind bars.

When it came flooding back, he called, "Rayna, are you still here?"

"Oh dear Lord, I thought you were dead. You haven't made a sound for hours." Surprise colored her voice. Clothing rustled as she moved closer to the bars separating them.

"Not dead yet, so don't get your hopes up," he joked weakly.

The iron door separating the cells from the sheriff's office rattled. Footsteps sounded, then a key grated in the lock to his cell. He turned his head to see a slight, spry man carrying a black medical bag.

"Doc?" Brett murmured.

The doctor hurried to the bunk and felt Brett's forehead. "Sheriff, he has a raging fever. This bullet has got to come out. I want him transported to my office right away."

Brett heard the sheriff's gravelly voice. "Nope. Ain't leaving here."

"Get me some light then," the doctor snapped. "Lanterns. Three of them, plus a pail of clean water and some cloths. And quick."

"A lot of fuss for a stinking half-breed," the sheriff grumbled.

Doc turned Brett onto his belly, and pain shot like a thunderbolt through him. He bit down on his lip until he tasted blood to keep from crying out. He couldn't suppress a moan though.

"It's all right, son. Not everyone in this town shares the sheriff's views. I'm going to take care of you."

Compassion showed in the gentle way the doctor removed Brett's shirt, and Brett relaxed for the first time since this nightmare began. His mind drifted like a lazy cloud on a summer's day. His ranch and beloved horses filled his mind. The smell of lush, sweet grass surrounded him, and the vivid blue sky stretched overhead as far as the eye could see.

Please help me get back to the Wild Horse. That's all he asked. The thought of not seeing his ranch again brought jagged pain. The Wild Horse was a buffer between him and the outside world. It was the one place where he'd always been happy and safe.

"Will I die, Doc?"

"Not if I can help it, son." Doc sounded reassuring at least.

A few minutes later, the sheriff and his deputy were back with the requested items. Brett could feel the hate from their eyes boring into him as Doc removed metal instruments from his bag and set them aside.

Finally the pair left, turning the lock in the door between the cells and the office.

"About damned time," the sawbones muttered and finished examining the wound. He asked Brett to sit up for a moment and held a bottle of whiskey to Brett's lips.

When Brett tried to refuse, the kindly man pressed, "You'll need something for the pain when I remove the slug. Don't try to be a hero."

Finally, Brett accepted a drink but instantly regretted it. The liquor left a burning trail down his throat to his belly and released a fit of coughing. "No more. I'll deal with the pain. Just get on with it."

"As you wish. Lie back down on your belly then, and I'll get started."

A few seconds later, Brett wished he'd not been so hasty in turning the whiskey away. The pain was far worse than anything he'd experienced, even in the orphanage when Mr. Simon took off his belt and whipped him as he curled into a ball on the floor.

He heard screams and realized they came from him. And then everything went black as he slipped beneath murky, swirling water.

❧

In the next cell, Rayna plugged her ears with her fingers to block out the noises. Though Brett's screams had ceased, fragments still echoed in the dim light. A drop of water fell onto her dress, and she realized she was crying.

The Indian was in such agony. And she couldn't help.

His plight told her he was one of the have-nots, like

her. Though she'd only just met him, it would kill a part of her if he died. He reminded her of a wounded animal—like the hawk she'd secretly cared for years ago after a storm snapped its wing in two.

Her father had raised a ruckus when he discovered she'd hidden the hawk in the wagon amongst the pile of bones. He'd cursed her, then yelled that bone-pickers had no business trying to be softhearted. Their only job was to collect the bleached buffalo skulls and fragments left behind after the hunters had passed through. The pickers received eight dollars a ton when they delivered them to be shipped back East, where factories used them to make bone china and ground them into fertilizer. That eight dollars barely kept them fed.

Raymond Harper had made her dump the hawk out beside the trail, saying that nature would take care of things.

Rayna shut her eyes against the memory of how it squawked and hopped around, desperately trying to fly. Her father calmly took out his gun and shot it, then turned to her. "Now quit your sniveling."

Six months ago, after her father passed out under the wagon, she finally ran away.

The lonely expanse of prairie was better than staying with him. Anything was better than being a bone-picker's daughter. Bone-pickers had no soul. But *she* did. She did her best to make sure of that. She removed her fingers from her ears to wipe away her tears.

The doctor was muttering to himself in Brett's cell, sounding frustrated. She guessed he was having a hard time finding the bullet fragment. She opened her eyes.

"Can I help, Doc?" she asked softly.

He whirled. "Rayna child, I didn't know he'd thrown you in jail again. Yes, I wish I had your good eyes. I can't see as well as I used to." Doc Perkins left Brett's cell and returned a moment later with Sheriff Oldham.

"I'll open her cell, but she better not try to escape. I hold you responsible for her," Oldham muttered.

"For God's sake, Sheriff, you have the door separating the cells from your office bolted. They don't even have a window."

"Can't be too careful."

The minute the key turned in the lock, Rayna rushed out and into Brett's cell. "Tell me what you want."

"The bullet fragment, child. There's so much blood. Take these forceps and see if you can get it."

As the sound of the sheriff's footsteps faded and the lock turned in the heavy metal door, she took the pointed metal instrument from him. He held a lantern up high. She stared at the open wound and again thought of that hawk. She couldn't save that bird, but maybe she could save Brett Liberty.

With a trembling hand, she moved the torn, raw flesh aside, trying not to gag. So much blood. Her stomach threatened to revolt. After willing her belly to settle, she took a deep breath and blocked out everything except her task. Repeated tries found no success, however.

Tears of frustration trickled down her cheeks. She wasn't a failure. She *wasn't*. And she wasn't going to give up.

Minutes ticked by and Brett's breathing became

more and more shallow. She had to do this, not only for him, but for herself. She couldn't fail again and prove Raymond Harper right, especially when a man's survival hung in the balance.

Finally, the light glinted off a piece of metal. Grabbing onto the spent bullet with the forceps, she pulled it out and dropped it into a tin pan beside the bed before she could lose it inside him again.

"You did it, child. He may well owe his life to you."

"Do you think Brett will live?"

"He has a lot better chance now." He took the stained forceps from her and added them to the pan with the metal fragment. "I'll wash the wound, and you can help me apply a bandage. Did you know you make a fine nurse?"

It was news to her that she made a fine anything. She was nothing but a picker. Of bones, of pockets, and now of bullet wounds. "I'm glad I could help. He seems nice."

Doc Perkins dipped a cloth into the water and began cleaning away the blood from Brett's shoulder. "I agree. He's not a monster to be locked up like some wild animal."

"I don't know why the sheriff wants to hang him."

"Hate. Pure hate. The Comanche massacred his entire family when he was a boy. Oldham never got over it."

Rayna rolled Brett onto his side so the doctor could get to the blood that had run down to the thin mattress beneath. Minutes later, she helped wrap the wound with gauze overlaid with strips of muslin they tied together.

Doc stood back. "We've done all we can for him.

The rest is up to the good Lord." He began gathering everything and putting it back into his bag. "I'll check on him again in a few hours."

"Thank you, Doc. I'll sit with him as long as Sheriff Oldham will let me."

"I'll tell him I've ordered you to." He laid a hand on her shoulder. "I'm guessing your life has always been between hay and grass, but you have a big heart. That's plain to see."

"I do care, and that's a fact."

The room felt empty after he left. She sat on the edge of the bunk and touched Brett's dark hair, which was tied back with a strip of leather. It was soft, just as the hawk's feathers had been. "Yes, I care. More's the pity."

She sensed a wound much deeper than that left by the bullet. One that had scarred his soul. Her brother had once told her that kisses held magic, healing. They never had for her, but maybe they would for Brett.

Rayna lightly traced his lips with her fingertips. She could steal a kiss and he'd never know. It was too tempting. She'd never kissed anyone before without being forced. Just one time, she wanted to know how it felt because *she* wanted to. Bending her head, she gently placed her mouth on his.

It felt nice. Real nice.

So much that she tried it again.

❧

Brett forced his eyes open, then promptly shut them against the glare of the lanterns. Why were there lanterns there? Where was he?

Someone moved beside him, and a cool hand touched his forehead.

"Who?" he murmured.

"Rayna. Don't you remember?"

Images of his flight from the posse, the bullet slamming into his back, and the jail in Steele's Hollow came flooding back. "Are you holding a wake? Am I dead?"

"No, silly."

"What are you doing in my cell?" He tried to joke. "Did you escape so you could steal my moccasins?"

"I thought about it. I do believe they're the right size if I stuff the toe with newspaper."

"Don't get any ideas," he muttered, but his lips curved a little against his will.

The light finally allowed him to see her clearly. He couldn't say she was especially pretty—not traditionally so, in any case—but her cloud of auburn curls reminded him of the flames of a campfire on a cold night. Her eyes danced with mischief. Their color was as difficult to nail down as she was. One minute they were blue, the next green. They changed with each movement. *They*, he decided, were beautiful.

As he pondered that, sleep overtook him again.

The next time he woke to find a hand in his trousers. His head jerked around as he flared back into full consciousness, and Rayna pulled away with a gasp. "Trying to pick my pockets now? I'm afraid you'll be sadly disappointed. I'm one of the have-nots."

Color flooded Rayna's cheeks. "I was only giving you something."

Brett threw his long legs over the side of the bunk and, with great effort, struggled to a sitting position. "Giving me something? Now that's a new wrinkle."

"It's true." She sat down beside him.

"Then I suppose I need to see what you left in my pocket. Does it bite?"

"Good Lord, what kind of a person do you think I am?"

"God only knows." He allowed a smile as he stuck his hand in his trouser pocket and found a small object. He pulled it out. It was a smooth piece of wood someone had carved into the shape of a heart. He stared into her blue-green eyes and raised a brow.

"You need it more than I do," she said. "My grandfather carved it a long time ago. It's always brought me good luck."

Brett fought the impulse to laugh and, except for a quirk of his lips, managed to keep a straight face. His gaze swept the iron bars, the plank floor, and the grim, windowless space. "Yes, I can certainly see that this brought you all manner of good fortune."

Rayna twisted a piece of her dirty, threadbare dress. "Well, it did before I got here to Steele's Hollow."

He caught the sorrow in her eyes before she looked down. Acting on impulse, he reached for her hand, only to stop, unsure of himself. But it was so clear she needed comfort. Finally, he took her small hand in his, keeping his grip light, fearing he might break it.

"Thank you," he said softly. "It's the best present anyone ever gave me."

"So you'll keep the heart? It would mean a lot."

"In that case, I can't refuse."

She brightened. "When they hang you, I'll take it back."

"Such overwhelming faith you have in this talisman." He tucked the small heart into his pocket. "You never told me why you're in my cell."

Her hand curled inside his, and he found the feeling shooting into his chest very pleasant. "I was helping Doc. He can't see well and had trouble locating the bullet fragment, so he got the sheriff to let me try."

"Then I owe you a debt of thanks." He squeezed her fingers just a tiny bit.

Strange sensations traveled the length of his arm. Rayna was the first woman he'd touched in this way. Her skin was as soft as the down on a baby wren.

"When the doctor left, he told Sheriff Oldham that he needed me to watch you. I'm awful glad you're doing better. Looked like you were a goner for a while. Doc said you had an infection, but it looks like you might beat it."

He took in the woman who'd saved his life. He doubted the top of her head would reach his chin. Both delicacy and strength showed in her face. It seemed apparent she'd had her share of disappointments. Still, it hadn't beaten her down. She had plenty of spunk and then some.

"What time do you think it is?" he asked, releasing her hand.

"Near to midnight, I would say."

"Then I think I'll lie back down if you don't mind."

She rose and stood beside the bunk, then hesitated. "I wonder…do you think I could stay? Just for a while? Maybe watch you sleep? Just in case you start feeling poorly again and need…something."

Brett studied her face and noticed the worry and fear darkening her eyes. Through the haze of his pain, he could clearly see that Rayna hungered for human contact. He couldn't deny her that. He turned on his side to make more room. "Lie down beside me. We'll watch each other sleep."

"Try not to snore too loud."

He frowned. "I didn't know I did at all."

"Just a little but it was probably from the pain." She curled up next to him and laid her head on his arm. "Good night, Brett."

"Good night." He hesitated a long minute, impulse warring with reserve…then slowly laid his other arm protectively across her stomach.

A sense of peace flooded over him. This slight woman who seemed to have no one had awakened a long-buried dream. He silently vowed to protect her for however long he had left.

Three

BRETT WOKE SOMETIME LATER. HE HAD NO IDEA OF the hour. In the lantern light, he stared at his bunk partner's mass of riotous curls, blowing one away from his nose.

Having a woman in his arms felt nice. It was something he'd never allowed before, something he'd never sought. Yet deep inside, his heart had desperately yearned for this sort of moment. She was very different from anyone he'd ever known. Somehow, even though he lay in a jail cell and listened to a gallows being constructed outside, she made him feel alive and happy.

Rayna stirred. "Are you awake?"

"Yes. Just curious about the time. I don't want the sheriff or anyone to catch us like this. I would feel great pain if he harmed you because of me."

She sat up, pushed back her cloud of russet hair, and got to her feet. It was then he saw that she wore a heavy pair of men's brogans. Where on earth had she gotten them? The shoes looked as though they might've come off a very poor dead man.

Her dress was dirty and had been mended so many times it looked like a patchwork quilt with none of the squares matching. But she seemed so spirited, so brave.

If society had ever allowed him to take a wife, he'd want someone like her. He hated to think he'd have spent all his life never knowing what it could be like to be happy like his brothers now were. While he waited to die, maybe they could pretend.

Maybe he could know what it was like to be loved.

Until they led him through those doors to a hangman, maybe he could have the bride prejudice had denied him. The bold notion made ripples dance under his skin.

Brett raised to a sitting position, ignoring the pain shooting through his back. "This may sound crazy, but I'm going to ask anyway. Rayna, do you think you could pretend to be my wife? Just until they take me away? No one will ever know but us, so they can't hurt you."

Turning, she dropped down beside him. Surprised tears bubbled in her eyes. "No one ever asked me to marry them before."

"Is that a no?"

"I'd be honored to be your pretend wife," she whispered, brushing his face with her fingers. "What do we do now?"

"Do you mind if I kiss you?"

"I'd like that…husband."

Under her bright gaze, he lowered his head. But before their lips touched, the sound of a key grating in the lock made him jerk back. "Quick, go to your cell before they catch you with me."

Rayna scurried into hers and quietly eased the door shut.

Just then a deputy sauntered in, taking care to keep his distance from Brett's cell. "You alive, breed?"

Brett glared. "Disappointed?"

The deputy—a squat man who reminded Brett of a possum with little weasel eyes, grunted, shifting his gaze to Rayna. "Give any thought to my offer, woman?"

No one had to spell out what the deputy meant. Brett sought to tamp down his rising anger. He watched Rayna tilt her head at a defiant angle.

"The answer is the same as all the other times."

The weasel shrugged and went back out. The minute the door locked shut, Rayna slowly walked into Brett's cell and sat down beside him again. "I wish I could see the sky and smell the fresh air."

"How long have you been in here?"

"Over a month, I think. With each sunrise I've been making a mark on the wall. The one today makes thirty-one. But no matter how much I want out, I'm not doing what that deputy wants," she whispered. "I'll never be a fine lady, but even I have my dignity. No one will ever take that."

Though still hesitant, Brett took her small, dainty hand. Her skin shone white against his. He couldn't remember the last time he'd touched someone who wasn't family, but his pretend wife was different somehow. "Always stand on your principles. In the end, we still have to live with ourselves, look at our faces in the mirror."

"I know."

The door opened again, and this time it was the doctor. Shuffling his feet, he ambled into the cell as though his shoes were two sizes too large and moving slow was the only way to keep them on. He carried a fresh pail of water.

"Our patient is looking better," he said to Rayna.

"I kept watch over him like you asked. He still has a fever though."

"I'll check his wound, and we'll change the bandage. Did he sleep and eat well enough?"

"I'm sitting right here, Doc. You don't have to act like I'm not in the room," Brett managed quietly.

The doctor stared at Brett like he'd just noticed him. "Indeed you are." He set his bag and pail of water down beside the bunk. "My hands aren't too steady, Rayna. Can you unwrap his bandage for me?"

"Yes, Doctor Perkins." She moved back into Brett's cell. He tensed when she stood in front of him.

Though they'd slept in the same bunk last night, this seemed different. The bandage had been a barrier of sorts between them. Now her fingers would be touching his bare skin. That was something wives did, he was sure—only not pretend ones.

She untied the muslin and began unwrapping all the strips. Feeling her sudden pause, he turned his head and saw that she was biting her lip.

"Doc, blood has seeped through, and the gauze is stuck."

"You'll have to loosen it by soaking. One thing we don't want is to pull the wound and start it bleeding again," Perkins said. "You can do it. I have faith in you, dear."

Rayna went back to work. She got some water from the pail and began gently dabbing his back.

Other than the coolness of the water, he didn't feel anything. No pulling, no stinging. But the minute her warm fingers touched his skin, he jumped. The brush of her hand was almost unbearable in its tenderness. His ragged breath was loud in his ears. He'd never known such gentleness.

The woman who excelled at picking pockets and giving to those in need had bestowed upon him a great prize, and she didn't even know it.

⁂

Over the next few days, Brett regained some of his strength.

But the clock had started ticking again.

Each day brought him closer to the meeting with his Creator. Hammering and sawing commenced at daybreak and didn't cease until dusk. The gallows would soon be ready, even though he had yet to see a trial.

At first he hadn't taken the threat seriously. It seemed too unlikely that they'd hang an innocent man. Now, worry set in. His only hope was that the farmer would get word to Cooper and Rand. Yet he admitted that the chances of them arriving in time were slim.

He sat up with effort and glanced into Rayna's cell, where the sheriff had again locked her after barring Doc Perkins from giving him any more medical treatment. It was difficult to see her without the lanterns that Oldham had taken away. In the shadows, he could barely make out her slight form.

Rayna Harper had been a bright spot in all this. She

was an exceptional woman. Through the false bravado and blunt talk, he glimpsed the scared little girl inside of her. Beneath it all lay a fierce yearning to better her circumstances. She had such a big heart that she could no more stop herself from caring about others than she could sprout wings and fly.

Eyes adjusting to the shadows and gloom, he finally saw her with her eye pressed to the hole in the wall, looking out.

"It's just about ready," Rayna announced. "Won't be long now. You need a miracle."

Brett took the carved wooden heart from his pocket. The talisman had again failed to deliver good luck—not that he'd had any faith in it anyway. He believed in what he could see. "Looks like you'll get my moccasins after all."

She rose and gripped the bars separating them. "I never thought they'd really do it." Her voice trembled.

"Makes two of us. Will you remember me, Rayna?"

"I'll think of you every time I put those moccasins on. You're really brave, Brett Liberty."

He forced a tight smile. "I have no choice."

Whether the credit for his bravery went to the blood of warriors in him or his years in the orphanage, Brett didn't know. He only knew that when his time came, he'd not beg or cry out. It didn't seem to serve much purpose. It wouldn't change the end result. He wouldn't show any weakness. He'd keep his honor as a man.

A key grated in the lock, and the squat deputy named Dingleby came through the outside door, bringing the stench of his unwashed body with him. He carried a tin plate.

"Rise and shine." He bypassed Brett's cell and slid the food under Rayna's iron door. "Nothing for you, breed, on account of Sheriff Oldham saying we ain't gonna feed you. It would be a waste, since you're fixin' to get your neck stretched an' all."

Brett stood to his full height and moved to his cell door. "Then I will see the judge today?"

"Nope." The deputy hugged the earthen wall in an effort to get well out of range of Brett's long arms. As he moved, his low-hanging holster slipped around his legs, tripping him. A silver pocket watch fell out. The weasel quickly raised the belt, gathered his watch, and hurried to the door. "Ain't gonna be no judge an' no trial. You ain't a citizen of this country. You're a savage, so we don't have to."

The slamming of the iron door echoed in Brett's head. Not a citizen? He'd been raised with whites, had white brothers. He didn't know any of the ways of his own people, how to speak their language, or any of their customs. He didn't even know to which tribe he belonged. He doubted they'd want him either.

Maybe they'd also put him to death for being born.

Rayna handed a piece of bread through the bars. "Take this, Brett. I'll share what I have."

"You eat it, Rayna. I'll be fine." He slowly returned to his bunk.

No judge. No trial. No hope.

The old woman at the orphanage who'd given him the name *Liberty* should've had her head examined. There was none to be had for people like him.

❧

Gnawing worry had chewed Cooper Thorne's gut for the last sixty miles. Something bad had happened to Brett. He never took this long delivering a string of horses.

"Are you sure he would've come this way, Coop?" Rand Sinclair swiveled in the saddle.

"He told me he had a horse to deliver to a man near Walnut Springs. He wanted to go a different route." Cooper stood in the stirrups, stretching his legs. "You know our brother's need to avoid people."

"I do indeed." Rand chuckled. "He'll go an extra hundred miles just so he won't have to talk to anyone."

They rode on in silence. Finally they came to a farm in a little valley. A man looked up as they approached the house.

"Can I help you gentlemen?" he said, rising from where he was working on the well pulley.

Cooper dismounted. "I hope so. I'm the sheriff over in Battle Creek, and I'm looking for my brother. He's tall and wears moccasins. Name's Brett Liberty."

"Oh, you must be talking about the half-breed." The farmer took a bandanna from around his neck and wiped his forehead.

Rand pushed his way forward. "Have you seen him?"

"He came this way. Nice enough sort. He was shot, bleeding something awful. The sheriff took him to Steele's Hollow. Your brother asked me to tell you that if you stopped by."

"Who shot him?" Cooper's brain tried to digest it all.

"Reckon it was Sheriff Oldham."

"Why?"

"He hates Indians. Thinks the only good one is a dead one."

Cooper touched the brim of his hat and turned toward his horse. Rand did the same.

"Reckon you'd best hurry," said the farmer.

"Why's that?" Rand put his foot in the stirrup.

"My neighbor said they're gonna hang him."

"Hang him? What for?" Hot anger swept through Cooper.

Rand let loose a string of cusswords. "Don't tell us. The sheriff hates Indians."

The farmer spat on the ground. "Yep."

Cooper vaulted into the saddle. Rebel danced around in a circle and sidestepped for a minute until Cooper gained control of the animal. Of all times to be skittish.

"Better hurry," the man repeated. "Gonna hang him today. A real shame. Your brother promised me five of his best horses if I told you where he was."

"You'll get your horses no matter what, mister," Rand said, slapping the hindquarters of his horse with his hat.

Steele's Hollow. The name struck Cooper Thorne with cold, paralyzing fear. That sheriff had some explaining to do, and Cooper meant to do some reckoning.

No one would hang Brett Liberty.

❧

The longer the day wore on, the tighter the knot in Brett's stomach clenched. His jagged, raw nerves jumped each time the hundred-pound sack of flour fell through the trapdoor in a test run.

He'd long forgotten the hunger he'd felt upon waking that morning. His fingers rubbed the smooth wooden heart Rayna had given him as he lay on his bunk waiting, staring…hoping.

His heightened senses heard every sound, felt every shift in Rayna's mood. She was being unusually quiet, and at times the sound of sniffling drifted into his cell.

"Pretend husband," she whispered now, "I just wanted to say you remind me of my brother, Hershel. He was older than me by several years. No one more capable and sure ever lived." She sighed. "I really miss him. My brother looked out for me."

He got painfully to his feet and padded to the bars. "What happened to him?"

"Hershel got into a fight with a stinking buffalo hunter. Over me. One night my father gave me to this man in exchange for a jug of corn liquor. My brother came after us. The buffalo hunter killed Hershel, knifed him in the back."

"I'm sorry," Brett said quietly. "How long ago?" Wanting to comfort but unsure how, he touched her face with a tentative fingertip and lightly traced the line of her jaw.

"About a year, I'd say. We buried Hershel in a desolate spot on the prairie. After that, I told Papa that I was sleeping with a knife. If anybody came near me, I'd kill 'em and then him."

"Where is your mother?"

"Don't know. She just wasn't there one day. My father told me he left her in the rough town of Mobeetie, Texas. Said she refused to go another step. I didn't believe him though. He lies. Do you have any family, Brett?"

"Two brothers, Cooper and Rand. And I recently

found out I have a sister, or a woman claiming to be my sister anyway." Brett didn't know what to think about that. He was afraid to put too much stock in the letter she'd sent.

None of that mattered now. If she came, she'd find him below ground. Maybe she'd visit his grave…if they saw fit to do that much for a half-breed. Likely they'd drag him out into a field and let the buzzards feast on him.

"What time do you think it is, Rayna?"

"Early afternoon, I think."

"I never got to kiss you."

"You can now," she said softly.

Just once before he died, he'd taste her lips. He lowered his head and gently pressed his mouth to hers. Despite the cold iron bars, the feeling that rushed through his body took his breath. A hunger rose up so strong it left him weak and trembling. Heat pooled in his belly and spread through his body like nothing he'd felt before.

Did she have these feelings too?

Brett raised his head, silently cursing his inexperience and lack of knowledge about such things. If only he had time to figure things…*her*…out.

"Thank you. I'm ready to die now."

"Don't say that," she cried.

They broke apart when the iron door swung open. Sheriff Oldham strode to Brett's cell and unlocked it. "Let's go, breed."

The sand in the hourglass had run out.

Brett silently turned and picked up his shirt.

"Don't need that," Oldham barked. "Men like you don't get to die with dignity."

The words cut through Brett like a knife. With great effort, he pulled his shirt over his head anyway and adjusted his hat on his head. "No one can steal my dignity. Not you or anyone. It's mine to keep."

Brett swung to the bars separating him from Rayna. He took her hand and pressed the heart into her palm. "You can use this. I hope it brings you better luck." Without turning, he spoke to Oldham. "See that she gets my moccasins."

Rayna angrily dashed away the tears streaming down her face. "I'll pray."

"Save it. Those don't do any good either." Brett gently caressed her cheek again with his finger.

The deputy entered and murmured something low to Oldham.

Brett took advantage of their turned backs. "Do you mind if I kiss you once more?"

When she shook her head, he lowered his mouth and pressed his lips to hers between the cold steel bars.

The tremble of her lips beneath his spoke of her struggle to keep from crying. Mixed with the salt of her tears was a hint of the berry jam the deputy had brought her for breakfast along with the chunk of bread she'd tried to offer Brett.

As with the first, the kiss sent a wave of tenderness through him that shook him to the core.

Taking one step back, he stared at her, wondering if it had been real. "Thank you, Rayna. Think of me with kindness."

The deputy cursed, trudging back toward the office. With a huff of annoyance, the sheriff shifted his focus back to Brett. "What the hell?" Oldham jerked

Brett's arms behind him and snapped on the handcuffs. "What's been happening in here anyway?"

Brett fought down nausea that came with the pain. No doubt the vicious yanking had opened his wound. He glared at the sheriff. "You harm her, and you'll pay. She's innocent."

The hate-filled sheriff laughed. "You'll do nothing, because you'll be dead, rotten half-breed."

"I have two brothers, and they don't take kindly to anyone who hurts a woman. They'll gladly do what I can't."

Without another word, the sheriff yanked him to the heavy iron door. Pain knifed Brett's body and spread downward. He suppressed a groan and looked back for one last glimpse of the wife he could never have who'd offered kindness and a gift he'd carry to the beyond.

Four

ONCE IN THE OUTER OFFICE, BRETT STARED AT THE faces of the deputies. Their eyes glittered with hate, except for an older man whose thick white mustache drooped like Brett's hopes.

The man stepped forward. "Sheriff, the storm that's been threatening just blew in. We can't hang this man in the driving rain."

Sheriff Oldham shot a glance out the window at the deluge and vented his frustration. "For two cents I'd go ahead with it, but I reckon everyone's already scurried inside like a bunch of lily-livered chickens, afraid a drop of rain will dampen their hair. Maybe Dingleby has the right idea. Put a bullet in his damn head and be done with the matter."

Another deputy spoke. "You do that, and we'll have a bigger problem. There's the prisoner's brothers to consider. If we hang him, at least we can claim *some* legal right."

Oldham spat a string a curses. "Reckon you get a reprieve, breed. Someone take him back to his cell."

The mustached man stepped forward. "I'll do it."

Seconds later, the old deputy opened Brett's cell door and removed the handcuffs. Brett thanked him.

"I don't hold with Sheriff Oldham's views," the jailor said. "He's eaten up with hate. My brother took a Comanche wife and had some kids. I got nothing against them. Would you like me to rustle you up something to eat? A piece of bread if nothing else?"

Brett rubbed his wrists. "I don't want to make trouble between you and your boss. I'll understand if you don't return."

The old jailor gave a short nod, then locked Brett's cell and strolled back into the office.

Rayna clutched the bars separating them and held out the carved wooden heart. "I knew your luck would change. You should take the charm back."

Shaking his head, he chuckled. "Fortune smiled on me only after I gave it to you. You keep it. Besides, at this rate, we're going to rub off any luck the token may have passing it back and forth."

"Maybe it was the kisses that swung things to your favor. My brother Hershel once told me that kisses are full of magic. Maybe this is what he meant." Wonderment colored her voice. "We should do it again. Just to see all the magic that comes out, of course."

The dimness hid the color of her eyes, but he suspected they were the shade of bluebonnets kissed by the morning rain.

He didn't believe in magic or good luck charms, but he sure wasn't going to pass up another chance to kiss the woman who'd shown him so much gentleness. "I suppose it couldn't hurt."

With the bars between them, he was unable to do

more than lightly caress her lips, but the contact shook him nonetheless. As much as the bars allowed, he drank in Rayna's sweetness, her innocence. This time, his movements were more confident.

Blood pounded in his ears as it sped through his body like his galloping wild horses. The depth of passion and hunger rocked him. He didn't know about magic, but this was more powerful than anything he'd ever felt. When the kiss ended, Brett stared at Rayna in wonder.

"What do you think?" He drew in a ragged breath.

"I almost missed knowing this," she whispered. "You're a tender, beautiful man, my pretend husband."

As he digested her words, he lightly ran the pad of his thumb over her eyes, cheek, and lips. Even though they'd only known each other such a short time, Rayna made him feel as though he really mattered. As though his being alive brought strength and worth to her.

It almost felt like what he imagined love to be.

Since he never had the opportunity to know his mother and father, Brett wondered if *they'd* loved, or if they'd been cold and distant, hurrying in the darkness when they created him. In his opinion, two people who brought a child into the world should have tender feelings for each other.

Or maybe making love tended to be more like making war.

Only that certainly wasn't the case between his brothers and their wives. He'd seen the raw hunger in their eyes when they were in the same room. "Did your parents ever kiss, Rayna?"

"Raymond Harper never once said a kind word to her, not even when she told him she lost the baby she was carrying. He looked at her and said that he was glad, because he had enough hungry brats. My mama cried. He always made her cry. My father is a hard, bitter man. I hate my name because half of it is his."

Brett brushed her cheek with the pad of his thumb. It was getting easier and easier to initiate these small touches. "I'm truly sorry."

She raised her eyes. "What were your parents like?"

"Don't know. I never knew them. People at the orphanage found me on the steps shortly after I was born."

"Sometimes I wish I'd have been an orphan." Her voice sounded wistful and full of regret. "Would've been better to have never known *my* father."

"You're saying that now because of the painful memories. It's hell never knowing where you came from. I have nothing tying me to the past, or maybe the future either. The way I see it, the two are woven together into a colorful blanket. Without one, the other is full of holes."

Brett turned at the sound of the door. The sympathetic jailor came in carrying a cloth-covered basket. He unlocked Brett's cell and set it on the bunk. "Be careful. There's a coffeepot and two cups in case Miss Rayna wants some too."

Hot coffee. The man might as well have offered him a pocketful of twenty-dollar gold pieces. "Thank you, sir. You don't know how much I appreciate this. What is your name?"

"Hank Maxwell. Only brought a few simple things

that I know can lift spirits. The sheriff and other deputies are out of the jail. I'll be back to collect the basket in an hour."

The footsteps had hardly faded before Brett removed the pot and cups. He poured some for Rayna then for himself.

Rayna's hand trembled when she accepted the cup, her fingers brushing his. "I haven't had coffee in a long while."

"Just enjoy it." Brett looked at what else the deputy had brought. His eyes widened. "Want some fried chicken? There's more than enough."

"Is there anything else in there besides chicken? Some bread or vegetables?"

He frowned. "What's wrong with chicken?"

"I don't like it."

Brett shook his head in disbelief. "Strangest thing I've ever heard." He pulled out some thick slices of bread, kept one for himself, and handed her the other three. "That's all that's in the basket. It's not enough to fill you up. If you change your mind about the chicken, let me know."

"Thank you, but I won't. This bread is good. It's not moldy like most they bring."

Each sat on their bunk and ate in silence. Brett had the best meal he'd had in a week. Between sips of coffee, he ate his fill. At least if they hung him tomorrow, his stomach wouldn't growl when they placed the noose around his neck.

With everything gone an hour later, he replaced the pot and cups in the basket. Then he lay on his bunk, staring at the ceiling.

"Thank you, Brett," Rayna said softly. "I was so hungry."

"You're full now?"

"Couldn't hold another bite." She stood, wrapping her fingers around the bars. "I think you've brought me good luck."

A smile curved Brett's lips. First she gave credit to the carved heart, then the kiss, and now to him. He found her childlike innocence refreshing. Rayna probably believed in fairy tales and magic. "I've never been anyone's good luck charm. Most likely it was due to our jailor remembering he has a heart."

"Maybe it'll rain tomorrow, maybe for a whole week."

It would only prolong the agony. He didn't wish to wake every morning with the inevitable hanging over his head.

"Brett?"

"What is it now?" He rose onto an elbow, careful not to pull the wound on his back.

"Would you hold me again?"

"Are you forgetting the bars between us?"

"Nope. You can still put your arms around me."

"Are you cold?"

"I'm lonely. And scared. I don't think the sheriff intends to let me out. I may die in here. In the darkness. With the rats and spiders and…bats."

"When did you get *bats* in your cell?"

"I don't have 'em yet, but I know by the time I die, I will. They like dark caves, and this resembles one. Bad things happen in the dark."

Her small voice touched him. He rose and stood in front of her. Slowly, he stuck his arms through the bars and around her slight frame. She sighed and pressed as close as she could get to him. Her nearness jolted his body, sending unexpected heat through him.

Here in the dark, it was easy to think Rayna was the woman he'd waited his whole life for. He'd like to wrap his arms around her and never let her go.

She might hide insecurity and fear from others, but he saw them clearly.

And it was in them that he recognized himself.

"I wish our cell doors would magically come open so I could sleep beside you again," she murmured. "You make me feel safe."

"You do me as well, Rayna Harper." And Brett realized he meant every word.

He made a decision. When they put that rope around his neck tomorrow, he'd close his eyes and take a calm breath. Rayna's face would be the last thing he saw. She'd given him an unbelievable gift—that of letting him pretend to have lived a full life and known love. He'd cherish that until his very last moment.

❦

Cooper and Rand arrived at Steele's Hollow that afternoon in a pouring rain. A sign at the edge of town met them: *Travel at your own risk.*

But it was the skull of a buffalo perched on the pole above it that sent chills skittering up Cooper's spine.

What the hell did that mean? He checked his Colt to make sure it was loaded and easily accessible before proceeding slowly down the street.

He dismounted at the jail. After giving the gallows next to it a narrowed look, he strode inside. Right behind him, Rand slammed the door shut with a good bit of force. Water cascaded from their dusters and dripped from the brims of their hats.

The man behind the desk jumped to his feet, his chair clattering to the floor. He was wearing a tin star. "What the hell? Who are you?"

"You must be Oldham." Cooper slowly removed his gloves. "I'm Cooper Thorne, the sheriff of Battle Creek, and me and Rand Sinclair have come for Brett Liberty. Get him out of his cell immediately."

From the corner of his eye, he saw Rand striding toward the metal door that presumably led to the prisoners.

"Hey, you can't go back there." The bearded, middle-aged sheriff started toward him.

"The hell I can't," Rand answered. When the door didn't open, he looked around for the keys.

Cooper spied them on a nail. His boot heels struck the floor like shots from a rifle. He took the ring of keys and pitched them to his brother. Rand unlocked the divider and disappeared.

"You can't barge in here and take over my jail and my prisoners. We have laws in this town. I caught the Indian dead to rights."

"Doing what? What are the charges?" Cooper's steely glare had the sheriff backing up. Cooper tucked his duster behind his holster to reveal his Colt for good measure. Best to let the man know he meant business, but he wouldn't use it unless he had no other choice.

The easy way or the hard, he would get Brett out.

"Uh...horse thievery." Oldham righted his chair and sat back down. Now that he had a barrier between himself and Cooper, his bravado returned. "He's due to hang tomorrow."

"Brett raises some of the finest horses in the state. He doesn't need to steal one."

"Maybe he liked the animal, so he took it."

"Show me this horse he's charged with stealing."

"Well…I can't rightly do that." Oldham licked his lips. "I believe… That's to say, it might've ran away."

"Mister, I'll have you know that Brett Liberty hasn't stolen so much as a penny candy in his entire life."

"How would you know? Are you with him every second? He ain't nothing but a greasy breed."

Cooper shoved the desk aside and grabbed Oldham by the shirtfront, yanking him to his feet. "He's my *brother*. I've lived with him for twenty-five years."

The color drained from Oldham's face. "You don't look like brothers," he said weakly.

"You don't look like a sack of shit either, but you are." Cooper tossed him back into the chair. "You move, and I'll shoot you."

Just then, Rand appeared with Brett, who leaned heavily on him.

"I'm glad to see you," Brett said, breathing hard. "What kept you?"

"A little matter of not knowing where you were." Cooper tossed five silver dollars at Sheriff Oldham. They scattered, rolling all over the floor. "This'll pay for his keep."

Brett pulled himself up straight with effort. "He took the bank draft from the sale of the horses."

Putting both hands on the desk, Cooper leaned within a few inches of the sheriff's face. "Hand it over, or I'll go through everything in here until I find it. I'll also have Brett's knife."

Glaring, Oldham reached into a drawer, jerked out the paper, then retrieved the knife. Cooper snatched them and straightened.

"Let's get out of this stink hole," Rand said, moving Brett toward the door.

Brett came to a dead stop. "Not yet. I'm not leaving without the woman in the cells."

Letting out a long sigh, Cooper swung back. "How much is the woman's fine?"

Oldham met his stare. Evidently now that they were about to leave, his bluster returned. "Ten dollars."

"She's been in here for over a month," Brett protested. "She's already paid double for her petty crime."

Whoever this woman was, Cooper knew Brett wouldn't budge without her. He fished out two more silver dollars and pitched them. "This is all you get. Argue, and we'll break her out also. Better to get something than nothing."

Though anger flushed the sheriff's face, he kept silent.

"I'm ready to wash the stench of this town off me." Rand leaned Brett against the door and vanished into the back.

Cooper kept his eyes on Oldham. "You're a disgrace to the office you hold. I promise I'm wiring the governor. I'd love to have the Texas Rangers ride in here and clean up this mess."

"I keep the peace here. You can't fault me for that."

Ignoring him, Cooper turned to Brett. "Where is your horse?"

"Oldham and his deputies shot him."

Rage shook Cooper to the core. He pinned Oldham with a hard glare. "If I ever see you again, you're a dead man."

Rand returned a minute later with a woman who probably didn't weigh ninety pounds soaking wet. Clutching a pitiful little gunnysack that probably held everything she owned, she gave Brett a smile and thanked him.

When Cooper jerked open the door to leave, a squatty man wearing a deputy's badge tumbled inside. Red-faced, he quickly straightened.

Cooper didn't miss how quickly the woman shrank against his side or the protective hand Brett laid on her. The actions told him the deputy was rotten to the core.

"Sorry," the beady-eyed deputy mumbled. Brushing against the woman, he shot Oldham a questioning glance.

"I released the prisoners," Oldham said as though feeling the need to explain.

Shooting the pair one last glare, Cooper held the door for his brothers, then ushered the woman out. They stood under the roof's overhang, staring at the dismal weather.

"We'll have to buy two more horses first thing," Cooper said. "Are you and your friend hungry, Brett?"

"No. I just want out of this town."

"Me too," the new addition to their party said in a low voice.

"By the way," Brett said, "this is Rayna Harper."

"Welcome aboard, Miss Rayna. I'm Cooper Thorne. Guess we'd best head to the livery."

"Little brother, we have lots of catching up to do," Rand said, grinning, then introduced himself to Rayna.

By the time they'd purchased two horses and saddles, the rain had stopped. Cooper mounted up, ready to lead the way. He was ready to get home to his beautiful wife and twins. He'd spent too many nights away from them.

He noticed Brett's grimace when he pulled himself into the saddle. "Do you think you can ride?"

"Don't think you're going to leave me here. Don't worry about me; I'm going to live."

"Yes, you are," Rayna said, reaching to lay a hand on him. "I told you the good luck charm would work. Or maybe it was the kiss."

Cooper swore he could see the color rising in Brett's face. Instead of teasing, he raised his arm and ordered, "Let's ride."

Within minutes they passed the travel-at-your-own-risk sign near the edge of town. He turned to Brett. "Didn't this tell you to watch for trouble?" his brother teased.

"It was pitch black when I rode through. Never saw it."

As the riders put the town and its corrupt sheriff behind them, the golden sun poked through the low-hanging clouds, seeming to promise happier days ahead.

"Look at that," Rayna breathed. "This means bright blessings."

Brett shook his head. "Everything to you is some sign or another. I hope you don't plan on doing this when we get home. Or trying to steal my moccasins. I'm going to keep my eye on you."

Home? Cooper didn't know what Brett had in mind, but it sounded like he'd issued an invitation to the Wild Horse. Possibly a lot more than that. All he knew was they were already acting like an old married couple.

Cooper grinned. Their little brother was taken with his auburn-haired cellmate.

And what was that about stealing Brett's moccasins? Cooper sensed quite a story there, but he knew his little brother would sooner cut out his tongue than reveal it.

Especially if he was in the process of losing his heart to Miss Rayna Harper.

From the looks of things, the last holdout might not remain a bachelor long.

Five

TWILIGHT BATHED THE ROLLING HILLS IN PLUM AND charcoal shadows before they stopped to make camp. They'd managed to put twenty miles between them and Steele's Hollow. Still, Brett wouldn't breathe deeply until he was back on his land. He watched his brothers head off to scare up something for supper while Rayna collected wood for a fire.

It irked Brett that he could only lie on a bedroll like some broken-down old man. In truth, though, the ride had exhausted him. It had taken all his willpower and a tight grip on the reins to stay in the saddle the last few miles.

He closed his eyes and let the rain-cooled air replace the dank stench that lingered in his nostrils.

Never would he take his freedom for granted. It was a precious thing and worth more than all the gold on earth.

At Rayna's cry, his eyes flew open in alarm. He struggled to his feet. As he drew closer, he saw a white owl flying from tree to tree, its wingspan impressive. Rayna dropped a load of branches to pluck something from the ground.

"Where are you bit? Tell me." His mind raced. It was still a little early for rattlesnakes to be out and moving around, but spiders and scorpions were. He hated both with a passion.

"Nowhere."

"What made you cry out?"

"It's terrible luck to see a white owl before dark."

"Oh." He grinned and relaxed, collecting the load of wood she'd dropped. "What was that you picked up off the ground?"

"An acorn. Carrying it will ward off evil."

They walked back into camp, and he dropped the firewood. "Rayna, do you truly believe all this?"

"My grandfather taught me all about omens and spells." She clearly knew her way around a campsite too. She laid twigs and some shaved tree bark inside a circle of rocks exactly as he would've done.

"I know, but do you really believe their power?"

"I certainly do." Rayna glanced up and met his stare. "What? Why are you smiling?"

"I love watching you. You're a constant mystery. You're afraid of the dark, have wild superstitions, and relieve people of the things in their pockets, yet you dove in and saved the life of a perfect stranger. I can't figure you out."

She shrugged. "Not much to figure. Sometimes you make the choices, and sometimes the choices make you."

"They do for a fact." He pondered over her surprising answer. It carried so much wisdom. But at least one of her choices had led her down the wrong path.

"You should've left me in that jail."

"Sorry, couldn't do that."

Bewilderment rippled across her face. "Why?"

"I saw someone worth saving," he said quietly.

Rayna turned away, but not before he saw sorrow fill her eyes. The silence stretched as she bent to her task.

At last Brett spoke. "You know a lot about making a fire."

"Ought to. It was my job when I was with my father." She lifted the matches wrapped in oilcloth that Cooper had left. She struck one and placed the flaming end to the twigs.

"You never told me what happened to him."

"No, I never did." She stared into the rising flames as though seeing something from the past.

An impenetrable wall had gone up. He lowered himself onto the bedroll. "I was lying here counting my blessings before all the commotion. Seems we never value what we have until it's taken away. Want to come sit with me like we did in the cell?"

Her face darkened. "I don't want to talk about that place."

"We don't have to. But we do need to talk." He'd thought pretending she was his wife wasn't going to hurt anything, since he'd faced certain death. But it was. It was going to hurt Rayna in ways he hadn't even considered.

Once the fire caught the twigs, he watched her add a few larger pieces. Then she came and perched beside him. "I like your brothers. They're nice."

"There's no better men to have with you in a fight. They don't back down, and they don't quit until they've eliminated the threat."

"I wish my Hershel was here. He was that way."

Brett reached for her hand. "I wish he was too. I'm sorry his life had to end the way it did."

"Why? Why do the good ones have to die and the rotten ones keep on living?"

"I don't know." Brett took a deep breath. "Rayna, the pretending we did in the jail is something we can't do anymore. You don't understand this life I'm forced to live, people who say I have no right to the same freedoms as a white man."

"That's wrong."

"Yes, it is. But because of that, we can't be together out here."

Her chin raised a trifle. "I thought you were different."

Two gunshots rent the air, then two more. Brett jumped before he could stop himself. It would take a while for his nerves to settle. He swore he still heard the sounds of the gallows being built. "Appears they found supper," he said after several heartbeats. "Are you hungry?"

"Not much." She tugged her hand free and got to her feet.

He hated the thick wall each was erecting. The freedom they'd had while they were jailed was gone, and nothing but sadness and longing remained. "Aren't you curious about where we're going?"

The firelight caressed the russet strands of her hair, bringing out a fair amount of gold. The result was the same bright color as the flames.

"No. It has to be better than where I've been." She turned. "I need to change your bandages before it gets too dark. Doc Perkins would have a conniption if he knew I wasn't tending to your wound."

"I'm tired. I figure morning will be soon enough."

She put her hands on her hips. "I'm changing those wrappings tonight, and I'll have no argument."

Color had swept into her face. He was wrong. She *was* pretty, especially when she was mad. Her softly parted lips drew him like a magnet. The thought crossed his mind to kiss her, and it didn't seem to want to leave. Yet the rustling brush told him his brothers were back. Their privacy had ended.

"Yes, ma'am," he said. "I know better than to mess with a determined woman."

"While I work, I hope you can clear up something."

"I'll try."

"Explain to me how you, Cooper, and Rand can be brothers. You all have different last names."

"We're brothers in here. The only place that counts." Brett tapped his chest where his heart beat out a rhythm that was as strong and true as the love he had for his brothers. "A deep bond formed between us in the orphanage, so one night we sat in a circle, pricked our fingers, and let our blood mix together. We declared ourselves brothers and became the only family we knew. Nothing has or will ever come between us."

"I love your loyalty to each other. It's beautiful. No one I know would travel so far to save me from the gallows. And not one person would want my blood to mingle with theirs."

Cooper and Rand came into the clearing, carrying three plump rabbits. While they skinned and cleaned them, Rayna tore a strip from her petticoat and wet it in a nearby stream.

Returning, she knelt in front of Brett, and his

well-honed senses sharpened as her fresh rain scent drifted into his yearning soul.

Fighting unbearable desire, he slowly removed his shirt. As she bent to the task of untying the strip of muslin that held his dressing, her gentle breath fanned his throat. Tendrils of hair tickled his chin, reminding him of the night they slept side by side. When her fingers brushed his bare skin, he closed his eyes and soaked up her gentle touch.

This closeness he felt between them aroused secret desires for everything he'd denied himself. Rayna showed him what he could have if he trusted enough to accept it.

Truth was, he didn't. He couldn't. Danger waited if he tried.

He walked between two worlds with neither embracing him as he was. He didn't fit in the white world any more than he did the Indian one.

A slight pull then sudden stinging made him wince. "Is the dressing stuck again?"

"I'm sorry I hurt you. I was trying to be very gentle. I'll need more water to loosen the wrappings. The wound busted open, soaked the gauze through to the muslin strips, and dried."

"I'll get some water," Rand volunteered. "Need to wash this rabbit and my hands anyway." He collected a canteen and sauntered to the stream, whistling.

Brett watched Rayna tear several more strips from her petticoat to bandage him once she'd washed his wound. He enjoyed the view of her trim ankles. "At this rate, you'll be naked by the time we get to the Wild Horse."

"Just focus on you getting there." Color stained her cheeks a pretty shade as she went to help Cooper put coffee on.

He swallowed a groan. What in the hell was he doing? A man didn't say things like that to a woman. He'd spent so much of his life in solitude he didn't even know how to carry on a proper conversation.

Brett watched the easy way she had with Cooper. He could learn things from his oldest brother. Cooper would never speak like that to a woman.

By the time Rand returned with the water, the heat in her cheeks seemed to have cooled. When at last she returned to loosen the dried bandage, Brett's muscles quivered beneath her careful touch, and he wished he could prolong the pleasurable sensations that ended all too soon.

"Thank you, Rayna," he said when she stood and gathered the bloodstained wrappings. "Doc was right. You make an excellent nurse. And I apologize for the teasing earlier. I'm sorry."

Her strange-colored eyes met his. "It's okay. There's a lot of difference between you and the things other men have said."

"I'd never hurt you."

"I know." She moved to the fire. Cooper handed her a pointed stick that had a rabbit skewered onto it and asked her to hold it over the flames. She looked as though she might retch. Still, she kept her head averted from the dead animal and did as he requested.

Funny thing though, as soon as Cooper relieved her of the rabbit, she rushed behind a tree and emptied her stomach.

Rand strolled over to Brett. "What's wrong with Rayna?"

"I'm not sure. Maybe she got something bad in the jail. The food they served was little better than slop for the most part."

When Rayna returned, Brett took her aside to ask if she was all right.

"I'm fine," she said, not meeting his eyes.

He knew a fib when he saw one, but he didn't press. She'd talk when she wanted. Or not. Being one who had never felt the need to do much conversing, he understood her desire for quiet.

His gaze followed her as she walked down to the stream. Suddenly, he remembered her refusal to eat the fried chicken the kind jailor had brought them. He suspected it wasn't just chicken she didn't eat. Without a word to anyone, he moved into the woods and found some wild berries, roots, and nuts. Wasn't much, but it would keep her from getting too weak to travel.

Her grateful smile was all the thanks he needed.

While the men devoured their supper, she ate what Brett had found. Every once in a while, she favored him with a smile.

Later, with a full stomach and a blanket of dark shadows around them, Brett moved to a log beside her. His gaze caressed her, doing things his hands could not. Light from the flames flickered and danced across her face, softening the angles. She raised her eyes and met his stare.

Yes, Rayna Harper was pretty. Real pretty.

Six

BRETT AND THEIR SMALL PARTY RODE INTO THE SMALL town of Hawk's Landing a little before noon. The community didn't offer much. But it had a mercantile, a saloon, and a café. The group scattered like buckshot the minute they stepped inside the general store.

Rayna marched off to get gauze and dressings. Cooper and Rand made tracks to the coffee and foodstuffs.

Intent on replacing the ruined shirt he wore, Brett went straight to the ready-made clothing and rifled through the lot. Finally he selected one of black wool.

A pretty blue dress peeking from behind a dull brown one hanging on a wall captured his interest. He pulled it out. "Rayna, please come over here," he called.

When she pried herself away from the gumdrops she'd been wistfully staring at, he held the dress up to her. "I think this might fit. At least until we get back to Battle Creek." No doubt it was a little big, because she was so small, but it was a damn sight better than her ragged, dirty one.

She pulled away, jamming a hand into her pocket. "I don't need that. Mine is perfectly fine. It'll wash up."

Brett snorted. "I doubt that. We'll take this one anyway."

Letting out a huff, Rayna jerked her hand from her pocket. A silver watch clattered to the wood floor. Her eyes grew wide as she stared at him.

Stooping, Brett picked up the timepiece. Sadness that she'd reverted to her old ways washed over him. He would've staked his life that she'd changed. "Do you want to get us arrested again?"

Rayna glared at him with burning, defiant eyes. "That didn't come from this store or even this town."

"Where?" he demanded.

"Steele's Hollow."

He wracked his brain and recalled the egotistical deputy handling a similar watch. "Deputy Dingleby?"

"He asked for it the way he pranced around and said all those things. Then he pinched my rear when we were leaving."

"Why didn't you say something? We would've taken care of that weasel-eyed, sawed-off runt."

"No one listens to the daughter of a bone-picker."

A bone-picker? He'd seen impoverished families who'd resorted to collecting bones in order to survive. Sometimes they drove their wagons across his land. He was about to ask her more when the clerk came over.

"I couldn't help but notice... Is everything all right?" the woman asked.

Brett opened the pocket watch and checked the time. "Everything is fine. We were just discussing

meeting some friends." He took two steps and turned.
"Does the stage pass through here by chance?"

The clerk brightened. "Indeed it does. The stage
lines added us to the route last year. It's due to arrive
at 1:10."

"Much obliged, ma'am." Brett captured Rayna's
hand. He wasn't going to let her out of his sight in case
she spied something she couldn't pass up.

At this rate, he didn't dare turn his back.

A few minutes later, everyone had finished shopping. Being the only one with money, Cooper paid
for their purchases, and they left the establishment.

Outside, Brett left her with Rand. Pulling Cooper
aside, he showed his brother the deputy's watch. "The
runt dropped it in my cell. I didn't remember even
sticking the timepiece in my pocket until just now.
Actually, I was going to leave it on my bunk."

"Damn!" Cooper said. "How are we going to
return it? We can't go back."

"I have a plan." Brett told him about the stage and
his idea to let the driver deliver it to Steele's Hollow.

"Good idea. We can get something to eat at that
little café while we wait."

❧

Rayna entered the little eatery with the men and
thanked Rand for pulling out her chair. She glanced at
Brett from beneath her lashes. She wished he'd let her
apologize so things could go back to the way they were.

Yet when she tried, he'd turned away.

If only she could go back and change things. She
hated that she'd let him down. He'd said she was

someone worth saving. No one had ever told her that. She'd never let herself harbor any thought that she might possibly amount to two cents.

It was strange how a heart adapted. When something ached for a long time, a person got used to it eventually and quit noticing the pain.

She sighed. Old habits were hard to break, especially when they involved someone like Deputy Newt Dingleby. He deserved everything he got. He reminded her of that buffalo hunter who killed Hershel, except that man was taller and heavier. They shared the same beady eyes and appetite for unwilling women.

"Miss Rayna, what would you like to eat?" Rand asked, breaking into her thoughts.

"I'm not sure," she muttered, glancing at Brett.

Rand squinted at the chalkboard menu on the wall. "Better decide. I'm going to have the special. Maybe two platefuls. I'm hungry enough to eat a cow— hooves, horns, and all."

Cooper laughed. "I always claimed you were hollow inside. Guess you're missing Callie's cooking."

Rand grinned. "Sure am. That wife of mine really knows how to fix a good meal. Her cooking was what turned me from my bachelor ways. That and her pretty eyes. Lord, I can look at her all day long." He paused. "Brett, you're awfully quiet."

"Reckon you and Coop are talking enough for all of us."

Rayna caught the glances Cooper and Rand exchanged. She'd seen Brett take Cooper aside, and wondered if he'd told his brother about the watch and her part in it. Embarrassment and shame crawled up her neck.

This was all because of that dumb owl she'd seen the previous day. She needed something more powerful than the little acorn to combat the bad omen. She'd keep her eyes peeled for a four-leaf clover. That should do it.

One thing for sure, she was not going to pick any more pockets. She wanted to measure up to the woman Brett thought she could be. He seemed to think she had potential, and she would show him or die trying.

He would see that she could be honest and trustworthy.

"Well, you could say something once in a while to let us know you're still alive," Rand grumbled. "Half the time I'm not too sure about you, little brother."

The waiter came and took their order, but Rayna wasn't positive she could force down her green beans, squash, and potatoes when they came. Knowing Brett was angry at her had stolen her appetite.

"Didn't you want any meat, Miss Rayna?" Rand asked.

"No, thank you."

Cooper frowned. "Never heard of anyone who turns down meat. You sick?"

"I'm fine. Please don't fret about me." Anxious to redirect the conversation, she addressed Brett. "Now that we have gauze and muslin, I'll clean your wound and change your bandages before we start down the trail. Doc Perkins will shoot me if your infection gets worse."

He swung his dark eyes to hers. "I'm fine."

"You'll damn well let her put a clean dressing on it if Rand and I have to hog-tie and sit on you." Cooper's deep voice indicated he wasn't putting up with any nonsense. "I don't know what's stuck in your craw, but you'd best get over it."

No one spoke.

When the food came, Rayna forced a few bites past the big lump blocking her throat.

"I'll sure be glad when we get off the trail," Rand said at last, taking a bite of his chicken leg. "I'll bet I could grow a crop of turnips with the dirt on my clothes."

Brett spoke quietly. "We have something to take care of before we can leave here."

Rand stopped chewing. "Mind filling me in on whatever it is that's going on? What were you and Coop discussing outside the mercantile?"

This was it. Rayna held her breath. Brett would tell them what she did. And then they'd most likely leave her in this little town alone to fend for herself.

She raised her chin a notch. She'd faced worse. She would survive. But seeing Rand's and Cooper's set, grim faces would hurt something deep inside.

Reaching into his pocket, Brett removed the watch. "You might as well know, I guess. This timepiece belongs to a deputy in Steele's Hollow. He dropped it in my cell, and I pocketed it without thinking. We were discussing how to return it."

She went weak with relief. Her eyes filled with tears at the realization that he would shoulder the blame. For her.

A frown wrinkled Rand's forehead. "Why didn't you give it back when we left?"

"Forgot I had it. I had intended to leave it on my bunk to let the runt know I'd bested him." Brett forked a bite of steak into his mouth. "There's a stage coming through here at 1:10. I'll put the watch on it."

When Brett's eyes met hers, she mouthed, *Thank you.*

A tiny smile flickered before it died. Sudden hope that Brett's coldness was beginning to thaw filled her.

She lifted her fork and dove into her food.

They finished eating and returned to the mercantile, which also served as the stage stop. After getting the watch aboard, they went down to a little creek.

Rayna unwrapped the strip of torn petticoat from around Brett's chest. The wound looked angry and red, but it didn't have any of the seepage around the edges that Doc Perkins told her to watch for. "I don't think there's cause for worry," she said. "But we need to make sure to keep it clean, Brett."

"I'm glad for that at least."

She washed and patted the injury dry. "Thank you for not telling your brothers I stole the watch. But why? Why did you take the blame?"

"Because I wanted to. Wasn't any reason to tell them."

A moment of silence followed as Rayna applied a new dressing. She loved the way her fingers brushed his smooth skin. It was a mystery to her, though, why he seemed almost to wince at the contact. "Brett, I've been thinking. Maybe you should go on without me. I can stay here."

"No." He unbuttoned his new shirt and slid his arms into the sleeves.

"You've done more than anyone else ever did. I won't be a burden."

"No."

When he glanced up with his dark stare, she thought he was the handsomest man she'd ever seen.

The black wool matched the midnight hair that he kept pulled back and tied with the rawhide strip. He was so tall that the top of her head didn't even reach his chin when he stood. The depth of his honor and strength filled her with wonder.

At the jail, they'd seemed bound by something deep and pure.

Only she had to go and ruin it.

"I can't bear to have you upset with me." Rayna chewed her lip. "You don't need to feel responsible. I'm a grown woman. It would be best if we go our separate ways."

"I'm not leaving you at the side of the road, and that's final." He put his hands on her shoulders and said quietly, "What you did saddened me, but I'm not one to keep chewing on the same piece of hide. You'll find lots of opportunities to turn over a new leaf in Battle Creek. I'll help you." He handed her the new garment he'd selected and gently pushed her toward some tall bushes. "Change so we can get going."

Shielded by the greenery, she quickly removed her dirty, ragged clothes and slid into the blue dress. The soft fabric felt heavenly next to her skin. For a long moment, she ran her hands down it, marveling at the delicate texture. She'd never had anything so fine. A bone-picker's daughter didn't know what it was to wear a dress no one else had ever worn.

Digging in the pockets of her threadbare garment, she pulled out the lucky heart and acorn. She stuffed them, along with her prized slingshot—her only weapon, since Sheriff Oldham had confiscated her knife—into the pockets of the new outfit.

The brothers' voices drifted on the breeze.

"We'll ride until dark before making camp," Cooper said. "I figure we can be home late tomorrow. How do you feel, Brett?"

"I'm all right. Don't slow down on my account."

"What about Miss Rayna?" Rand asked.

Brett answered, "Don't worry about her. She'll keep up. The lady has plenty of grit."

"What's her story?" Cooper asked. "Why did Oldham have her in jail?"

"He didn't need much of a reason to lock people in his cells. From what little she's told me, she's had a hard life. Her mother vanished, and a buffalo hunter killed her brother. Not sure what happened to her father. Seems to be all alone though."

Hidden by the thick brush, Rayna put her dirty, threadbare dress into the small bag that held all her belongings. She fought to swallow past the tears clogging her throat.

Alone. Despite the turn her life seemed to be taking, she knew that was to be her fate for what she'd done.

Her sins would catch up with her sooner or later.

Seven

Streaks of copper and orange splashed across the red evening sky like splattered paint when Battle Creek came into view at last. Brett paused, taking in the sight. The buildings, decked out in whitewash by the Women of Vision garden club, sat like pretty brides waiting on their grooms. And the fragrance of freshly cut lumber from the new sawmill put the jagged edges of his soul at rest.

He was home.

Every bone ached with weary exhaustion, and Brett wanted nothing more than to crawl into his tepee that he'd erected a year ago, smell the earth beneath him that was home, and sleep.

At the edge of town, his brothers rode on toward their ranches, anxious to see their families.

Now he wondered what he was going to do with Rayna. His thoughts hadn't gone beyond getting her here. Guilt for that weighed heavy.

After his ordeal in Steele's Hollow, he was extremely conscious of the way people viewed him. In light of that, he couldn't take her to the Wild Horse. He wouldn't do anything to invite people's cruelty. He wouldn't have them calling her squaw or any of the other names he was always braced for. Bone-picker was mild in contrast to some slurs they might resort to using.

She needed someone to take her under their wing, to show her how to do more than lifting people's valuables. He'd gladly do that, but he wasn't sure how often he could come to town. Besides, she needed female guidance, something she hadn't had much of. Maybe someone like Mabel King.

Riding beside Rayna, he glanced at the dress he'd bought her. She looked pretty with her russet curls and the vivid blue-green of her eyes. Like the rest of them, she could probably do with a long bath, a plate of hot food, and a month of sleep.

Even if he wasn't afraid of what people would say, his ranch didn't have any of the things a woman needed. He lived in a tepee, for God's sake.

Brett caught her horse's bridle, bringing the mare to a stop. "Rayna, I'm going to put you up at Mrs. King's boardinghouse. A lady needs a bed, a hot bath, some food, and to get her bearings."

Her eyes widened in the waning light. "I thought I was going with you. I thought—"

"I can't, I won't, sully your reputation. I care too much. People would talk, and they can be very spiteful."

The tremble of her bottom lip nearly did him in.

"You're still upset with me?" she asked.

"No, it's because I have a fierce need to protect you." He pushed back a curl from her face. "I'll find work for you and make sure you have everything a woman needs, such as clothes."

"I have a dress."

"One patched dress isn't a wardrobe. You need shoes other than those clodhoppers you're wearing, and a nightgown, and all that girlie stuff. When I come back into town tomorrow to put a draft for the sale of my horses into the bank, I'll take you shopping. Really, this is for the best."

She narrowed her eyes. "For you. Isn't that what you're saying?"

"Best for you. I explained all of this that first night on the trail. I thought you understood. I have no culture fully my own. I can take people treating me as lesser." A muscle worked in his jaw. "It's what they'll do to you that scares the daylights out of me."

"That talk, those kisses, pretending to be married in Steele's Hollow has to be like it never happened? I can't forget those things," she whispered.

The words hurt, but what he had to say pained him more. There was no other way. "We have no choice. For those few hours, I tried to grab hold of a life I had always wanted and knew I could never have. I said and did things then that are impossible now. I'm sorry."

"But everyone is a stranger here. I'm scared. Maybe you can pretend just a little that you want me. These people will hate me when they find out who I am."

The tip of his bowie knife plunging into him wouldn't hurt like her desperate cries. Damn!

"I shouldn't have come. I've made a mistake. I'm only going to make things worse." She pulled the reins to the right and turned the horse around to leave.

Just before she galloped back the way they'd come, Brett managed to grab her with his good arm.

He lifted her from the animal, surprised at how little she weighed.

"Let me down." She squirmed and kicked.

"Not until you quit fighting." When she calmed, he slid her to the ground and dismounted. "Rayna, what is it *you* really want?"

He'd been so concerned with himself he hadn't truly considered her wishes. He was trying to force this town on her. He'd take her anywhere except to the Wild Horse.

She stared down at the ground. "Not to be somebody's trouble for once in my life."

Her soft words struck him with blunt force. He didn't know what it would feel like for people to help only because he was a burden, but he could see how deeply it hurt Rayna. She deserved better. He had to find a solution, but not at this late hour. "I'll make you a deal. Stay at the boardinghouse tonight. We'll talk about everything tomorrow. All right?"

With a jerk of her head signaling agreement, she reached for her horse. They rode to Mabel King's and went inside. Brett explained the situation, and the woman assured him she would take care of Rayna's needs.

Breathing a sigh of relief, he took her horse to the livery and turned at last toward the land he loved outside of town.

Rayna was a wounded soul. Maybe that was what drew him to her. Even though he couldn't change his circumstances, maybe he could fix her, give her a better life where she wouldn't feel the need to resort to criminal behavior. There was something hidden beneath the layers of hurt and fear. Something worth fighting for.

He prayed he hadn't made a mistake bringing her here. How could he make her understand that what they'd had in the jail cell couldn't exist out in the real world? That only the certainty that he was about to die had given him the freedom to ask for what he knew he could never have?

First thing tomorrow, he'd try again to make her see and pray she wouldn't hate him.

❦

Brett's footsteps had barely faded before Mrs. King set to work. Mabel, as she asked to be called, scrambled eggs and sliced thick pieces of bread, then added strawberry preserves and a big glass of milk. Rayna didn't stop eating until every bite disappeared. Food had never tasted so good.

While she ate, she heard Mabel bustling about the kitchen. The minute she put down her fork and leaned back, the round woman with kind eyes took her hand and led her into the kitchen.

A tub of warm water beckoned. Rayna clasped her hands in wonder as a big lump rose in her throat.

"Go ahead, dear. I won't let anyone interrupt your privacy," Mabel urged.

"I don't know what to say except thank you."

After making sure she was safe from prying eyes, Rayna slid off her dress and petticoats, then eased herself into the heavenly water. With a long sigh, she leaned back.

The icy stream in Steele's Hollow where she'd done

her best to keep clean offered no comparison. Yet she'd braved the chill because the smell of unwashed bodies turned her stomach, and she was determined to be better than her lowly station in life.

She picked up the fragrant soap that carried the scent of roses and lost no time in scrubbing every inch of her body. Afterward, she washed her hair.

An hour later, feeling clean for the first time in a while, she lay in her bed upstairs in a borrowed nightgown and stared at the ceiling, willing sleep to come. But despite everything, her busy thoughts kept her wide awake.

Her mind drifted to Brett. Would he return for that talk like he promised?

And if he didn't, what then?

Hopefully, she could convince him she'd be better off with him at the Wild Horse. She didn't care what people said. But convincing him of that…

A tear trickled from her eye and wet the pillow.

Would she ever find a place where she fit in? She'd tried so hard and waited so long. Surely her punishment wouldn't last a lifetime.

Biting her trembling lip, she turned to the wall. Brett Liberty could help her.

But would he?

～

Safe at last at the Wild Horse, Brett fed and bedded down his horse as the sounds of the night swirled around him.

After making a fire to banish the night's chill, he stared out over the land that brought peace to his wounded soul. The lush meadow, ringed by trees, provided feed for the horses and wide-open space for his tepee he'd made two years ago after studying drawings of one in a book. Living in something made from buffalo hides had appealed to him, drawn him. He'd wanted to find some small connection to that part of his blood. Now, he couldn't imagine living inside walls that didn't whisper as he slept. The babbling creek nearby offered plenty of fresh water for him and his horses. He had everything he needed.

Almost.

Bending, he picked up a handful of dirt and let it fall from his fingers. His soul was at peace here. He could forget his parents had abandoned him at the orphanage as a babe. Forget he was unwanted and unloved.

And he could forget the deep scars he carried where no one dared to look.

He let his gaze roam the rolling hills and the clearing where his horses bunched together to ride out the night. Worry teased the fringes of his mind. He'd taken his last trip to Fort Concho. The quartermaster had informed him they were closing the fort and would have no further need for his animals.

For years he'd caught wild mustangs that lived up in the hills and gentled them. But when the army needed larger ones, he'd started a line of Thoroughbreds.

What was he supposed to do? How would he make a living just selling one now and again to ranchers?

That wasn't his only worry. He was also in a dilemma about Rayna. He couldn't turn her over to Mabel King and go his merry way. He took her from everything she knew and brought her to a strange place where she knew no one.

You should've left me in that jail. Her words echoed in his head.

Yet, he couldn't have lived with himself if he had.

He had a debt to repay. She'd made the difference in maintaining his sanity when it would've been so easy to lose all hope.

That wasn't the only thing though. What he felt went far deeper. Somehow during those days, she had wiggled her way past the iron shield he'd put up.

The woman with hair the color of swirling autumn leaves and blue-green eyes made him willing to give everything he possessed for just one more night with her in his arms. The ache never went away. It only grew stronger. When she'd curled up beside him on that jailhouse bunk, she'd also curled up inside his heart.

Yet no matter how much he wanted the pretty lady, in the world they lived in, she could never be his.

∽

Golden rays of dawn peeked through the lace curtains the next morning. Rayna opened her eyes and stared at the pretty filigree the light had created on the ceiling. For a long moment, she wondered where she was. As one who depended on her quick thinking in order to stay alive, she hated this muddled sense of not recognizing her surroundings.

Relief came when her memories washed back. She stretched then snuggled deep in the quilt. She was clean and had slept in a real bed for the very first time in her life.

The ground, surrounded by sun-bleached bones, had served as a bed when she'd been with her father, and nearly every night since, minus the bones.

The only exception had been the hard bunk with its thin, moldy mattress in the jail. But when she stretched out beside Brett that one night with his arm protectively across her stomach, it felt like pure heaven. She'd been safe and free from the terror that often plagued her during the nighttime hours.

Rayna closed her eyes for a second, remembering the feel of his arms around her and his warm breath ruffling her hair. If only she could feel that again. It would be worth all the pain and misery she'd gone through.

Brett was coming to talk to her today. Maybe he would relent and take her to his ranch. It could be cut off and private, like the jail. She would do her best at convincing him. Her heart raced at the thought of seeing him.

The Wild Horse Ranch with Brett was where she wanted to be.

No other place.

Feeling optimistic that her life was changing for the better, she threw back the covers and quickly dressed.

Mabel King met her at the foot of the stairs. "Good morning, dear. I trust you slept well."

"Yes, ma'am. The bed was like lying on a cloud."

"Come and sit at the table with the other diners. I have breakfast ready."

Apprehension crawled up her spine. She wasn't one to make friends easily. Her footsteps dragged as she followed Mabel. Taking her seat, Rayna tried to remember all the proper things to say as Mabel introduced her. She supposed she must've said all the right things, because the three boarders—a man and two women—warmly welcomed her.

After eating and assisting Mabel with the cleanup, Rayna wandered outside to wait for Brett and sat in one of the rockers that were lined up on the front porch. Taking deep breaths, she tried to calm her jitters.

Maybe he wouldn't come.

Maybe he'd only made an empty promise and dumped her here.

Maybe she was a fool to believe some men still had honor.

In the midst of struggling to tamp down her fears, Mabel joined her, taking the rocker next to hers. The wide porch offered a good view of the town and people bustling to and fro.

Rayna's gaze caught on four gravestones surrounded by a fence that townsfolk and horses alike stepped around. Puzzled, she leaned forward. She found it strange that someone would place a burial plot in the middle of the main street. Curious, she asked Mrs. King about it.

Mabel smiled. "All newcomers want to know the same thing. No one really knows who's buried there, but we believe the graves hold the bones of four men who were massacred in 1838. They were part of a group of government surveyors numbering twenty-five. Only seven lived to tell about the fight."

Brett was an Indian. Were some of his ancestors to blame? She frowned at that possibility. "But why bury them in the middle of the street? It creates a hazard for those having to avoid them."

"Actually, the plot was here first. The town just grew around it."

"Were Brett Liberty's people part of the attackers?"

Mabel ceased rocking. "Oh good heavens, no. Brett isn't from around here. He and his brothers didn't arrive until several years ago. I heard they came from Missouri."

"So the folks of Battle Creek accept him?"

"Yes, we do, and others like him. They're people just like us. Don't see a reason to shun them for something they have no control over." Mabel leaned forward. "Why do you ask?"

Rayna told the kind woman about Steele's Hollow and ended with, "I wasn't sure he'd get out of there alive."

"I'm glad he did. And you too, dear. That's not a fit place to live."

"I like it here in Battle Creek."

The light caught just right on a piece of metal, and Rayna spied Brett coming down the street on a beautiful black horse. She noticed he had a long feather sticking from the hat pulled low onto his forehead. Her heart beat faster.

He came. Just like he said he would.

Once he'd dismounted near the porch, he said, "Morning, ladies. Enjoying the pretty day?"

The sound of his low voice sent delicious thrills over her.

"How did you guess?" Mabel grinned and pushed back a strand of hair that had escaped the bun at the nape of her neck.

"Just lucky that way, I suppose." With the sun's rays

kissing his bronze face and neck, he climbed the steps and propped his lean body against the rail, crossing his legs at the ankles. The knee-high moccasins made his legs appear even longer than they already were. Rayna found her breath trapped somewhere inside her chest. "Are you ready to go shopping, Rayna?" he asked.

"I really don't—"

"I didn't ask that," he interrupted softly. "I'm sure you think you have everything you need, but I want to do this. Please." He swung his attention to Mabel. "Would you please come with her? She could use your help. *I* could use your help."

The round woman's kind eyes lit up. She immediately began smoothing her graying hair and stood. "Give me a minute to get this apron off." She disappeared into the house.

Brett sat down in the rocker she'd vacated. Though they'd shared close quarters while being held in Steele's Hollow, Rayna had no idea what to say to him now. Her tongue seemed tied in a knot, and jitters made her insides hop like jumping beans.

Finally, she cleared her throat. "How is your wound? I probably need to take a look."

His dark eyes met hers. "I'll have Doc Yates here in Battle Creek check it."

"That's probably best…with him being a doctor and all."

"I didn't mean that I think you're not good enough. You did an excellent job, Rayna. As Doc Perkins said, you seem to have a knack for doctoring."

"Thought we were going to have a talk. At least that's what you said last night."

"We will. I promise. Right after the shopping. I have a little more thinking to do first." He rose, took her hand, and gently pulled her from the rocker. "I know you're scared, so I intend to show you the town so you can get used to it. I meant what I said about helping you. And if you decide this is not the place for you, I'll take you to another and another until you find what you're looking for."

His soft words brought warmth to her face. Her pulse raced as she tilted toward him a little. The yearning to be close, feel his strong arms around her, his lips on hers, made her knees tremble with wanting. All sights and sounds melted away. They were in their own silent world like before. She couldn't focus on anything except the nearness of Brett's firm mouth and the fact that they were alone. The force between them was undeniable. And real.

His dark eyes were locked on hers. He started to lean in.

But she'd never know if he'd intended to kiss her, because Mabel returned at that moment, and Brett pulled away with a flush.

"I'm ready," the woman announced cheerfully.

"Then let's head to the mercantile." Brett offered each lady an arm and they set off.

Rayna took in the construction everywhere she turned. It appeared the town was undergoing a growth spurt. When they came to a ladder leaning over the boardwalk, she stopped in her tracks.

Brett turned. "What's the matter?"

"It's bad luck to walk under a ladder."

"Unless you walk in the street, you have no choice."

"You go ahead, and I'll go around."

"It's only a ladder, dear," Mabel said.

"I know." Rayna stepped off the boardwalk and onto the dirt thoroughfare. They were waiting when she rejoined them.

The remainder of the walk passed without any more hindrances. Outside the mercantile, Brett turned. "I will leave you ladies for a bit. I have some errands to run. Mabel, don't listen to anything Rayna says. She needs everything. Especially shoes."

Rayna put her hands on her hips. "What's wrong with my shoes?"

"Those men's clodhoppers aren't fit for a woman. Besides, if you have better shoes, maybe you'll leave my moccasins alone." He leaned in to whisper, "Remember that Cooper is the sheriff in this town."

⁂

Guilt left a trail inside Brett as he strode to the bank. He shouldn't have said that last bit, even as a joke. He either trusted her or he didn't. There shouldn't be any half measures. So which was it? Did he trust this woman he barely knew…or didn't he?

He tried not to worry, yet it was in the back of his mind as he went about his business. A short time later, he emerged just as the nine o'clock stage rolled down the street and stopped at the Franklin Stage Line office across from the bank.

Ever since getting the letter from the woman claiming to be his sister, he'd begun paying attention to the stage arrivals. Just in case. Not that he believed she would come for a second.

He didn't have a sister. She was either some deranged woman, or she had him mixed up with someone else.

Cooper and Rand were all the family he needed.

But still…just in case.

Brett leaned against the building's shadowed wall and watched the passengers getting off. The first person through the door was a thin woman who fanned her face furiously against the swirling dust the horses had kicked up. A small child clutched her dress. Brett was about to head over to the mercantile when a second woman accepted the driver's hand and stepped out.

This mysterious woman stood in the midst of the churning dust without fanning or choking. Instead, she stared unflinching toward the horizon, her pale face a beautiful, calm mask. He took in her fancy hat, kid gloves, and clothes that probably cost what twenty of his best horses would bring.

Something told him this woman never let much disturb her. She seemed to notice everything around her and took it in stride. Even if she was disappointed by what she'd found.

The sun caught on strands of hair beneath her hat and painted them the color of newly plowed earth. She moved aside, and a boy around fourteen or so, who was tall and as lanky as a colt, alighted to join her. In contrast to her pale skin, he was clearly of Indian blood. A jolt rushed through him. He straightened, pushing away from the wall of the building.

A second later, he crossed the street in time to hear the woman speak to the stage driver. "I was told Brett Liberty lives near. Can you give me directions please?"

Eight

THE DRIVER, WHO HAPPENED TO BE AN OLD FRIEND, spied Brett. "I can do better than that, ma'am. Here's Brett Liberty now."

Brett moved forward. "May I help you?"

The woman, who was clearly white, held out her hand. "I'm Sarah Woodbridge, your sister."

Ripples of shock wound through him. How could he and Sarah be siblings? "Miss Woodbridge, there seems to be some kind of mistake. We can't possibly be related."

"There is no mistake. I am your sister. Just hear me out, that's all I ask. I think I can convince you. If not, I'll climb back onto the stage, and you'll never see me again."

That sounded fair enough. She didn't seem to be forcing herself or her crazy notions on him. He had lots of questions, but not in the middle of milling people. Brett swallowed his questions back for later in private.

Without smiling, she turned to the boy who would soon become a man. "This is my son, Adam."

"Nice to meet you, Adam."

"Can we eat now?" The boy rudely turned away, spurning Brett's outstretched hand.

"We will eat when you can show some manners, young man," Sarah said firmly. "I'll not tolerate disrespect."

"Sorry," the boy mumbled. "I apologize, *Uncle* Brett."

"It's fine." After all, they couldn't be kin. Brett's attention swung to Sarah. "If you can point out your trunk and other bags, I'll see they get to the hotel. We have two hotels, the Lexington Arms and the Texas Cattleman's. Do you have a preference?"

"I trust your judgment. I have very limited funds, though."

"Then I suggest the newly renovated Lexington Arms."

"Sounds perfect."

Thinking her statement about a lack of cash a little odd, given her manner of dress, Brett made arrangements to return for her trunk. He escorted Sarah and Adam to the hotel, pointing out the Three Roses Café along the way.

"Will you join us at the café, Brett?" She lifted her long skirts in order to maneuver the steps. "We have some things to discuss."

Brett glanced toward the mercantile, but saw no sign of Rayna and Mabel. "I have to be somewhere. Besides, it's too noisy at the café. I can meet you at two o'clock. There's a boardinghouse up the street—Mabel's. You'll have no trouble finding it. It's quiet there."

"See? I told you," Adam blurted angrily. "He doesn't want us either."

Brett swung around. "I don't believe I said that."

Fidgeting under Brett's piercing stare, Adam mumbled, "Sorry."

Satisfied, Brett opened the hotel door and ushered them inside.

Once Sarah had gotten a room that was furnished with a sofa for Adam to sleep on, she laid a gloved hand on Brett's arm. "I'll see you at two o'clock. I'm so glad to finally find my brother. I've waited a long while for this moment."

Unease gripped Brett as he left the hotel. He didn't know what he'd expected when Tom Mason told him about Sarah two months ago, but this wasn't it. He'd expected her to be more like him, not some rich, cultured woman with pale skin.

Yet the record of birth, in addition to Sarah's letter Mason had provided, seemed to suggest that possibly they were related.

A sister.

He suddenly smiled.

If the evidence didn't lie, he had blood kin.

But he'd learned that even the most fervent hopes could flame and turn to ash in the blink of an eye.

❦

Rayna glanced out the mercantile window in time to see Brett entering the hotel with a well-dressed woman.

A painful lump in her throat blocked her ability to breathe.

Though she vaguely wondered about the woman's identity, she couldn't stop staring at her fine clothes. Those, in addition to the way she carried herself, told

Rayna she was a lady. The kind Rayna desperately wanted to be but never would. That was something a person was born with.

She was a bone-picker's daughter, a girl who would always be on the outside with her nose pressed against the glass.

The new clothes and the first real pair of ladies' shoes she'd ever owned wouldn't make her into anything better. You couldn't make a silk purse out of a sow's ear. She would always be someone's problem.

"Can you think of anything else you need, dear?" Mabel asked.

Only the man who had given her hope of a new start, but Rayna didn't voice it aloud. "No, Mabel. I have more than enough." She turned away from the window and the bitter disappointment strangling her.

"Then I suppose I should tell Mr. Abercrombie to wrap our purchases, and we'll return to the boardinghouse."

"I suppose." She watched Mabel King speak to the proprietor and wondered where she would go from Battle Creek. One thing about it, she wouldn't stay. It would hurt too much seeing Brett and not being able to have him.

She vaguely heard the bell over the door jingle as she tried to swallow past the lump blocking her throat.

A man spoke from behind. "Are you finished?"

Rayna whirled to find Brett standing there, smiling, holding his black hat. Her heart melted at the sight of him even as she knew now he'd never be for her. "I…I am."

"You look surprised. I told you I'd be back."

"Learned a long time ago not to count too much on anyone. Saves disappointment." *And a broken heart*, she added silently.

He took the packages from her. "Rayna, I never say anything I don't mean. I know it'll take some time before you realize that though. Seems we both have a ways to go before we trust. Life has kicked us around too much for it to be easy."

His softly spoken words were like a soothing ointment on a deep cut. She wanted to trust him more than anything in the world.

Only where she came from, trust wasn't discussed, because it didn't exist. She didn't even know how to begin. She knew so little about such things. The more she was with good, kind people, the more ignorant of the world she realized she was.

Brett leaned close. "I'll never toss you aside. No matter what, you'll have me."

The gloom suddenly lifted, and her heart soared with hope. Rayna smiled. "All I know to do is keep trying to find the goodness."

"Me also." He looked down at her feet and frowned. "Where are your shoes? Why are you still wearing these brogans?"

"I did what you asked. I do have new shoes."

"Then shouldn't they be on your feet?"

"I didn't want to get them all dirty on the way back to the boardinghouse. They're the first shoes I've ever had that have belonged only to me."

Brett smiled. "All right."

"I promise to change at Mabel's." Her heart swelled.

Despite her fears, she couldn't help clinging to hope. She decided she'd stick around for just a while longer.

She could always leave later.

❦

Brett was acutely aware of Rayna's small hand clutching his arm as they strolled to the boardinghouse with Mabel. This time he walked around the ladder with her. Whether walking under it gave you bad luck or not, Brett wasn't going to take a chance, since he would meet Sarah in a few hours.

He shifted Rayna's purchases and thought of what she had revealed. How could she not have had at least one pair of new shoes? He couldn't imagine that. Even as an orphan, he usually always got a new pair at Christmas when donations flowed in from charitable folk. Though more often than not, they hadn't fit.

And she'd been surprised that he'd kept his word to come back for her. Something inside his chest had cracked when she said she'd learned a long time ago never to count on anyone. Someone had tried to destroy her. Maybe they almost had.

Raymond Harper? He knew she had no love for her father. For her to be so damaged, it was likely others had tried as well.

Mabel had been walking beside them, but she now turned. "Do you mind if I run on ahead? I forgot I have to get some beans on to cook."

"We don't mind, Mabel. We'll be along," he said.

After watching her stride off for a minute, Brett stopped and thrust the packages underneath his arm.

Then he took Rayna's hand in his. The shadows in her face vanished, and her smile was like the sun peeking through the clouds. "Thank you, Rayna."

Her strange-colored eyes stared up at him. "What for?"

"For being you. You're easy to be around. And for sharing your good luck heart with me."

"The charm you scoffed at. You simply had to believe."

"How can you put so much faith in a carved piece of wood but none in people?"

"Easy. A piece of wood never lies," she said quietly.

"No, I guess it doesn't."

"Would you like to carry it? I wouldn't mind. Really." Thinking of his impending talk with Sarah Woodbridge, he considered taking the good luck charm. But only for a moment. He feared he'd need something more than a wooden talisman before it was all over and done with. "No, you hang on to it. The thing brings you comfort."

"I suppose you'll go back to your ranch pretty soon." Rayna's skirts brushed his legs.

"Not until later. I have to meet with someone first. She'll come here to the boardinghouse."

"You don't sound pleased about it."

"I don't know what this woman's motives are."

"It sure would save in the long run to know ahead of time. But we can't. My grandfather used to say putting the cart before the horse never got you where you want to go. You'll just have to see what she has to say first."

"She's bringing a young boy with her." Brett gave Rayna a half smile. "I wonder if you could do me a favor and keep him company until we finish our conversation. I know it's a lot to ask, but we need some privacy."

Rayna tightened her hold on the crook of his arm. "Of course I don't mind. Tell me a little about him. How old is he?"

"I'd say thirteen or fourteen. He's Indian like me. His name is Adam. Other than that, I really don't know anything else. Sorry." He leaned to kiss her cheek but pulled back, remembering he couldn't keep touching her, kissing her cheek, holding her hand. Deep sorrow that he couldn't do what he most wished sent a blow to his heart. "Thank you. It's good to have a friend I can count on."

❧

At two o'clock sharp, Sarah Woodbridge knocked on the door. She had a woven bag on her arm. Brett let her and Adam in and made the introductions, omitting the fact that Sarah claimed to be his sister. Wasn't any need until she proved it beyond a doubt.

This could all be a hoax of some kind.

His heart lurched painfully. If it turned out to be false…

Once Rayna took the boy outside to the stream that ran behind the boardinghouse, Brett led Sarah into the parlor. Every nerve was stretched as tight as a piece of rawhide.

Maybe after all these years he was finally going to get some answers about who he was.

Sarah declined some refreshment and sat on the settee while he lowered himself into a chair opposite her. She dropped her bag to the floor and pulled off her gloves.

Smoothing back her light brown hair, Sarah met his gaze. "I know you're having a difficult time accepting me as your sister. I had hoped the letter I sent with Tom Mason would prepare you, but I can tell it's a shock to see me."

"To put it mildly. But I'll hear you out. Your letter didn't say much except that my father was English and my mother of an Indian tribe."

"I thought it best to wait for more until we were face-to-face."

Steepling his fingers, he took in her high cheekbones, straight nose, and chin that resembled his. They both had the same proud bearing. And perhaps her skin wasn't as pale as he'd initially thought. They were more alike than he'd thought at first. "What happened to you? Were you taken to an orphanage also, Sarah?"

"No. I was seven years old when you were born. I hid when our grandfather came and took you away. After it was safe, Mother and I lived among her people, the Iroquois tribe." Though Sarah's face remained impassive, tears swam in her eyes.

"You remember it all, I suppose."

"Sometimes I wish I didn't."

"Continue. Why did this grandfather hate us?" She appeared genuine, and if money was her motive for coming, she hadn't asked for any yet.

She rose and went to the window to stare out as though seeing events and people from the past. "First you will have to know our father, Thomas Woodbridge III. He was English and quite wealthy.

He was also an artist. He loved to draw and paint, especially the Native Americans. His wanderings took him to an Iroquois village, and he met the chief's daughter. They fell in love. The chief performed a marriage ceremony, and I was born nine months later. This angered Thomas's father."

Sarah paused then turned away from the window. "Grandfather sent men to order Father to return to England, but he refused. One night, Father was walking along a high cliff in a driving rain. He must've stumbled and fell over the side. Mother found his broken body lying at the bottom. Grandfather arrived shortly after, accusing members of the tribe of pushing his son to his death. Tightly in the grips of raging fury, he destroyed the village."

Brett rose and moved beside her. This woman who shared the same blood that flowed through him needed comfort, but he wasn't sure what to do. Finally, he awkwardly laid his hand on her shoulder and felt her tremble like a leaf in a summer storm. "I'm sorry. This is painful for you. It's all right if you want to stop."

Despite himself, he felt drawn to Sarah. Comfortable, almost. It was easy to be with her. Remarkable, really, since he felt this way only with his brothers and their families.

"No, I need to make you understand what happened."

"Come and sit down then." He led her to the settee and sat beside her.

"Mother had just given birth to you. Grandfather grabbed you out of the cradle Father had built and disappeared. We never knew where he'd taken you.

He would've taken me too if I hadn't hid. He terrified me."

Thick emotion clogged Brett's throat. "All this time I thought my parents had thrown me away."

"They didn't." She laid her hand on his arm. "You were so loved. By them and by me." She took a picture from the bag at her feet and handed it to him. "Our father painted this."

The portrait was of Sarah holding an infant. He knew he had to be the raven-haired babe in her arms. He stared at it for a long minute, lightly running his finger across the babe's face. This was how he must've looked when he arrived at the orphanage.

"I never stopped looking for you after our mother died of a broken heart," Sarah went on. "Upon her death two years later, the tribe sent me to some missionaries, who gave me an education."

"I wish I could've known our parents. Before today, I had no idea to which tribe I belonged." Knowing he belonged somewhere eased the longing in his heart. "But tell me, Sarah, why do we look so different? Why do you appear white? And why am I and your son brown?"

"A doctor once told me that it's not uncommon when there's a mix of white and Indian blood. And as for Adam, the coloring that missed me came out in him. My husband refused to believe the doctor. Jonas Black took one look at Adam and walked out on us. He accused me of being unfaithful and promptly obtained a divorce."

"I'm sorry. I guess that's why you're using the Woodbridge name."

"It is. I gave Adam the choice of taking my name or

his father's, and he chose Black. I think he's clinging to the hope that one day Jonas will want him."

"Give the boy some time. He's going through a difficult phase."

Sarah gave a tremulous sigh. "I'm trying. I was hoping you might help. That is, if you'll let us stay. I used every cent I had looking for you. Then when Tom Mason told me he'd found you, I sold everything I owned to come. Please tell me I haven't made a fool's journey."

Her voice broke as she looked away. "If you can't take me, will you take my son? He needs…"

Brett set his surprise aside. After a moment's hesitation of again being unsure of how she would take his touch, he took her trembling hands in his. Her deep anguish, and embarrassment even, bruised something inside him. Her breaking voice told him how great the cost had been to ask the favor. He cleared his throat. "Of course you can stay. Both of you. I can't find out I have a sister and nephew only to let you waltz out of my life."

"Thank you. I wasn't sure where I would go if you turned us away."

"I may not be much help with Adam, but I'll try."

After all, they were family. Families stuck together and helped each other. He'd learned that from his brothers.

Suddenly, the front door opened and Rayna ran inside. "Come quick. It's Adam."

Nine

BRETT'S MIND RACED AS HE STRODE TO THE DOOR. He couldn't imagine what trouble Adam might've gotten into this soon after his arrival. "What is it, Rayna? Is the boy hurt?"

A gentle breeze blew a russet curl across beautiful blue-green eyes that clouded with worry. "Tried to stop him."

"From doing what? What happened?"

"He took your horse from back of the house where you'd staked it. Then he lit out, heading north."

"I'm so sorry, Brett." Sarah straightened her spine and sucked in a breath. "I have no excuse for him. He'll get lost out there."

"Don't worry. I'll find him." It would take time though. He had to locate another horse first. "Stay here, and don't worry. We'll figure this out after I bring him back...*Sis*."

Brett stumbled over the word that had formed in his throat and curled around his tongue so strangely. It seemed odd that *Sis* seemed to have found a home inside his head this soon.

Dragging his thoughts back to the immediate problem, he tried to consider what he needed to do.

If Adam knew his way around this area, Brett would say leave him be and let him come home when he got hungry and cold. That would be the best thing for him. That strategy had always worked with his wild mustangs. Give them enough rope and time, and pretty soon they figured out he wasn't going to hurt them, that he had their best interests at heart.

But his nephew wasn't a mustang, and he'd never seen this part of the country before. Brett had better find him before he got into more trouble than he could wrestle out of.

Conscious of losing precious seconds, Brett sprinted to the livery and collected the mare Rayna had ridden from Steele's Hollow. He galloped north, keeping his eyes peeled, trying to figure out where his nephew would go.

Maybe Brushy Lake. The glistening water would certainly tempt a normal boy into stopping to skip rocks if nothing else.

Hoping that's where he'd find him, Brett slowed to a trot. He couldn't afford to lose another horse. His heart still ached over the loss of Soldier.

Almost a mile out of town, he rounded a bend and spied the boy limping down the road. Both relief and concern filled him at once. Brett slowed the horse to a walk. Adam kept hobbling, refusing to look at him.

Since it appeared the rebellious young man wasn't seriously hurt, Brett remained silent, riding the mare along beside him. They continued this way until Adam sat down to rest on a fallen log beside the road.

At this rate, it would be dark before they got home, but still Brett would give the troubled youth as much time as he needed.

Brett finally dismounted and joined him. "Where's my horse?" he asked quietly.

"Go away. I don't want you. I don't need you. I don't want anybody. I shouldn't have been born."

He didn't know what had happened, but he knew a cry for help when he heard one. "We all need someone."

"Not me."

Sadness washed over Brett. His sidelong glance caught a muscle working in Adam's jaw as he tried to control his feelings. "I used to think I was unwanted, that my parents threw me away like a pair of holey socks."

Adam glared. "Well, I ain't you. My father did throw me away, and he made sure I knew it. If I was white, he'd have kept me. And sometimes I think my mother would be glad if she didn't have to pretend to like me. I hate being a half-breed."

Sadness colored Brett's words. "There is nothing wrong with being who you are."

His nephew glared. "Name one benefit."

The boy had Brett there. He'd just escaped a hanging for being born. He suspected Adam already knew about that kind of hate. "I don't have all the answers, but maybe we can figure this out together."

"Well, I won't be here long enough for that."

Brett wanted to rest his hand on Adam's shoulder but knew the boy wouldn't welcome his touch. Not yet. He had to get the fourteen-year-old to trust him first. His nephew needed gentling as much as the wild mustangs did.

"Don't know where I'll go yet." Adam stared down the road. "Just know I ain't staying."

"All right," Brett said evenly. "Now again, where is my horse?"

"Don't know. Something spooked the nag, and he reared up, leaving me in the dirt. Ran off down the road."

Though the *nag* comment got under Brett's skin, he overlooked it for now. "Were you hurt?"

"My leg. It's not busted but hurts when I walk."

"Want me to take a look at it?"

Adam shrugged. "Suit yourself."

Crouching in front of the sullen boy, Brett raised his trouser leg and ran his hand over the knee and ankle. "You have swelling. Probably sprained. We'll have Doc Yates check it out when I get you back to town."

"Ain't asking for any favors."

"Not giving any. You have to earn favors. I'm taking you to Doc for your mother's sake. And besides, when you get ready to hit the trail, you won't have to hobble. Wild animals attack those who can't fight back. Keeping you from being eaten is the least I can do."

His nephew glanced nervously around.

"This your first time out West, Adam?"

The short nod confirmed Brett's suspicions. "Lived in New Orleans. Never been to Texas before. There's so much...land. Sky."

"I think you'll like it here if you give yourself a chance."

"Don't hold your breath."

Brett wouldn't, but he looked forward to building some trust between them.

After a few minutes in which the silence stretched like a line of white buttermilk clouds, Brett helped his nephew onto the mare and they headed back. Adam's problem was much larger than he'd thought. Sarah did need help. Lots of it.

He couldn't wait to start replacing some of that anger with a respect for the land and his cherished horses.

But that was the easiest part of his task. The other would take much more work, and he wasn't entirely sure how to go about teaching something he hadn't yet figured out for himself.

How could he teach Adam to embrace his Indian heritage when Brett struggled daily to try to fit into a world that saw the color of a man's skin but not what was in his heart?

❦

Rayna sat waiting with Sarah Woodbridge on Mabel's porch, trying to sort everything out. Had she heard Brett right? Had he called Sarah "Sis"?

If so, that would make Adam his nephew.

The boy had angrily told her that they came to Battle Creek because they had nowhere else to go. That he'd rather die than to live as a half-breed.

Suddenly she wondered if Brett also carried resentment. It seemed possible. He definitely had good reason. Though she'd faced her share of people looking down their noses, no one had ever tried to hang her for being destitute. It must be horrible for Brett and Adam to live with such hate directed at them.

She took in Sarah's beautiful skin that had just a hint of color, like she spent a lot of time outdoors without a hat.

How was it possible that Adam's mother could be white and her son bronze? And if Sarah was indeed Brett's sister, how could they be so different?

"I thought I heard Brett call you 'Sis,'" Rayna remarked casually.

"Yes. He's my brother." Sarah shifted her gaze to Rayna. "I know what you think. It's what everyone thinks when they look at me and Adam." She explained how they could look so different.

"I've never heard of such a thing before," Rayna said, thinking she would've counted it a curse to look like her drunken father. "Did it take a long time to find Brett?"

"Twenty-five years. We've been separated since he was a babe. I found him today only after the man I hired tracked him here."

Rayna stopped rocking. "I'm glad you found him. I had a brother once. If someone told me he was suddenly alive, I'd be so happy."

"I am. I never stopped looking for Brett. I promised my mother I'd find him, and I didn't rest until I did."

"Adam has Brett's features. They're both handsome men."

"My son is fighting against having Iroquois blood. His father walked out on us when Adam was born because he refused to accept a wife or son bearing Indian stock."

"I'm sorry."

Deep sorrow in Sarah's voice told Rayna it would

be a good idea to change the subject. "Is Brett all you'd hoped?"

"More." A smile spread across Sarah's face and briefly lit her eyes. "He's much taller than I thought he'd be. He carries himself like our father. He has such kindness and compassion about him too. I'm so proud of the man he became. He's the brother I always dreamed of finding."

A thought hit Rayna and made her chin quiver. Now that Brett had real family, he surely wouldn't want her. She glanced down at her new high-top boots. They laced up, were made of the softest kid leather, and fit like a glove.

She'd give anything to fit into Brett's world as easily as her feet had slid into the boots. But it seemed her life now was full of firsts.

First new dress.

First new shoes.

And first time she'd saved a man only to lose him.

༺✦༻

As the afternoon waned, Rayna helped Mabel fix some hot tea and took it out to the porch where Sarah kept a vigil.

"Thank you, Rayna." Sarah settled back into the chair with a full cup. "This is nice."

"My mama loved hot tea, but she didn't get any except once in a blue moon." Rayna poured some for herself and got comfortable.

Lord, how she missed her mama. One of these days, if she ever saw her papa again—which she wouldn't if she had anything to say about it—she was going to insist he tell her the truth about what happened to Elna Harper.

Not knowing sat like a boulder on Rayna's chest.

Full of melancholy, she took a sip and glanced at Brett's sister. She liked Sarah. The woman wasn't one to show the turmoil that must be twisting and turning inside her. No tears, no hysterics. Only serene acceptance for whatever came.

A lady like Sarah would never be one to carry a carved wooden heart and acorn in her pocket, much less a slingshot. If Rayna stayed, maybe Sarah could teach her how to be a lady, someone Brett would be proud to claim.

She could learn. She'd try real hard.

In Steele's Hollow, she'd secretly watched the ladies who walked down the street in their fancy clothes. They had fine manners, always knowing what to say and how to act.

No one ever called *them* names; they wouldn't dare. She always told herself that one day she'd be a lady. But she was born to bone-pickers, and *one day* had never come.

With a sigh, she turned back toward the road.

They both must've seen Brett and Adam at the same time, but it was Rayna who breathed the words, "They're here."

She followed Sarah down the steps as they raced to meet the pair, her heart pounding at the sight of Brett. But when she reached them, she hung back, unsure of what to do or say.

Brett dismounted and gave Adam a hand down. Sarah hugged her son despite his efforts to push her away.

Rayna felt the boy's indecision. She saw the yearning on his face to throw himself into his mother's arms despite his best efforts to hide the urge behind cold, sullen features. He was left with pretending that he didn't love his mother and her attention. Rayna saw through the pretense and sensed the truth.

Adam was just as lost as she was.

Brett moved to Rayna and stood with his shoulder barely brushing hers. "I see you're still wearing the new shoes. I figured you'd yank them off and put those god-awful brogans on the minute I turned my back."

"Since you paid good money for them, the least I can do is wear them." She glanced at Sarah and her son. "Other than the limp, Adam looks okay."

"When Sarah gets through hugging on the boy, I'll take him over to Doc's office. I think his knee is just sprained, but need to make sure that's all that's wrong."

"Wouldn't hurt to get Doc's opinion. You didn't find your horse?"

"Nope. I just hope the animal remembers the way home. Instead, my nephew and I had a long talk, the first of many, I suspect."

"If anyone can get through to him, you can."

He gave a short laugh. "Thanks for the confidence."

"I can let you have the lucky heart for good measure."

"You mean the one that doesn't work? No thanks."

Rayna frowned and said softly, "It might've if you'd believed."

His dark eyes twinkled. "I decided I'd leave that to you. I'm much more the facts type. We escaped from that jail because of Cooper and Rand."

"We can believe what we want." And she chose to

credit Brett's near miss with the hangman to the magical kisses. Just like Hershel said. Her brother knew about such things. He had experience.

"Last night I woke up drenched with sweat, and for a second I thought I was back there about to be hanged," Brett murmured.

She nodded, hungering to touch him, to curl up in his arms. "It'll take some time, I reckon. For both of us. When I woke up here at Mabel's, I panicked. Staying alive has often depended on quick thinking. A muddled brain always spelled trouble for me."

Panic washed over her as he stared deep into her eyes, almost clear down to the blackness she wanted no one to see. "I can't imagine what you've gone through. From what little you've said, it wasn't easy."

Talking about herself made her skittish. But the way he looked at her…if she didn't watch it, she'd tell too much.

Things that were better left unsaid. Like the blood on her hands that she couldn't wash off. Killing a man tended to stick in your mind, even if it had been justified. "Brett, we never had that talk you promised. At your ranch, it can be like it was before. No one will even know I'm there."

"They'll know." His solemn face was like an iron fist closing around her heart. "I admit that things are complicated, but I didn't bring you here to dump you. Life in Battle Creek is different from anywhere you've been. You can finally grow and flourish."

"I can do that on the Wild Horse."

"No." He brushed back her curl then suddenly

dropped his hand as agony crossed his face. "I won't let them look down on you and call you names."

"I've been called names all my life. Spat on when I walked by."

"It's not only names. Being with me is dangerous," he said softly. "I'll find you a good job where you can make an honest living, something you can be proud of doing."

Crushing disappointment and confusion swept over her. He'd seemed to hint at something more between them. Hadn't he? Or had she only desperately hoped for love and made it fact, like she'd done with other things so often in her life? "I told you I didn't want to be somebody's problem. Not ever again," she said tightly.

But she *was* a problem—Brett's problem.

"You won't be after you learn a skill other than the one that landed you in jail. Helping you make a new life is the best I can do. Forget about me and the things that happened between us. Rayna, we can't pretend anymore."

Unexpected pain shot into her chest.

Frightening stillness washed over her. There was always stillness before a storm crashed down around her. "I've been pretending all my life."

She watched Brett wince as his piercing brown stare met hers. "Rayna, I never meant to hurt you. I was wrong, and I led you to believe things that just aren't possible. This world isn't safe for people like me, and if you were mine… I just couldn't do that to you. I can't offer more than friendship, but if you're willing, we can give that a try."

Though he'd wrapped the words in gentle softness, they left a harsh sting. She'd been stupid to believe that a man like Brett would want her in his life for real. She didn't need protecting. She needed someone to hold her. "Why did you bring me here, buy all those pretty things? What is the real reason?"

Brett glanced away. "I wanted to give you better than what you had."

A layer of ice formed in her veins. She was nothing more than a shivering mutt he'd rescued from the side of the road.

Her chin rose. "I understand everything. You said you took me from the jail because you saw someone worth saving. I can *save myself*. I don't need you. You're no better than those tambourine bangers always preaching that I'm bound for hell."

Taking a deep, shuddering breath, she continued, her voice barely louder than a whisper. "You consider it your duty to care for the poor, pitiful bone-picker's daughter." Her lips trembled. "I can manage on my own. You can keep your pity and the fancy clothes and shoes." She whirled and ran toward the house.

Rayna had gotten only a few steps when Brett caught her arm, halting her progress. His dark eyes glittered like stones. "Pity? Is that what you think? Lady, the last thing I feel is pity. Good God! I said what I did just now because I don't want false pretenses between us. You deserve honesty."

What she deserved…how about a handful of broken dreams and empty hopes?

Nothing ever changed—hope and despair just

repeated in one endless cycle. Over and over and over again.

She jerked free. Plopping down on the porch steps, she untied her kid leather boots and hurled one at him. He caught it with ease. Infuriated, she threw the second one. She muttered an oath when he made a left-handed catch, his dark brows knitted.

Shooting the buttery-soft footwear as well as the man holding them a glare, she raced into the house and up the stairs.

By the time she made it to her room, the burning behind her eyes materialized. Silent tears trickled down her cheeks. She swept the purchases of that morning onto the floor and curled up on the bed.

She had to get out of Battle Creek.

But how would she be able to leave when her heart desperately wanted to stay?

Ten

AFTER A FEW MINUTES, RAYNA ROSE. SHE UNBUTTONED the new dress that Brett had bought her in Hawk's Landing on the way to Battle Creek and left it on the floor like a puddle of melted dreams.

She stared at the dress for several heartbeats then went and picked it up. Sitting on the side of the bed, she smoothed the folds. Never had she worn anything so fine. After thinking a few more minutes, she folded it neatly and stacked it on top of the purchases from that morning. Getting her old patched dress from her little burlap bag, she shimmied into it, then pulled on the pair of dried, cracked men's brogans.

How sad that she could slip back into her old life as easily as she'd slipped out of it.

Only this time it felt a little dirtier than before.

She glanced down at her ragged dress that had seen her through some tough times. She should've known she could never be a lady. It had been a wasted effort to try. A lady wouldn't have thrown shoes no matter how mad she got.

No wonder Brett didn't want to marry her. She

didn't even know how to act, much less any of the other things ladies knew about.

She began to pace, thinking about what to do. A knock at the door made her jump.

"Dear, supper is ready," Mabel announced. "Brett and his sister and nephew are joining us."

Embarrassment crawled up her neck. She couldn't face Brett after what she'd done. She wanted to dig a hole and pull the dirt on top of her. "No thanks, Mabel. I'm not hungry."

"I'm sorry to hear that. Are you ill?"

"No, ma'am. I'm fine, just fine."

"I'll leave something out for you in case you change your mind later."

"Thank you, but I probably won't be hungry later either."

She might not eat anything again. The knot in her stomach was growing.

So Brett had decided to stay in town. Most likely to get acquainted with the sister he hadn't known he had. She was glad. They needed this time. She imagined they had lots to talk about.

Her thoughts went to Adam. He struggled under a load much too heavy for a young man. Sometimes a body never figured out the world and his place in it. She was still trying after all these years. But if anyone could get him on the right track, it would be Brett. He had a gentle soul.

Anger no longer burned in her stomach. She realized she'd been the one in the wrong, not Brett. The fault lay with her and her bad habit of thinking things meant more than they did. She hadn't listened to what he'd been trying to tell her because she hadn't wanted it to be true. She wasn't sure she agreed that it would be too dangerous for them to be together—that the world they lived in wasn't ready for that—but she believed *he* thought so, and she had to respect that, even if it stung.

At least she could cherish his friendship.

But how would she ever be able to face him again, to look into his eyes and see nothing except what could have been? She'd offered the only thing she had—her heart—and he gave it back. Staying in Battle Creek would be pure torment.

Rayna waited until she was sure everyone was eating supper, then she crept down the back stairs that came out into the kitchen. Quietly, she eased the door open and escaped into the cool night air.

A short while later, she stood in front of the Franklin Stage Lines staring at the schedule posted on the outside of the locked building. The first stage left at 8:15 the following morning. Though she didn't much care where it went, she froze when the words said Steele's Hollow. The second departure was to Corsicana.

That would work. But the cost was one dollar and fifty cents—a hefty sum.

Maybe she should give up on the stage. She thought of *borrowing* a horse like Adam had but quickly dismissed that. They hanged horse thieves.

Bad as they were, her problems were trivial next to horse thieving.

Sitting down on a bench, she stared at the men going in and out of the Lily of the West Saloon across the street. A tinny piano's lively tune drifted in the breeze. She couldn't keep from tapping her foot. While she waited, a plan crossed her mind of how to obtain money for the stage ride out of town.

It wouldn't take any skill to reach into the men's pockets and lift a little change. She wouldn't take it all. They wouldn't even miss it.

A little voice inside her head whispered, *You promised Brett you wouldn't do this anymore.*

But that was before. Now she was nothing but his problem—exactly what she'd never wanted to be.

Well, she'd soon remedy that.

Rayna rose and crossed the street to the brightly lit establishment. She stood to one side of the bat-wing doors, testing herself.

One drunk then two stumbled out and into her.

"What'cha doin', lil' darlin'?" the short one mumbled. "Wanna ha…have some fun?"

When she didn't answer, he lurched back and forth, trying to navigate the boardwalk that evidently pitched and dipped. She took a deep breath. She was ready. She decided that the next drunk through the door would be her target.

The second stumbled far worse than any of the others, and the strong stench of liquor nearly knocked her down. She shivered when he turned his mean, icy stare on her. Before she chickened out, she deftly slipped her hand into his pocket and felt some loose change.

Intent on her task, she nearly screamed when a hand clamped around her wrist.

"No you don't," a man's voice said in her ear.

Rayna swiveled and peered up into Brett's dark eyes. "What are you doing here?"

"Trying to save your pretty neck. I thought you might try something like this. Did you forget your promise to give up a life of crime?"

"That was before I learned I had made a fool of myself in believing I could have my dream."

"Hey," the mean-eyed drunk hollered, "what is your hand doing in my pocket, girlie?"

"Only a mistake, mister," Brett apologized. "I surprised her just as you fell into her. She didn't mean anything."

The drunk pulled himself to his full height, straightening his vest. "I should com…complain to the sheriff."

"I assure you, there's no need. We'll move on."

Giving a huff, the man staggered to his horse at the hitching rail.

Brett took her arm and propelled her to a bench a good ways down the boardwalk. "We need to talk."

The night air seemed to quiver like the hitch between thunder and lightning.

"We've done that," she pointed out. "Go back to your sister. You've done your duty. I don't need you to keep *saving* me." The sharp glare she hid behind should've hurried him on his way. Instead, he sat down beside her.

He stretched out his long legs, crossing them at the ankles as though he planned to stay awhile. "You might not need me, but you've got me, and right now, I'm the only thing standing between you and a jail cell. I thought your promise meant something."

The pain of disappointing him again shot through her, breaking sharp pieces off along the way. In trying to fix the problem and relieve him of his burden, she'd made things worse. She had to get away before her resistance vanished and she did something even more stupid.

Why couldn't she learn how to do things the right way? She felt as though she always lagged behind everyone else. Despite racing to catch up, she never could.

When she tried to rise, he held on to her. She gave a deep sigh. "I didn't plan on breaking my word. I was trying to help, but I have this teensy little problem—no money. In my desperation, I saw all those drunks at the saloon. Picking pockets was the only way I knew of getting out of town on the morning stage."

Even as she said it, she knew that wasn't true. She'd walked for days across the prairie to escape her father. She could walk now.

Had a part of her truly wanted to get caught?

Brett was silent so long she thought he wouldn't trouble himself with a reply. He reminded her of the different seasons that no one could rush.

Finally, he spoke. "I don't want you to go, Rayna. I thought earning your own money would allow you freedom to pick and choose. You wouldn't have to depend on marriage for the security you want."

"I had some dreams once—and hope." She hated the bitterness that crept into her voice. "But I learned that hoping and dreaming were for other folks, not me."

Brett took her hand. "That's crazy. Those aren't allotted only to certain people. Anyone can have them."

"Not me. My heart can't take any more blows."

"Courage is getting back up once we've been knocked down. Shame is in not trying. I'll help you get back up."

"Why?"

"Because I want to. I see a spark inside you just waiting to flare brightly."

"My father hammered into me that people like us don't get to be normal…or liked. We're outcasts. We stay with our own kind. I made a mistake in forgetting that."

"As Cooper would say, that's hogwash. You're just as normal as anyone. Stop limiting yourself."

Rayna inhaled the fragrant breeze, wishing she didn't have to keep hobbling the yearning welling up inside, at times so strong she couldn't breathe. "I have to. It's a lot less painful. If you don't pin your hopes on things, your heart doesn't get broken as often. Our fight is my fault. I have this problem of always thinking things mean more than they do. It's just that I wanted so bad for what we had to be true that I got lost in pretending."

He hesitated only a moment before putting his arm around her shoulders. "If I was able to take a wife for real, I'd want it to be you. But I'll never marry anyone. I'm a color no one appears to have a particular fondness for."

"It doesn't make any difference to me. I see your heart, not your skin."

"Thank you, but it does matter a great deal to some."

Rayna rested her head on his shoulder. "Not to the people of Battle Creek. Mabel told me everyone loves and accepts you."

"This town is only one place in thousands, and the resentment others harbor outside of here would fall to you also. I refuse to let that happen. No one will hate you because of me."

"It's not because I'm no lady?"

"No. I swear it."

"Do you think all this hating will ever change?"

"I hope so."

Relief flooded Rayna. "Then I will wait for you."

"I can't let you do that."

She lifted her head from his shoulder and sat up straighter. "I'm volunteering. I will wait however long it takes."

"Change may not happen in this lifetime," he warned.

"Then we'll try to hurry it along."

"Dear sweet Rayna, I wish others could see things through your eyes. So you'll let me try to help you?"

"I suppose." Rayna picked at a loose thread on her patched dress. "I'll need something to do while I wait for the world to get some sense."

"In the meantime, I can't be anything but a friend."

"I'm glad. I need a friend."

"Let's get you back to Mabel's." Brett rose and pulled her to her feet. She placed her hand in the crook of his elbow. "I have to say that you have an awfully good pitching arm. Maybe I can find you something that requires throwing things. What else are you skilled at?"

A layer of sadness and misery lay beneath Rayna's laugh. She didn't want to discuss the only two things she was good at.

The bottom of her skirt swished against Brett's

moccasins. She cast him a sideways glance as she changed the subject. "What did the doctor say about Adam?"

"Only a sprain. The boy's lucky. I'll spend tonight in town. When I head out to the Wild Horse, I'm going to take him with me. I have a feeling the best thing is distance between him and his mother. Also, hard work. In my experience, that seems to be an excellent attitude adjustor."

"Seems to." They walked in silence for a minute. "Brett, I'm sorry for getting angry. Thank you for coming after me."

"You're welcome."

With her arm tucked in the curve of Brett's, Rayna's heart settled. She swallowed the last of her resistance and bitter disappointment.

As they passed under the shielding overhang of a big evergreen tree, away from the glare of the saloon lights, she turned to stare into the dark shadows of his face. "Could I have something to remember the time when someone almost loved me? One final kiss? After this moment, we'll be nothing but friends."

"I don't think that's wise."

She sensed Brett's yearning as he raised his hand to touch her, only to let it fall.

Powerful need for one last feel of his fingers on her skin gave her the courage to beg. "One light brush of the lips between friends here in the darkness. It won't mean anything."

"Rayna…" The word came out hoarse and wounded.

Tingles raced up her spine as he gently traced the curve of her lips, as though he, too, was filing a memory away. She lowered her lids in an effort to soak up the sensations. Her breath hitched when his sensuous mouth touched hers.

Hunger…

Sweet ache…

Torment…

Desire blazed with the heat of a raging prairie fire.

This first kiss without steel bars between them was full of raw power, danger, and beauty.

Brett's hands plunged into her hated curls, holding her just like she dreamed. This man, hunted and despised, seemed to pour all the secrets of his soul into this kiss. With a low moan, she slid her hand around his neck, drawing him closer.

Delicious agony arced out like the branches of the old tree they were under, reaching, straining for more of the sweetness.

There was a jolt as his thigh brushed her hip when she leaned into him. She knew she'd overstepped the boundaries he'd set, but she couldn't stop herself. Her need to store up memories for the lonely times ahead was too great.

When he ended the kiss, she felt all quivery inside. Flutters in her stomach reminded her of butterfly wings, and Rayna knew from now on she'd never be the same.

She also knew friends probably *didn't* kiss like this.

Despite Brett's vow that they couldn't be anything but dear acquaintances, something appeared to have gotten lost…again. Maybe it would always be this way whenever he was near.

If only Hershel was here so she could ask him what the kiss had meant. But he wasn't. She was on her own.

Touching Brett's face, she met his dark stare. "I think my brother was right."

"What about?"

"Kisses do have magic."

Her promise to wait for him would severely stretch her limits. She wanted Brett Liberty now, not years in the future. Minds usually changed with the passage of time. On this night, even though shadows and uncertainty surrounded them, she would secretly hold him in her heart and relish the love impossible to deny.

~∾~

Rising early the next morning, Brett climbed from the loft of the livery where he'd slept. If you could call what he'd done sleeping. Thoughts filled with Rayna Harper had kept him awake the biggest part of the night.

That earth-shattering kiss had left him shaken.

The moment he thrust his hands into her wild, fiery hair, touched his lips to hers, he knew he was lost.

Before last night, he'd felt their shared time in Steele's Hollow had bound them with a silken cord, but he was wrong. Like it or not, the kiss had tethered them with something stronger—an unseen strip of rawhide.

The funny thing about rawhide…when left under the rays of the sun, it shrank, drawing tighter and tighter and tighter.

He squirmed. The way he'd kissed her wasn't something friends did. He owed her an apology and a promise not to let the hunger for her show again.

Yet deep in his heart, he knew the only way to

keep from repeating it was to stay away from her. And he couldn't do that. Not even if someone marched him up the steps of a gallows and placed a noose around his neck.

The passion they'd shared only made him want her more.

He wasn't quite sure how he felt about her pledge to wait for him. On one hand, a nice feeling spread inside his chest, knowing that she thought he was worth waiting for.

On the other side of the coin, he didn't want her to waste her life sticking around for a happenchance.

Spending all day mulling that over wouldn't get much accomplished, and he had lots to do. But as he strode past the horses in their stalls, her words were in his head. *I don't need you to keep saving me.*

Brett sighed and mumbled, "Sorry, lady. It might make you mad enough to spit nails, but you've got me anyway. You're worth saving, and I'm going to do it if it kills you and me both."

Without an inkling of how to go about that, he stepped from the livery and stared at the town that was rubbing sleep from its eyes. He missed his tepee and the silent, haunting beauty of his land. He also missed his horses and promised himself he'd not leave them again once he'd taken care of a few things.

First, he had to find jobs for Rayna and his sister. And he would keep his word to the farmer who'd told Cooper and Rand where the sheriff had taken him. Parting with five of his best horses was the least he could do to repay the favor.

Cooper rode past him and dismounted at the café.

Brett hurried to join his oldest brother. He opened the door of the small establishment and pulled up a chair at Coop's table. "Morning, Brother. Haven't seen you since we returned from Steele's Hollow." Brett accepted a cup of coffee from the waitress.

"Seems we've both been a mite busy." Cooper lifted his cup and sipped the strong brew. "How's the bullet wound?"

"Fine. I wish people would stop asking me about it every time I turn around."

"They care about you. What are you doing in town so early in the morning? I'm guessing you passed the night here, but why? I've never known you to spend this much time with those of us who walk on two legs." Cooper's grin crinkled the lines at the corners of his gray eyes.

"Stop. It's too early in the morning."

"Can't help if you make it so easy."

"I have problems, if you must know," Brett muttered, scowling. He told Cooper about his sister and nephew's arrival, and Adam's surly attitude. "I'm going to take the boy to the Wild Horse after I help Sarah find a job."

"Sounds like a good plan. My money's on you. Being out there with those horses will help Adam. I swear, you have more patience than Noah when he set out to build that big boat." Cooper lifted his cup again, giving Brett a sideways glance. "How's Miss Rayna?"

Brett had hoped to avoid discussing her. He wasn't ready to share his thoughts. "She's fine. Staying at Mabel's. I promised to find her honest work."

"*Honest* work. That's an odd way of stating it." Cooper scowled over his cup. "What did you mean?"

"Nothing." Brett was thankful for his coloring. It would help hide the heat creeping into his face. He'd said too much. He needed to be more careful if he wanted to protect Rayna from ugly talk. "I only meant that I'd make sure she finds a nice job after all she's been through. Would you know of any openings?"

"Does she have certain skills?"

Did she ever, but none Brett could share. "Forget I asked."

"I heard the schoolteacher is getting married and moving back East."

"Don't think so." Nope, Brett certainly couldn't see Rayna teaching school, besides, she wasn't qualified. He doubted she'd had much schooling going from pillar to post as she had.

Cooper waved at an acquaintance. "Waiting tables at the Three Roses Café? Or cleaning rooms at one of the hotels?"

Those were all right, but Brett wanted something more.

It seemed a good idea to change the subject. "Did you wire Governor Roberts about the mess in Steele's Hollow?"

"Certainly did. He said he wasn't going to have that going on in his state. I'm sure the Texas Rangers are on the way. They'll clean up that riffraff and won't take all day doing it." The conviction in Cooper's deep voice filled the Three Roses Café.

Brett was proud of the way his brother handled himself and the job of sheriff. All the more reason why he couldn't let Coop get wind of Rayna's past. He couldn't bear him thinking less of her. "That's good, seeing as how I'm heading back that way once I get free here."

"Taking the farmer those horses?"

"Yep." Brett took a drink of his coffee. "Owe him a lot more than a few horses. I wouldn't be here if not for that man."

"Don't forget to take your rifle. You might need it. Besides, it'll make finding supper easier than your way of trapping."

"I think I can manage." He hated when his big brother started acting like a father. "Speaking of horses…have to make sure the one Adam *borrowed* made it back to the ranch. If not, I'll have to take time to find it."

"I'd help, but I have to meet the stage." Cooper lowered his voice. "The bank has a shipment coming in, and I have to see that it gets over there all right."

"That's okay, Coop." Brett stood and picked up his hat. He was wasting daylight.

His heart hammered at the thought of seeing a certain head full of flaming curls. He'd just had an idea.

Eleven

RAYNA SAT AT THE EMPTY DINING TABLE EATING EGGS and toast when Brett let himself into the boarding-house. She was glad she'd put her blue dress back on, including the new shoes she'd found outside her door when she returned last evening.

She put down her fork and stared as he strode toward her with confidence. He laid his hat on the sideboard in passing. His dark hair glistened in the sunshine spilling through the windows. "Morning, Rayna." He pulled out the chair beside her and sat down. "I was having coffee with Cooper when an idea struck me. How about working for Doc Yates at the small hospital here?"

"A nurse for a real doctor?" She frowned. "I don't know enough."

"You're good at it. And he can teach you things."

Rayna watched as Mabel silently plunked down a plate of bacon and eggs, along with silverware, in front of him and went back to the kitchen.

This would probably be a good time to tell Brett that she couldn't stand the sight of blood or raw meat. Only then Rayna would have to explain why.

She didn't want to do that. Not yet. It was too painful.

Her gaze lowered to her plate. "I'm not sure this is a good idea."

"Why? Already spoke with him, and you could sure help him out if you wanted. One of his nurses left, and he's shorthanded. He's so desperate he offered to hire you sight unseen. I could take you over there after we eat." He lifted his fork and shoveled eggs into his mouth.

Oh dear. What was she going to do? She would end up making a total fool of herself. The only way she'd handled his wound in the Steele's Hollow jail that night was because of sheer willpower. She knew she had to find that bullet fragment or Brett would die. She had been determined not to have that on her conscience, along with everything else.

Rayna picked up her glass of milk, staring at the man whose kisses had branded themselves in her memory. Brett Liberty made her believe that anything was possible.

Even hoping and dreaming.

As unusual as it was, she'd felt a dream beating inside her when she awoke that morning. A lot had shifted in her life since Sheriff Oldham threw Brett into the cell next to her that fateful day.

The little carved heart she carried had to have changed her luck. She reached into her pocket for the charm, caressing it for a minute. Perhaps it was worth giving nursing a try.

After they finished eating and she washed dishes for Mabel, she walked beside Brett to the small hospital. Despite having misgivings, excitement beat in her heart when she opened the door. She had a *real* job.

Maybe she could finally be like normal people. It seemed a start.

A short, stooped man rushed to meet them, his disheveled shock of snow-white hair fluttering in the wake created by his hurry. "There you are, my dear." He took her hand. "I'm Doc Yates. You don't know how grateful I am to have your help."

"It's a privilege to have the chance, Doctor." She immediately felt at ease. Behind a pair of spectacles were the kindest, wisest eyes she'd ever seen. "I'm Rayna Harper."

"When can you begin, Miss Rayna?"

She met Brett's warm stare before she answered, "Today, if you need me."

"Perfect. I admitted three new patients and haven't had time to get them settled in properly. If you can do that for me, we'll start their treatment sooner. Brett tells me you're excellent at changing dressings. Says you have the gentlest touch." Doc's faded blue eyes twinkled. "I think he's quite smitten, if you ask me."

Her face flamed. "Oh, no, sir. We're only friends."

Doc patted her hand and winked. "Better than being enemies."

"No fair having fun at my expense, Doc," Brett replied, frowning. "I will leave Rayna in your hands and get about my business. Promised to help my sister find employment also."

"Try the Texas Cattleman's Hotel if she's got a good head for numbers. Heard they're looking to hire someone."

"Thanks, Doc." He turned to Rayna. "I probably

won't see you for a few days. I have to return to a farm outside of Steele's Hollow to repay a debt."

Instant fear seared a path up her spine. She sucked in a breath and reached for him. "Please don't go. They'll kill you."

"Don't worry. I'm not going into town, but even so, the Texas Rangers are riding toward there now to clean up that mess."

"All the same, please be careful."

"I will," he promised.

A flash of tears blurred his tall form as he strode to the door. For two cents she'd delay starting the nursing job and go with him. He needed someone to look out for him.

Someone to change his bandage and guard his moccasins.

Someone like her.

❦

Brett left the hospital with a warm feeling of satisfaction, glad she'd been willing to give the job a chance. The more he learned about her, the more his heart broke. Both life and her father had beaten her down until she hadn't been able to see any way out of her circumstances.

Hopefully now things would change for the better.

He strolled down the street and met Sarah in the lobby of the Lexington Arms Hotel where she and Adam were staying. He hesitated only a moment before he kissed her cheek and took a chair beside her. "Where's Adam?"

"He's upstairs in our room. Why?"

"Just curious. I'd like your permission to take him on a trip I have to make. We'd be gone a week. It'd be good for him."

"I think it would also. He's bored, Brett. He needs something to do."

"Then the trip would be perfect. Also, when I get back, I'll keep him with me at the ranch for a while."

"You don't know how much I appreciate this."

Brett flashed a wry smile. "Don't hold your breath just yet. I'm not a miracle worker."

"You've given me hope. That's more than I've had in months."

"I may have news. Doc Perkins heard that the Texas Cattleman's Hotel is looking to hire someone who has experience in keeping books. What kind of job did you have before you came here?"

Sarah lowered her eyes. "I worked for Madame Duchaine's in New Orleans."

The name wasn't familiar, but from her deep embarrassment, he guessed it to be an establishment in the red-light district. Certainly no place for a boy, or his sister.

"What was the nature of your employment?" he asked quietly.

Resting her hand on his arm, she lifted her head and shot him a gray stare. "Not what you think. I was their bookkeeper. Adam and I had our own separate living arrangements outside the establishment. I never exposed him to that sordid life. I love my son and wouldn't do anything to harm him."

"Don't get so defensive, but you can't mention any of this to Potter Gray when he interviews you for the position."

"I know. What *do* I say?"

"I'm out of ideas."

"How about that I was a private bookkeeper to a wealthy man who recently died? That way I wouldn't have to explain the lack of a letter of reference."

For a long moment, Brett didn't speak. He'd never told an outright lie in his life, and the thought of doing so now soured his stomach. But this was necessary, he told himself. He had to help an outcast like himself. Sarah had nothing. She needed this job to survive. "It might work."

"I need a name to give him."

A man strolled by at that moment wearing a Prince Albert hat. Brett's gaze followed him. "Albert. Albert Wynn."

"All right. I'm going to head over to see Potter Gray." She rose and smoothed the front of her dress. "I'm a little nervous. How do I look?"

Brett got to his feet and gazed at his sister. She was a beautiful woman. Her upswept hair, the color of a brown robin's wing, combined with the cut of her dress, added elegance and warmth. "You look very pretty. And smart."

She laughed. "Thank you. I certainly hope so." She kissed his cheek, then worry darkened her eyes. "If I get the position, I'll need to ask a favor."

"You know I'll help."

"I'll need more clothes similar to what I'm wearing." She glanced down. "I had to borrow this dress from a friend so I'd have something suitable. I wanted to make a good impression. I have others, but they're not good enough for a fancy hotel like the Texas Cattleman's."

The admission surprised Brett. He'd never have guessed her circumstances by looking at her. "I would've thought you had plenty of nice dresses from the work you did for this Madame Duchaine."

"I never went to the establishment, so had no need for fancy dresses. She brought receipts and bills to my home weekly."

"All right. I'll set up accounts for you at the mercantile and anywhere else. Get whatever you need, Sarah."

She finally looked up and smiled. "You don't know what a relief it is to get that off my chest. Having to ask for favors wasn't the way I wanted to start off our relationship. Go on up and visit with Adam until I return. First room on the right."

He waited until she left, then went upstairs. Pausing outside the door Sarah had indicated, he took a deep breath before knocking.

When Adam didn't come, he knocked again.

This time the boy jerked the door open and glared. "You. What?"

"Why didn't you answer the door?"

"Didn't want to. Thought whoever it was would have sense enough to go away."

"I'm not ever going away, no matter how angry you get," Brett said quietly. "Your mother asked me to wait up here with you until she gets back. May I come in?"

"Suit yourself." Adam turned, hobbled to the sofa, and plopped down.

Brett slowly entered and crossed to the window, where he looked out. He knew what needed to be said, and he chose his words carefully. "I'm glad you didn't have to grow up in an orphanage without a soft bed, plenty of food, or family. I sure didn't have a mother who loved me more than she loved anything in this world."

"You expect me to cry?"

Brett whirled. "I want you to wake up. Look at all the beauty and the gifts around you. You were granted life for a reason. You should appreciate all you've been given."

Adam crossed his arms. "Oh, you mean being a breed? And having a father who hates the very sight of me? Sure thing, *Uncle*."

"I don't know about a father, but I'm no stranger to hate."

"People hate Indians, but breeds worst of all."

"Your attitude doesn't make it better. One day you'll see that."

"Yeah? Well…"

Seeing he was making no progress, Brett walked to the door. "I was going to take you on a trip. If you want to go, find me."

With that, he turned the knob and strode downstairs to wait.

The situation reminded him of an Indian parable a wise old man had told him about everyone having two wolves inside. One was good, the other bad. Only one could survive all a man's life. Whichever one you fed would win.

Sadness filled Brett to see the bad wolf winning the fight for Adam's soul.

The wise man who'd told him the story was Isaac Daffern. Daffern had rescued Brett, Cooper, and Rand when they were boys. They'd escaped an orphan train and walked for days to Hannibal, Missouri, where they worked hauling water in a bathhouse. One night when Brett was only eight years old, a man accused him of stealing his watch. Tolbert Early beat him really bad. Cooper—who was fourteen—shot Early, and they had to run for their lives.

Daffern took them to his ranch and taught them to be men. He showed them how to run a ranch, have love for the land and animals, and most of all to love themselves.

Brett missed that old man who'd been like a father. He could sure use Daffern's wisdom now. He glanced out the window at the people hurrying by. Opening the door, he found a seat on a bench in front of the hotel.

Pretty soon, Rand rode into town, spied Brett sitting there, and dismounted at the hitching rail. "Now, I sure don't ever recall seeing you sitting on this bench—or any bench in town for that matter—in the middle of the day, little brother. What are you doing?"

"Waiting for my sister."

Rand sat down next to him. "When did she get here?"

"Yesterday." It was hard to imagine. Seemed like Sarah and Adam had already been there a week.

"How's it going?" Rand slapped at a fly buzzing around his head.

"Everything is fine. I like her. She answered a lot of my questions about who I was and where I came from."

"Glad to hear it. The mystery really bothered you.

But if it's going so well with your sister, why do you look like you just went to someone's funeral?"

Great. Now Brett would have to rehash the whole thing. Why couldn't Cooper and Rand get together when he was telling something so he'd only have to say it once? "Ask Coop."

"Not around. Busy with sheriffing duties, I'm told." An ever-present grin spread across Rand's face. "So shoot. Why the dark scowl?"

Brett gave a long-suffering sigh and went over all the problems with his disrespectful nephew once more. Hopefully for the last damn time. "He's breaking his mother's heart. I don't know if I can help him."

"I'm betting on you, little brother. It takes time for a kid to accept who he is and look for the best in himself. My son Toby had to do this, and he's only six. Guilt ate him up two months ago when Nate Fleming tried to take him from us and was killing everyone who got in his way. Toby saw it as his duty to take on the sins of his outlaw father and his evil rampage."

"How is the boy doing?" Brett asked quietly, remembering that horrifying time, not knowing when Fleming would strike next, or where.

"Healthy and happy and loving every minute of life with his sisters. He's the best kid. Adam can be also, under your expert tutelage."

"Tutelage? When did you learn to speak so fancy? And what have you done with my brother?"

"Callie's been teaching me these big words like *peruse* and *flagellate*. Says she's broadening my horizons, whatever the heck that means."

"Well, when you're with us common folk, just

speak it plain so we can understand you." Brett sighed, stretching out his long legs.

"Where's Miss Rayna? How's she doing?"

"She started working for Doc this morning. He needed a nurse, and she seems to have a gift for patching up people."

"That's great news. She does seem suited for it."

"How are the rest of the kids?"

"Wren is growing like a weed. She's almost six months old. And Mariah is looking more and more like her mother. It's amazing what can happen in a short time. It's as though Mariah has always lived with us. She doesn't even have nightmares anymore."

"Poor kid. Fleming did his best to kill her."

"Yeah, but he didn't. She's tough."

"How's Callie?"

"Just fine." Rand's eyes lit up. "That wife of mine is something else. I'm a lucky man."

Rand's life had really changed over the last four months. He went from a determined bachelor to a family man with three children who he loved more than his land and the ranch he bought from the sale of his saloon.

It just showed that a man didn't always know what waited around the next corner.

The Bachelors of Battle Creek had shrunk to one.

And that's where it would stay.

Brett's thoughts turned to Rayna. A little more than a week ago, she had no hope. She was locked in a cell, with no future. Now she was making friends and had a job in a hospital.

She was no longer an outcast and had discovered she could be one of the *normal* people she'd envied.

Just proved anything was possible.

Even more possible was the fact that with her new freedom and money, she wouldn't want him. Waiting got tedious. Just a matter of time before she found someone else to settle down with and have a houseful of children.

Throbbing pain shot into his heart, nearly doubling him over.

Twelve

ONCE RAYNA PUT ON A WHITE APRON, DOC YATES kept her moving from one patient to the next. The small hospital had eight beds, and seven were full.

She visited every person and acquainted herself with their case, plumped pillows, spread blankets, and in general made them comfortable. Doc even let her change a dressing under his watchful eye. More than one told her they'd never received better care or felt a more comforting touch. Her chest swelled with pride.

It neared lunchtime when Doc Yates rounded the corner and headed for her. "Nurse Harper, I couldn't be happier with your work. You've been a godsend."

"Thank you, Doctor. I'm enjoying being of help."

"Would you like to go pick up the patients' food at the café? They usually have it ready about now."

"I'd love to."

Still smiling five minutes later, she strolled toward the Three Roses. Everyone she met said hello and wished her a nice day.

Maybe Brett was right in saying she could be just as normal as anyone.

But when she reached Main Street and turned left, her smile vanished, and she froze.

A wagon piled high with sun-bleached bones was parked next to the mercantile.

A dull-eyed woman and three raggedy children stood beside it. A man whose eyes showed the same dullness sat on the wagon bench. People were giving the family a wide berth. She didn't recognize them, just their pitiful circumstances. Though she wished she could walk by without sparing them a glance, she could not.

Even though it took every bit of courage she had. Her heart went out to the family, especially the children, who didn't have a say in how their parents made a living. As painful as it was to admit, she had been one of them.

A thick lump blocked her throat as she forced herself toward them.

Holding back a sob, Rayna drew closer to the mother, who didn't look much older than she. The woman coughed into a dingy rag that, like the clothes they wore, had seen better days. When she lowered the cloth, it was blood spattered.

Rayna sucked in a breath and touched the woman's thin shoulder with a trembling hand. "Ma'am, do you need help?"

With panic-stricken eyes, the woman shrank back, shaking her head furiously. Her man leaped from the wagon seat and planted himself between them. His matted, shaggy beard gave no hint of his age. "Leave my wife alone. She's fine. We don't want no trouble. We ask for nothin'; we take nothin'."

"Sir, I only want to help. I work as a nurse for Doc. Your wife is sick."

"She'll be good as new in a few days. Only tired." He laid a gentle hand on his wife and helped her to a seat on the boardwalk. He hurried to the wagon and came back with a cup of water.

A flock of crows suddenly flew down from the roof and perched on the bones. When Rayna counted five, her breath hitched painfully. Five crows were a sign of sickness.

At least there weren't six. That meant death.

The children—two girls and a little boy who hadn't been walking long—crowded around Rayna. She gave them a smile, wishing she had a few coins to press into their palms. By the way they shyly touched her dress, she knew they'd never seen anything so pretty.

An ache that went bone deep pierced her chest. "Hello, my name's Rayna. What's yours?"

The biggest of the children—who was around eight years old—whispered, "Alice."

"That's a beautiful name, Alice."

The girl's straggly, pale blonde hair hid her face. She ducked her head and hurried to her mother. The other children followed.

Rayna turned to the father. "Please let Doc take a look at your wife. These children need her."

"We must go." He pulled his wife to her feet and moved her toward the wagon. "We don't have money for doctors. Get in the wagon, kids."

"I know how desperate things are, sir, but if you change your mind, there's a hospital one street over. You'll be welcome."

"No one welcomes us."

Tears filled Rayna's eyes as the pair of oxen pulled the wagon slowly down the street. He hadn't lied. No one *ever* wanted bone-pickers in their town. They were outcasts.

Her heart broke for the little family. What would become of the children? Especially if their mother died. She knew how it was to lose a mother. She wouldn't wish that on anyone.

She clutched a post that held up the building's overhang and swallowed a rising sob. Where was justice for outcasts and lost mothers?

After a few minutes, she regained her self-control and remembered she had food to fetch for the patients.

Still, as she strolled toward the café, she was heart-sore and raw inside, recognizing that at least part of it came from worry for Brett. What if that sheriff caught him again? What if Brett didn't come back?

Such a thing would destroy her soul.

⚶

By the time noon arrived, Brett had everything he needed to make his trip. Leading the string of five horses, he neared the Lexington Arms Hotel, intending to try one more time with Adam.

Sarah had returned from her interview that morning with Potter Gray, and the man had hired her to keep the Texas Cattleman's Hotel books.

Brett thought he should give up raising horses and just go around town finding people jobs.

And then he saw her, and his breath caught.

How could he miss that hair? Or the blue dress that brought out the color of her eyes.

Or the way his heart skipped a beat at the sight of her. Memories of the kiss beneath the moon-washed evergreen crowded into his head. How could they just be friends when his heart hungered for more?

He had to be satisfied with what he had and not yearn for the impossible. Wishing for more would end in failure and disappointment. Slowly he dragged his attention back to the woman who had his insides in an uproar.

Rayna walked slowly toward a bone-picker's wagon. Her steps were hesitant, but she didn't stop. He pulled to the side, out of the traffic, to watch.

Maybe she knew them. Though given his age, the man couldn't be her father, and her brother was dead.

She seemed concerned about the woman, who didn't look well. Though he couldn't hear the conversation, he could see Rayna's kindness toward them. But then, having lived that life would probably make her more sympathetic. She knew firsthand how hard bone-pickers had it.

When the family loaded up and drove slowly down the street, he crossed to the other side to speak to her.

A smile teased her lips and lit up her sad eyes when she saw him. "What a nice surprise. I thought you'd left."

"Had some things to do first. Just came back into town to see if Adam changed his mind. He was dead set against it earlier." Brett paused, then said low, "Saw you talking to that family. You have a big heart, Rayna Harper."

"The mother is sick and coughing up blood. I was trying to get her to come to the hospital to see Doc, but her husband refused. I'm worried about her, Brett."

The slight tremble in her voice revealed her concern. He saw that she was a hair away from tears, wanting to help but frustrated that she couldn't. "You can't make people do something they don't want to."

"Those children need her. And then five crows flew down and lit on the bones in the wagon."

Brett was hard-pressed to keep from grinning. "What do five crows have to do with anything?"

"They foretell of sickness." She sighed. "At least there weren't six."

He took it that six would've been real bad. "Given the woman's symptoms, you didn't need some birds to tell you what you already knew, did you?"

"Well, no."

"I rest my case. Where are you headed?"

A light came into her eyes. "Doc Yates sent me to the café to pick up food for the patients. I love my job. Thank you for talking me into trying."

"That's what I'm here for. Do you mind if I walk with you to the café?"

"I'd love it." She waited while Brett tied the horses to the hitching rail, then took his arm. "I'm gonna miss you."

He glanced down at her small hand and smiled. Rayna made him feel special. Somehow, he saw his worth mirrored in her blue-green gaze. "I'll miss you as well. Tell me the favorite part of your job so far."

"Helping the patients. They're stuck in bed and in such pain, but they're immensely grateful for even the smallest things I do for them. It makes me feel good."

"I'm glad. You have so much to give."

Holding the door to the café, he wished he could

accept what she'd offered him. He wanted more than a token of friendship.

Much more.

After carrying the lunches back to the hospital, he stood awkwardly, fighting the yearning to touch her but knowing that would be wrong. Finally, he tucked her smile into his heart, promised to be careful, and left. Collecting the horses, he moved down to the Lexington. His heart leaped when he saw Adam leaning up against a pole in front. "Glad you changed your mind, Nephew."

Adam straightened. "Beats listening to that ticking clock in the hotel room. Just don't talk."

"Don't worry on that account." Brett handed him the reins to the horse he'd brought for the boy, just in case. He waited for him to mount, then silently turned and trotted out of town.

An hour later, they stopped to rest the horses and let them drink from a spring.

Brett didn't speak a word to Adam. If the boy wanted silence, that's what he'd give him.

Not a word left Brett's mouth for the remainder of the day. He rode, listening to the clip-clop of hooves and the animals' snorts. Every once in a while he glanced at Adam's features, frozen in sullen lines.

The sun had slipped below the horizon before they made camp for the night. Brett went about his chores, paying Adam no mind. He laid a fire, boiled coffee, bedded the horses down, and killed a rabbit with the rifle Cooper had insisted he bring.

Adam watched it all. Finally, he asked, "Aren't you going to say anything?"

"You didn't want me to talk. I was only respecting your wishes."

"I didn't mean ever."

"Would you like to help cook our supper?"

At Adam's shrug, Brett handed him a skewer with pieces of the rabbit on it, and made room on the log where he sat by the fire.

Side by side, they each held the meat over the flames while the moon rose above the treetops.

Brett recalled another such recent night with Rayna after Cooper and Rand had gotten them out of jail. How she refused to eat any of the rabbits. He'd meant to ask her more about that, but he'd forgotten in the wake of Sarah and Adam's arrival.

When he got back, he'd try to get her to talk about it. He sensed a story there.

But it was more than idle curiosity. He wanted to know everything about her and the life she'd lived before he met her. She was one of those before and afters that divided an important part of his life.

Everything before he'd found her seemed trivial. Only the *after* interested him. He hadn't been really alive until Rayna.

She's just a friend, he reminded himself. That's the way it had to be if he truly cared.

But convincing his heart…now that would take some time.

A coyote's howl sent Adam scooting closer to him.

"The animal won't hurt you unless it's traveling in a pack," Brett reassured the boy. "That one's not. Our supper's ready. Let's eat."

Adam pulled some meat off the sharpened stick and

cautiously stuck it in his mouth. "Where are we going to sleep?"

Though Brett wanted to tell him to look around, he didn't. "On the ground. On a bedroll. Haven't you ever slept under the stars before?"

"Nope."

The boy must've liked the taste of rabbit, because he crammed more into his mouth. Plainly his nephew had even more catching up to do than Brett thought. He just hoped he could teach him enough survival skills before the boy actually needed to use them.

"Tell me again why we're taking these horses all this way." Adam bit off another big bite.

"To pay a debt I owe."

"What kind of debt?"

Brett wished Adam would sink back into moody silence. If he kept asking questions, Brett would wind up revealing too much. It wasn't that he didn't want Adam to know about the ordeal in Steele's Hollow. He was concerned that learning about the near hanging would worsen Adam's internal struggle. "For saving my life. Always pay your debts, Adam. It brings honor," he said quietly. "No more questions."

Sounds of the night filled the silence. The coyote's howl, the hoot of an owl, the musical babble of the spring, the soft nicker of the horses…

…the sound of a snapping twig.

On instinct, Brett jumped to his feet and hauled Adam into the darkness, whispering to keep quiet while he slid his bowie knife from its sheath.

"Hello the camp," someone called. "Don't want no trouble. Just want to share your fire."

"Come on in, but keep your hands where I can see them," Brett answered. He whispered to Adam, "Stay here until I tell you to come out. Understand?"

When Adam nodded, Brett emerged from the shadows as a lone rider came into view. The man positioned his horse so he dismounted facing the campfire, showing Brett he meant no harm.

"Thanks for the invite," the rider said. "I'm saddle sore."

As the man turned, Brett recognized Hank Maxwell, the old deputy from Steele's Hollow. "You alone, Maxwell?" Brett stepped toward the light.

The deputy's eyes widened beneath his bushy eyebrows. "Never thought I'd see you again, Mr. Liberty. What are you doing with all the horses?"

Brett stiffened. "They're not stolen."

Maxwell lifted his hands in protest. "Not accusing you. Besides, I ain't a deputy anymore. I quit when the Texas Rangers rode into town. Do you mind if I have a shot of that coffee? Sure does smell good."

Brett poured some and turned toward where he'd left his nephew. "You can come out, Adam."

Taking the cup, Maxwell asked, "Who's Adam?"

"My nephew." When Adam came into the firelight, Brett introduced the former deputy.

"Never thought you'd mosey back this way again after your brothers got you out of jail. Shouldn't you be riding away from Steele's Hollow instead of toward it, Liberty?"

So much for trying to keep things from Adam. Now Brett would have to explain the whole mess.

And Adam's hate for who he was would grow.

"I'm taking five of my horses to the farmer who told my brothers where I was. I keep my promises," Brett said quietly.

He could already see the questions forming in Adam's head. The boy had seated himself on the log and took in every word.

"Yeah, saving your life calls for a little settling up." Maxwell's droopy white mustache twitched with his sudden smile. "Things are different in Steele's Hollow. The rangers put Newt Dingleby behind bars when the fool shot one of them. Oldham is on the loose, but it's only a matter of time till they catch him."

"I'm glad to hear it. Where are you headed?"

"Got a little spread up by Flat Creek over in Henderson County. Not much." Maxwell stared into the flames. "But it's a good place to die."

If a man was lucky, he'd have one of those places staked out. For Brett, his soul would be at peace only on the Wild Horse.

And if he was lucky and the world would allow it, Rayna Harper would lie beside him. He'd take comfort in that.

Thirteen

THOUGH RAYNA TRIED TO KEEP HER MIND OCCUPIED the following morning as she worked under Doc Yates, her thoughts were far away on a certain man with bronze skin. She'd never known what a grin could do to her until he came along. He didn't smile often, but when his mouth deepened at the corners to show his white teeth, her heart ran away with hope and possibilities.

Pleasing as his looks were, there was much more to him than that.

Brett Liberty was one of those men who was forged by a hotter fire. The fire gave him power, and the blows he'd taken provided strength so he was able to stand when other men fell. She'd seen this with her own eyes in Steele's Hollow. No one else would've faced death with dignity like he had.

She couldn't wait for him to return. Even though she might not see him much, just knowing he was near would put her at ease.

Finding a free minute between patients, she closed her eyes and said a silent prayer. She'd seen inside a church only twice in her life, so she didn't know if praying worked, but she wanted to try anyway.

Pain rose up, swift and powerful. She'd gotten up early one Sunday morning a few months ago and bathed in the icy water of the creek so she wouldn't smell. She'd washed her dress, and after it dried, she went down to the church and took a seat near the back. Just as the singing started, two men came and told her they didn't allow her kind in there.

With her face flaming, she ran from the building. That was the last time she'd made that mistake. She decided if she wasn't good enough for the churchgoers, maybe she'd just stay with her own kind—whoever they were—and not think too much about praying.

Those preachers preached about repenting, and Lord knew she had a lot of things weighing on her heart. Only she couldn't face up to them. If only she had a trace of Brett's steely courage, she would own up to her sins.

Rayna sighed, ignoring the worry rising up, and turned to the task of rolling bandages.

Shortly after the doctor had finished his rounds, the door banged open. She glanced toward the noise and saw the man she'd spoken to on the street yesterday. He carried his frail wife in his arms.

"Doc, come quick." Rayna's heart thudded against her chest as she hurried toward the bone-picker.

His wife must've taken a turn for the worse. Rayna had lain awake thinking about their wagon moving slowly down the street with those five crows perched on the bones piled high.

Doc Yates directed the husband toward a curtained area where he examined patients. Rayna didn't know if she was supposed to follow, but the couple's three children standing in the doorway caught her attention. All three had tears streaming down their cheeks as they watched both parents disappear behind the curtain.

Going to them, she spoke to the oldest. "Hello, do you remember me? You told me your name is Alice. Mine is Rayna."

The eight-year-old sniffled. "My mama is sick. I'm scared."

"I know you are, honey." Rayna knelt and put her arms around the girl. "Doc is going to make her all better."

"Promise?"

Could Rayna state with certainty that Alice's mother would get well, when she knew too often people didn't make it? All three children stared, waiting for reassurance. "Doc will do everything in his power to give her back to you. I promise." At least she could pledge that.

She led them to an area in the corner where three straight-back chairs stood. "You sit here quietly, and I'll see what Doc says about what's wrong with your mama. Okay?"

"Can you hurry?" Alice pulled her baby brother into her lap. "Ain't askin' for me. I'm big. But my little sister an' brother ain't never been away from her. They need Mama."

A lump blocked Rayna's throat. "Yes, honey, I'll hurry."

Mamas left such a hole when they suddenly weren't

there. She glanced back at the children who were trying so hard to be brave.

After the doctor's examination, he announced that Mrs. Clark had pneumonia and would need to stay in the hospital. Rayna's heart sank. She knew it was very bad.

"For how long?" Mr. Clark asked.

"It's as tough a case as I've ever seen. I can't tell you how long it'll take to clear up. I don't know how fast she'll respond to treatment."

Mr. Clark set his jaw. "Then I'll be thanking you for your time an' taking my wife."

Doc Yates laid a hand on his shoulder. "You do, and you'd better dig her grave, because she'll be dead in a few days."

"I have three children who need their mother. What am I supposed to do? I need Elizabeth." The man sank into a chair and buried his head in his hands.

"I can help with the children, sir," Rayna said quietly.

When he raised his eyes, he wore the look of a man who'd been battered and bruised by life. "I've never left my young'uns with strangers, an' won't do so now."

Rayna pressed on. "It's the only choice you got, sir. Just an hour or two a day while you visit your wife."

"Listen to her, Clark." Doc Yates peered over his wire-rimmed glasses. "My nurse makes a whole lot of sense."

Finally, Mr. Clark gave a curt nod and rose. He turned to Rayna. "Thank you for your kindness yesterday. We camped outside of town, but I saw how weak an' sick Elizabeth was gettin' each passin' second. I knew the only thing to do was bring her to this hospital you told us about."

"I'm glad you did." Rayna held out her hand and introduced herself.

He briefly touched her palm as though he feared he'd taint her. "I'm Silas. Silas Clark. I won't be forgettin' what you done."

Alice and her siblings ran to him when he stepped around the curtain. A little of the heaviness in Rayna's chest lifted to see the love Silas showed his children. This was how it was supposed to be—a father who thought his children hung the moon.

A father who didn't try to sell his daughter for a jug of corn liquor.

The powerful memory rose like a sudden summer storm, churning and black. Rayna squeezed her eyes shut against the pain stabbing her chest, so severe it hurt to breathe.

Shoving the memories to the back of her mind, she turned toward the Clarks. Nothing washed away heartache like helping other folks deal with theirs.

❧

Brett parted ways with the former deputy as the sun peeked over the horizon. The frisky horses nickered in the cool air, talking to each other and swishing their tails happily.

Riding beside him, Adam glanced back at the man who'd shared their campfire. "This town—Steele's Hollow—what happened there?"

Brett winced. So much for hoping to avoid this. "Trouble."

"What kind?"

Pulling back on the reins, Brett sighed and stopped. He should probably get this over with. "I had a bad time there. You might as well know that the sheriff tried to hang me."

"Why?"

"For being born, he said. He hates people with our skin color."

Adam's anger returned. "See? It's never gonna change. People hate us. They won't give us a chance."

"Some like Hank Maxwell do. He's one of the good ones. So is the farmer I'm taking these horses to. I wouldn't be here if he hadn't cared. For every person who clings to hatred, there is one who's willing to go the extra mile. In a way, I guess it all evens out."

"Says you," Adam spat, galloping off down the trail.

Things had gone as Brett feared. Learning about the near-hanging had added more fuel to the boy's anger.

They didn't say two words to each other until time to make camp that night. As soon as Brett found a good spot in a clearing near water, he dismounted and handed Adam the rifle. "I guess you know how to shoot."

"I ain't stupid. Learned a long time ago. Why?"

"Your turn to find some supper."

Adam wore a puzzled look. "Me? What's wrong with you?"

"I'm not going to do it all. It's your turn to step up and shoulder more responsibility. I let you by last night because I realized this is all new and you're hurt. But it's time you learned that no one is going to carry you through life. If you want to eat tonight, you'll kill it." Without waiting for Adam to think of a reply, Brett turned and led the horses to the stream to drink. When he glanced back, he saw no sign of his nephew.

He prayed he made the right decision. Maybe he was wrong and should've given the fourteen-year-old something easier. It ate at him that Adam might've stretched the truth about being able to shoot.

Sarah would have his hide if her son shot himself in the foot.

Still, he hadn't been wrong in showing the youth he trusted him. Even if Adam messed up, this could give him some confidence in himself. He needed to know that he was capable of seeing to his own welfare when he had to. Brett had a feeling that Sarah had been far too protective.

An incident with Isaac Daffern crossed his mind. Brett had probably been about eleven at the time. Daffern told him about a magnificent white stallion up in the hills that he wanted brought down and gentled. Cooper and Rand wanted to go along, but the old rancher wouldn't let them. He said this was Brett's time to find out what he was made of.

Brett had gathered up a week's worth of supplies and saddled a horse. For six days he chased that animal. On the seventh day, he managed to throw a rope around the stallion's neck.

He still remembered the satisfaction he felt and the look of pleased surprise on Daffern's face when he rode in with the stallion.

This was what he wanted for Adam—a chance to find his self-worth.

An hour passed as Brett laid a fire and sat down to wait.

At pitch dark two hours later, he still hadn't heard the sound of a shot. His stomach rumbled. Maybe he needed to go look for Adam. Something might've happened, and he lay hurt in the trees. Brett got to his feet and made it to the edge of the clearing before he retraced his steps. He'd wait a while longer.

A blanket of stars popped out overhead, and the moon rose.

The rifle shot made Brett jump out of his skin. A smile slowly crossed his face. Now the only thing to do was to see if the boy had killed something. Brett sure hoped it wouldn't be a skunk.

Thirty minutes later, just as he finally decided to go look for him, Adam raced into camp carrying a turkey. "I did it. I got us some supper."

The happiness shining in his eyes did Brett proud. Adam had done something he'd never known he could do. And over the shared cleaning of the bird, he talked, relating every detail of how he stalked the turkey and didn't take a shot until he was sure.

Brett was quick with praise, keeping to himself that he could find no sign of a bullet fragment or hole. He guessed the shot came so close it had given the bird a heart attack.

What was important was for Adam to know he had inner strength worth discovering.

It probably neared midnight by the time they finished eating and lay down on their bedrolls.

Thoughts of Rayna filled Brett's head. He prayed she was staying busy and out of trouble, though something told him she'd given up her pickpocketing for good.

She was learning new skills and thriving in a strange place.

And she was waiting for him.

He frowned when a thought occurred to him. What if someone else came along in the meantime, and she decided she didn't want to waste her time on a happenchance? After all, he hadn't exactly given her much of an incentive. He groaned silently, remembering his offer of friendship—if she was willing to give that a try.

What woman would leap at that chance when she could have more with someone else?

He was conflicted, torn between what he wanted and a powerful fear beaten into him by years of facing men like Sheriff Oldham.

Or maybe he needed to forget Rayna Harper and stay with his horses. Long as he gave them plenty of sweet grass and water, they were content, and being near him could never hurt them.

But one thing worried him.

How did a man go about forgetting someone who'd made him feel truly alive for the first time in his life?

～

On the third night following Brett's leaving, the boardinghouse clock downstairs struck twelve times, and Rayna hadn't closed her eyes yet. She rose from her bed and went to the window overlooking the town.

A lantern still burned next to the Clarks' wagon that Silas had pulled up on the property at Mabel's insistence.

Rayna frowned. Was one of the children sick? She hoped not. The little family didn't need anything else to come their way, unless it was good fortune. They could sure use some of that. Elizabeth Clark seemed to be a tad better. Doc Yates appeared happy with her progress. Maybe soon the children could have their mother back.

And then what? Where would they go? And what would happen to them when work dried up? Everything came to an end eventually, and so it would with their trade. Once the buffalo were gone, there wouldn't be any more.

She remembered the grueling days under the hot sun, picking up bone after bone and throwing them into the wagon until her arms ached. It was no kind of life, especially for children.

As she stared out, she saw Silas Clark lift Leo and cradle the two-year-old in his lap. He was a good papa. She wondered if he had hopes and dreams, or if he was like her and didn't let them come. Maybe like her he, too, felt he didn't deserve them.

Brett had told her they weren't restricted to only a few, that everyone could have them. He'd been right about a lot of things—maybe he was right about this.

She hoped so, because she couldn't stand any more disappointment. Still, what if he was mistaken?

Leaning her head against the windowpane, she thought of the tall man who made heat rise to her cheeks.

Where was he? Was he thinking of her?

Touching her fingers to her lips, she remembered the kiss under the evergreen tree. She remembered the way her hands had slid around his neck, the way she'd drawn him closer. Just recalling how her heart had raced when he'd touched his lips to hers made her feel as quivery inside as she had that night.

Oh, to feel that every night.

"Come home, Brett," she murmured against the windowpane. "And please don't forget I'm waiting. I'll wait as long as I have to." All she had was time.

Fourteen

AT SUNDOWN, SIX DAYS FROM WHEN THEY'D LEFT, Brett and Adam rode back into Battle Creek. The trip went without a hitch, and the farmer was really excited that Brett kept his promise.

The return to the farm had been a far cry from the previous time. You'd have thought Brett was an honored guest. The couple invited them in, and the wife cooked a real feast. The farmer said it was the least they could do.

After the meal, he and Brett walked down to the horses. "You know, I've never owned anything but a few mules, and they died," the farmer said with tears in his eyes. "These horses will change our lives. Thank you."

"You're welcome, sir."

At least Adam had seen there were good people in the world, and that was worth all the days and nights away from Rayna.

They'd left the following morning at sunrise and pushed harder on the return.

Pausing now at the edge of town, Brett glanced at Adam. He'd left a kid and come back a man. His surly attitude was gone for the most part. Every once in a while Brett caught a glimpse of it, but he loved the way Adam had grown inside.

He turned to Adam. "You make your mama proud. Let her fuss over you for a bit so she can see that you still have your arms, legs, ten toes and fingers, then we'll head to the Wild Horse."

Adam gave his customary nod when he didn't have much to say, which was still more frequent than not. The boy wasn't a talker.

Since Brett wasn't either, they got along fine.

As he moved slowly down the street toward the Lexington Hotel, his thoughts turned to Rayna. He wondered if she was still at the hospital. He needed to see her, just to make sure she was doing all right and hadn't left town, he told himself.

She was a friend, and friends looked out for each other. That's all he was doing.

Not a thing anyone else wouldn't do. Almost.

"I'll be back to get you in about an hour," he told Adam when they stopped in front of the hotel. "Tell your mama hello and that she doesn't have to worry about you. You both have me now."

Again, Adam nodded and tied his horse to the hitching rail.

A few minutes later, Brett dismounted at the hospital and went inside. His gaze swept the room, landing on her right away, sitting beside a patient, holding her hand. He stood for a minute, drinking in the sight. Light from the lamps danced in her auburn hair. Glancing up, she saw him, and a happy smile lit her face. She rose and came to meet him.

"You're back! I'm so glad." She tilted those glistening blue-green eyes up to stare at him. "How did it go?"

The overwhelming need to touch her, to settle his weary spirit, became too great. With so many eyes on them, he settled for taking her hand and squeezing her palm. He remembered how scared he was of touching her in the beginning and was surprised how easily it came now.

"No problems. The farmer was glad to get the horses."

"And Adam?"

"I think I might've turned a corner with him. We'll see. Who is that woman you were sitting with?"

"Doc calls her Granny Ketchum. Said she won't last the night. She has no family. I can't let her die alone."

Deep sadness settled over him. "I didn't know Granny was sick."

"It's her heart. Is she a friend?"

Brett nodded. "She was one of the first people to welcome us when Cooper, Rand, and me came to town almost eight years ago. I thought she'd always be here. The town won't be the same without her. I wonder if Cooper's wife, Delta, knows. They are very close."

"That's where Doc is now. Rode out to tell her."

"Good. Those two have a special bond." He reached for Rayna's other hand, needing something to ground him. Aching sadness tightened, making it hard to breathe. "Do you think I could see her for a minute?"

"The old dear would probably like that. She hasn't opened her eyes since Mr. Abercrombie at the mercantile brought her here."

Still keeping one hand in Rayna's, he moved to the

bedside and sat down in the chair. He released Rayna's hand and took Granny's wrinkled one. "Granny, it's Brett," he said softly. "Came to thank you for the gift of your friendship. You're finally going to be with Elmer again. He's waiting for you."

Granny Ketchum's eyes opened. Staring at the ceiling, she smiled.

"I think she heard you," Rayna whispered.

Just then Delta Thorne strode hurriedly into the hospital. Tears streamed down her beautiful face. "Please tell me I'm not too late."

"She's still alive." Brett gave Delta his chair and walked toward the sitting area in the corner. Rayna followed and sat next to him and rested her hand on his arm. He needed her warmth to banish the chill surrounding his heart.

Neither felt the need to talk. Silently, they watched Delta Thorne crawl into bed with Granny and take her in her arms. "I'm here, Granny. I'll hold you and help you across. I love you more than words can say. You opened your arms and your heart to me when I had no one. I'll never forget you. I know you're tired and it's time to go, but my heart is breaking."

Brett found it hard to breathe. He would really miss Granny Ketchum.

They sat in silence for some time, Delta's soft murmurs to Granny the only sound.

Finally, Rayna spoke in a hushed voice. "Will you go the Wild Horse tonight?"

"As soon as Adam spends a few minutes with his mother. I'm ready to get back to my land and care for the horses."

"I wish I could go with you, but I'm needed here." Rayna leaned closer. "There's another woman in the hospital that I'm looking after. Elizabeth Clark was passing through town. She was the woman you saw me talking to beside the bone-pickers' wagon. She has pneumonia, but she's getting lots better. Doc says she'll probably get to leave in another couple of days. I'm helping the father care for their children."

"I'm sure he's grateful." He yearned to touch her hair, take one of her curls between his thumb and forefinger, and feel the softness.

"Mr. Clark is lost without his wife."

"I can tell how much you love this job." Though she looked tired, she had a glow about her that hadn't been there when he'd left.

"It's the best thing that could've happened. I can make a difference here. For the first time in my life, I have a purpose. I'm not just existing anymore. I'm really living. You told me I could grow and thrive here, but I really didn't believe you. I couldn't see it. But that's what I'm doing. I'm thriving."

Like Adam, Rayna Harper was finding self-worth and becoming confident. All they needed was someone to believe in them.

"I'm glad." He stood with one last glance toward Delta and Granny. "I've got to get going. Adam will wonder."

Rayna got to her feet. Her softly parted lips awakened the memory of their kiss on a moonlit night. "Brett, please don't stay away too long. I've missed you."

"I'm back now. I promise to come into town often."

He brushed a curl from her face. Tamping down the deep yearning to kiss her cheek, he strode to the door without looking back. If he'd turned for one last glimpse, he'd have hauled her against his chest and crushed his mouth to hers.

The red-haired lady had him under a spell of some kind, and he didn't know how to break it.

Or even if he wanted to.

༄

Under the pale glow of the moon that bathed everything in silvery shadows, Brett turned from the main road and took a hidden path through the trees. Before long, his tepee came into view. He dismounted in front of his abode.

"Where's your house?" Adam asked.

"Right here. This is my house."

"I should've known. You expect me to sleep in that?"

"Sleep wherever you want. Makes no difference to me." Brett unfastened the cinch and removed his saddle. "I'm too tired to argue."

Adam slid to the ground and stalked to the tepee.

"Not so fast. Take care of your horse first," Brett called, wondering where the spirit of cooperation had gone.

Giving a huff, Adam turned. "I guess you're gonna have a bunch of rules now."

"Only one." Brett removed the saddle blanket. "You will take care of your animal before you see to your own needs unless you're unable. I've already made this clear."

"I thought that was just on the trail. Now we're on your land. You can do it."

"The same applies no matter where we are," Brett said firmly. He hoped the fourteen-year-old wasn't going to slip backward after making such strides.

Without a word, Adam did as he was told while Brett took his mount to the corral and then made a fire. As was his custom, he gazed over his land, soaking up the peace that came from finding a place of refuge where he didn't have to worry about being accepted.

He thought of Granny Ketchum and said a prayer that she'd found an easy crossing.

Memories swirled. One in particular came to mind. In tears, she'd asked his help in finding her cat. He looked everywhere he could think of but saw no sign of it. Just about to give up, he noticed the flicker of a campfire down by the creek that ran behind her house. Everyone knew about Granny's soft heart. She couldn't turn any soul in need away from her door.

Two men were hunkered down by that fire, trying to keep warm. Though one was shivering and shaking, he'd used his one blanket to wrap Granny's cat. It was warm and snug. Brett had had hell getting it loose from its new home.

He remembered how Granny had let the cat go back, unable to take it from the stranger who desperately needed something to care for.

Not long after, she found another cat to take its place. As long as he knew her, she'd had a mess of cats.

Maybe he'd ride into town in a few days and bring one of those cats to the Wild Horse in her memory, as a thank-you for her kindness.

Adam walked back from the corral and stood beside him. "It's not bad here. You have a nice place. I think I'll sleep inside the tepee."

"You'll like it."

He watched the kid push the flap aside and disappear. The youth had simply needed a reminder of where the boundaries were. Just like Brett had earlier when he'd been with Rayna. He'd set boundaries on how far he was willing to go with her.

Redrawing the line would only confuse them both.

But how he'd hated it. She tempted him at every turn. He didn't know how long he'd be able to resist. She was danger. His need to be near her, to touch her…he couldn't trust himself when he was with her.

Neither could he stand being away from her.

This battle was ripping his heart to shreds.

Fifteen

OVER THE NEXT WEEK, BRETT KEPT ADAM BUSY from daylight to dark. By the end of each day, Adam was so exhausted he ate and collapsed onto his bedroll. The work had been a tremendous attitude fixer. Brett could see the pride Adam took in working with the horses. A real love for them was growing.

On Saturday, they went into town. Just so the boy could see his mother, he told himself. Yet Brett knew the real reason, and it involved a certain friend.

Battle Creek was a beehive of activity when they navigated the burial plot in the center of Main Street and proceeded to the Texas Cattleman's. Since weekends were the busiest, Sarah would be working. They tied their horses and went inside.

She came around the registration desk and hugged Adam, even though he pulled away. "I'm really happy to see you. How is it going, Son?"

"Fine. I like working with the horses and hunting and swimming in the creek. Uncle Brett is teaching me a lot."

Going to Brett, she hugged him and said low, "Thank you."

"My nephew is a fast learner. How do you like your job?"

"I'll bet you haven't had breakfast. Come into the dining room, and I'll tell you."

"I could use some food," Adam said, grinning. "Uncle Brett doesn't feed me anything but jerky."

"Complaining, boy?" Brett loved seeing how Adam was opening up enough where he could joke. A far cry from two weeks ago.

"Nope." Adam followed his mother into the dining room.

Sarah indicated a table, and Brett pulled out her chair. His sister had changed as well. She didn't have that closed expression she'd worn when she arrived. Maybe things were working out for both mother and son.

For Brett, his life was set in the only path it could go.

He just had to tell it to his heart, because it didn't appear to be listening.

Firmly, he forced his thoughts back to the matter at hand. After giving the waitress his order, he glanced around the dining room. His gaze landed on one of his neighbors, a new one by the name of Edgar Dowlen. Dowlen had owned his land for only a few months, so Brett hadn't had time to really get to know him. The man stared at Adam, then shifted his attention to Brett. Edgar didn't even try to hide his cold contempt. His eyes held the same loathing that the sheriff's of Steele's Hollow had.

Though Brett and Dowlen had never exchanged

anything other than hellos, he'd never considered that
his neighbor despised him. The revulsion written on
Edgar's face brought gut-wrenching pain.

Brett met his stare with a hard one of his own, finally
forcing the man to look away. Dowlen rose. Slamming
his chair against the table, he stalked from the hotel.

With turmoil churning in his gut, Brett dragged his
attention back to Sarah. "Now, you promised to tell
us about your job...*Sis.*" There was that strange word
again, only this time it came out a little easier. Maybe
it just took some practice.

"I love working here. The people are very friendly,
and my boss is free with his praise. He seems satisfied
with the way I'm doing things."

Just then Potter Gray entered the dining room, and
Brett was quick to notice how Sarah's gaze followed
him. The tall, broad-shouldered hotel owner did cut
quite a figure. Brett studied his blond hair, brown
eyes, and closely cropped beard. He had something
that the ladies...Sarah...seemed drawn to.

Brett scowled. This protectiveness of his sister was
something that caught him off guard and he didn't
like it.

Potter went around the room, then stopped at their
table. "Good morning, Sarah. How do you do it?"

"What, Mr. Gray?"

"You always look so pretty, whether early in the
morning or after a hard day's work. I'm fortunate to
have snagged you before any of the other business
owners in town. They're all envious."

After Sarah introduced Adam, she turned to Brett.
"Do you know my brother?"

"Indeed I do. Hello, Brett. I didn't know you two were related."

Brett stiffened. "Does it make a difference?"

He readied for some kind of remark, to have Potter Gray say that he'd made a big mistake in hiring Sarah.

Instead, the hotel owner laughed. "Heck no. I was just surprised."

"Would you like to join us, Mr. Gray?" Sarah asked.

Relief washed over Brett. Maybe he was being too sensitive, but the eye-opener he'd just had with Dowlen made him a little jumpy.

"I wish I could, Miss Sarah," Potter said, "but I have matters to attend to in my office. I'll see you later after you've eaten."

Brett wanted to ask what Sarah's feelings for the hotel owner were, but he couldn't quite find the words. Besides, Adam launched into an excited account of life at the Wild Horse until their meal came. Then the youth shoveled food into his mouth so fast, Brett was afraid he'd choke. You'd have thought Adam hadn't eaten in a month of Sundays.

Brett sat there silently watching his family, grateful that they'd come into his life.

And if anyone got it into his head to hurt them…

❧

Rayna thought surely her eyes must be playing tricks on her when she saw Brett strolling into the hospital. Standing in the doorway with the sun beaming brightly behind him, he seemed larger than life.

Her pulse raced as she ran to meet him. But when she reached his side, everything she wanted to say left her head. Finally, she murmured, "I'm so happy to see you."

The minute he took her hand and gave her that slow, lazy smile that showed his white teeth, she melted inside and heat rose to her face.

"I brought Adam into town and thought I'd invite you to lunch. You do take lunch, don't you?"

"Not normally, but I'll make an exception today."

"Good. I have a feeling you've been working too hard. You're getting too skinny. I'll meet you at the Three Roses." He released her hand. "Sharing a meal with a friend is an excellent way to pass the time."

"Thank you, Brett." Her gaze followed him to the door, admiring the view of his nicely formed backside. And the way he walked, of course. His loose-jointed saunter made her think of a cougar.

Rayna could scarcely keep her mind on her work, and when the clock in town struck twelve, she was halfway to the Three Roses Café. The minute she pushed inside, she saw Brett at a table. He rose and pulled out her chair.

"I'm glad you could come." He sat down and leaned back to stare at her.

The close examination made Rayna a bit uncomfortable. She fidgeted, afraid of what his probing gaze would see.

The pain lurking beneath the surface.

The despair she'd lived with for so long.

And her lack of knowledge about how to conduct herself with a gentleman. She didn't want him to discover the things she hid. Like the fact that he still made her pulse race, and she had to fight the need to be in his arms. "Seeing you is the best part of my week. How's Adam working out?"

"We kinda got off to a rocky start, but everything's going well."

While they ate, Brett told her how Adam had found a true love of horses and was coming to respect the land. In return, Rayna talked about her work and getting used to Doc Yates's way of doing things.

"I've made blunders, I'm afraid." The words were out of her mouth before she could call them back. She hadn't intended to admit that. Oh Lord! She could feel her face heating.

"Do you want to talk about it?"

"It's just that I get carried away. Doc used a word— overzealous, I think he said. I forget that I don't have to make all the decisions anymore about everything. But he's very patient and forgiving. Doc reminds me a lot of my grandfather."

"It's a wise man who patiently teaches. I hope that's how I am. I'm trying anyway."

"Don't worry. You are." Rayna noticed a shift in Brett when a shaggy, gray-haired man with a pock-marked face entered. Brett seemed to tense up, and his eyes never left the newcomer. "Who is that?"

"My neighbor, Edgar Dowlen. He seems to have a problem with me for some reason."

"Has something happened between you?"

"No, and I don't know of anything I've done. But please go on. Tell me more about your job."

"The only part I hate is when patients die. It breaks my heart. I kept a vigil along with Delta Thorne when Granny Ketchum passed. I haven't seen anyone more

devastated about losing someone. My heart broke for
Delta. Doc had to give her some medicine to calm
her. Right before the light went out of Granny's eyes,
she mumbled something that sounded like, 'I missed
you, little darling.' Doc said she was probably thinking
about her only child that she lost a long time ago."

"Probably. Did she have a nice funeral?"

"The whole town turned out, and the band led
the procession down Main Street all the way to the
cemetery. It was like a parade in honor of someone
real important."

"Granny would've liked that. Wish I could've been
here, but me and funerals don't mix. Never have liked
'em." Brett's gaze flickered to Edgar Dowlen, then
back to her. "Let's get out of here if you're finished."

"Of course." She rose, took Brett's arm, and
walked to the door.

Once outside, he seemed more his old self. "I know
you have to get back to the hospital soon, but let's take
a walk down to the stream back of the boardinghouse.
I won't make you late."

"That sounds nice." She enjoyed the leisurely stroll.
In the hospital she went in a run, so the slower pace
was nice. "How long will you be in town?"

"Young Adam and I will head back in an hour
or two."

Rayna nodded and fell silent. She hated the thought
of him leaving so soon. When they reached the creek,
she lay in the wild grass while Brett stretched out
beside her, staring up at the sky. The gentle babble of
the water was peaceful.

His silence made her wonder if she'd done

something wrong. She fidgeted under his quiet study of her. "What are you thinking?" she asked.

He raised on an elbow. Slowly, he lifted a curl, rubbing it between his thumb and forefinger. "Your hair fascinates me. It's beautiful. The softness reminds me of a newborn colt. All shiny and fresh."

"I've always hated my hair," she murmured, grimacing.

"I don't see why."

"Because it's always drawn the wrong kind of attention, for one thing. And two—I can never smooth it back into the kind of style an elegant lady would wear. My curls are like springs, and there's no taming them. It's so frustrating."

"We always want what we can't have." Deep sadness and a little anger tinged his voice.

She met his dark, mysterious gaze. One day she hoped to know what secrets he kept. She thought about asking what it was he wanted that lay beyond reach, but she reckoned she probably already knew. He yearned for a world where he could live in harmony.

"Hard as I try, I can't forget that night I caught you picking pockets outside the saloon. You were so sure your life here in Battle Creek was over."

"And I begged you to kiss me," she whispered.

Leaning closer, Brett traced the curve of her cheek with a fingertip. Anguish flared in his eyes and tightened the lines of his face. He was in obvious pain, and she didn't know what to do, what to say. Clearly he wanted more, but had forbidden himself to have her. He denied the one thing that might possibly bring him peace.

She lay silent and still. Waiting. Hoping. Daring to dream.

With a cry that might have come from a wounded animal, Brett lowered his mouth, crushing his lips to hers. Instant warmth flooded her. She laid her hand against his heart, feeling the wild beating, like the thunder of hooves, that matched her own.

Heat raced from her core, blazing a searing path through her, arousing hunger for something more, something indefinable.

As he deepened the kiss, his hand followed the outside curves of her body to rest at the indentation of her waist. A yearning like she'd never felt burned inside as she gave herself over to the pleasure of a touch that only he could deliver.

Her nipples hardened to stiff peaks, straining for his caress.

What they'd shared before, including the night she lay beside him on his bunk, paled in comparison to this raw hunger sweeping through her, devouring her.

In the fragrant grass, surrounded by the scent of wild sage, she ached with the sweet sensations rolling over her. Some strange craving pushed her toward a need for a completion of some sort.

While she didn't know much, she knew beyond any doubt there would never be any other man for her.

Rayna clutched his shirt, releasing a soft cry.

As if the sound jolted him back to himself, Brett groaned and jerked back. "Sorry. It seems I can't control myself when I get within a foot of you. I shouldn't have done that. It was wrong." He got to his feet and stood rigid with his back to her, gazing into the water.

Stinging tears lurked behind her eyelids. His

statement about it being human nature to want what she couldn't have was certainly true.

Only she wasn't thinking about her curly hair anymore.

❧

Brett thought of Rayna all the way back to the Wild Horse. Once he got there, he removed two of Granny's sleeping cats from inside his shirt. After making them a bed, he threw himself into his chores, even though the sun was fast disappearing on the far horizon.

Work was something he knew. Something he was good at.

He'd do well to keep remembering that.

When he could think of no more work to do until morning, he saddled a fresh horse and told Adam he'd be gone for a few hours. Without further explanation, he rode to the top of a hill that overlooked the ranch. Dismounting, he sat on a huge limestone boulder and watched the moon rise.

This thing he felt for Rayna had him tied in knots. He hated this burning hunger that ran through him like molten steel.

He was a man with needs and desires.

She was an innocent, beautiful woman who was caught between his need and his fear.

Cursing, he looked up at the millions of stars dotting the sky. He acted worse than a fool every time he was with her. He groaned with frustration, still feeling her warm lips beneath his, her silky auburn hair between his fingers.

Yes, he'd saved her. But from what? He certainly

hadn't saved her from him. And in saving her, had he destroyed her?

Dawn was beginning to break when he rode down to his tepee and put the coffee on. The two cats he'd brought from town rubbed against his legs. He scooped one up, stroking its fur. He'd spent the whole night thinking, but it hadn't done a bit of good. He was still as messed up and exasperated.

The only decision he'd arrived at was to cram his days full of work. If he didn't give himself any free time, he wouldn't think about her.

~❧~

The sun was high in the sky two days later when Brett spied a man in a black stovepipe hat stumbling across his meadow. At first Brett thought he must be drunk the way his legs wobbled, refusing to hold him up.

Though cautious, Brett went to meet him. Adam must've also seen the stranger with long, snow-white hair, because he stopped in the corral to watch.

Upon nearing the visitor, Brett noticed the wrinkled bronze skin of an Indian. Surprise rippled through him. "Hello? Can I help you?" he asked.

The man collapsed in Brett's arms, no longer able to stand. Hefting the unconscious old Indian onto his shoulder, he carried him into the tepee.

Adam appeared in the opening. "Who is he? Do you know him?"

"Never saw him before." Brett touched the old man's forehead. He was burning with fever, and his dry lips were cracked.

"What's wrong with him?"

"Don't know. Could be anything." He turned to his nephew. "I need you to go into town for Doc Yates. Do you think you can do that?"

Wide-eyed, Adam nodded.

"And bring Rayna too. Whatever he has, it might be best to keep him away from town."

While Brett waited, he got some cold water and bathed the man's face. Then, not knowing what else to do, he sat cross-legged beside the bedroll and stared at the Indian's clothing.

It was the first time he'd gotten a close look at those kinds of garments, and he was curious.

The shapeless pants and shirt adorned with beads were made of doeskin. A leather pouch of some kind hung around the stranger's neck. Seeing that last item jolted Brett's memory. He had a similar one. A woman at the orphanage had given it to him when he was about six years old, saying it had been the only thing in the woven basket when they found him on the steps.

Not knowing what the pouch meant, he'd stuck it away and forgotten about it all these years. In truth, he'd stashed it out of sight, along with the memories of that horrible time. He'd never opened it for fear of what he'd find. He stilled.

Or was his fear rooted more in what he *wouldn't* find?

He jerked to his feet and went to the box where he kept his things. Digging to the bottom, he found what he was looking for and pulled it out. Maybe all men like him had one of these.

But why?

A lump of something was inside. He loosened the

strip of rawhide holding it shut. His fingers closed around something cold. Bringing the object into the light, he saw the rock, a black onyx. Fragrant sprigs of sage came out with it.

A feeling he was supposed to know what these signified washed over him. He wished the old Indian would wake up so he could ask.

But he showed no sign of opening his eyes.

Brett went outside, staring in the direction the stranger had come from. The only thing nestled between two jutting limestone cliffs was a box canyon. He used the canyon often as a natural corral for his horses.

The wind whistled through a nearby stand of trees, moaning, almost as though the breeze was sobbing.

He had a feeling that trouble rode the wind, and he needed to do something—but what?

Sixteen

THE CLOSER SHE AND DOC YATES CAME TO THE WILD Horse, the more Rayna's heart thumped against her ribs. She would finally see Brett's horse ranch, though she wished it was under different circumstances.

Adam had run into the hospital, saying a stranger had stumbled onto the ranch from out of nowhere and collapsed.

All Rayna knew was that Brett needed her.

Her mind went back to the afternoon by the little stream behind Mabel's and the way his lips had settled hard on her mouth. The kiss had surprised her and, from the look on his face, it had startled him too.

The anger afterward had bewildered her. He'd been cold and distant when he had escorted her back to the hospital.

Had he been mad at her? Or himself?

Now he needed her help, and she was more than willing. The unconscious stranger concerned her. Maybe he'd been shot. Oh Lord, she hoped not.

She calmed. Doc Yates was more than capable of digging out a bullet if that's what had happened.

Adam said the man had worn a tall stovepipe hat. No one wore those anymore, at least not that she'd noticed.

A tepee caught Rayna's attention first. As the doctor's buggy began slowing, she glanced around for a dwelling of some sort. Seeing nothing else, she realized Brett lived very simply.

The pointed tepee fit a man like Brett, who seemed as free and unfettered as the wind. She shouldn't have expected anything else.

He must've heard their approach, because he stood waiting outside the home made of buffalo skins. Her breath caught. His rolled-up shirtsleeves revealed strong brown forearms. His dark gaze meeting hers beneath the brim of his hat showed relief…and something else. Happiness?

"I'm glad you came." He put his hands around her waist and lifted her from the buggy. "I wasn't sure you would or could."

Rayna trembled beneath his touch and felt a sense of loss when he removed his hands. "Doc said he might need me, so a nurse who works only at night agreed to take care of the patients until we get back. What's wrong with the stranger?"

"Beyond a burning fever, I don't know." He held the flap of the tepee aside for her. Doc Yates followed.

She'd expected the interior of the dwelling to be shrouded in shadows, but was amazed at the light streaming in from the opening above.

Immediately, her focus shifted to the white-haired man lying on a bedroll, his black stovepipe hat next to him on a large rug. She figured he had to be in his seventies at least, or maybe older.

Doc Yates took a stethoscope from his black bag and stuck it inside the patient's shirt. "Weak heartbeat," he murmured.

After checking the man's fever and completing his examination, Doc rose. "He's very dehydrated, and I suspect he hasn't eaten in a while. He could have any number of other complaints, but we won't know until he wakes up. If he wakes up. Miss Rayna, let's get some water into him right away."

"I tried to get him to drink," Brett offered, "but it ran out his mouth."

"Then wet a cloth and get some into him that way." Doc put his instruments back into his bag and turned to Rayna. "Keep trying, and if he comes to, ask about other ailments. I have to return to Battle Creek, but I want you to stay. It would be best to leave him out here until we determine he doesn't have anything contagious."

"Yes, Doc." While she was sad about the old man, her heart sang with the news that she could stay. She brushed past Brett as she went to the nearby creek for water. Filling a bucket, she waved to the doctor, who was driving off, and hurried back to her patient.

Brett sat cross-legged beside the old Indian. He lifted the man's head while she held a cup to his mouth. At first, the water ran out and onto his chest. After repeated tries, he finally began to swallow some. Hope grew that he would wake up soon and tell them who he was.

"We'll need to get some broth into him," she said.

Brett got to his feet. "Adam killed a pheasant this morning. I'll make a fire and put the bones on to cook. Rayna, I'm glad you're here."

"Me too." She fidgeted under his piercing stare that seemed to see clear down to her soul. "Between us, I know we can fix him up." Turning at last, she wet a cloth and laid it on the man's fevered brow.

The mysterious patient interested her. He was someone's father and grandfather. Maybe he even had a wife. His family must miss him. She prayed he wouldn't die. Nothing was sadder than dying in a strange place among people you didn't know. She'd seen so many die beside the trail, only to be left there. For years she'd carried that fear inside her.

Only the slight movement of his chest when he breathed let her know he was still alive. She gave him a few more sips of water, praying it wasn't too late for their efforts. Seeing nothing more she could do, she went to join Brett.

He swung around when she stepped out. "How is he?"

"About the same. I think the broth might help. He's very weak. I wonder where he came from. Is a reservation close?"

"No. He must've walked quite a distance."

Her gaze scanned the haunting beauty of the land that lay in a valley bordered by high cliffs. A herd of horses grazed on tall grass. The glistening creek where she went for water ran like a silk thread, cutting into the land. It was peaceful. And free.

"I can see why you love this place so much. It's breathtaking. The Wild Horse is like you—bold and untamable."

"This land is embedded into my soul. I'm not comfortable anywhere else."

She noticed Adam working with a horse in the corral. He stood in the center with the animal running in a circle around the edge. Every so often it would stop and reverse course. "What is Adam doing?"

"Talking to the horse, gaining its trust."

"I've never seen anyone do this."

"Most ranchers break horses by forceful domination. I hate that method because it's unnecessary and cruel. I show my horses respect and let them know that I'm not going to hurt them. Over days, or sometimes weeks, I gain their trust. We become lifelong friends."

"Like us?"

He brushed her cheek with his forefinger and stared at her for a long moment. The world seemed to hold its breath. "Yes, like us."

"I feel I've known you forever," she whispered, leaning into his feathery touch. "And you know more about me than anyone. Things I've never told a living soul. What comes next with us?"

"I don't know." His words sounded ragged and bruised, as though they'd had to squeeze through the narrow opening in his throat. He jerked his hand away and turned to the boiling pot.

Knowing the conversation was over, she went back to her patient. Though unconscious, surprisingly *he* spoke in a language she could understand.

Brett confused her. One minute he seemed happy she was there, and the next totally miserable. How could she ever hope to make sense of him? It appeared impossible.

An hour or more passed before Brett entered the tepee with a cup of cooling broth. She took it, blew on a spoonful, then dribbled it into the old Indian's mouth. After repeating that for about ten minutes, she set it aside so she could give him more later.

Maybe it was only wishful thinking, but he appeared to be improving. His breathing seemed stronger.

Shadows filling the tepee told her the day was waning. Where would she sleep? Rayna looked around the enclosure. Except for the small fire pit in the center that was surrounded by stones, the floor was covered with rugs.

Bedrolls indicated where Brett and Adam bedded down each night. Her gaze swung to three crates stacked to one side, with a small drum sitting beside them that appeared to get regular use. For some reason, she had no trouble picturing Brett sitting cross-legged on the rugs, playing the drum.

She guessed the crates probably contained personal items. Clothing was neatly folded on a box, and she assumed the leather satchel at the end of the other bedroll belonged to Adam.

The fact that everything was neat and orderly told her a good deal about Brett. He'd made a place for each of his belongings and kept them there.

Maybe that was what disturbed him about her. He didn't know where to put her.

He didn't know how to make a place for her.

An ache developed behind her eyes. She was still his problem, something she'd never wanted to be.

The rumble of male voices drifted inside as Brett and Adam talked low over the campfire. They had each other and shared a common interest in horses. The two of them were family. She had no one, no friends or family, only Brett. Just a job and a little money that could take her far away. If she wanted that.

Her lip trembled. There would never be a home for her. This was the way it was, and nothing could change it.

No matter where she traveled, she'd always be nothing more than a bone-picker's daughter.

❦

Brett poured a cup of coffee and took it inside to Rayna. He found her washing the old Indian's face with a cool cloth.

"I thought you might need some coffee. It won't be long until supper."

She wearily pushed back a curl that appeared to irritate her and took the cup. "Thank you."

"Any change?"

"His eyes fluttered a little while ago. I think he might be trying to wake up."

"That's good. Maybe we'll find out who he is."

"I gave him the last of the broth. I think it helped."

"Hope so." He touched a match to the kindling in the small fire pit and sat down beside her. The soft light caressed her hair and the lines of her face. "What I have isn't much, but I'll make sure you have a place to sleep. You look exhausted."

"I got up very early this morning."

"Is Doc working you too hard?"

"No. I volunteer for extra hours. It keeps me from thinking about certain things."

He wondered at her deep sadness. "Such as?"

"A past I'm trying to forget. And a future I can't claim."

"I haven't been much help with the latter. I struggle with that too. There's this thing between us that refuses to die. I would like nothing better than to be able to..." His words faded into the dream he carried in his heart. He'd give anything to change people's views about his race, to be able to make her his wife.

Rayna laid her hand on his, and her touch burned. "I said I'd wait for you, and I meant it."

"What if someone else comes along, someone you can't live without?"

"No one sees me except you."

"Just know that I won't hold you to your promise," he said hoarsely.

"I've decided to believe in miracles."

If only it was that simple, and he could have what he wanted by thinking it true. But he'd learned a long time ago that such things existed only in daydreams and fantasy. Life had taught painful lessons and hard truths. "I hope you can weather the disappointment."

Memories swirled inside his head. Once in the orphanage—during a rare occasion of letting him play outside—he'd seen a man and woman come for one of the other little boys they'd adopted. That child was so excited and happy. He told Brett that he had a family at last. That he was finally wanted.

The jagged pain Brett had felt then flooded back so strong that it left the bitter taste of gall on his tongue.

No one ever came for him. No one ever wanted him to be part of their family. No one had seen his tears at night when he'd buried his face in the pillow and wept. And even now, years later, he was stuck watching the brothers he'd chosen find love and settle that past heartbreak, leaving him all alone.

So yeah, tell someone else that a ragged little boy could have his heart's desire. That would be a lie. Though he had his brothers, and now Sarah and Adam, he could never have the thing he most wanted. He could never have Rayna.

Glancing at her, he felt guilt eating him. He would not ask her to wait. He couldn't. He knew what being alone did to a person, how the yearning for someone to care crowded into a man's mind, leaving room for nothing else. She deserved a happy life, even if it wasn't with him.

He sighed, got to his feet, and pulled her up. "Let's eat."

"I'm not hungry," she protested.

"You're too skinny." He led her through the flap made of buffalo hide to the feast he'd prepared.

Her eyes lit up when she saw the winter squash and corn he'd cooked over the open fire, along with baked apples and fry bread. "Oh, Brett, you remembered."

"Sit and eat. I'm going to fatten you up." The gruff words came from seeing sheer happiness on her face at the simple fare. The smallest things were like great treasures to her.

Adam grinned and winked at her. "Better listen, Miss Rayna. Or else he'll hand you some jerky and send you to work."

Knowing she didn't eat meat had provided a challenge, but Brett wasn't about to let her starve. Only after she'd gotten her food and sat in a chair he'd hewn from an oak tree did he move toward the quail roasting on the fire. Sitting beside Rayna on an upturned crate, he watched her tackle her food. She asked for so little and appreciated every kindness.

She was everything he needed.

He fought back the thickness of his tongue and burning behind his eyes that seemed hell-bent on embarrassing him. He cursed everything that kept them apart—including himself.

Seventeen

JUST AS THE FIRST RAYS OF DAWN BROKE THROUGH THE low-hanging clouds the following morning, the old Indian woke up. Brett moved closer into his line of vision and laid a hand on the man's chest. Before he could ask the question he wanted to know, the Indian's gaze shifted to Rayna. She'd kept a vigil by the old man's side through the night, even though Brett had made her a bed of soft blankets.

The mystery patient's confused gaze came as no surprise. After all, he'd never seen them before.

Brett smiled and introduced himself, then explained, "You're in my tepee. This lady is Rayna Harper. Can you tell us your name?"

When their patient frowned but didn't utter a word, Brett considered that maybe he didn't speak English.

Rayna spoke very slowly and several degrees louder. "We don't know what to call you. What is your name?"

"I am not deaf. You call me Poechna Quahip."

She pursed her lips, smiled, and laid her hand on his shoulder. "Do you mind if I just call you Bob? The other tends to tie my brain in knots."

Brett had to turn his head and cough to contain hoots of laughter. Rayna always did like things straight and simple.

"Bob?" The old man thought for several seconds, then grinned. "I am Bob."

Rayna clasped her hands together. "Excellent! You've been very sick. Are you hungry?"

He nodded. When she went out to collect the breakfast she'd made, the old man turned to Brett. "Crazy white woman."

Not willing to go that far, Brett felt the need to paint her in a favorable light. "She's a good nurse. Loyal and committed, real committed. She sat by you while you slept."

"Keep away evil spirits."

"Mr. Poechna Quahip—"

"Bob," the old man corrected.

"All right." Brett knew then that she'd cast a spell over the old man. "Bob, you came staggering across my meadow yesterday. Where did you come from?"

"Canyon." He grabbed Brett's shirt with his bony fingers and pulled him closer. "Children need help. Hurry."

"Which canyon?"

"Narrow, steep sides." Bob drew a square in the air. "Four horses wide."

"The box canyon?"

The man frowned. "Go! Not last long."

Brett ran outside past Rayna, who was bent over the fire, yelling an explanation on the way. He woke Adam, asleep in his bedroll on the dew-kissed grass. "I need you to come with me. We've got some children to rescue."

Yawning, the boy rubbed sleep from his eyes. "What children? And how do you know they need rescuing?"

"Bob told me."

"Who's Bob? Did we get more company?"

"No. He's the old Indian."

"Funny name for a red man."

"Rayna gave it to him."

"Figures." Adam got to his feet, already fully dressed. "I'll hitch the horses to the wagon." Brett sprinted to the corral where they always kept a few horses. Saved having to round one up every time he wanted to go somewhere.

By the time he got halters on two and led them out, Adam was waiting by the wagon with the rigging. Within a few minutes, Brett drove full out toward the canyon that lay about a mile away at the edge of the Wild Horse.

When he drove into the small canyon, he thought the old man must've sent him on a wild-goose chase. Brett saw no one. His gaze scanned the low brush that littered the canyon floor.

At last, he called, "Hello? Is anyone here? I'm Brett Liberty from the Wild Horse Ranch, and I was told you need help."

Eyes peered over a rock. Then another pair.

"I won't hurt you. You can come out." Brett set the brake and climbed down from the wagon.

A ragged boy of about six or seven edged out from behind the rock. Like a skittish animal, he slowly came, inch by inch. When he reached Brett, the boy took his hand and tugged. Brett followed him around the rock formation.

He was unprepared for the sight. There had to be around two dozen children easily, ranging in age from three or four years old to about eight. None were older than nine, and most lay listlessly on the ground or huddled in groups. The older ones were trying as best they could to care for the younger. All were Indian.

Neither did he expect an old nun with a wrinkled, leathery face, who had to be at least a hundred. She struggled to her feet and approached, hunched over, apparently unable to stand straight.

"Hello, ma'am. Bob told me that you needed help."

"Bob?" Her faded, rheumy eyes stared up at him blankly.

"Poechna Quahip."

"Oh. The old goat left here two days ago. I assume he made it, since you're here."

"Yes, ma'am. He's been unconscious though. Just woke up this morning."

She snorted. "Probably faking it."

"No, ma'am, not this time at least." Brett introduced himself and Adam.

"I'm Sister Bronwen."

Brett tipped his hat. "Nice to meet you, Sister. Adam and I will start loading the children. We need to get them back to the ranch as soon as possible."

"Bless you, my brother. I'm thankful for your help. Many days we waited for the Lord to save us."

He laid his hand on her shoulder. "I don't know much about your Lord, but you don't need to worry anymore. We're here now."

Some children walked to the wagon, while others had to be carried. He didn't know what they suffered from, but all had dry, cracked lips. He wished he'd have thought to bring water, but he'd been in such a hurry.

Considering the bad shape Bob had been in, Brett had feared he'd find them all dead. They were obviously children no one cared about. Probably orphans.

As soon as they'd loaded everyone, he helped Sister Bronwen onto the wagon seat, and they set off over the bumpy ground. It was slow going until he reached his meadow. At last they pulled to a stop in Brett's camp.

Rayna rushed from the tepee and made the children comfortable on the grass. Brett was painfully aware of his lack of space for them. He'd been sewing skins together so Adam could have his own living quarters, but Brett had them only halfway done. He'd have to think of something else.

For the next two hours, he and Adam gave the children as much water as they wanted and cooked a simple soup made with onions, carrots, and potatoes. It was all he could pull from thin air. When it was done, he and Adam fed them, as well as Bob.

Then Brett pulled Rayna aside. "What's wrong with them?"

"They're dehydrated and starving, for one thing, but I think there's something really wrong with some. Half of them have a high fever and rashes. We need Doc Yates to come look at them."

It didn't sound good. Smallpox came to mind, though he didn't want to voice those fears to Rayna. "I'll send Adam to fetch Doc."

"Also, can you have him bring back as many blankets as he can find?"

"All right. If I had some large muslin, I could rig up a shelter for them. It won't have sides, but it'll keep the sun off them in the daytime and the dew at night."

Rayna laid her hand on his arm. "Thank you, Brett. You saved them. No telling how long these poor children have been out there."

He got tangled up in her blue-green stare and forgot how to talk. Nodding, he quickly turned to find Adam before he did something stupid, like crush her to him and kiss her soundly.

Calling himself a big fool, he gave instructions to his nephew and told the boy not to dawdle.

As he watched Adam stride away on his long, gangly legs, he admired the strength and purpose that Adam had shown. His nephew seemed to have grown in so many ways since he stepped off the stage. Brett didn't have to worry if he was capable of doing the job. He knew he could. And would.

While Brett waited, he helped Rayna however he could. Once when he glanced up, he noticed Bob had come from the tepee wearing his stovepipe hat. He sat in the sunlight with both cats on his lap, watching everything.

Sister Bronwen shot the old Indian a black scowl. Brett got the feeling that they were like two snarling old dogs that didn't have enough energy to engage in combat but wanted to give each other grief however they could.

"How are you doing, Sister?" Brett asked.

"I'd be a lot better if that old coot wasn't staring at me. He doesn't have sense enough to go in out of the rain."

The sister's terrible attitude seemed odd, but then he'd never known a holy person before. "I'm curious, Sister. What are you two doing with all these children?"

"They're all Comanche orphans. Someone set fire to the mission, so we're taking them down to Cristobal. A group of men started chasing us four days ago. We hid in the little canyon."

"I didn't see any horses or wagons."

"Our mules ran off while we slept one night. Poechna Quahip forgot to tie them." She shot Bob another glare. Baring his teeth, he answered back with a glare of his own. "We had no choice but to leave the wagons and walk."

"How exactly did you evade the men on horseback?" It seemed a miracle that they escaped.

"God provided. Just as the ambushers seemed to have us, U.S. Cavalry came from nowhere with their guns, which allowed us to run into the canyon. Then the orphans started getting sick, so we hunkered down. I told Bob he had to go for help, or I'd know the reason why."

"You should be proud of him, Sister."

"Humph! He's worthless."

"At least he got help," Brett couldn't help pointing out.

"Humph!"

When Sister Bronwen glanced Bob's way again, he stuck his finger up his nose. Brett hid a laugh and shook his head. The two elders acted worse than children.

Brett's gaze wandered back to Rayna. She wouldn't leave the children, even though they were all sleeping or resting. Her dedication and the depth of her heart warmed him.

With nothing else to do at the moment, he took a seat beside Bob. He felt a kinship with the old man. A sudden gust whipped strands of the old Indian's snow-white hair across his face.

"You seem to be better, Bob. It's good to see you up and around."

"Have to. Battle-ax wants to slit my throat."

"You're safe. I don't allow bloodshed on my land."

"What did she speak about me? Tongue lies."

"She said she's grateful for your help. Can't imagine what she'd have done without you." The lie seemed necessary for the well-being of all parties.

"Humph!"

Brett stretched out his legs. "I want to ask you about something. What is that leather pouch around your neck, and what does it signify?"

"Dumb question. Did Battle-ax send you?"

"No. This may sound strange, but I grew up in a white orphanage. I don't know anything about being Indian. But I have a leather pouch like yours, only I don't know what to call it or what to do with it. When I was left on the steps of the orphanage, a woman found it in the basket."

"It is medicine bag."

"What is it for?"

"Holds your power. Sacred. What is inside?"

"A stone and some sage. Let me show you." Brett rose and went into the tepee. He lifted a soft leather pouch from the box and hurried back out, excited that he was getting answers. Sitting back down, he handed it to Bob, who opened it and emptied the contents in his wrinkled hand.

"Black onyx protects you. Traps bad spirits, keep you safe. Sage purifies." Bob put the items back inside and thrust the bag into his hand. "Wear."

Brett tied it around his neck. A medicine bag. He'd learned something valuable.

"Find things of meaning to *you*," Bob said. "Put inside. Good medicine."

Glancing at Rayna, Brett knew he had to put something belonging to her inside. She gave him more power than anything he knew. Everything about her was sacred to him. A smile curved his mouth. The ones who denied him from having her would never know she lay next to his heart.

"I am Comanche. What is your tribe?" Bob asked.

"Iroquois. I didn't know until two weeks ago, after my sister told me. In fact, I didn't even know I had a sister for a long time. It's strange how we sometimes think we're all alone, and then out of the blue we find out we have family. Adam is her son. My nephew is having a hard time being Indian. But to correct myself, actually we're only half Indian. How do you feel about half bloods?" Brett steeled himself for the answer.

"Some Comanche not like. You saved the children. I welcome in my tepee."

Brett clasped Bob's hand. "Thank you, brother. Do you think you can teach me some of the ways of your people? I want to learn."

"Yes. If Battle-ax does not kill me while I sleep."

"I'll make sure that doesn't happen."

Brett looked up as the sound of a galloping horse grew near. When it came closer, he made out Edgar Dowlen. Getting to his feet, Brett moved toward his neighbor before he could dismount. Something told Brett this wasn't a social call.

"What can I do for you, Dowlen?"

The cattle rancher's eyes glittered. He leaned on his saddle horn, waving his arm toward the orphans. "I want them gone. All of them."

"You have a hell of a lot of nerve telling me what I can do on my own land." Anger crept up the back of Brett's neck.

"When it affects the rest of us, I think I have the right."

"What is this about? We've never had a problem between us until now." Though Brett kept his voice low and even, mind-numbing cold swept over him.

"There was only one of you before. I was willing to let that go. Then you brought the boy out here, and *now* you've got a whole damn reservation. I ain't gonna stand for it. No one else will either. Give your kind an inch, an' you take a mile. You'll be overrunning me next, stealing my cattle."

Brett was vaguely aware that Bob stood beside him.

"You kick us, treat us like dogs." Bob thrust out his bony chest. "Spit on us. Orphans are sick. Dying."

Dowlen dismounted and stalked to where one child lay. "Smallpox!" He leaped back, grabbed his neckerchief from around his neck, and slapped it over his nose and mouth.

"Hold on, Dowlen," Brett said. "We don't know that. We've sent for Doc. Meanwhile, we don't want to cause panic."

The rancher marched to his horse and put his foot

in the stirrup. "You have until sundown. If they're not gone, you'll pay the consequences."

A muscle worked in Brett's jaw. "They're staying where they are. This is *my* land. I say who comes and goes, not you."

"You've heard my warning, half-breed." With that, Dowlen turned his horse and galloped toward his property line.

Bob shook his fist at the neighbor's retreating back. "Not brave like Comanche or Iroquois."

Thick foreboding crawled up Brett's spine. Edgar Dowlen was going to be trouble. Even so, Brett knew he wouldn't back down. He'd fight to the last breath for these orphans who had no one else.

Eighteen

ADAM AND DOC YATES ARRIVED SOON AFTER DOWLEN left. Rayna welcomed the warmth of Brett's hand as they hurried to meet Doc. She prayed they weren't dealing with a smallpox epidemic. She'd seen what it did amongst the poor families of bone-pickers, and had even caught it herself, but survived. She was thankful because it would protect her now as she cared for these children.

"Thank you for coming back so soon, Doc." She held his black bag while he climbed from the buggy.

"Adam said you found a bunch of sick children in a canyon."

"We did," Brett answered, falling into step with the sawbones. "Some were only dehydrated like Bob, but others have a high fever."

"Bob?"

Rayna allowed a tired smile. "It's the name I gave the old Indian."

"Oh." The old doctor blinked rapidly, as if trying to make sense of what she'd said. "Well, let's see what these children have, Nurse."

For the next twenty minutes she followed him from patient to patient, answering each question. The knot that had formed inside her chest when Brett first unloaded the orphans grew. She knew the meaning of Doc's grim expression. It didn't look good.

Finally he straightened. "I can't be sure until more time has passed. They're just starting to break out. It could be smallpox, though it's most likely chicken pox. We'll keep our fingers crossed that it's the latter, or it's going to cause panic."

That had already happened with Edgar Dowlen. She shuddered to think what he'd do if the doctor confirmed smallpox. "What is the treatment?"

"Try to keep the fever down and give them plenty of water. Not sure they'll be too hungry, but if so, only vegetables and fruits if you have any. No meat. Where did these orphans come from?"

Rayna told him what Sister Bronwen had said and added, "I feel sorry for them."

"The Indian wars several years ago left hundreds without parents. Then sickness and disease are taking even more lives. Now we're dealing with the aftermath." Doc Yates rolled down his sleeves and picked up his bag. "I'll be back tomorrow."

"If we're here." She told him about Dowlen's threats.

"That man is evidently a lunatic. Be careful. Send word if you have to move the children."

"I will." She saw him off, then her gaze sought Brett's tall form. So proud and strong, his muscles straining against the black shirt he wore. She'd never known a man with so much honor and depth of heart. She'd seen how he faced up to Dowlen and knew he'd die trying to save these children from anyone who wanted to hurt them. He and Adam were putting up some shelters. They stuck poles into the ground and stretched canvas over them. Simple but effective. Bob and Sister Bronwen supervised whenever they could stop fighting long enough, which wasn't often.

With one shelter ready, Rayna hurried to the wagon and unloaded the blankets Adam had brought from town. Then she laid them under the canvas and began moving some of the children.

Dusk fell all too soon, and with it came a mass of jitters. Sitting around the campfire eating, she felt Brett's unease. Every noise startled him, and sometimes he stood, silently gazing toward Dowlen's land. She prayed trouble wouldn't find them. And if it came, she prayed it waited until they could reinforce their small band.

But she knew from experience trouble had a mind of its own and didn't come head-on. It sneaked up from behind and caught you before you could hide.

Trembling, she set her coffee cup aside and rose to go check on the children. Most were sleeping, but one girl about six years old was awake. The child smiled up at Rayna, shyly touching her hair when she bent over to tuck the blanket around the small body.

"You have the prettiest smile," Rayna said, feeling her forehead and finding no fever. "Can you tell me your name?"

"Flower."

"I like that. Do you hurt anywhere, Flower?"

The dark-haired child shook her head. "Water?"

"You sure can." Rayna reached for a cup, dipped it

into the pail she'd brought with her, and handed it to Flower. "Are you hungry?"

"No." The child drank and lay back down.

When Rayna glanced up, she found Brett watching her. "You have a mothering touch. So gentle."

"I care about these children. What's going to happen to them? I'd take them all if I could." Rayna stood.

"Haven't figured that out yet." He took the pail from her, and they walked toward the campfire. "I want you to sleep in the tepee tonight with Bob and the sister."

"Why?" Rayna tried to read what he *wasn't* saying.

"If Dowlen comes, I want to know exactly where you are. I may not have time to hunt for you."

Her heart hammered. "Where are you going to sleep?"

"I'm not. Adam and I will stand guard." He added a piece of wood to the fire. "After everyone beds down, will you take a walk with me?"

His voice was low and hoarse, as though he didn't think he had a right to ask.

"Yes, as long as we stay close." She turned to help Bob and Sister Bronwen into the tepee, and made herself a bed on the rugs for later.

Bob sat on his bedroll and bared his teeth at the nun. "I sleep with knife. Stay on your side, old woman."

The sister inhaled a deep breath and blew out the lamp, plunging the abode into darkness.

"I warn you, Battle-ax."

"Shut up, Bob, before I come over there and give you a good shaking," the sister warned.

Rayna let out a sigh. It was going to be a long night. She left the two still bickering in the pitch black and went to sit by the campfire. She didn't see Brett. As the night fell like a heavy wool cloak around her, she closed her eyes for a moment, thinking of Edgar Dowlen's threat. She was so weary of trouble. Before she could stop it, her mind drifted back in time. Frightening memories rose up, their intensity suffocating her.

She could see blood pooling beneath the man's body, smelled the stench, tasted the fear that clogged in her throat so thick she couldn't breathe. She had taken a life, and now his ghost haunted her, determined to make her pay for what she'd done.

"Oh, Mama, where are you? I need you." Her whispered words melted into the still air. A sound made her jump.

"Tell me about her." Brett stood beside her with a folded blanket under his arm.

"Nothing to tell," she said a bit too sharply, embarrassed he'd overheard.

"If it's not something, you wouldn't have said it."

"Just me being crazy. Sometimes I talk to myself. Forget you heard me. Is everything all right? I take it you've been checking for trespassers."

"No sign of anyone, but the night's young." He held out his hand. "You said you'd walk with me."

The minute Brett's hand curled around hers, her pulse started racing. An invisible thread seemed to tie them together. His gentle touch went straight to her heart. He was just a friend, she reminded herself. For now, anyway.

Rayna swung into step beside him, but her short legs were no match for his long ones, and she was huffing, trying to keep up.

Finally he noticed and slowed. They took a few more steps to a flat boulder and sat down.

She tried not to notice the hard feel of his body settling next to hers, but every fiber of her being was alive with excitement as the essence of him washed over her. His hands brushed against her as he unfolded the blanket and draped the warm wool around her shoulders.

Gazing up at the brilliant stars overhead, she inhaled deeply. "The sky is so beautiful. My grandfather once told me to make a wish on the first star of the night and it'll come true. But I learned not to believe him."

"My wishes didn't come true either," Brett said softly.

She turned to look at him. "Tell me one thing you've never told anyone, and I'll tell you something about me."

Brett was silent for so long she thought he wasn't going to answer. Finally he said in a quiet voice, "One time in the orphanage, I tried to run away. I was about seven years old, and Mr. Simon had laid into me with this thick razor strop after I laughed during the blessing of the food. This kid next to me was imitating the hawk-nosed Simon, and I couldn't help myself. Each time the strop hit my backside, Simon called me a red savage heathen. Said he would beat that out of me if it was the last thing he did. That I never cried always worked him into a fury."

Her heart ached to think of how he suffered. "I'm so sorry. I don't blame you for running away."

"They caught me right away. After whipping me again in front of the whole group of ragged kids, Mr. Simon tied me to the orphanage gates like some dog and left me there for three days as a warning to the others."

Rayna clasped her hand over her mouth. The scars he carried were as deep and lasting as hers.

"Cooper and Rand hid scraps of food in their pockets and snuck it out to me at night. They stayed with me until almost daylight. A year later, we escaped from that orphan train they put all their troublemakers on."

"I can't imagine how horrible your life must've been."

"The orphanage was pure hell. But I survived, and I'm stronger for it. These children are never going to have to endure anything like that if I have a say in the matter."

"Me either. They have no one to protect them except us."

"It's your turn," Brett reminded her. "What one thing have you never told anyone?"

Stillness washed over her. Her hand trembled as she clutched the blanket tighter. Why had she suggested this? She'd buried so much inside. Too many painful things she never wanted to share. "Forget this game. We need to go back."

Brett laid a hand on her arm, anchoring her to the rock. "Nice try. You started this, lady. I told you mine."

Which one would be easiest without revealing too much? She glanced at the horses huddling together nearby. For warmth? Or for companionship, so they wouldn't be alone? After her mother and Hershel were gone, she'd had to face the darkness by herself.

Now that Brett was with her, the horrors didn't seem so bad. She reached for his hand and clutched it for more courage.

After a minute, she sighed. "I'm sure you've wondered why I can't bring myself to eat meat."

"I have been curious."

"My father never needed an excuse to be cruel. He took such delight in it, especially when he'd been drinking. This one time he thought he'd put the fear of God in me. He didn't know I lived with that fear every second of every day. I tried to run, but he grabbed my hair and dragged me through a thorn patch and then…"

She took a shuddering breath, still shaken by the memory. "He took a handful of this raw meat black with flies that had been sitting out in the hot sun all day and stuffed it into my mouth. I gagged the second it went in and that awful smell went up my nose. When I tried to spit it out, he sat on top of me, holding his hand over my mouth and nose until I swallowed every last rotten morsel of it."

Brett put his arm around her shoulders and gently wiped the tears streaming down her cheeks. "Why?"

"To teach me a lesson to eat whatever he said. *Do* whatever he said. Raymond Harper was always in control, and when I didn't obey, he found ways to bend me to his will. Though I puked most of the meat up later, I was sick for two weeks. Couldn't even keep water down. I've never eaten meat since."

"Easy to understand why. I wish I'd have been there. If I had, I probably would've tried to kill your father."

Rayna laid her head against his broad chest. She was so tired. But it felt good to get one nightmare out. She'd bottled it up too long inside. "Why do we have to go through so much grief and misery?"

Brett pulled her closer, and she heard his heart beating against her ear. "I guess so we'd be stronger. Or maybe it's so we'd recognize the good times when they came. You're away from him, and you'll never have to go back."

"Sometimes I dream I'm back there. I hear his gravelly voice saying such hurtful things, feel the force of his fist. And when I wake up, I'm drenched with sweat." She felt Brett's chin lightly resting on the top of her head. She snuggled against him, placing her palm on his chest, reminding herself that she was free of the likes of Raymond Harper.

But would that ever truly be possible?

Her hand came in contact with a soft leather pouch she'd never seen him wear before. "What's this?"

"A medicine bag. I've always had it, but until today I didn't know what it was or why it was in the basket when I was left at the orphanage. Bob told me it holds my power, things that have meaning only to me."

He paused a moment, and when he spoke, his voice sounded rusty. "Rayna, I have a request that may sound odd."

"You know I'll do anything I can."

"Would you mind if I cut a small piece of your hair to put inside?"

His request surprised her at first, then warmth rose at the thought that she meant this much to him. She raised her head. "I would be honored to have a lock of my hair in your medicine bag."

She moved from the circle of his arm. He pulled his knife from its sheath and, holding a curl between his thumb and forefinger, cut it. Then he opened his leather pouch and laid it inside. A pleasant glow spread through her chest.

Part of her would always be with him. Her eyes misted.

Brett placed his lips to her ear. His soft breath ruffled her hair. "Thank you, Rayna."

Flutters quivered in her stomach. When she leaned into him, he dropped a kiss on her cheek before moving away.

Though she wished for more, she'd learned to be grateful for what she got.

She had these peaceful moments and shared secrets with Brett to cherish forever. Maybe she was starting to heal.

A glance toward the sleeping children told her with certainty that there was no time for Brett and her now.

Even more things blocked their future.

Adam's dark figure moved next to the fire. The kid seemed to be adjusting. Rayna knew the calming balm the Wild Horse offered had been exactly what he needed.

Maybe this land could heal her ragged spirit, too, and help her live with the things she couldn't go back and fix. If she had a mind to.

But some things just needed doing even if they scarred your soul.

Nineteen

ACCORDING TO THE MOON, IT WAS NEARING MIDNIGHT as Brett sat propped against a tree where his property butted up to Dowlen's. His rifle lay across his lap. The things Rayna had told him crowded his mind. It certainly explained the loathing she had for her father, and it was no wonder she steered clear of meat. What else had Raymond Harper done to her? Somehow, Brett knew she'd suffered more.

Anger rose up so fast it startled him. One day he hoped to make the man pay for the horrors forced upon his daughter.

Rayna deserved a life free of abuse and suffering.

He touched the medicine bag hanging around his neck. Her hair would mean nothing to anyone but him. It was his most treasured possession. He brought the supple leather to his mouth and kissed it.

His eyes sought Adam's lanky figure and found his nephew crouching under a tree about a hundred yards away. He also had a rifle that he'd brought back from town.

A sudden sound alerted Brett. He made out the

form of two men moving by foot onto his land. One would most likely be Edgar Dowlen, by his size, but the other?

Brett got to his feet and raised the rifle to his shoulder. "I hope you have a good reason for trespassing, gentlemen. Sneeze, and I'll blow you into hell."

Hands slowly raised.

Brett moved toward them. "What are you doing on my land?"

"Get rid of the sick orphans," Dowlen spat. "I'm warning you."

"Guess I'm happy with them right where they are. The only question I have is where do we go from here? Do I cart your mangy carcasses into town draped over a horse or sitting upright?"

"Ain't no law against protecting yourself from disease," whined Dowlen's accomplice.

"What is your name, mister?"

"Oscar. Oscar Fenton."

"Well, Fenton, if you're so all-fired worried about catching something, why are you coming toward it instead of going away from it?"

"Doin' a service to the community," the man mumbled. "We were just gonna scare you into gettin' rid of 'em."

Though Fenton's hat shielded his eyes, Brett recognized a shifty sort when he saw one.

Adam came up beside Brett with his rifle pointed at the men. "You don't want this fight, so go home or go to jail. Your choice."

The hardness of Adam's words had Brett doing a double take. The fourteen-year-old sounded like a grown man. The youth had come a far piece from the belligerent boy who'd gotten off the stage over two weeks ago. Brett was proud to have Adam stand beside him.

"Threatening us, Injun boy?" Dowlen sneered.

"Nope. Just statin' facts."

"So what's your choice?" Brett prodded. "My nephew gave you a better deal than I did. I think I'd take it."

Dowlen spat tobacco on the ground. "I think I like my chances."

When Brett inched closer, sudden gunshots came from the direction of the trees. Brett and Adam dove for cover beneath the low, overhanging branches they'd been under, and returned the unknown gunman's fire.

In the pitch black, everything blurred. Brett couldn't tell for sure where Dowlen went. Since they were on foot, they had to be near.

Orange flame shot from the darkness on Dowlen's land. Deciding it was crazy to blindly return fire, Brett settled back and tried to focus on where his neighbor might be. Seconds passed as he watched, waited, listened. Every muscle tensed for the next bullet that might come his way. His finger never left the trigger of the rifle, nor did he lower it.

Hoofbeats and the blowing sound made by a galloping horse first alerted him. Suddenly a horseman burst from the trees, leading two riderless horses. They headed straight toward Brett. As the animals drew closer, Dowlen and Fenton tore from the dense cover of cedar and ran shouting toward the horses.

Brett's heart hammered as he opened fire, managing to wound Oscar Fenton. Though it made his gut clench to know he'd harmed anyone, strange satisfaction filled him.

The man gave a loud curse and grabbed his arm. Brett ratcheted another bullet into the chamber and fired again, this time missing. Both Fenton and Dowlen grabbed one of the extra mounts and pulled themselves into the saddle. Two more shots missed, but Brett kept firing until the hoofbeats faded into the night and the only sound was a low moan.

With his breath coming in raspy pants, Brett ran toward the sound. "Are you hurt, Adam?"

The boy stood but was visibly shaken. "I'm fine. Is it always like this?"

"What do you mean?"

"The fear. The danger. My hand's shaking so bad I couldn't fire my rifle."

"I'm afraid to tell you it's always like this. A man who remains unaffected by getting shot at has ice in his veins. You wouldn't be normal if you weren't scared."

"Do you think they'll be back, Uncle Brett?"

"Maybe not tonight, but we haven't seen the last of them." Through narrowed gaze, Brett stared toward his neighbor's land. "Men like Dowlen don't give up. The hate inside them is too strong. They don't stop until they're dead or someone makes them."

Someone like him, Cooper, and Rand. This wasn't the first time they'd faced such men before.

"Why can't people leave us alone?"

Brett put his hand on Adam's shoulder. "That's a question I wish I knew the answer to. I'm really proud of you. You're a man with a heart. You care about the fate of these orphans and the two elders."

His nephew shrugged. "They can't help who they are."

"No, they can't. And neither can you." Brett prayed that Adam had gotten his eyes opened for good. "Let's settle back down. See if they return."

Adam went back to his post, and Brett resumed his position under the tree. He took off his medicine bag. Opening it, he took out Rayna's curl and held it up to the moonlight, watching a silvery ray kindle a flare of fiery warmth. He'd been right. She'd brought him powerful medicine. When Bob had spoken with reverence of the Great Spirit, it had sounded foreign. Brett had never heard it before and had always referred to the heavenly being as his creator or God. Somehow he liked the idea of a Great Spirit, a commanding force who watched over people like them.

It was nice not to feel alone anymore.

With a warm glow in his chest, he rubbed the few treasured strands of hair Rayna had let him cut. The thought hit him that he hadn't given her anything. He needed to make her a medicine bag. She could wear it under her dress if she didn't want anyone to see. Knowing she was safe meant everything to him, and if the bag helped keep her that way, then she'd need it.

❧

Cooper rode in the following day. Brett was happy to see him. Even though Dowlen or his men hadn't returned, he knew it was a matter of when, not if.

Brett went to greet his older brother. "What brings you out this way, Coop?"

"Trouble." The sun glinted off Cooper's tin star as he dismounted. "Dowlen's in town, hiring drunks right and left out of the saloon. When he's done in Battle Creek, he'll probably hit China Wells and all the other little towns. He's shooting off his mouth about a smallpox epidemic out here on your place."

"Figured as much." Brett told him about his run-in with Dowlen and the trespassing last night. "Managed to shoot one."

"Bad?"

"Looked like I only grazed him."

"It gets worse. Dowlen's trying his best to get regular God-fearing folks, not just the drunks, to take up arms. Battle Creek's citizens aren't going to listen, but those in China Wells and other places will be a different story."

Brett recalled that the Comanche had nearly wiped out China Wells a few months before he, Cooper, and Rand arrived a little over seven years ago. Those people still carried a grudge.

"The feeling in my gut says that we're about to have a war," Cooper added.

Though Brett thought the same thing, hearing it put into words froze the fear in his chest. "I think you're right."

"What are you doing to prepare?" Cooper asked.

"Just guarding at night. Me and Adam. Too much ground to cover for just us." Brett stared off toward Dowlen's land. "How about a cup of coffee while we finish talking?"

"Sounds good."

Bob strode from the tepee in his stovepipe hat with his arms folded across his chest. "Gonna arrest us now?"

"Nope." Cooper held out his cup to Brett, who had the pot. "Have you done anything wrong?"

"Stole this hat from a dead man. And last night dreamed I killed the nun. Stabbed her a hundred times, but she only kept laughing at me."

Brett watched Cooper struggle to keep a straight face. He introduced them and explained how Bob came by his name. Curiosity apparently was killing Sister Bronwen, because she wasted no time in joining them.

Bob bared his teeth and growled low, which prompted the nun to stick out her tongue. Finally, Brett and Cooper walked away, leaving them to their game.

Cooper shook his head. "You've got a mess with those two, Brother."

"Don't I know it. I'm hoping it won't lead to bloodshed. But back to Dowlen. This could get really ugly."

"I have to ask…*do* the children have smallpox?"

"Doc says it's too soon to tell. He's leaning more toward chicken pox, but that's bad enough."

"Some people think they're related." Cooper tossed his coffee dregs into the tall grass. "They might join forces with Dowlen. Disease can cause panic, and once it does, you can't reason with them. Fear takes over, and they become desperate."

"I'm prepared to protect these orphans with my life. They're innocent."

"Rand and I can bring our hands to help you fight. I'll put eight at your disposal, but only count on two from Rand, since he doesn't have as many to pull from. It'll take a few days to get everything situated so they can come."

Ten extra guns would be better than nothing. They'd have fourteen, counting Brett, his two brothers, and Adam.

"That's probably best anyway. I don't want to overreact. Maybe Dowlen will come to his senses and call off this war." Brett stared toward his neighbor's cattle ranch.

"Hopefully. But range wars have started for less."

A bad feeling clawed up the back of Brett's neck. He knew Cooper was right. This fight was far from over, and it would take everything he had to win it.

∽

After Cooper left, Brett got out the buffalo hides he'd put back for another tepee, and set Bob to work sewing them together. Give the old man something to do, and he'd leave Sister Bronwen alone. Peace might prevail for a short time.

Once Brett had Bob occupied and Rayna assured him she didn't need his help with the children, who were breaking out in red raised spots, he located a small piece of supple leather.

While they worked, Brett asked Bob about some of the customs and traditions of their people. Through the old man, he learned about life in a Comanche village and the tribal laws that governed them. The elders were held in high esteem and settled disputes, assessed penalties for crimes, and taught the youth the ways of their people. He hated the deep sadness that oozed from Bob's voice when he spoke about losing the land the Comanche loved and a way of life that simply vanished as though it had never been.

"Gone. All gone. People. Land. Villages. I will die soon."

Brett laid a hand on Bob's shoulder. "I'm sure you feel you've outlived your purpose, but I assure you that isn't true. You still have value. These children need someone to teach them the old ways. They need what you can give."

Bob stared toward the horizon with faded eyes. "They will have you."

"I don't know what to teach them. You do."

"You will learn." Bob turned back to his needle and hides and lapsed into silence that no amount of prodding could break.

An hour later, Brett had finished a simple medicine bag. Of course it needed decorating with beads, but that could come another time.

He strode to a patch of wild sage and broke off a few small stems. Then some sweet grass. This was a start. The rest would have to be up to Rayna. He couldn't say what held meaning for her.

The sun was high overhead when he found an opportunity to give it to her.

Her blue-green eyes lit up. "Oh, Brett, no one ever gave me a gift before. I'll cherish it." She lifted her hair and immediately asked him to tie it around her neck.

The soft auburn curls brushed his knuckles, arousing feelings he constantly strove to hide.

"You needed something to keep you safe," he said gruffly.

Turning, she quickly brushed his cheek with her lips. "I already have you, but I'll take more. Thank you."

"Put what you want inside." His cheek burned where she'd kissed him.

"I intend to. Can I borrow your knife?" Her eyes danced. "That is, if you'll let me a have a piece of fringe from your moccasins."

Brett stilled, overcome with emotion. His breath froze in his chest. That she would put such value on one piece of worn fringe—and its connection to him—rendered him speechless. Touched. After a long moment, he handed her his knife.

Kneeling, she cut a small piece off and tucked it inside her bag. He helped her stand and stuck his knife back into the sheath.

"How are the children?" he asked, low. "I saw the spots."

"I wish Doc would come." She drew her eyebrows together and chewed her lip. "I don't know if it's smallpox or not. While it may not help, all I can do is to keep on with what I've been doing."

Brett took her hand. "He'll be here soon. Maybe he got held up at the hospital."

But though midday arrived with still no sign of the buggy, he wasn't sure. An hour later, he went to Adam. "Saddle a horse. I need you to ride into town to see what's holding up Doc."

The boy seemed grateful for something to do. Like the rest, he could do nothing but stand around waiting for whatever was coming. He lost no time saddling a mount, and within a short space, galloped out.

With Adam gone, Brett strode to Rayna's side and helped her soothe the sick ones. She seemed to appreciate his help, since Sister Bronwen had gone to lie down.

Brett was holding a small bucket for Flower to throw up in when Adam raced onto the land and jumped off the horse before it completely stopped.

The hair on Brett's neck rose in warning.

Rayna took the bucket. "Go. See what's happening."

Frustration spewed from Adam's mouth before Brett reached him. "Never got to town. Men blocked the road. Must be why Doc couldn't get here."

"Did they see you?"

"Nope. Got out of sight before they could."

"I'm glad you're safe. You did well, Adam." Brett's heart sank. This had to be Dowlen's doing. He hurried to tell Rayna the doctor wasn't coming.

Panic and worry deepened the shade of her eyes before he even said a word. She seemed to know what he was going to say.

"What are we going to do?" Her voice trembled, and he could see how scared she was. "Without Doc…"

Brett pulled her into his arms and held her close. "We'll get through this. You're smart. You'll know what to do. In the meantime, the minute Doc tells Cooper, he'll lay a blazing path and go through hell if he has to. One thing about my brother is that he doesn't put up with troublemakers. Has no patience with them."

"I'm just so scared. I've never had so many lives

depending on me. I don't know enough." She clutched his shirt. "What if I do the wrong thing?"

He rubbed her back. "You won't. Trust your instincts. Do your best. How can I help?"

Dark, thick lashes framed her eyes when she looked up. "Can you make more of your special vegetable soup? The children could eat some of that."

Lightly pressing a kiss to her forehead, he smiled. "I certainly can." He could hop over the moon if she asked him.

She gave him a smile. The thing about Rayna was she bounced back fast. She never let despair drag her down for long. Stepping out of his arms, she smoothed her hair, pasted on a smile, and became all business. It was time to get back to work.

Brett admired her gumption as she marched toward her patients. Such big things lay in that small package.

He knew one thing for certain—if he dared, she could sure fill his arms.

And his heart.

Twenty

A SOUND LIKE ROLLING THUNDER CAME ABOUT MID-night, sending chills up Brett's spine and knotting his stomach. The noise vibrated the air, shaking the ground beneath his feet. Though their task seemed futile, he and Adam had taken up guard duty near the property line, hoping to stop any trespassers they could. From the fury in the air, he knew it was hopeless.

Dowlen was back and, judging from the pounding hooves, he'd brought many more with him this time.

How could two men hold their own against a mob?

Brett wasn't afraid for himself. It was Rayna and Adam and the others who concerned him. He had to somehow protect them even if it cost him everything. He flinched, breaking out in a cold sweat.

Despite the odds, he couldn't quit. He had to give this fight his all, and if he died doing it, then the Great Spirit would reward him for bravery.

Taking a deep breath, he tightened his grip on the rifle and readied for the assault.

"Make every shot count," he murmured to himself.

The invaders—at least two dozen strong—swarmed

across the pasture between his position and Adam's like a horde of hungry locusts.

Brett took aim and fired, but it didn't slow the attackers a bit. He fired again, and this time managed to get one, although the shot didn't knock the man from his horse.

On the riders galloped—toward the crude shelters where the children slept.

Cold fear gripped his heart, freezing him in his tracks for only a second.

Then his moccasins skimmed the ground as he ran, yelling at the top of his lungs, hoping and praying everyone would wake up and get out of the way. He cursed the fact that he hadn't ridden a horse to the place where he'd lain in wait. Fact was, he'd been afraid the animals would've given away his and Adam's positions. He'd thought to lure them across, thinking no one stood watch. He called himself a damn fool.

Now, one of his mustangs could've covered the distance in nothing flat.

When he reached the camp, he thought he'd descended into some type of grisly hell. Everywhere he looked he saw chaos and destruction. The carnage twisted his insides into knots until he could barely draw breath.

Children shrieked in terror. Horses gave high-pitched screams into the night. Others reared up on their back legs, unseating their bellowing riders.

The sounds of the frightened children and animals blended into the sort of helpless nightmare from which he could not escape.

Brett raised his rifle and fired at the nearest invaders,

but with the flurry of constant movement, most of his shots missed.

When he emptied his rifle, he tossed it aside. Reaching up, he jerked the man closest to him from his horse. Drawing back, Brett hit the attacker with every bit of strength he possessed and watched him crumple to the ground.

He whirled in time to see a beefy figure on foot lunging at him from behind.

Managing to sidestep a crushing blow, he delivered a quick uppercut to the invader's jaw.

The stocky man returned one that came near to shattering the bones in his face—and would have if he'd hit him square. As it was, it knocked Brett back several feet, but thankfully, he still remained standing. He staggered and shook his head to clear the cobwebs.

Taking a second breath, he went at his opponent again, marshaling all his power. With a mighty swing, he connected with bone and tissue, and the man fell like a huge oak, lying still upon the ground.

From the corner of his eye, Brett saw a dark figure duck under one of the canvas shelters he'd erected. Whatever evil the man thought to do, he'd find a way to stop him.

He was still several yards away when a child's bloodcurdling scream filled the air.

With his breath harsh in his ears, he scrambled into the shelter. The dimness couldn't hide the man standing over one of the sick orphans with his arm raised.

He wielded a club of some sort above his head.

Before he could strike, Brett made a flying leap and tackled him. The momentum carried them outside, taking the canvas with them. He quickly bounded to his feet with his fists doubled, as did the enemy.

The man wore some kind of carved wooden mask that was frozen in a gruesome smile. He turned, and with a guttural cry, launched himself at Brett. Brett caught him under an arm and threw the attacker over his head.

Spinning, Brett delivered two quick kicks to the devil's midsection. He was about to put an end to the grunting mask-wearer when a horse galloped straight for him. With not a minute to spare, Brett leaped to the side.

The rider reached down and pulled his disguised accomplice up onto the horse behind him. In the effort of trying to get away, the man's mask tumbled to the ground.

Edgar Dowlen's face shone in the moonlight.

"Get the hell out of here!" Dowlen thundered the order to his men. "Retreat! Retreat!"

While Brett went to check on the child, a little girl about six years old, the unseated riders somehow managed to find horses, and they all melted into the darkness.

The trembling child threw her arms around his neck. "Save me."

"It's all right, honey. I'm not going to let the bad man get you." Not even if he had to put a bullet through Dowlen's black heart and drive him back into hell.

Brett couldn't shake a dark thought: it was strange that Rayna hadn't come running, and that terrified him. It could only mean something had happened to her.

With gentle hands, he picked up the girl and carried her near the fire where the others had gathered. "You'll be safe for a minute. I have something I need to do."

Trying to contain the worry gripping him, Brett raced into the tepee. "Rayna!"

Though his hands shook, he managed to light the lamp. Bob and Sister Bronwen huddled low against one side, staring back.

There was no sign of the woman who filled his dreams.

"Rayna, where are you?" he yelled, stepping into the cool night. He whirled in a circle, searching for her.

The instant he saw her, all the chaos of the night faded, and his world righted. She walked out of the darkness toward him, holding the hands of two of the orphans and carrying a third.

"Rayna," he said on a trembling breath.

She began to run, and he went to meet her. Putting down the little boy she held, she threw herself in his arms and clutched his shirt for dear life. "I was so scared. I thought they'd kill us all."

Brett kissed her as his trembling hands smoothed back her wild curls. "Are you hurt?"

"I'm fine. When I heard the horses coming, I grabbed these children and ran. I hated that I couldn't take everyone to safety." She pushed away from him. "I've got to check on the rest."

The sob in her voice said she expected to find some hurt. Or worse. He scooped up the little boy she'd been carrying—who was probably no older than four—and scanned the camp the raiders had left in shambles.

Only one of the three canvas shelters remained

standing. Dazed orphans wailed as they walked amongst the ruins. Brett's heart ached for them. They'd fled terror only to find more here where they thought they were safe. He bent and picked up the hideous wooden mask where it had fallen. A muscle worked in his jaw.

Somehow, someway, Dowlen would pay.

The man who had instilled so much terror fueled by his own ignorance and fear would know retribution. But that would have to come later. He had things to do that took priority.

Namely, finding Adam.

He'd not seen his nephew since before the attack, and he didn't like what his gut was telling him. Without a word, he handed the little boy in his arms to Sister Bronwen, who'd come from the tepee. Sprinting to the corral, he grabbed the first horse. Swinging onto its bare back, he galloped to Adam's position on the property line.

"Adam! Adam!"

There was no answer. All of a sudden he spotted a dark form lying in a patch of trampled grass. No! He rushed to the boy's side.

Please let him be alive. That was all he asked.

Adam's eyes were open, but he seemed in shock. Brett talked while he looked for the source of blood. Finding no visible gunshot wound, he turned his attention to his nephew's torn clothing and deep cuts. Adam appeared to have been trampled by one of the raiders' horses.

Using great care, Brett got him on the mustang and climbed up behind to hold him.

Rayna came running the minute they rode into camp and helped lower Adam to the ground and into the tepee. Then she shooed Brett away. "Let me do my job. If I need you, I'll call."

"Just tell me this—how many of the children were hurt?"

"Six, though none are serious. I've already tended to their scrapes and bruises. They're terrified though."

Since none had lost their lives, it appeared the main reason for the attack had been to frighten the children so badly that he'd take them far away from the Wild Horse. But where could he take them that they would be free of men like Dowlen? He knew of no place.

Brett gave Rayna a weary nod. While she cared for Adam, he turned to calming the orphans. One by one, he held them, wiped their tears, and spoke quietly until their trembling stopped. Then he spread their blankets on the grass and got them to lie down.

He looked at them a good while. Some slept and others stared blankly into the sky. Tomorrow he would put the canvas shelters back up. He sat down and dropped his head onto his folded arms.

Heartsick, Brett didn't know how long he sat there numb and hurting. Suddenly, the four-year-old he'd taken earlier from Rayna crawled into his lap.

The child's small hand patted Brett's chest as the orphan began to softly sing in the only language he knew. The comfort the little boy offered soothed some of the misery and anger bubbling inside Brett.

As the first rays of dawn began to lighten the eastern sky, bringing hope for a better day, Rayna came from the tepee. He gave her an expectant glance.

"Of course, Doc will have to check Adam for internal injuries that I don't know how to look for, but I don't think he's too hurt," she reported. "He has a broken rib or two—probably some are cracked as well—and he's bruised and battered something awful. All in all, he's lucky. It could've been worse, lots worse."

"I'm glad. I was just sitting here wondering how I was going to tell his mother that I didn't take care of him like I promised."

Rayna laid a hand on his shoulder and said softly, "You can't protect him or any of the rest of us from everything. It's impossible." Her gaze shifted to the child in his arms. "Your little friend is sound asleep. Want me to carry him to a blanket?"

"I'd probably drop him if I tried. I'm so tired."

Sliding her hands around the snoozing boy, she laid him on a blanket with another small boy. Brett thought they must be brothers, because he always saw them together.

If the bond between these two boys was as strong as it was between him, Cooper, and Rand, they'd be all right.

Brett's gaze followed Rayna as she returned and sat next to him. She looked tired. He rose and stood behind her. He moved her hair aside and kneaded her neck and shoulders in firm, swirling motions.

"Oh, Brett, that feels so good."

"Thought it might."

"You need it worse than I do though. You've been working like mad and going without sleep, trying to keep us safe."

"I'll rest when this is over." He let one hand move to a shell-like ear and traced the curve. Bending, he kissed her cheek. "You're quite beautiful, Rayna. I've loved watching you blossom. You're not the same woman I met in that jail cell. When I couldn't find you after the raid, I thought I'd lose my mind. If I lost you…"

"I felt the same way when you left to go stand guard," she whispered. "I've developed a great need to see your face and know you're all right."

He mulled over her confession as he rubbed her neck and shoulders until he felt the tension leave. Would it ever be possible for them to be open with everything they felt? He sure hoped so.

Sighing, he moved beside her and reached for her hand. "I'll get some coffee on in a minute. I hate to miss a second of our time, because we don't get this often. The kids will be stirring soon, and we'll have to go about taking care of them."

Rayna's gaze swept the damage. "Looks like we have our work cut out for us. Only…what if those men come back and tear it all down again?"

Brett wished he could tell her that wasn't going to happen, but it would be a lie. He *knew* they'd be back, and when they came, it would be far worse.

For the first time since he was very young, he doubted his abilities. He couldn't stop this madness.

⁂

The sun had burned off most of the heavy dew across Wild Horse land as Brett sat beside Bob by the dying embers of the campfire, listening to the old Comanche telling stories of when he was young. Some of the healthier children had gathered around, enthralled.

At the sound of approaching horses, Brett's stomach clenched. He grabbed his rifle and raced toward the thump of hooves and the clatter of a vehicle of some kind. His only thought was to meet trouble head-on and do his best to stop it before it reached the others.

Flanked by two columns of men on horseback, the doctor's black buggy rumbled onto his land. He gave a sigh of relief.

Cooper rode in the lead. When he reached the camp, he held up his hand for his men to halt and dismounted. "Sorry it took so long to get Doc here. Looks like a tornado came through."

Brett clasped Cooper's hand. "Have to say I'm mighty glad to see you. I sent Adam toward town late yesterday, and he found the road blocked, so I knew the barricade prevented Doc from reaching us."

"I take it those same men are to blame for this mess."

"Yep. Visited us again last night. My nephew and some of the children were injured."

"Damn Edgar Dowlen!" Cooper swore. "Doc couldn't find me to let me know about the situation until a few hours ago when I went into town."

"I figured it was something like that."

"This morning, I threatened to shoot the whole damn bunch of rabble-rousers if they didn't get going back to where they came from," Cooper thundered. "Hell and be damned! I better not find that road blocked again, or someone will pay."

"Want some coffee?" Brett asked.

"Always," his brother replied.

"How about your men? They want some? I can make more. It's the least I can do for bringing Doc Yates."

Cooper grinned. "Never knew those fellows to pass up coffee."

The motley group of ranch hands dismounted and untied bedrolls from behind their saddles. Brett counted ten in all, the number Cooper had promised.

Brett filled a cup and handed it to him. "Thought you said it would take a couple of days before they'd be free to come."

"The blockaded road hurried them along."

"Glad for the help. I was wondering how I was going to patrol the entire property line tonight." Brett cast his brother a glance and lowered his voice. "The children began to break out in red raised spots. Rayna is afraid it's smallpox. If she's right, stay away from them. I don't want you taking the disease back to your twins. That's all you need."

Cooper took a swig of coffee and nodded. "I see a few are able to be up." He motioned toward the ones sitting at Bob's feet.

"I think those were only dehydrated and had gone too long without food. Once we got something to eat and water into them, they seemed to feel better." Brett watched Rayna with Doc as they made their rounds. He sure hoped the report would not mention deadly smallpox. Bob had told him it wiped out entire Comanche villages years ago.

Brett's heart froze.

As closely as Rayna worked with the orphans, she could take ill. She could die.

If he lost her…

He couldn't finish the thought. The mere possibility brought crushing pain.

Over the next hour, Brett made many more pots of coffee and shared his thoughts with the ranch hands. They'd get the shelters for the children back up first, then go from there.

He and Cooper were talking when Doc Yates shuffled over. "It's clear. The children have chicken pox, not smallpox."

Relief made Brett's knees weak. "That's good news."

"The disease is still making them very sick, but they should get through it." Doc scratched his head. "Now, I'll see about that nephew of yours. Rayna told me he got trampled."

"He's just inside the tepee, Doc," Brett said and turned to Cooper. "You and I should ride over and tell Dowlen so he'll call off this war."

"I hope it makes a difference, but I doubt it," Cooper said. "He's bound and determined to get rid of you and these orphans. One excuse is as good as another to people like him. I'll mosey over that way and let him know though."

Brett tightened his jaw and reached for the black, carved wooden mask. "I'm coming with you. I've got a score to settle, and I'm returning this."

Thirty minutes later, Cooper and Brett crossed onto Dowlen's land. At least three dozen small tents dotted the area around the house, and men gave them sinister stares. Cooper slid his Colt from its holster, sending a message that he was ready if they wanted to start trouble. Brett noticed most looked down when they rode past.

They pulled up in front of the quiet house.

Dowlen jerked the door open and stomped onto the broken-down porch when they dismounted. "Wha'd'ya want now, Sheriff?"

Still holding the Colt, Cooper ordered, "Call off your men. The orphans have chicken pox, not small-pox. Doc just confirmed it."

A black bruise covered the side of Dowlen's face and along his jaw, and he sported a bloody lip. He leaned against the doorjamb, staring at Brett. "They're still diseased. They spread their vermin an' filth to good folk tryin' to take care of their families."

"You don't speak for everyone in this county," Brett said.

"I will before I'm done. Mark my words, no one wants a mess of savages livin' next to them."

Brett's hand curled into a fist, itching to slam it into Dowlen's face again. Forcing himself to stay calm, he pitched the wooden mask at his neighbor's feet. "You left this on my property last night. Thought I'd return it, that being the *neighborly* thing to do. I catch you trespassing again, and I won't be so forgiving. Heed *my* words."

"Threatenin' me, breed?"

"You'll know it if I threaten you. You won't have to ask." When Brett took a step toward him, Dowlen quickly straightened and moved back.

Cooper stepped between them. "Dowlen, stay on your own property. You should know I brought some men to fortify the Wild Horse. I won't stand for any more trouble. I'll haul you to jail so fast you won't know what's happening. Got it?"

"Got it, Sheriff." With that he stepped inside and slammed the door so hard it shook the windowpanes.

"That went well, Coop."

"I just hope he listens."

That made two of them. Brett's soul craved peace. He'd never been one who thrived on fighting and disharmony, like a few others seemed to.

Meanwhile, he'd keep his guard up. Rayna and the orphans were his life, and their welfare occupied his every thought.

All doubt about his abilities was gone. If anyone messed with them again, they'd find out how unforgiving a warrior he could be.

Twenty-one

With everyone pitching in, it didn't take long to set the camp to rights. Even some of the children helped in making them a place to sleep.

As Brett restored some semblance of order, his blood boiled anew when he discovered a rope around one of the poles sticking from the top of the tepee and dangling down the side, where one of the attackers had attempted to pull it over. Deep sadness and anger permeated his very being and seeped down into his soul.

They'd invaded his home…his one place of peace.

At what point would it all end? His heart cried out for the tranquillity that had been stripped from the land he loved.

This must be how the Comanche felt after the white men took away their land and destroyed their way of life. His gaze found Bob, who was still working on the buffalo hides for another tepee. Though Brett could've finished the job in half the time, he knew the old Comanche needed to feel useful.

After Bob finally completed the sewing, Brett and

some of the men cut poles and erected a second tepee. He put Rayna and Sister Bronwen, plus a few of the weakest children, into it.

While he worked, Brett made a point to check on Adam several times. His nephew had been in a lot of pain, so Doc had given him a big dose of medicine. Now Adam was in a deep sleep. But early afternoon when Brett stepped into the tepee again, he was awake. "I'm sorry, Uncle Brett. I couldn't get out of the way quick enough."

"No need to apologize. You did nothing wrong. You manned your post every bit as well as I did mine."

"I left you to face them alone," Adam pointed out. "You needed me."

Touching Adam's bandaged shoulder and chest, Brett blinked hard. The apology was his to make, not Adam's. He cleared his throat. "You didn't let me down, so don't even think it. I'm sorry I put your life at risk. I should've kept you with me."

Adam's glare hardened. "Because you think I'm still a kid and need to have someone watch me like a hawk? I'm a man. I'm not as tall as you or have your muscles, but I'm a man all the same."

"I know that, son. I'm proud to have you stand beside me. But maybe I needed the reminder. I'd send for your mother, but it's too dangerous out here."

"I don't want her to see me like this anyway," Adam said. "She'd make me go into town. I'm tired of being safe. I want to do something important."

Brett touched his shoulder. "I think I understand what you mean."

"When those men came last night, all I could think

about was making sure they didn't hurt these orphans. I didn't even care what happened to me as long as I could stop 'em." Adam's sudden outburst revealed the rage inside.

When Brett spoke, his voice was thick and a bit raspy. "That's what being a man is about. How old you are doesn't make any difference. You've grown up since you came West."

"Where's my rifle?" Adam glanced around. "I can still shoot. I want to keep it beside me."

"I'll bring it to you. The help is appreciated."

Adam nodded and closed his eyes. He seemed relieved that his request wasn't met with an argument. Brett found the rifle he'd retrieved from the grass where his nephew had fallen and took it to him. Finding him asleep, Brett laid it beside his bedroll.

He stood for a moment watching Adam get the rest he needed, thinking how close he'd come to losing him. The hole that would leave would never fill. Adam was his now, thrown away by a father that, from all accounts, was like Dowlen. In a lot of ways Adam was like a son instead of a nephew.

Heaviness filled Brett. Rayna was the only one who understood that kind of pain. He needed her wisdom and gentleness.

With Doc and Cooper spending the night, Brett found time to seek her out around dusk. "Take a walk with me, Rayna?"

Her eyes lit up. "I'd love to."

He felt his muscles quiver when she wrapped her arm around his and fell into step with him.

As they walked, the horses crowded around,

wanting his attention. He petted, rubbed, and spoke to each of his friends and, in turn, they talked back in their own language of kindred souls. One, a beautiful gray with black markings, mane, and tail, nuzzled his shirt. Brett laughed, stroking the mare's face. "You're out of luck. Don't have any apples today, girl."

"She's so sweet." Rayna ran her hand over the sleek sides. "What is her name?"

"Doesn't have one."

"That's mean. She needs a name."

"I usually let my customers name the horses. Why is it so important?"

"Because they love you and they need to belong, just like we do," Rayna said softly. "At least that's my thinking on the subject."

"When did you learn about horses?"

"I don't have to be an expert to know that they're the same as people, only hairy." Rayna dropped a kiss on the mare's nose and crooned to her.

Brett watched in amusement. He would never doubt Rayna's feelings for all living creatures. "Why don't you name her?"

"Are you sure about this?" she asked.

"I am."

"I'll have to think of a good one." She wrinkled her forehead in thought. "Names are serious business. Mind if I take some time? But why have you changed your mind?"

"You convinced me she needs one, and I don't like disappointing a lady. Take all the time you need." He took Rayna's hand, curling his fingers around hers. "I want to show you something."

She hesitated. "I can't go too far from the children."

"We won't. I promise. It's very near."

A little ways farther, they walked around a rock outcropping, and she sucked in a breath. "Oh, Brett! This is beautiful."

A pool of blue water surrounded by lush grass and trees lay nestled in a hidden alcove. The flowing sound of a small waterfall added charm and music to their ears.

"This is my oasis," Brett said, watching her. "It's where I come when I need to think or to find solace after a trying day. This place always soothes my soul." When she sat down on the thick grass, he dropped next to her with their shoulders touching. "I thought you'd like it. If ever we need peace and serenity, it's now."

Rayna's face glowed in the last rays of remaining light. "I never would've known this was here. It's like how I picture heaven to be. My heart can't take in all the beauty."

Neither could his. Brett stared spellbound at how the light played on her glorious hair and gentle face. Rayna was the woman of his dreams. If he couldn't run his fingers across her lips, kiss her, he would lose his mind. The weariness of fighting folded around him like a heavy gray shroud. He had no more resistance against desires that refused to be locked away.

A sudden thought niggled in his brain, exciting him. Right now, the Wild Horse offered as much privacy as their jail cell in Steele's Hollow. They were apart from the world. It was safe to give in to what they wanted if only for a little while. If she were willing, perhaps they could find peace together in these quiet, stolen moments.

Perhaps he would know the taste of her again.

Happiness replaced gloom for the first time in days. Brett traced the curve of her cheek, hope making his heart pound. It had been so hard denying himself the feel of her. "Do you mind if I kiss you?"

Her eyes shone as she leaned into him at once, her upturned face a silent invitation.

Very gently, he lowered his mouth to her moist, slightly parted lips. A current ran through him the second he touched her, and he realized the quick kiss he'd had in mind wouldn't satisfy this time.

With a ragged groan, he slipped his arms around her, crushing her to him.

His need was too great to pull back. Her breasts pressing against his chest, her heart beating next to his, brought instant peace.

Hungering for everything he'd denied himself, he thrust a hand in the silkiness of her fiery curls. Her scent swirled around him like a caress, touching him everywhere as it burrowed beneath his skin.

When he ended the kiss, his lips remained at the corner of her mouth, their breaths mingling. "Thank you, Rayna. You are like this oasis. You set the jagged edges of my soul at rest. I wish…"

Rayna caressed his face with her fingers. "Me too. I would give anything to spend the rest of my life with you right here in this hidden place where nothing can hurt us."

"We're safe here," he said, reassuring himself as much as her. He nibbled her ear and left a trail of kisses down the slender curve of her neck to the collar of her dress. When he raised his glance, he saw expectation in her blue-green eyes.

"Brett, I dreamed of this moment but was too afraid to hope it might happen." A smile trembled over her lips.

The palm she rested on his chest sent heat shooting beneath the fabric. His skin quivered everywhere she touched as hunger consumed him. He lifted her hand to his lips. "Never wonder if I want you," he murmured hoarsely. "I will to the day I die."

Gently, he laid her back in the lush grass and leaned over her, probing the fathomless depths of her eyes. "This *friends* thing isn't working too well."

"What do you mean?" Her breathless question was hushed.

"What I feel for you is far more than a friend would. I need you to sleep beside me forever."

"I'll wait however long it takes." Rayna paused as worry rippled across her face. "But—"

"But what?"

"You may change your mind when you find out some things about me."

He smoothed back her hair, taking a tendril between his thumb and forefinger. "I know all I need to. Keep the past where it is. What matters is what's before us."

With a hand under her chin, he left feathery kisses along the seam of her mouth before taking her lips in earnest. His touch followed the contours of her body and rested on the flat plane of her stomach. Rayna had brought light to his world, and he cherished every moment spent with her. The depth of emotion running through him shook his being as they kissed for what felt like a very long time—and not near long enough.

Pulling back, wrestling back control of the heat that raged between them, he gazed at her in wonder. How could his feelings be so strong in such a short time? A month ago, he didn't even know she existed.

Finally, he gave a ragged sigh. "As much as I'd love to stay here, we can't. We have people depending on us." Getting to his feet, he offered her a hand up.

Rayna stood on tiptoe and kissed his cheek. "I'm glad you showed me your special place. I needed this bit of beauty. Thank you for finally being honest about your feelings."

She walked to the edge of the pool, staring into the blue water. Bending, she picked up something.

"What did you find?"

Holding out her palm, she showed him a glittering green stone. "I'll put this in my medicine bag so I'll always remember you and the Wild Horse."

"It's pretty."

Unfastening the top two buttons on her dress, she pulled out the leather pouch he'd made and dropped the stone inside. The glimpse of her creamy skin dried the spit in Brett's mouth.

Only that peek wasn't enough. That one brief view just whetted his appetite. A powerful hunger rose again.

After tucking the medicine bag back into its place, she buttoned her dress and smiled up at him.

Walking back, he thought about the new direction their relationship had taken. They weren't just friends. He'd been a fool to think they could be.

But what exactly was she to him?

They hadn't made love—even though his body cried out for her—so they weren't lovers.

Companions?

He frowned. That didn't seem right either. All he knew was that her curves perfectly fit his hands. One day he wanted to touch her bare skin beneath the layers of clothing. He dreamed of someday exploring her soft, satiny skin to his heart's content.

Suddenly he knew what to call her.

The mercantile owner kept a Montgomery Ward catalog on the counter, and sometimes Brett liked to thumb through and look at all the stuff beyond his means.

Rayna was what he wished for. She was his Wish Book woman.

❧

The night seemed to whisper a warning in Brett's ear two hours later. Trouble was coming. He felt it.

This time they were ready, complete with horses so they could mount and pursue at a moment's notice. The ten ranch hands, plus Brett and Cooper, were spaced along the side that joined Dowlen's land. Every one hundred yards they'd built a bonfire, which lit up the countryside. Dowlen wouldn't have to strain in order to see his way across if he chose.

And when he violated Wild Horse land, a hail of gunfire would greet him.

Brett moved into the shadows to wait. Nothing moved on either side of the property line that had already seen too much trouble.

The night was young. Dowlen preferred midnight or after, but Brett swung around at the sudden noise behind him.

The dark form sneaking upon his position came from the direction of the camp. He could see the outline of a horse behind the person.

"Brett," a voice whispered. "Where are you?"

The skirted figure had to be Rayna. His heart stood still. All he'd need would be for someone to shoot. He moved toward her. "Rayna, what are you doing out here?"

"I brought coffee. Thought you might need it to keep you warm and awake."

"It's too dangerous. Go back to camp."

She moved closer into the light from the bonfire, and time stood still. He ached to hold her, to tell her how beautiful she was with the dancing flames brushing her features and firing the golden red glints of her curls.

"I will in just a minute." She removed a blanket from around the coffeepot and drew a cup out of her pocket.

Brett took the cup from her and held it as she poured. The fragrance of the brew filled the night. He gazed at her features, taking a sip. "Shouldn't you be sleeping instead of gallivanting across the countryside?"

"Couldn't sleep. I kept thinking about our secret spot and how you kissed me. I've never known anyone like you. Do you ever think of me sometimes?"

He stroked her cheek with his fingertips. "You are impossible to forget." He should know, because he'd tried.

"I'm glad." Rayna set the pot down in the grass. "I was afraid you'd be angry with me for coming. My father gave me a terrible whipping once because I followed him when he went to visit Mrs. Vager's wagon. He was always sneaking over there after her husband left."

"I'll never raise a hand to you."

She stared over his shoulder with fear in her eyes. Her breath came in harsh gasps. "No!"

Brett whirled with his finger on the trigger of the Winchester. What he saw could certainly frighten anyone, but bullets were useless.

The full moon that appeared so near on this night began to darken at the left edge. Slowly, the black shadow crossed the moon's surface until it blocked all light. A dark, ominous red was all that remained.

A blood moon. Large and mysterious, it loomed in the sky like a giant bird searching for prey.

Though he'd seen the sight before, the orb still struck fear in his heart. He didn't mind fighting the things within reach, but this gave him a helpless feeling. It seemed to be taunting. Or sending a warning of some kind.

Rayna made a strangling sound. "This is a bad, bad omen."

He tried to reason with her. "It's nothing to be afraid of. It'll go back the way it was."

Far in the distance, Brett could hear Bob chanting and calling on the spirits to save him.

"It means death," she whispered, grabbing the coffeepot. "I've got to get back to the children."

Putting his arm around her, he walked her to the

horse. She placed the coffeepot into a basket she'd rigged onto the side of the animal.

Before he helped her up, he drew her against him, feeling the wild beating of her heart. "Please be careful. If you hear shots, gather the children and run to our secret spot. They won't find you there."

"I'm worried for you." Rayna fisted a handful of his shirt. A little sob sneaked from her mouth. "Please be safe. I don't think I could bear it if something happened to you."

"It won't." His mouth found hers, and he kissed her until calm replaced his worry for her. He hated to let her go. "Thanks for the coffee. I'll see you in a bit."

He formed a step with his hands for her foot and boosted her into the saddle. Then he watched the darkness swallow her, wishing she wasn't so scared. Trying to dispel the omens she saw everywhere around her was a job. He hoped the children were asleep and oblivious to the fear. They sensed such things.

Sighing, he listened to the measured incantation in the distance for a moment, then went back to watch for evil he knew how to fight.

Sitting down in the shadows, he glanced up at the sky as a shiver crept up his spine.

A few hours later, thick fog rolled in, blocking out that red-as-blood ominous moon and encasing him in a damp blanket. He could barely see the fires that burned up and down the Wild Horse eastern boundary.

Alarms sounded in his head.

Dowlen would take advantage of the blinding haze.

But there was one thing his neighbor needed to know and know it well—Brett didn't intend to lose this fight he'd never asked for. He *would* still stand when this was all over with.

Could Edgar Dowlen say the same?

Twenty-two

RAYNA SAT DOWN OUTSIDE THE TEPEE BRETT HAD
erected for her and Sister Bronwen, listening as Bob
chanted in his strange tongue. She didn't need anyone
to tell her about fear. She'd lived with it, breathed it,
smelled it until she sometimes gagged.

Memories crowded the edges of her mind. She
thought of the night she left her father passed out
under the wagon filled with bones, still clutching the
empty jug of liquor. The large harvest moon lighting
her way had been yellow as she struck out across the
dark prairie. Maybe if it had been red like the one
above, she wouldn't have found the courage.

She still remembered her first cleansing breath of
freedom as the wagon disappeared behind her.

If only she could've saved her mother. Rayna
had killed a man for Elna Harper but, in the end, it
hadn't mattered. She still lost her when Raymond
Harper took his wife into town and came back
alone. She'd never known what happened, but she
had her suspicions.

Steeling herself, Rayna glanced up once more at the

ill-boding blood moon hanging over her so round and full and close. Fear of what it meant made her shudder.

She couldn't stop whatever rode toward them.

Just as she couldn't keep her father from ridding himself of her mother, despite Rayna's pleading and bargaining. He'd threatened to get rid of her, and he'd carried through.

No one could prevent what this moon set in motion either.

Bob's chanting stopped. Rayna glanced in his direction and, through the smoke of the juniper he'd laid on the fire, saw he'd fallen. She hurried to his side and helped him to the log she'd been sitting on.

"Are you hurt, Bob?"

His heavy breathing and the bowed head told of his exhaustion.

"No. Must call the spirits." When he tried to rise, she laid a hand on his thin arm.

"Rest a while. Your legs have given out." Rayna felt his despair and fear. "Bob, what does the blood moon mean to your people?"

"Comanche know. Much fighting. Big battle. Call spirits to protect."

The flap on the tepee opened, and Sister Bronwen emerged. "You old fool. God is the only one who can offer protection. Your chants and mumbo jumbo are useless and getting on my nerves. I'm trying to get some rest."

"Go inside, Battle-ax. Make prayer beads smoke."

Probably to irritate Bob, the sister crowded next to him on the log. Removing a rosary from the sash at her waist where it hung, Bronwen began to call on her saints.

Huffing, Bob promptly rose and renewed his chanting.

Great. The moon had brought war all right—a war of beliefs. Rayna was tempted to go to bed and stuff something in her ears, let the two old war birds fight it out and hope their differences wouldn't lead to bloodshed. But before she could move away, a heavy fog rolled in, settling over them.

Maybe it was a sign, but she couldn't recall any omen concerning fog.

Bob and the sister hushed their prayer duel. Without a word, both turned toward their respective tepees and left Rayna to a peaceful, silent vigil.

She listened for the sound of gunshots, praying in her own way that they wouldn't come. She didn't know if she could find her way to the hidden waterfall in the heavy fog.

Footsteps sounded, echoing off the fog. She looked up to find Doc Yates standing outside the men's tepee.

"Couldn't sleep either, Doc?"

"What in Sam Hill was all that racket? I've never heard such in all my born days." He lowered himself to the log.

"A clash of Indian ways with the rigid Sister." She told him about the problem. "But this fog silenced them both. They decided they needed their sleep. I was afraid they'd wake up the children."

"If they slept through that, they can sleep through anything." He took her hand. "I sense something is troubling you."

"I'm afraid for Brett. Every time I start to care for someone, something bad happens to them."

"You think sitting up all night will ward off evil?"

"No. I just want to be ready in case I have to grab the children and run." She told him about Brett's last words to her. "So I'm listening for gunshots."

"Makes sense." He patted the back of her hand. "I noticed from the first how much Brett means to you. Your eyes glow when he's around, and you lose your focus."

"I've never met anyone like him, Doc. I think I'd die if something happened to him."

"That's the way it is when you're in love. I'm not so old that I can't remember what it was like. He loves you back. That man wears his heart on his sleeve, though I'm sure he'd insist that you're just friends if I were to ask."

"Oh no, not anymore." At Doc's raised eyebrows, she went on. "He decided that we can't be friends right after he kissed me last evening."

Doc laughed. "I'm guessing he recognized that friends don't feel the way he does. It's not proper."

"I've never been in love before," she said softly. "How will I know when I am?"

"Didn't your mother ever talk to you about these things?"

She shook her head. "Mama only told me never to settle for someone who would hurt me. My father isn't a nice man. He took my mother into the town of Mobeetie and came back alone. I don't know what happened to her."

"What did he say when you asked?"

"That I'd have to do the cooking and everything." Her voice lowered. "He said I'd wind up like her if I didn't watch it."

"I'm sorry. You deserve better than what you got."

"I wish I'd have been an orphan like these children."

Just then Brett's confession about that mean ol' Mr. Simon came back. She wouldn't have wanted to be whipped and tied to the gates like a dog.

Air couldn't get past the sudden lump blocking her throat.

Would they ever get rid of the ghosts of the past? All she and Brett wanted was to be free. *But is anyone ever free of their past?* she wondered. It seemed to follow behind wherever she went, like a dark, looming shadow.

❧

Brett strained to see through the soupy muck that had silenced everything except the birds. A meadowlark's call to its mate indicated approaching dawn. It couldn't come too soon. Once he thought he heard a muffled noise and went to investigate, but didn't find anything. He could hardly wait for the sun to come out so it would burn off the fog.

He added more wood to the blazing fire and sat down to wait and listen.

Maybe Dowlen and his men were afraid to try anything with Cooper and the reinforcements there. Men like Edgar Dowlen would wait until everyone left. They'd want to stack the odds heavily in their favor.

Brett stifled a yawn and rose to stretch his legs. He could sure do with more of Rayna's coffee. He was stiff and cold, not to mention being sleepy enough to hibernate for six months like an old bear.

But then, thinking of sleeping aroused memories of Rayna.

How she'd curled up beside him in the cell in Steele's Hollow.

How her curves had fit perfectly against him.

And how he'd known he'd never be able to be apart from her.

The pretty lady had woven some sort of spell over him. He couldn't be a hundred feet away without wanting her in his arms, pressing his lips to hers.

A form leading a horse strode from the mist. Brett's finger tightened on the trigger.

"Don't shoot, Brett, it's me," said Cooper.

Brett relaxed. "What's up? Any sign of anything?"

"Nope. I don't think they're coming."

"Either you being here or the fog probably scared 'em off."

Cooper shook his head. "Wasn't me. Dowlen isn't afraid of jail. Hell, I saw that when we confronted him. But this is damn poor weather for mounting an attack. Can't see anything."

Brett cupped his hands and blew on them. "Wish we had a pot of coffee."

"Ain't that the truth? We might as well go make some."

"You and the boys go ahead. I'm going to lag behind a while longer just in case. The sun will be up soon."

Nodding, Cooper collected the reins of his horse and went to tell the men. Brett sighed and glanced wistfully at the mustang tied to a low branch.

Soon, he told himself. Soon he'd see Rayna's bright smile, and the cold and misery of the night would vanish.

❧

By the time Brett allowed himself to mount up and go search for coffee, the sky had lightened considerably. Though the fog hadn't lifted, he could see a lot better.

About a hundred yards out of camp, he spotted a dark form on the ground. He slid from the saddle and walked over to the carcass. A huge amount of blood and entrails spilled onto the ground. Someone had cut the steer's throat and gutted it. Brett's spirit cried out against the senseless carnage.

No doubt Dowlen bore responsibility. While Brett couldn't be positive, this appeared to be his handiwork.

A check of the brand made his heart sink. Dowlen's. Brett took out his bowie knife, intending to cut out the twisted S design registered to his neighbor. Before he could move, men on horseback swarmed from the gray fog to encircle him. Dowlen's pockmarked face stared down at him.

"Caught you red-handed, breed. You killed my steer."

A rope whirred, then trapped Brett's arms to his sides. "You know I didn't do this."

"I have you dead to rights. You still got the knife in your hand. Reckon you needed something to feed those heathen kids and looked to my beeves. Took advantage of the fog in order to hide your thieving ways."

Brett glared. "Loosen this rope, and we'll settle this once and for all. You and me. No weapons."

"Ain't got a prayer this time, breed." A horseman moved closer. There was something familiar about that voice.

The bearded rider moved through the fog to

Dowlen's side, and Brett saw the ugly twist of the man's mouth.

Sheriff Oldham.

The former sheriff must have heard word of Dowlen's plan spreading through the nearby towns. With a hate as strong as his, it was no wonder he joined in the cause. Foreboding crawled up Brett's spine. Defiance seemed his best bet. If he could keep them talking, he might have a chance. Voices traveled pretty far across flat land. Someone had to hear. "Last I heard, the Texas Rangers were chasing you, Oldham. About like you to throw in with Edgar Dowlen. You're always going to be on the wrong side of a fight, because you're nothing but scum of the earth."

Oldham's face flushed. "I'm happy to help good people get rid of your kind once and for all. This time, I'll do the job right."

At the sound of galloping horses, Dowlen and Oldham moved to face the riders coming through the fog.

Cooper, followed by the ranch hands, leaped from his saddle. "Get that rope off right now. What are you doin' on Wild Horse land?"

"Catching a cattle rustler. I'm taking him over to China Wells where I can get justice." Dowlen spat a stream of tobacco juice onto the ground.

"You'll go through me to do it."

"Hide and watch. You'd take up for your brother no matter how much evidence I got. He's still got that long knife in his hand. He cut this cow's throat." Dowlen wallowed around a big plug of tobacco in his mouth.

"I know my brother, and he's never stolen anything in his life."

Oldham snorted. "Well, that was before he got his reservation to feed." He turned to his men. "Get the rustler on a horse. We're ridin'."

Cooper slid his Colt from the holster in one fluid movement. Steel reinforced his deadly words. "I'll shoot the first man who tries. Move, and I'll blow your head off. In case you're thinking of challenging me, I have to tell you that I never miss what I'm aiming for."

Dowlen's men glanced from one to another.

"Get that rope off my brother," Cooper barked. "Now. Or my finger might just press this trigger a little too hard. Sometimes it has a mind of its own, boys."

Dowlen spat another stream of tobacco. "Do as he says."

The man holding the rope released it, and Brett stepped out of the loop. He gave each of the trespassers a hard glare. "Stay off my land. And take your dead steer with you. I have no need of it."

The former sheriff of Steele's Hollow shot Cooper a glare. "You've crossed me twice now, Thorne. There won't be a third time."

"You know where to find me," Cooper answered, taking a wider stance. "I seem to recall you being a man on the run. A telegram giving your whereabouts to the right people will fix everything."

With a curse, Oldham spat, "Ain't no charges against me."

"I'll check for myself."

With Cooper's Colt still keeping them in its sights,

several of the interlopers dismounted. One tied the rope that had been around Brett moments earlier to the slaughtered cow's hind leg. Brett, Cooper, and the ranch hands watched until they disappeared from sight, dragging the carcass behind them. Only then did Brett return his knife to the sheath and Cooper holster his weapon.

"Coop, this is going to get real ugly." Brett gazed into the thick soup. "They're trying everything to turn China Wells against me. Dowlen and Oldham will have the whole town up in arms. Maybe some of Battle Creek's citizens too, unless I miss my guess."

"I know, Brett. I fear the same thing." Cooper laid a hand on his back. "Dowlen was bad enough. Now that he's in cahoots with Oldham, the situation will be totally out of hand."

"I'm just wondering…how did they ride up so fast?" Brett couldn't shake the feeling he'd been in their crosshairs and hadn't even known it. He should've been more careful.

Suddenly he froze. What if they'd caught Rayna a few hours earlier? His hand shook. He would tear them limb from limb if he could get to them. He drew a shaky breath and wiped the thought from his mind, reminding himself she was safe. "I had just gotten off my horse and walked over there to check the brand," he continued. "Once I saw it was Dowlen's twisted S, I got my knife to cut it out. It looked to be hair-branded, not all the way to the hide. I wanted proof."

"They probably caught a maverick and quickly slapped a brand on it," Cooper said. "Dowlen wouldn't kill one of his own beeves. I heard that man is after the almighty dollar."

"But how did they know to ride up at the right moment?"

"With this fog, they wouldn't have seen you unless they were lurking like vultures close by. That's all I can figure." Cooper climbed into the saddle. "Rayna's cooking breakfast. Bet you're hungry."

Brett mounted up. "You guessed right."

He didn't waste any time heading toward the grub. A minute later, his heart leaped when he saw Rayna standing apart from the others, seeming to search for sight of someone—him? Suddenly, the prospect of hot food didn't hold much importance. Her eyes lit up when she spied him. She lifted her skirts and ran to meet him.

"I'm so glad you're all right," she said, out of breath. "I was afraid…"

"I'm none the worse for wear." Brett slid from the saddle and faced her. He would've given anything not to feel men staring, because he wanted to hold her against him and run his fingers through her wild hair. Though the help was necessary and he was glad they were there, the Wild Horse had gotten a mite crowded.

Now that they stood eye to eye, it seemed neither knew what to say next.

Finally, she murmured, "I just boiled a fresh pot of coffee. Bob's been helping to cook. I don't recognize anything, but it smells good."

"Oh Lord! Did he put any meat in it?"

Rayna smiled happily. "No, I made sure."

"Then let's go taste it." He offered his arm as

though they were on Battle Creek's main thoroughfare. When she giggled, linking her arm through his,
he remarked, "Maybe Bob has found a calling."

He glanced toward the campfire. The sister, with
the white-and-black thingamajig on her head, was
giving Bob heck. She was trying her best to put
something into the pot that Bob held out of reach. But
the latest skirmish between the two didn't hold much
interest for him.

The lady beside him captured all his attention.
She'd left the top button of her dress unfastened.

A gift he'd be sure to thank her for later.

Twenty-three

RAYNA SAT ON THE LOG NEXT TO BRETT, WATCHING him eat his second plateful. Though she'd had to pester him before he'd talk about it, he finally told her about the trouble with Dowlen and Oldham coming in. She realized how narrowly Brett had escaped. The thought of losing him terrified her. She let her leg brush his as he seemed to enjoy the unknown dish Bob had cooked. "How is it?" she whispered.

"Not half-bad. Ol' Bob is full of surprises. How about you?"

"It's delicious."

Brett's fork paused in midair. "How is Adam doing? I should have checked on him."

"You wouldn't have found him in the tepee. He's down by the corral."

She didn't miss how quickly his gaze shifted to find his nephew, or the worry that lined his face.

"Isn't this too soon?" he asked.

"He's sore but said he's tired of sleeping." Rayna cleared her throat, praying that she wouldn't sound bossy. "Speaking of that, you need to lie down at least for a couple of hours. You can't keep up this pace. Your body won't let you."

Brett gave a wry grin. "I'm afraid if I do lie down I won't wake up until next year."

"I won't let you sleep too long."

"All right. What are your plans?"

"I'm not sure." She'd already gone with Doc to check on the children, and they'd made remarkable progress. Now that they'd broken out in a rash, the fever had left. The worst complaint to speak of was the horrible itching. Most were running around and playing.

Little Flower left a group of kids, picked up one of the cats, and crawled up in Rayna's lap. Brett tickled the girl under her arms and was rewarded for his efforts with peals of laughter. The sound was a balm to Rayna's heart.

Only... Now that the children were better, would she have to go back to town with Doc? She didn't want to leave Brett.

Spending precious moments on the Wild Horse had provided healing in a way. This land, even during this dangerous time, had brought the peace she'd sought so she could start forgiving herself.

"How are you today, Flower?" She smiled down at the girl. "Are you feeling better?"

Flower nodded shyly, twisting one of Rayna's curls around her finger.

Rayna smoothed back the six-year-old's tangles that wouldn't stay out of her face. "Do you want me to comb and braid your hair in a minute? I love the color of it. I always wanted black hair, or any color except red."

"I love the color of your hair," Brett mumbled, low. "It reminds me of the leaves in autumn."

The unspoken things lying beneath his words made her heart skitter. She flashed him a smile.

"Comb." Flower put her hands on her head and grinned.

"All right." Rayna stood after Flower hopped down. She took the child's hand. Turning, she spoke low to Brett. "Will you be free for another walk later today?"

He smiled up at her, and her heart skipped a few beats. "I'll make time."

With happiness doing flips inside her, she led Flower into the tepee she shared with the nun. The next opportunity to see Brett didn't come until around noon, and then he was in a huddle with Cooper and the men. She guessed they were mapping out a plan for the coming darkness. The thought sent quivers the length of her. After the blood moon last night, and Dowlen and Oldham almost capturing Brett in the morning dawn, she didn't know what to expect, but something told her things were going to get much worse.

Shortly after lunch, Doc Yates found her soothing a young boy's tears over a spat he'd had with another. "I'm going back to town, Rayna. Have to check on my other patients."

Her breath struggled to get out as she pressed a hand to her stomach. There wouldn't be any more walks with Brett. "I'll get my things."

"No, I want you to stay here. The children need you. These men are too busy, and the old nun is incapable of caring for them."

A smile spread over her face. "I agree. But if you need me in town…"

"I don't. Not right now."

"Thank you, Doc."

A glint sparkled in his faded blue eyes. "I was young once. I remember."

Rayna blushed. She couldn't imagine why she'd discussed love with him. "About that talk we had early this mornin'. I wouldn't want—"

"It's our secret." He patted her hand and picked up his black bag. "I'm available anytime. I've grown very close to you. You're the daughter I never had."

"Oh, Doc." She leaned to kiss his cheek. "I'd be proud if you'd be my father."

Just then Adam brought the buggy around. Doc waved and climbed in. Tears blurred her vision as she watched him take the reins and head toward town with Cooper riding alongside. Doc's kindness put an ache in her chest. If only she could've had someone like him for a parent.

❧

Midafternoon, Rayna went to wake Brett. He'd agreed to sleep for a bit only if she'd come to get him up. She paused inside his tepee, listening to his soft breathing.

Kneeling down beside him, she placed her hand on the gentle rise and fall of his chest. Tears stung her eyes. Too many people wanted to do him harm. Right now, if Dowlen had his way, Brett would be in jail in China Wells.

Most likely, he never would have even made it to

China Wells. The thought of his lifeless body hanging from a tree along the road chilled her heart.

She touched his face and outlined the curve of his firm mouth with a fingertip.

Becoming bolder, Rayna bent and pressed her lips to his as she had in the jail cell when he was unconscious. Taking liberties appeared to be a bad habit of hers, especially where Brett was concerned.

With a sudden, unexpected move, his arms pinned her, pulling her on top of him. He muffled her surprised squeal with a kiss. Rayna melted in his arms.

"I hope you have a good explanation for taking advantage of a man when he's dead to the world," he growled.

Her heart hammered, and she grinned. "I do."

"Is everyone still here?"

"Afraid so."

Brett groaned. "I dreamed they'd all left, and we had the place to ourselves. I was about to have my way with you."

Tingles danced the length of her spine. "It sounds like a wonderful dream."

"It was. You should've been there."

"Next time I'll go with you."

"Dreams are nice in a pinch, but I'd rather have the real thing." He gently touched her throat.

Rayna smoothed back his hair. "Maybe one day."

"You promise?"

"I make a solemn vow."

"I'll hold you to it."

Rolling, Brett was suddenly on top of her. He kissed her brow and nibbled her throat. Then very gently, he captured her bottom lip and pulled it inside his mouth.

His warm breath was like a caress to her senses and made her shiver with longing.

Then he kissed her, and it shook her to her toes. What the kiss lacked in gentleness, it made up for in his velvet touch that brought raw heat to her skin.

Maybe Brett's urgency and hunger came from being unfairly branded a rustler. When a man lived with the fear of having his freedom taken away, he probably cherished things more, felt them more deeply, needed to know he was truly alive.

High-pitched squeals came from near the tepee's flap. Rayna murmured, "One of those children is going to peek inside."

Brett sighed and rose. "I know. Or else Adam or Bob."

Rayna accepted his strong hand, and he pulled her up.

As she moved toward the opening, he stopped her. "Thank you. I've never been awakened so pleasurably. We'll take that walk I promised you in a bit and… maybe finish what we started here in private."

The expectation of more sent heat spiraling through her. Bob's faded gray eyes twinkled like stars when she stepped into the sunshine. His big grin and wink told her the sly old Comanche knew what they'd been doing. Rayna felt her face flush. She managed to smile and nod before going down to the creek to wash some of the children's things.

She turned at the sound of a galloping horse, recognizing Brett's middle brother, Rand. For a few moments, she watched them clasp hands and slap each other's backs. The love between them was easy to see.

But the thing that struck home was how fiercely they fought for one another. These brothers, who weren't brothers at all, cared so deeply about the health and welfare of one another.

Rand had come, she supposed, because Cooper left. Brett told her earlier that Cooper thought it important to go into town to see if Dowlen and the ex-sheriff were stirring up the folks in Battle Creek, as Dowlen had in China Wells.

"Wanted to put out any fires before they got out of control," Brett had said.

It made sense. Who knew what Dowlen would do?

Rayna's gaze lingered on the two brothers a minute longer, then she set about her chore. She was on the last muddy stain in the pile when a long shadow fell across her. She turned to find Brett.

"Walk with me to the waterfall?" he asked.

"Just let me hang up these wet clothes."

"I'll help."

When she remembered his promise in the tepee to finish what they'd started, she became all thumbs. She wasn't exactly sure what he'd meant, but simply being with him, hidden away behind the rocks, excited her.

At last she took his hand, and they strolled toward their private hideaway. It seemed even more beautiful the second time.

She sat near the pool's edge, trailing her hand in the water. The sweet sound of the waterfall was nature's music, a balm to her spirit. It was nothing like the noises made by man. Not the loud banging of the

Salvation Army's drum or the rattle of the bones in her father's wagon, but more like a flock of bluebirds singing. Brett sat down beside her. She could feel him studying her.

"You once said that you don't want to be anyone's trouble." He tucked a strand of hair behind her ear. "I know at the time you felt you were, and that angered you. Now that you have a job and income, do you still feel that way, Rayna?"

She turned. "Sometimes, but not as much."

"I'm glad. It must be a horrible burden to bear. When you woke me earlier…" He paused as if unsure of what to say. He took off his hat and laid it beside him. "I'm not going to apologize, or fight against how I feel anymore. Seems that's all I do. The fact is, I enjoy holding you, feeling your breath on my skin. Whether it's right or wrong, I want you, Rayna Harper."

"I want you too."

Brett caressed her face, his touch light, his soothing voice gentle. "Do you know what I meant when I said I'd finish what we started here in our private spot?"

Rayna chewed her lip. "That you want to take off my clothes and lie on me?"

"Sort of, only I'd rather say we'd make love. There's a great difference. I'd never force you." He tucked a curl behind her ear.

Memories of the other times flooded her mind. Pain so sharp it felt like someone had taken a knife to her and left her unable to draw a breath.

"Will it hurt?" she whispered.

"I will be very gentle. But…forget it. It was a bad idea." He started to get to his feet.

Rayna clutched his arm. "No, please. If you say it can be different from those times, I believe you. I love when you kiss and hold me. Until now, I've never had a man show me tenderness. You shield me from darkness when I'm with you."

"I'm glad, because I only want you to know joy." Brett took her hand in his and kissed each finger. She shivered under his gentle touches. "From the start, I sensed deep wounds that have only begun to scab over. You're like one of my mustangs after it got tangled up in a barbed wire fence. The wounds are deep, and you have so many. I'm here if you want to talk."

She chewed her lip, knowing she had to tell him. "I'm so ashamed, but the times before I had no choice. Raymond Harper called me his little whore and said I had to obey him, because he was my sire. He traded me for things he wanted. I hate what he made me do, and I despise *him*."

Brett pulled her close and held her trembling body for a long while, stroking her back, murmuring quietly, like someone would calm a frightened child. She thought it must be how he soothed his horses.

At last he spoke low, as though struggling to control his anger. "The shame is not yours. It belongs to those who preyed on you. We'll build so many memories, they'll erase all the bad and leave only good ones."

"I don't deserve you." She moved out of his arms and ran her fingers along his strong jaw and down his muscular neck. She couldn't stop this need to touch him. "The feelings you awoke in me earlier... I want to have more of that. It was a lot like standing too close to a bolt of lightning and feeling the energy rush through me. It was an exciting sensation."

"How about if we agree to go slow? Take this a little at a time."

Relief eased her strangling fears. She smiled. "I'd like that. You're a special kind of man, Brett."

"Let's start with me holding you some more."

When he opened his arms, she leaned into his embrace. The fresh scent of sage and the wild Texas land that defined Brett swirled around her. Closing her eyes, she buried her face in his throat.

With the hushed, protected pool and the sound of the waterfall in the background, he held her safe against him. After a while, she raised her face to meet his warm gaze. "I've never known this kind of peace," she murmured. "No one ever respected my wishes before."

"Dearest Rayna, I always will."

Brett traced the curve of her jaw, then lowered his mouth. Passion and hunger exploded the moment his lips touched hers, igniting smoldering embers left from earlier in the afternoon. Heat spiraled through her body. She had to touch him, had to feel his bare skin.

Pulling away, she tugged his shirt over his head. He was magnificent, just as she'd imagined. His muscles quivered under her light touch. She pressed her mouth to his warm flesh.

Rayna had never felt so achy. As she began to unfasten her buttons, Brett's hand replaced hers, and in seconds, the welcome cool air caressed her. Her dress and chemise fell away, dropping at her feet. Stepping out of them, she lay in the cushioning softness of the thick grass.

Brett propped himself next to her on an elbow, the feather from his hat in his hand. "You're exactly as I dreamed. No one ever stole my breath before."

Using the feather, he drew it slowly from her throat, down the valley between her breasts. Rayna quivered under the waves of unexpected pleasure that increased the achy need for this man. Then as he dragged the feather across the raised tips of her breasts, a hunger she'd never felt before enveloped her.

His heated breath brushed her skin when he moved to kiss each hardened peak before pulling one into his mouth.

Gasping, she arched her back, rising to meet him, needing everything he offered. She'd known how things could be. Tears came into her eyes. Never again would she remember the violence of her past. Each stroke of Brett's touch seemed to erase the horrible memories locked deep inside, replacing them with good ones.

He was showing her how it felt to be valued, to have real purpose, real worth.

Shyly, she brushed across the hard planes of his back, tracing the marks Mr. Simon's razor strop had once left on his tender flesh.

They both needed this in order to forget and focus on what lay ahead.

Dropping another kiss on her breasts, Brett raised his head. Taking the feather, he lazily inched to her bared stomach and drew circles and swirls. Down each leg and up the inside to her secret place.

Shivers of longing for something deeper washed over her. Just when she thought she could bear no more pleasure, he moved the feather upward. He stretched her arms over her head, then trailed the tip of the quill the length of each.

Finally, he laid it aside and crushed her to him. The passion of the kiss left her weak and gasping.

"Do you know what I call you?" he murmured into her ear.

"What?"

"My Wish Book woman. You're like something that's dangling out of my reach, something that I might see in a catalog, that I can't afford."

Rayna had never heard anything so beautiful. She wanted to be more than his Wish Book woman though. She wanted him to be able to hold her, kiss her, and know the price was well within his grasp.

"One day I'm going be more than something to wish for."

"You will," he said softly, reaching for her dress.

That's all? They weren't going to do more? Confusion must've shown in her face. "But—"

"I want you to get used to my touch before we move on," he explained. "Besides, we have children to feed. There's not much daylight left. Rand and I need to discuss some things."

Suddenly, the threatening world in which they lived lowered on top of them. They had managed to block it out only for a while.

Whatever happened, she would have the memory of today. No one could ever steal that from her.

Twenty-four

THE VIVID IMAGE OF RAYNA'S BARE BODY STILL burned in Brett's memory two hours later—so much so that he kept losing focus on his conversation with Rand over hot cups of coffee. His gaze kept wandering to Rayna as she tucked the children into their blankets. He watched how she smoothed back their hair and kissed them good night.

Her loving ways struck him. The woman who'd never seen any love sure had plenty to give.

"Don't you agree, Brett?" Rand asked.

"About what?"

"Where have you been, Brother? You haven't heard a word I've said for the last ten minutes. Guess I've just been talking to the wind. I'll bet Bob was listening, weren't you, Bob?"

The old Comanche stared. "Talk too much."

"Yeah, reckon you might have a point," Rand agreed. "Both of my brothers have always said so. Hey, Bob, what does your Indian name Poechna Quahip mean anyway?"

"Buffalo piss."

Brett and Rand hooted with laughter. Though the more Brett thought about it, the more it fit the old Comanche.

Rand wiped his eyes. "Who gave you a name like that?"

"My brother. Father passed naming honor to him."

"Buffalo piss." Rand collapsed into another fit of laughter.

Evidently curious about what was so funny, Sister Bronwen came over. "Old coot, I demand to know what you're saying about me."

Bob bared his teeth and growled. "Man business, Battle-ax. No place for woman. Go back to prayer beads."

Brett hid a smile. The two were like axle grease and water—you could stir all you wanted, but they'd never blend.

"I'll pray for your rotten soul, old coot, though I doubt God wants anything to do with you either." Bronwen sniffed and hobbled into the tepee she shared with Rayna and the youngest orphans.

"Battle-ax?" Rand quirked an eyebrow.

"Wants to slit my throat." Bob sighed and touched the leather pouch around his neck. "Powerful medicine keep safe."

Pointing to Brett's similar bag, Rand asked, "When did you start wearing that, little brother?"

"After I remembered I had it, and Bob told me what it was."

"What's in it?"

"Things."

"What kind of things?"

"I'd rather not talk about it, if you don't mind. It's personal."

Rand crossed his arms. "What *do* you want to talk about?"

"Silence might be nice." Smiling, Brett rose to throw his coffee dregs into the fire and watched the flare of the flames.

The sun had already sunk below the horizon. This was his favorite time of day. Work was done, the sleepy-eyed horses were looking for a place to ride out the night, and the world readied for slumber. It was time for quiet and peaceful reflection.

Though whether Brett got that would depend on Dowlen.

"I'll speak to Rayna, then we'll head out," he announced.

"Sounds good." Rand stood and moved toward his horse.

Brett found Rayna gathering the sun-dried clothes she'd washed. "I'm glad I caught you apart from the others. We're about to take up our positions for the night."

"I was hoping you'd tell me good night." Her blue-green eyes glistened in the low light. "This afternoon was very special."

He touched her hair, then let his hand slide to her cheek. "You'll never know what it meant to have you offer your body to me. No matter what happens, no matter what evil touches our lives, you are the keeper of my heart."

"One day it'll be different. Until then, we'll take whatever happiness we can get."

Brett's arms went around her. He lowered his mouth to hers—one last taste of her to carry him through the lonely night. The tender kiss gave him strength in case trouble found them before morning.

"Be safe, Brett." She slipped something into his hand. "I saw a white butterfly in my tepee. It's a sign of good luck. I think it might've replaced the bad omen of the blood moon. That and Bob's chants to his spirits. But if not, the butterfly indicated you're going to be all right tonight. Hold to that."

He laughed. "Hope you're right. I'll welcome it. If you'd told me sooner, I'd have rounded up a whole bag full of 'em."

Before turning away, he opened his hand to see what she'd pressed into his palm. It was the carved wooden heart her grandfather had given her. "Are you sure, Rayna?"

"I want you to have it."

"Thank you." He slipped it inside his medicine bag and kissed her again. Leaving her was the hardest thing he'd done, but he could see Rand, Adam, and the ranch hands waiting for him beside the horses. He was out of time. "See you in the morning. Stay in camp tonight. I want you here with the children."

"I'll have coffee on," she called as he strode away.

Rand looked up when Brett reached the horses. "Marry that woman, Brett. She's a keeper." He slid his foot in the stirrup, settling in the saddle. "Did I ever tell you about how Callie asked me to marry her?"

"I don't believe you did." Brett mounted, and they set off.

"Well, she was god-awful determined to give little

Wren a home, soon to be orphaned as she was. Only Wren's dying mother had stipulated that we had to be married, so Callie hauled off and asked me to tie the knot. 'Course, I was already smitten with that woman. Loved her from the first time I laid eyes on her. Never thought I'd find anyone with so much love inside to give. If anything happened to her, a part of me would die."

Rand took a deep breath and plunged on. "That's what love is. It completes you and makes you see yourself in your woman's eyes. It's a wonderful thing to know all you can be and that you make her proud. When you find the right person, grab hold and ride the thunderbolt."

Fifteen minutes later, Rand was still talking about love and his Callie Rose when Brett announced, "We're here."

Thank goodness. His ears couldn't take much more. He loved Rand and was grateful to him for helping out, but he never knew when to hobble his tongue. One thing for sure though—his brother worshipped the ground Callie walked on. Brett did too, only in a different way. She was one special woman. She'd been through hard times aplenty but had emerged all the stronger.

Frustration wound through Brett like a persistent trumpet vine. He'd give anything to share the love growing in his heart for Rayna. But he still hesitated, afraid of what loving him could bring to her life. Giving a sigh, he showed Rand where he wanted him and left before his brother could get wound up again.

As on the previous night, they lit bonfires up and

down the boundary line, and each man took a position. Brett settled down to wait, enjoying the blessed silence that was broken only by the crackling fire.

The stars came out, lighting a path for the moon. Though it was round, the orb wasn't red or as large as the previous night. It lit up the countryside. He sat watching it rise, contemplating the mysteries of life and love.

The snorts of horses jerked his attention back to the task at hand. He looked toward Dowlen's land, and fear crawled up the back of his neck.

Riders on horseback moved into place, side by side, up and down where his neighbor's property met the Wild Horse. They all carried torches that, with the bonfires going, illuminated everything.

What was their plan?

Brett gripped the rifle and moved toward his mustang, never taking his eyes off the formidable line. His twelve were no match.

Then he remembered Cooper saying that Dowlen had scoured the saloons in all the towns around, even down to Mexia, asking for recruits. Most of these lined up across from them were probably drunks who might not shoot straight. Maybe they didn't have the heart for Edgar Dowlen's fight.

That would suit Brett just fine. But he had a feeling even if Edgar called off his feud, Oldham would take up the war. The hate glittering in Oldham's eyes called for blood—his blood and that of anyone on the Wild Horse.

Both Rayna and Bob believed the blood moon indicated a big battle. Brett didn't need the moon to tell him that. His gut whispered a warning that it was coming.

Brett wished he had time to learn more about his ancestors' beliefs. He was curious about their blood running through his body. If he could understand himself better, he could live a fuller life.

With effort, he forced himself to breathe normally, even though he remained beside his horse, readying for anything. If Dowlen and his men decided to cross, Brett and the others would have a big problem on their hands. Even with the ranch hands, they were stretched too thin.

Adjacent to where he waited, Adam stood and walked toward him. The boy needed to be back at camp. He still had his chest bound, and hobbled around, but he'd insisted on helping Brett stand his ground. His nephew had pure grit—a lot of it. He admired that in a man, and tall, lanky Adam had it in spades.

"What are they doing, Uncle Brett?" Adam said when he reached him.

"Waiting. Not sure what for though."

"They sure make me jittery the way they just stand there lined up."

"They want to make us nervous, hoping…" Brett stopped. Suddenly he knew what they were trying to do. "Adam, no matter how spooked they make you, don't fire at them. If they can goad us into shooting, they'll be justified in riding across. The law will be on their side, and they can call in the Texas Rangers to help them. I've got to warn the others. You stay here and keep watch."

"Don't worry, I can handle this. Hurry."

Brett slid into the saddle and rode from one man to the next, telling him not to fire his weapon unless the marauders applied their spurs and galloped across the boundary. Rand was the last for Brett to warn.

"You're right," Rand agreed. "I was scratching my head, wondering what kind of game they were playing, but you figured it out. I heard about this tactic used once before. Never seen it though."

"Dowlen knows he's not going to scare me and these orphans off," Brett said. "And he's not going to be able to frame me for cattle rustling. His only hope is to force us to make a mistake that puts him in a good light and us in a bad one. He'll make all kinds of claims."

Rand stared toward the line of blazing torches. "I don't know the man, since he hasn't been here long. Haven't ever run across him even to say howdy. But you can bet he's scared of a hangman's noose. He's not gonna risk a necktie party over this."

Brett's eyes narrowed. "You might be right. But he's eaten up with hate, and that makes men like him dangerous. I'm going to fight like hell for these children. He's not getting close to them again."

"Cooper and I will stand beside you. We'll whip this man then run him out of the state."

"Thanks for the support, Rand. I'd better get back to my post. Keep a sharp eye out, my brother."

With all the men clear on the orders, Brett returned to Adam. "Anything new to report?"

"Just that they've started passing a jug around. Bet it's not water."

Brett spared a smile for the first time since leaving Rayna. This might just work out in their favor. If they didn't fall off their horses first, they wouldn't be able to shoot too well. He just prayed that their liquor supply didn't run out. But if it did, they might give up and head off to scrounge up another jug or two. That could be even better.

Feeling more hopeful, Brett sat down to see what developed. It promised to be another long night. He yawned and huddled deeper into his leather jacket.

No more than an hour passed before the first insubordinate rider left. Dowlen yelled something as the man galloped away.

It wasn't long before another of Dowlen's drunken army began singing "Buffalo Gals," softly at the start, then getting louder. Every man it seemed lent his voice to the lyrics.

Buffalo Gals, won't you come out tonight and dance by the light of the moon.

Brett could feel Dowlen's fury. He began to scream at them to hush, to take their job seriously. One by one, what had seemed a formidable army collapsed into drunken revelry and abandonment of their leader. At last, only Brett's neighbor and a handful remained.

"Appears you lost your men, Dowlen," Brett called. "I'd go find some hot coffee and a bed if I were you."

"Good thing you're not me, Liberty. They'll be back. Maybe you're the one who needs sleep. You haven't had any the last two nights by my count. A man might fall asleep out here."

"You're awful considerate," Brett answered back

in a lazy tone. "Maybe I'm growing on you. Could be you don't hate me as much as you think you do."

Oldham answered back this time. "He only wants you gone. I want you dead. Before this is over, I'll put your heathen carcass six feet under."

"I'm afraid you're gonna be mighty disappointed. This is my land, and I'm staying. There's not enough men in the whole state of Texas to make me leave."

"We have you outmanned," Dowlen said. "When are you gonna see reason?"

A muscle worked in Brett's jaw as he glanced in the direction of his camp and the orphans. He had a whole bunch of reasons to stand and protect. In fact, over two dozen of them.

In his book, that put right and justice on his side. Dowlen would find running him off the Wild Horse a mite difficult in the face of that.

Twenty-five

RAYNA BREATHED A SIGH OF RELIEF WHEN SHE TURNED from the campfire to see Brett leading the tired men. She grabbed a cup, filling it with hot coffee, and stood waiting with it when he swung from the saddle.

Some of the weariness left his face as he took the cup. "Thank you. Rand said you were a keeper, and darn if I don't think he might be right."

Warmth flooded her face. That others saw her value brought a wonderful glow. Coming to Battle Creek had been a godsend. "Things went all right?"

"The white butterfly you saw must've brought us good luck. You're starting to get me believing in this." His hand sought hers.

She smiled happily and curled her fingers inside his grasp. "See? I told you. These omens are worth watching for. Sometimes a good one cancels out the bad."

"Did you have a good night?"

"It was a light sleep. I kept listening for the children or trouble coming. No dreams." She leaned closer and whispered, "I kept thinking about what we did before you left. About how good it felt and how your touches didn't frighten me. They were so gentle, like the wind sighing over me."

His dark eyes searched hers as though trying to see inside her head. "You never have to be afraid of me. I won't hurt you."

"I know. Thank you, Brett."

If she hadn't felt so many eyes on her, she'd have stood on tiptoe and boldly pressed a kiss on his lips. Since she couldn't, she pulled away and began breakfast. The little ones would be stirring soon.

With thoughts of Brett filling her head, she prepared a big pot of the dish Bob had made the previous morning. It was simple to fix. The three sisters, Bob called it—beans, squash, and corn. While it cooked, she sent one of the men for some venison from a small smokehouse Brett had built. Men needed their meat. And, though she still couldn't bear the thought of eating it, she could now cook it without retching.

Maybe that was a sign she'd begun to heal here, where she'd found her first real peace.

They were about ready to sit down to eat when a strange horse with a woman astride rode toward the camp.

Rayna squinted, making out Brett's sister, Sarah. She was happy to see her and figured why she'd come.

Adam and Brett rose and went to meet her. Rayna was glad to see Adam's big smile. She knew he'd missed his mother, especially following the accident that laid him up for almost two days.

"Morning, Sis." Brett helped her down. "You're just in time for breakfast."

"I've already eaten, but thank you." Worry clouded Sarah's eyes. "Cooper told me about the orphans and the trouble that followed them. He said my son was hurt."

Adam put his arms around his mother's shoulders and kissed her cheek. "As you can see, I'm just fine."

She patted his chest. "Don't tell me that. I can feel the bandages Doc used to bind your ribs."

"I'm walking though, ain't I?" His grin persisted.

Rayna had to hide her chuckle. The fourteen-year-old who stood almost a foot taller than his mother had answers for everything. He was cut from the same cloth as Brett. Both were men of courage and a fine-tuned sense of justice.

She hurried forward. "Sarah, you're a sight for sore eyes. I hope you don't have to rush right back."

Sarah's attention wandered to the two dozen children eating their breakfast on blankets. "It looks like you can use some help. These poor dears. I plan to stay for a few days at least. When Potter Gray learned of the situation, he gave me some time off, told me to come and help."

"I don't need mothering," Adam said low. "But I'm glad you can spend a day or two, Mama. I'll show you around. The Wild Horse is amazing."

With a sweeping gaze, Sarah took in the green landscape and the grazing horses. "I had no idea, Brett. This is beautiful. You've done quite well for yourself, Brother."

"Thank you, Sarah. I've worked very hard," Brett said quietly. "Come, let me introduce you to my tribe."

Bob wobbled to his feet as they reached the

campfire, took off his tall hat, and grinned. "Young Adam have strong mother. Much power."

"Thank you. I'm honored."

After Brett made the introductions, she leaned to whisper in Rayna's ear. "Bob? That's a little strange."

Rayna colored and explained, saying, "It's easier to remember."

A real lady wouldn't go around changing people's names on a whim. She thought she had made progress until Sarah came. Being with her for only a few minutes, she realized how far she yet had to go. She gave Sarah's plain dress a glance of approval. Fancy clothes did no good out on a ranch. But even in the plain dress with only one limp petticoat, the woman still put Rayna to shame.

Brett completed the introductions of Sister Bronwen, Rand, and the ranch hands. While he went to pour coffee for Sarah, Rayna and she talked about the children.

"They're a lot of work for one person, but I'm glad I'm here," Rayna said.

"Exactly why I came. Cooper told me you needed help. Has anyone given any thought about what to do with these orphans once they're well?"

"Frankly, no. We haven't had time for that. Do you have any ideas?"

"Not really. Where were they going before they arrived?"

"Sister Bronwen said they were taking them to a mission farther south. The one they were at burned."

"Missions everywhere are overrun with orphans," Sarah said. "They simply have no more room. Such a sad situation. Let me think about it. Maybe I can come up with a plan."

Rayna hoped so. They would have to go some-where soon.

Sarah rolled up her sleeves. "Tell me what you need. I'm ready to work."

Laughing, Rayna laid her hand on Sarah's arm. "There's nothing to do until the children finish eating. Here's Brett with your coffee. Sit down and enjoy it."

Sarah nodded and took the cup, then went to sit beside Bob. Rayna noticed how he beamed at the attention she paid him. It must be horrible to be left with nothing but memories as the body slowly crum-bled. The old Comanche couldn't do much except sit in the sunshine and wait to die. Though he irritated everyone at times, he was only trying to hold on to a little dignity in a cold world that had passed him by.

The stern-faced nun with her sharp tongue was bound and determined to steal that from him. Sure, Bob had messed up—everyone did some time or other—but Bronwen needed to let go.

Rayna had become defensive of Bob, who was like a grandfather to not only her, but Brett also, she suspected. She'd watched his face as Bob taught him things about the Comanche people. It was as if he was discovering lost pieces of himself.

She thought of Brett's pride when he asked his sister to come meet his tribe. Warmth spread through her, remembering the way he'd said it. It was as if she felt long-absent sunshine on her face.

She belonged here—maybe not as part of his family, but his tribe. Here on the Wild Horse Ranch everyone had purpose and worth. Maybe together, she and Bob could find theirs.

Hoofbeats interrupted the sound of low talk around the fire. She glanced up and saw Cooper Thorne sitting tall in the saddle. That he rode in a hurry couldn't be good. Alarm that was never far from the surface these days skittered through her veins as Brett strode to meet him.

Cooper's favorite mount, a buckskin named Rebel, had barely stopped before Battle Creek's sheriff swung to the ground. "Wanted to warn you of the latest."

"I smell bad news. Let me have it," Brett said quietly.

"Dowlen has rallied the entire town of China Wells to his cause, not just the drunks now. He told them that you're stealing his cattle, and that the orphans have smallpox, and the disease is spreading. If that's not bad enough, Oldham has convinced a good many who lost family in Comanche raids that you're gathering all these so they can rise up against them."

"Children and one old man?" Standing close, Rayna could feel the fury sweeping through Brett. "If I had that in mind, I'd reach out to the young warriors, men who know how to fight. Surely they aren't buying that bunch of hogwash."

"Fear clouds folks' ability to reason. Oldham is counting on that."

"What if I go and try to talk to these people? Maybe I can calm them down."

Sad hopelessness crossed Cooper's bloodshot eyes. "That's what I've spent the night and this morning doing. They refuse to listen."

Rayna tightly clutched a piece of wood she'd lifted

to add to the fire. Dowlen just wasn't going to leave them alone.

"Outright lies, all of them," Brett murmured.

She watched his weary glance shoot to the playing children and felt his frustration.

"There's also a rumor he's called for the Texas Rangers, which would be a very good thing," Cooper went on. "Though I'm sure it's not true. Those two don't want lawmen here."

The lines of Brett's face froze into a mask of stone. "Figured as much. We exchanged words last night in a tense standoff."

Rayna sucked in her breath. He hadn't told her that. Maybe he hadn't wanted her to worry. She listened as Brett relayed how Dowlen's men had gotten drunk, and one by one they'd left, leaving their leader alone.

"Dowlen is recruiting a better class of men who will fight for his cause," Cooper said. "He's dangerous."

"Has he tried in Battle Creek?"

"Tried, but didn't get far."

"That's good news at least."

Cooper nodded. "They won't give him the time of day, especially after I told them Edgar Dowlen's accusations were just lies. We need to think about moving the children to my place."

Brett shook his head. "Your babies are still too fragile. They're just getting a hold in life. These orphans could give them this disease. I won't have that on my conscience."

"Probably right. Delta wouldn't be too happy if the twins take sick," Cooper agreed. "Still, keep it in the back of your mind as a last resort. Delta would be the first to insist that we have to protect these innocent orphans."

Worry plagued Rayna as she put her coffee cup aside and dove into work. She'd wondered herself about moving the Comanche youngsters.

While she cleaned up the breakfast dishes, Sarah took charge of the children. Brett's sister was a natural. After getting faces washed, hair combed, and salve smeared on their blisters, Sarah played games with them. She even managed to get Adam involved. It was a sight, watching tall, lanky Adam run around in a circle, flapping his arms like a chicken.

She needed to talk to Brett. She had to lend her voice to Cooper's.

The minute Rayna caught Brett apart from the others, she hurried to him. "I apologize for overhearing your conversation with Cooper, but I think he's right. We need to move the children somewhere safe."

Brett brushed a curl from her face. "I would if I knew where. Both Cooper and Rand have families they need to keep safe. Wherever these little ones go, Edgar Dowlen and Oldham will simply move the fight there. Cooper has two tiny babies, and Rand three children, one of which is a half-breed like me. Pulling every available ranch hand away from those ranches to fight here has left them exposed."

"Is there anywhere else?" Her heart ached. She knew about being unloved and unwanted. It was a horrible burden for a child to bear.

"Not that I can see. We absolutely cannot take them into town."

"How about the box canyon where you found them?"

"Doesn't have any water, and the sharp rocks offer few places to bed down. I'd already have taken them there if it was an option." He touched her cheek. "I share your concern. I've thought of their safety every second since they came, and I'll do my best to think of a solution."

She leaned against him. "I'll help any way I can."

"You already are. I can't imagine having to deal with all this alone. You give me strength. I'm able to stand guard night after night because of you. Thank you, Rayna. Thank you for your deep heart."

❧

Now that both his brothers were there and Sarah provided relief for Rayna, Brett took Rayna's hand, and they walked to their favorite spot after the noontime meal.

He couldn't wait to undress her. Her body was small but flawlessly formed.

Of course, he had nothing to judge her by, since she was the first woman he'd been with. He'd watched with curiosity women walking down the street and wondered what it must be like to hold them in his arms, to kiss them. Cooper had once suggested he visit Miss Sybil's on the edge of town, but the thought of paying a stranger to let him undress her seemed wrong.

To his way of thinking, he had to feel something for the woman, and somehow he felt sure he never would in places like those.

Glancing at the happiness shining in Rayna's eyes made Brett glad he'd waited. He loved this excitement in his chest when he was with her.

As they slipped around the rock wall into their sanctuary, Brett knew there would never be another woman for him, not even if something happened and they could never be together outside of the Wild Horse.

Rayna stood looking at the water and breathing the fresh air. He moved up behind her and slid his arms around her narrow waist.

"I never get tired of looking at this beauty," he murmured.

"Me either. Each time we come, I see something different that I never noticed before. See the robin's nest to the left of the waterfall on that little ledge? They're getting ready to welcome their babies. And there's a small hole over by the banks of the pool where a ground squirrel lives. I saw one sticking his head out."

His gaze shifted to the spot she mentioned. "I meant the beauty standing in front of me. But I've never seen that nest or ground squirrel hole either. You have a way of seeing what others don't. You're right about our secret place."

"It's magical."

When she turned in his arms, he traced the outline of her rosy mouth with a finger. She tempted him in so many ways. Tenderly, he pressed his lips to hers.

She closed her eyes, and the fringe of her lashes brushed her cheek. Being with Rayna gave him joy and peace. She was his salvation in a world that despised his kind. The short time measured in fleeting moments together gave him strength to fight.

He laid his hand beneath the curve of her jaw,

knowing he'd throw himself in front of a bullet to protect her. Rayna Harper colored his world with love and grace.

No one would take her from him.

At a faint sound, Brett raised his head for a look but saw only the ground squirrel she'd spoken of scurrying along the bank. It stopped and stared for a moment, then went on its way.

Overcome by the immense gift he'd been given, he gave a hoarse cry and settled his mouth against hers once more. He wanted to fill every curve and indentation of her with the passion that was building inside him.

Twenty-six

BRETT LAID RAYNA ON THE GRASS BED NEXT TO THE lapping water. Slowly, he removed her clothing, pressing his lips to each section of bared skin. Little trembles shook her as piece by piece he bared her enticing, perfect body.

He sucked in a sharp breath as, at that moment, a cloud that had blocked the sun drifted away, and glorious golden rays suddenly bathed her where she lay on the carpet of green with her russet hair spread in disarray.

The sight made his knees shake. If angels walked on earth, he was looking at one.

Rayna wagged a finger. "Huh-uh. Your clothes too, mister. I've waited long enough."

"Are you sure?"

"I am. I trust you. You've shown me how it can be when there is respect and caring. I never had that before. I know you would die if you ever thought for one second that you hurt me."

Nothing she asked of him would be too great.

He pulled his shirt over his head. Unlacing his tall

moccasins, he removed them. Then turning away so the sight of his nudity wouldn't scare her, he took off his trousers.

If only it was dark. He tried one more time. "I don't think I should do this. Not after what you've been through."

"I love that you want to shield me, Brett. But I'm not afraid to see all of you. You have a beautiful body."

"Just promise to tell me if any of this brings back bad memories. Promise."

"Nothing we do here could ever awaken those."

When she held out her arm, he turned and dropped down beside her.

"See? I'm not running or screaming. But I have one more thing to get rid of."

Before he knew it, she'd removed the leather strip holding back his hair and run her fingers through the long black strands.

"Your hair is so soft," she murmured. "Almost the way I remember a bird's wing."

As she told him about trying to fix up sick and wounded feathered friends when she was younger, Brett stroked her supple skin. The softness reminded him of a newborn colt that had spent months nourished by its mother's womb, untouched by the sun and wind.

Abruptly, Rayna stopped, her voice strained. "Enough talk about that. I've bored you with my silly ramblings."

The sudden change baffled Brett. He wondered if she recalled something too painful to bear. Knowing Raymond Harper, it was likely.

Silently cursing the man, he drew her into his arms, sheltering her from terrifying memories and the harshness of life. "You can never bore me. I want to know whatever you wish to share."

"I'd rather not say more." She lowered her eyes, and when she looked up at him, the light was back. "Will you do more things with your feather?"

"Possibly." He grinned, relieved that she seemed so eager.

"May I see the feather please?"

He rolled over to pull the quill from his hatband, then placed it in her fingers.

"Now, lie back," she commanded. "It's my turn."

Brett stretched out, putting his hands behind his head. She started with his face, dragging the feather across his cheek and jaw, down the strong column of his neck to his chest.

Unfamiliar sensations rolled over him, making his muscles jump at the gentle caress. His body hungered for some kind of release, the desire almost more than he could take. But he knew he had to exert patience, even though the snail's pace killed him.

Rayna continued her slow trek downward to his belly and legs. But when she drew the feather up and down the length of his maleness, he came near to exploding with need. He inhaled sharply, then began to count until he'd tamped down the immediate urge.

"Unless you want to end this before we start, that's all with the feather," he said firmly, taking the quill from her.

Her little giggle caught on the gentle breeze.

Raising up, Brett stared into her sparkling eyes.

"I'm a lucky man to have found you, Rayna Harper." With the lightest touch, he put one hand behind her ear and lifted her face to meet his kiss.

When both needed air, he pulled back and trailed kisses down her slender neck, pausing to press his lips in the hollow of her throat where her pulse throbbed.

Reveling in the feel of her pliable breast in his hand, he touched the tip and took the rigid peak between his thumb and forefinger. He was instantly rewarded as she arched her back.

"More," Rayna pleaded, trying to pull him down to her.

But Brett wasn't about to rush. Instinctively, he realized that this called for a slow, gentle hand. For the melding of minds as well as flesh.

Besides, he wanted to make the experience last as long as possible. He'd learned never to take life for granted, especially since evil had touched the Wild Horse. This may be the last time they could be together. The need to store up every feeling, sight, and sound came over him.

With that in the back of his mind, he slowed even more.

Rayna gasped as he moved his tongue across the peak of a rounded breast before drawing the tip into his mouth. He felt need building in her tightening muscles.

Her hands were doing things to him also. When she slid her hand between their bodies to caress him, he found himself once again struggling to control himself.

"You're flirting with danger, my lady," he growled.

She jerked her hand back. "I'm sorry. I was only trying to give you pleasure in return."

A smile curved Brett's lips. "You're doing plenty of that."

As he touched, kissed, and stroked every inch of her responsive body, she seemed to liquefy in his arms.

"Please, Brett. I can't take any more torture. I never knew it could be like this."

"I didn't either," he mumbled against her ear.

Crawling on top, he gently lowered into her. He closed his eyes to fully absorb the sensations of warmth and tightness that surrounded him. Nothing, it seemed, was comparable to making love to a woman who hung the stars.

As their bodies joined, so did their hearts. They became one in every sense.

"Oh, Brett," she gasped. "I can't... I don't... Oh!"

"Just ride the river, my darling," he murmured in her ear.

His heart hammered as raging passion hurtled him higher and higher toward the point of no return.

When at last she shuddered beneath him, he found himself running free like his horses, feeling the wind in his hair, knowing true happiness in giving fully of himself to her.

The gentle waterfall in the background blended with the swirling sensations and liquid fire as he rode to great heights.

At last the intense emotions released him. On the slow journey back to earth, he lowered his mouth and kissed her.

Panting, he rolled to the side and lay for a minute,

trying to control his ragged breathing, to sort through the experience of making love for the first time. It was like pouring everything inside him into her and becoming part of her flesh, muscle, and bone, not knowing where he stopped and she began.

How glad he was that he'd waited until Rayna came along. He knew beyond a doubt making love would never have been this soul shattering and complete with anyone but her.

A little sob slipped from her mouth, drawing his concern. He raised himself up on an elbow and gently brushed back her hair. "Are you all right, Rayna? Did I hurt you?"

"No," she sobbed.

He wiped her tears with his thumb. "What is it?"

"Nothing."

"You don't cry over nothing." In fact, this was the first time he'd ever seen tears in her eyes. She never cried, not even when she spoke of Raymond Harper and his cruelty.

"Making love to you was the most beautiful thing I've ever done." She stared into his eyes and touched his cheek. "I felt this hot ache, and then I was consumed by wonderful heat that took my breath. I wanted to climb into the middle of it and stay. Being with you is so different. There is no comparison to the times…"

"When those men forced you," he supplied, fighting rising anger. He only prayed to come face-to-face with the bastards someday. If so, they'd know the sting of revenge by the time he got through with their sorry hides.

Brett ran his fingers through her luxurious hair and gently kissed her forehead, letting his lips slide to her cheek where her lashes lay, and finally, to her moist, parted lips. "You are my lady, Rayna Harper. I will never let anyone hurt you again."

Rayna stared up at him, laying her hand on the side of his face. "Being your lady gives me great happiness. Thank you, Brett, for making me believe that I matter."

"You do a sight more than matter." His voice was rough with emotion.

"Do you think when we're old and gray, we'll remember this moment?" Her hushed voice hung in the air.

Nothing would ever erase the memory from his mind. Not even death. They were bound by that piece of strong rawhide, tempered by the sun, the wind, and blessed hope.

Taking her palm, he held it to his mouth and kissed the tender flesh. "I will never forget," he vowed. "This time is branded into my heart."

"Me either. Whatever happens, I'll always have this day when I discovered what it meant to be cherished."

Twenty-seven

MIDAFTERNOON, BRETT STOOD WITH HIS BROTHERS and Adam down by the corral, discussing guard duty, when suddenly the ground began to tremble under his feet.

As he whirled toward the sound, the spit dried in his mouth. A herd of mustangs was coming directly toward them.

"Get the children and head for the trees!"

Brett didn't wait to see if they were following. He started snatching up the smaller kids and urging the bigger ones to run. His heart pounded in his throat as the noise became louder, vibrating inside him like the crash of thunder during a summer squall.

He could almost feel the hot breath of the horses on his neck.

From the corner of his eye, he spied Rayna and Sarah. Both had children in tow. Everyone ran in a desperate attempt to save the orphans.

"Hurry!"

Whether he'd screamed it aloud or the word froze in his brain, he couldn't tell.

Wishing he could grab them all up and whisk them to safety, he raced for the trees. The thick woods probably offered the group's best chance of escaping this stampede alive. The horses would head for the wide-open spaces.

But what about Bob and Sister Bronwen? They were too old to run.

If he could just make the trees, he would go back for them.

Please don't let anyone be killed, he prayed.

To save even one life, he'd sacrifice his own. He couldn't bear it if death helped Dowlen achieve his goal. It couldn't end this way.

The feeling he had earlier with Rayna that maybe time was running out must've been a premonition. He might never get another chance to be with her. Suddenly he wished he'd kissed her once more.

But reality told him not even a lifetime of kisses would've been enough.

What must've been a sob stuck in his throat as his moccasins pounded the uneven ground. With each stride, he urged himself faster.

The small, wriggling boy in his arms suddenly slipped from his grasp. Brett grabbed hold of the child's shirt as he fell and pulled him back up with the other two. Wrapping an arm tightly around them all, Brett increased his pace.

The tree line was getting closer. No more than twenty yards now.

Dragging in a painful breath that hurt his lungs, he gave the race everything he had.

Ten yards.

Brett turned to glance back. Rayna and Sarah were right behind him, sprinting as fast as their legs could carry them.

Glancing farther back past his brothers and the ranch hands, who all carried children, he noticed that Sister Bronwen had fallen, and Bob was trying to help her up.

Surely the horses would trample them. The frightened animals were gaining.

And in the midst of the charging beasts, Brett could just make out the figure of two men astride, driving the herd toward them.

Hot anger crept up his neck. That was proof this was no accident.

Dowlen was to blame.

Eaten by malice and poison, the man was making good on his threat to rid the county of Brett's kind.

Within a few more long strides, Brett finally reached the trees and set the children down. "Stay here," he ordered.

Turning on his heel, he raced to save the old ones. He met Rayna and Sarah, demanding they keep running. Feeling sure they'd make it to safety, he set his sights on Bob and the nun, who had managed to get to her feet, but they were moving slow.

Cooper and Rand made the trees, freed their arms of the children, and raced to help.

All were in the mustangs' path.

Brett's mouth dried. It was daunting to run headlong into a stampede. The herd could trample him into the ground, leaving nothing but his broken body behind in their mad rush to escape what they feared.

Yet, he didn't have time to worry about that.

Save as many as you can was a chant inside his head.

But he knew he wasn't going to make it in time. With his mind whirling, he frantically searched for an alternate plan.

"Turn the horses," he muttered to himself.

Yanking off his shirt, he yelled loudly, waving it over his head. Driven by mindless panic, the horses paid him no heed, galloping straight for him.

If he wore a gun, a blast might possibly turn them—or maybe it was already too late. As panicked as the spooked herd was, maybe they'd still keep coming. Even so, he'd never worn a Colt like his brothers, only carried a rifle sometimes, and his Winchester was back in the tepee the horses had already flattened.

That left only one choice.

He'd have to find a way to get on horseback. Astride, he'd have a fighting chance. He threw down his shirt and flexed his hands.

Suddenly, a conversation he'd had with Cooper when he bought the Wild Horse came back, calming him.

Every rancher made some kind of plan for a stampede. They had to. Brett's had always been to get on horseback, ride to the front of the herd, and turn them to the right into a wide arc—always the right, since animals naturally had an instinct to go that way. He and Cooper agreed that firing weapons before the arc was complete would kill a lot of the animals, plus the man astride, because they'd double back into themselves.

His head throbbed, and sweat formed on his

palms. If he didn't succeed, he'd have to bury Bob, the nun, and his brothers, who'd charged to help the old people.

They wouldn't make it to safety. They didn't have time.

One gamble, one chance to save them.

He prepared himself for the task of grabbing a mane and leaping onto the back of a racing horse. Mindful that he could fall beneath the pounding hooves and be killed instantly, he bent his knees, readying to jump.

Four lives depended on him.

Brett stood on the fringes and reached for the first mustang to pass by.

He grabbed the mane only to have it slip from his hands.

The contact nearly knocked him off his feet. He scrambled to stay upright.

With a deep breath, he ignored the hammering in his head and gave it another try. This time he managed to keep his grip. Marshaling all his strength, he pulled himself onto the panicked sorrel's sweat-lathered back.

For a moment, they engaged in a test of wills as the animal resisted his efforts to force it to the right. Locked in a desperate battle, Brett felt the taut muscles beneath him and the sorrel's mind-numbing fear. He leaned onto its neck and stroked the wet hair, hoping his gentle touch would instill some calm. Finally, he was able to gain control.

Yelling and waving his hat, he got ahead of the herd, and just as they bore down on his brothers and the two elders, he swung the stampede to the right.

The horses began to sweep into a wide circle,

riding away from his brothers, the children, Rayna—everything he loved.

Relief left him weak and shaken.

Now that he'd averted the immediate danger, Brett turned his attention to the men who'd caused the crisis. When they saw him coming, both tried to outrun him.

Brett gripped the sorrel's mane and slapped its flank with his hat. Coming alongside one man straggling behind, he leaped onto the culprit, the forward lunge sending them both tumbling to the ground.

The fall addled him for a moment, and apparently the other man also.

Finally, dragging in a harsh breath, Brett drew back a fist and slammed it into his opponent's jaw with all his might.

The man's head snapped back, hitting the hard ground.

Though dazed, he rose and made a lunge, attempting to throw his body on top of Brett.

Before he came down, Brett planted his moccasins in the middle of the adversary's chest, pushing him backward. Then scrambling, he crawled onto him, pinning him down so he couldn't move.

"Who are you working for?" Brett demanded, breathing heavily.

"No one," came the sullen reply.

"I know someone put you up to this. Edgar Dowlen? Oldham?"

"Not saying."

"Do you even care that you came close to killing a bunch of innocent orphans?"

"Be a lot better off." The piece of cow dung wiped

blood from his mouth. "Who'll miss a bunch of snot-nosed Comanches?"

Breathing hard and struggling to control his rage, Brett grabbed the man's shirt and hauled him to his feet. "What is your name, mister?"

"Why?"

"Makes it easier for the sheriff to know who he has in his jail, and for the judge when he sentences you to prison."

The sullen man spat, "I'm done talking."

Dusty and bleeding from cuts on his arm, Cooper strode over. "Nice work, little brother, both in turning the horses and in catching this weasel. I'll take charge of him."

"He refuses to say anything."

"Not surprised. He'll talk when I get him to jail." Cooper jerked his prisoner toward the camp that the horses had left in shambles. "March."

Brett stalked to his hat that lay in the dirt. Dusting it off, he jammed it on his head and turned to look around, his gaze searching for his Wish Book woman.

The knot in his stomach didn't unkink until he spotted her with Sarah and the children. His knees got weak, thinking about losing her. The possibility had been too close for comfort today.

Suddenly, he needed to be near her to see for himself that she was all right.

On his way to Rayna, he met Rand. "How are the elders?"

Rand pushed back his hat with a forefinger. "None the worse for wear. Have to say I lost three years off my life though. Thanks for turning them in the nick of time. Thought we were all goners."

"You and me both. Are the children okay?"

"Seem to be. Bet they'll have nightmares for a while."

"Probably." Brett swung away before Rand could get wound up. He had a pretty lady to see before he set to work.

But before he took more than two steps, Rayna came running to meet him. Laughing, he caught her up and swung her around. Almost dying had given him a deeper appreciation for being alive…with her.

As he gripped her tightly to him, burying his face in her hair, it suddenly occurred to him that he wore no shirt. She didn't seem to mind though. Having her in his arms, feeling her racing heart, made the world settle around him at last.

"I was terrified, Brett. For us, then for you when you decided to tackle those crazed horses without a rope or anything." Remnants of terror clouded her blue-green stare.

"I'm unhurt. Are you sure you're all right?"

Though she nodded, he let his gaze roam over her just to make sure.

He relaxed when he didn't see any scrapes or bruises. "Do you think I could have a kiss? I'm sorry it has to be in front an audience, but I can't wait unless—"

Rising on tiptoe, she covered his mouth with hers, silencing the rest of his apology. The kiss made him feel as though he stood at the bottom of a powerful waterfall with the rushing warm water, not swirling around him, but passing through his muscle and bone.

His lady was safe and in his arms.

Twenty-eight

WITH BRETT'S STRENGTH AROUND HER, THEY JOINED the others walking back to what was left of the camp. An ache filled Rayna's heart as she looked at the destruction. The tepee that had stood as a proud symbol of everything Brett was lay flattened, along with just about everything else, with the exception of the corral. His dream that he'd worked for with his blood and sweat was gone, and his beloved horses scattered.

"Brett, I'm so sorry. My heart is breaking."

He kissed her temple. "These are just things. I can rebuild and round up my herd. What I can't replace are people…you. Everyone I care about is safe, and that makes me a happy man."

Rayna laid her hand on his bare chest and felt the strong beat of his heart. "I feel the same way about you. We can go on. I'll help you make this ranch even better. But what are we going to do about the children? Where will they sleep? And what about Bob and the sister?" A sob escaped before she could stop it.

"We'll move everyone to Cooper's. I don't see we have much choice until this gets settled."

"I agree. I'll get the children ready. Will you stay here?"

"I won't leave my land."

That meant they'd be separated just when things were going so well between them. And he'd be here alone when trouble came. She trembled. It would kill her to leave him. Who knew what else the enemy would try. But she knew his mind was set, and nothing she could say would change it.

He went to get the wagon.

She gathered the children. "We're going to take you someplace safe."

"Where?" Flower's bottom lip quivered. She clutched the cat she held tighter.

"Somewhere safe, sweetheart."

"I don't wanna leave. Can I stay here?" This time it was an older boy named Joseph. "It's like home."

"I wish you could, but it's not possible," Rayna explained.

A handful of questions later, Rayna looked up to see Brett striding toward her. His stormy face told her he had bad news. With the frantic beating of her heart, she went to meet him out of range of the children.

"What's wrong?"

"The wagon is busted. There's no way to move them."

Rayna stiffened her spine, glancing at the trees that had shielded them in the stampede. "Then we'll make them a bed in the shadows of the trees. No one will look for them there, and the canopy will keep off the night dew while they sleep."

"You're right." He looked exhausted. She reached out to touch a trickle of sweat running down his throat.

"We can go after another wagon tomorrow. You have an excellent head on your shoulders, Rayna."

Happy that they would be together longer, she laughed. "Every once in a blue moon, I do have something worth sharing."

"I welcome each of your thoughts," Brett said, his lips brushing her hair. "And more."

"I'm glad." She wished they were in their oasis, where trouble couldn't find them. She desperately needed what only Brett could give—a little pleasure in the midst of madness. But it might be an eternity before they could have that again.

She sighed and told the children of the new plan. Their clapping indicated approval. A few minutes later, she and Sarah enlisted their help in finding the blankets and shaking them out. Then while the men set about putting the tepees back up and picking up the pieces of the camp, she and Sarah took the orphans to the woods to find a good spot to spread their blankets.

This was going to work out.

But when a rider galloped onto the Wild Horse, her blood turned to ice. He reined up in front of Cooper and dismounted.

She hurried, arriving in time to hear the stranger say that Cooper's wife, Delta, had taken very sick, and Doc Yates wanted him to come immediately.

Something about appendix and that it might've burst.

Rayna didn't know what that was but suspected the condition could kill a person.

Cooper handed his prisoner over to Rand with a request to take him into town to jail and sprinted to the thankfully still-standing corral for his buckskin.

A few minutes later, Cooper raced toward his ailing wife. Rayna hoped Delta Thorne would be all right. She liked the woman who'd sat up all night beside a dying friend.

After Rand left with the prisoner, who had not given any information, everyone went to work. Even Bob and Sister Bronwen. A turtle could walk faster, and their legs wobbled with each step, but they helped as much as they were able.

The place she'd decided the children would sleep was by a small pond with thick trees surrounding it. And the spot wasn't too far from the main camp, which was an added bonus. She and Sarah were happy with the find.

The orphans would be safe.

By nightfall, the main camp didn't look half-bad either.

They sat around the campfire, eating a meager meal of venison, squash, and corn. As long as the vegetables held out, she'd be okay.

When Brett finished, he and the others collected their horses. She watched him stride toward her and recalled the image of him during the height of the stampede. Somehow in all the pandemonium of those horrifying minutes, the leather strip that held his hair back had disappeared. His hair hung loose and free, swinging wild in the wind as he'd raced to save them.

His intense focus had frozen his face into a stone mask. She remembered thinking if he wore slashes of paint under his eyes, he'd resemble a fierce warrior, like those of his ancestors.

She'd never forget that look on his face. He wore

the same expression now as he padded closer with the fluid motion of a wildcat. Her heart thudded with excitement.

Flashing a brief smile, he went to share some words with Bob. She turned back to her chores, knowing he'd come to her in a bit.

Sure enough, before riding out to stand guard, he took Rayna's hand and pulled her into the shadows. There, he kissed her long and hard, stealing her breath.

She leaned into him and laid her hand on the muscled wall of his chest. She trembled with the realization that she loved this man who'd showed her his hidden sanctuary, then blazed a path to the stars.

A tingling of excitement swept through her as his fingers trailed down her arm before seeking the curve of her breast. He awakened the smoldering embers, making them flame. Aching heat and a hunger for his muscular body filled her.

A soft moan rose as Rayna clutched a handful of shirt, trying to draw him even closer.

Yes, she loved him and would until the day she died.

⁘

Brett hunched down on the eastern boundary of his property, scanning for any sign of movement. Since he hadn't wanted to advertise that they stood watch, he'd given the order for no bonfires. It might be best for Dowlen to think they'd left.

He swung around to the direction of the camp, thinking of Rayna, Sarah, and the children sleeping in the woods. The night held a chill, and they would be cold.

If only he could put his arms around Rayna, pull her up next to him, and warm her.

The kiss they'd shared in the night shadows haunted his mind. That kiss had seared into his brain.

Hunger for the bone-picker's daughter was growing stronger instead of weaker. He couldn't imagine going for even one day without touching her, kissing her, wanting to pull her inside of him where nothing could harm her. The sweet ache was becoming unbearable.

How could it be forbidden when it felt so right?

Why should he have to squash his desire for her and keep telling himself no, when evil men did whatever they pleased without a second thought?

What was it Rayna had said about choices? Oh yes, he remembered. *Sometimes we make the choices, and sometimes they make us.* That had never been truer. Right now, they had little say in the choice-making. Everything seemed driven by outside forces shaping their lives.

All he and Rayna could do was hang on for dear life.

A rider coming from the camp appeared in Brett's line of vision. He recognized Rand's blue roan and relaxed. Rand drew up next to his mustang, dismounted, and strode toward Brett.

"Got the prisoner delivered to the jail," Rand announced. "He got awful talkative before we got there. We pretty much knew all he said. Dowlen hired him and his friend to start the stampede. I think it's enough for Cooper to arrest your neighbor."

"That's good. I just hope he can before Dowlen kills one of us or the orphans. How are things in camp?"

"Quiet except for the snoring coming from Sister Bronwen's tepee. Man, that'll wake the dead."

"Are you sure it's not Bob?"

"Not unless ol' Buffalo Piss is in her tepee." Rand grinned. "Anything's possible, I reckon. Maybe pretending to hate each other is just a game. Think so?"

"Nothing those two do surprises me. How did things look in the woods?"

"No sign of anyone moving around there. Seem to be asleep."

"Nothing happening here either," Brett said. "If Dowlen thinks we've left, they might not try anything tonight."

"You should know that I heard in town that he's recruited almost every man from China Wells, and quite a few already from Corsicana. Looks like he's gearing up for a huge push to run you out of the country."

"Appreciate the warning."

"Brett, I don't think we can defend the Wild Horse with what we have. Just not enough men."

"I know." That worried Brett. But what choice did he have except to try? He wasn't about to roll over and play dead.

"I think some in Battle Creek would help if we ask," Rand suggested.

"Maybe." Brett knew he could count a good number as friends. Still, asking them to fight for him went against the grain. It was one thing to be a friend to his kind, and completely another to ask them to risk their lives. "Did you learn any more about Delta?"

"Ran into old lady Jones, and she said Delta is on death's door. 'Course in her opinion, anyone with a sore toe is fighting the grim reaper. I don't put much stock in what she says."

"Maybe Cooper will ride in tomorrow with news."

Rand stretched. "Reckon I'll find a place to hunker down for the night. I'm sure missing Callie and the kids. Lord, I'd like to snuggle up to her in a warm bed and get some shut-eye."

Brett watched his middle brother move farther down the line. He knew how Rand was feeling, but right then he could've shot him for awakening the need for Rayna that was winding through his body like a determined gourd vine after he'd just gotten it tamped down.

Though the existence of men like Dowlen proved he could never let himself speak of it, he knew he loved her. He had since he first laid eyes on her in that jail and she kept talking about wanting his moccasins.

Rayna Harper was a special woman.

And she had his heart. Even if one day all this had to end.

Twenty-nine

BRETT'S FIRST GLIMPSE OF RAYNA AS HE RODE INTO camp the next morning stopped him in his tracks.

The way the newly risen sun glimmered in her auburn hair took his breath.

She stood by the corral, stroking the gray mare that had taken her fancy. The look of love in her eyes for the animal caused a lump in his throat. He dismounted and went to join her. As he neared, he could hear her crooning to the mare like a mother to her baby.

"Morning. I hope you're not thinking of cajoling my mustang away from me." He watched her jump, followed by rising color to her cheeks.

"Morning yourself." She frowned. "You scared me. I didn't know anyone was around. I feel foolish that you caught me."

Brett moved closer and brushed her face with his fingers. "Don't ever think you're being foolish. Talking to a horse is entirely natural. I do it all the time. They like people talking to them. Have you thought about what you want to name her?"

"I have." She smiled. "Her name is Lady Pearl."

"That's real pretty." Just like Rayna.

"She's sort of the color of a pearl and, of course, she's a real lady, like your sister."

"Rayna, you're as much a lady as Sarah," he said softly.

A sudden breeze caught her curls, blowing them in her face. "I'm glad you think so, but I'm far from Sarah's elegance and grace. My words are simple and at times too coarse. And I never know how to act in certain situations."

"You're being too hard on yourself." The pain and insecurity in her eyes pierced his heart. He knew what it was to believe you weren't enough. She didn't know that she'd always be enough for him, no matter what. He pulled her close and kissed her. Coaxing her mouth open, he tasted her sweetness. Sliding his hand into her silky red curls, he murmured, "You'll always be my lady in every way."

"That gives me hope. I only pray you'll never change your mind." As the ranch hands brought their mounts to the corral, she moved back a step. "I took the absence of gunfire during the night as a good sign."

"Not a peep from Dowlen's side."

"I'm glad. We need our nerves to settle a bit."

"How about you?" he asked. "Did you rest well enough in the woods?"

"I did, except for several of the children crying out from their nightmares. We got lucky yesterday, didn't we?"

Brett nodded. "I never want to get that close to death again. Not for my sake, but for everyone else. We almost didn't make it."

"Yes, but we did. My grandfather used to say that a

near miss is as good as a mile. We're alive and greeting a new day." She smiled up at him, squinting in the sunlight. "I have coffee made and waiting. I've got to get breakfast cooking. The children are probably waking up."

Brett put his arm around her waist as they strolled toward the campfire. "I'll help you. It takes a lot of food to feed all these mouths."

But Rand latched onto him before Brett even got his coffee. "I've been doing a lot of thinking. Between us, I think it's time we took some ranch hands and paid Edgar Dowlen a visit."

"And do what exactly? You think he'll offer us a cup of tea and some cookies? Coop and I tried reasoning with him."

"Nope." Rand grinned. "One of his men might cooperate though. We need to know what he's planning. We're blind here. Be nice if we could get a head start on his next move. As it is, we don't know what to plan for."

That made sense. If they could just see how many men Dowlen had.

"All right, but it'll have to wait until after breakfast. I won't leave Rayna to take care of this bunch alone."

"Of course. Besides, my stomach's growling."

"No news there. Your stomach is always complaining." Brett watched him head toward the coffeepot then focused on the meal.

As he strode to the smokehouse to cut strips of venison, he thought about Rand's harebrained plan. In theory, it had merit. But if Dowlen caught them, there would be hell to pay. No telling what the man might do.

Getting rid of Rand, the ranch hands, and him would leave the Wild Horse wide open. Brett knew for a fact his neighbor would go straight for the orphans first.

And when Dowlen was done, he'd leave nothing but a bloodbath behind. He'd kill everyone, even Rayna and Sarah.

Cold fear squeezed around Brett's heart.

Could he risk it?

He decided right then and there that no one would go but Rand and him. The other men would stay.

The next hour, he worked by Rayna's side, feeling a jolt each time his hand brushed hers or their shoulders touched. He'd heard cowboys talk about being smitten, but had never known what they meant. He supposed it was something like how he felt about Rayna. If so, he found being smitten pretty nice.

Except for the fear of speaking what was in his heart. Hampered by the rules that others imposed, he would never voice his overwhelming love for her. He had to keep it locked away. They could kiss and touch and pretend here on the Wild Horse, but there was still no future for them.

That was his only choice.

Brett stared into the glowing red coals of the campfire. For a second, he let himself imagine the freedom to express the love beating so fiercely inside him.

Allowed himself to picture the light in her eyes when he kissed her awake, and the contentment in her smile as she held their babe.

"What is it, Brett?" Rayna's gaze met his. "First you scowl as if someone stole your knife, and the next minute you're smiling, all in the space of a few heartbeats."

"Just thinking. Some would claim I've lost my mind."

"You need more sleep. You're dead on your feet."

"Don't worry about me, Rayna. I'll be fine."

She put down the fork she was using to stir the eggs and put her hands on her hips. "I'll worry if I want to, Mr. Liberty."

What a sight she was, standing there all indignant and flustered with her wild curls dancing in the wind. Brett wanted to sweep her up in his arms and carry her to their private spot, away from prying eyes and trouble. Just his lady and him with the waterfall gently splashing into the pool.

Unbearable longing raged inside him.

He sucked in a deep breath, closing his eyes to block out the pain.

❧

The sun had risen high in the sky before Brett rode with Rand to Dowlen's ranch. They left the horses in a thick grove of trees and crept toward the sound of voices. It was painstaking and tedious because of the care each took to avoid snapping twigs or rustling the low brush.

Brett was determined to make sure no one caught wind of them. As they got closer to the voices, escaping detection became even more crucial, so they slowed even more.

The last three yards, they got on their bellies and crawled through the dense growth.

Finally, they reached the two men speaking.

"I don't hold with killin' little kids. What do you think, George? Does it set right with you?" one man asked.

"Let me tell you." A stream of tobacco juice landed inches from Brett's hand. "I lost my wife and three kids seven years ago by Comanche hands. The Good Book says 'An eye for an eye.' Reckon we're just obeying the scripture."

Brett shook with anger. How could the man speak so calmly of the murder of innocents? Nothing could justify what they planned. It was crazy. What the Comanche had done—*if* they'd committed the act— was wrong, but this wouldn't bring back that woman and kids.

His soul wearied of anger and fighting. He didn't know why everyone couldn't live in peace. They were all human beings. Color shouldn't divide people and cause them to turn on each other.

Leaves crunched, then a new voice spoke. "Boss said to come. He called a meeting to discuss the next move. And you'd better look lively. Edgar says he'll fire the next man that lifts a bottle to his mouth."

The man named George grumbled, "Next he'll be telling us when and how often we can piss."

Neither Brett nor Rand moved until the footsteps faded. At last they rose and peered through the trees. Row upon row of small tents filled the yard surrounding the house that was thick with milling people. There had to be upwards of fifty men gathering beneath a big oak tree.

Brett's breath froze in his chest. This army would have no trouble overrunning the puny dozen people guarding the Wild Horse.

How could they hope to defeat them?

They didn't speak until they reached the horses.

Finally Rand said, "Reckon we know two things, little brother. First is that Dowlen and this former sheriff are planning something big. And second, we need a couple of cannons. We can't defeat them with what we have."

"Nope. Wish we knew where we could get our hands on some big artillery and a couple hundred soldiers. Rand, I'm going to need you to get a wagon from your place. We have no choice but to move these children and the women."

"I'll head after it right now. I should be back by dark. If you want to bring them to my ranch, you know we'll welcome them."

"Thanks, Brother. I don't want to bring the trouble to your door, but I have little choice." He sighed, stuck his foot in the stirrup, and pulled himself into the saddle.

Rand moved to his saddlebags and brought out a gun belt and Colt. "I know how you feel about wearing a gun, but you're going to need this before it's all over and done with."

"Keep it. I have a rifle."

"All the same, I'd feel better knowing you have it." Rand moved to Brett's horse and stuck it in the saddlebag. "It's here if you need it. Cooper made me promise to give it to you."

"Then you kept your promise." Brett tugged the reins to the right, turning the horse around.

"Since Cooper's Long Odds Ranch is closest, I'll go there. I can fill Cooper in and see how Delta is. If she's better, maybe he can come."

"Good plan, Rand." In the meantime, he'd do some thinking.

If only there was a way to make Dowlen think they had more men.

"When do you think they'll hit?" Rand asked.

"Soon. He has everything in place for a raid. Daylight or dark won't make any difference now." Unspoken fear lodged in Brett's chest like a patch of devil's claw, hooking the tender flesh with no way of getting it out. "You probably won't be back in time."

Twelve men against an army of warring invaders.

"Maybe I shouldn't go. My gun can help," Rand argued.

"No, we need the wagon. While I wait, I'll hide the children deeper in the trees and keep them there."

They rode the rest of the way in silence. Brett thought of the children and Rayna and Sarah—all those lives depended on him. Somehow, someway, he'd protect them.

He had to. To fail would steal his reason for living.

❧

While Rayna waited for Brett to return, she sat with Bob, talking quietly. She adored the old Comanche who felt such a need to be valued. It wasn't so much what he said aloud, but how dull his eyes had become, especially when Sister Bronwen said the things she did.

"Bob, do you have family?"

"No. Had wife, but she died of sickness." He stared off into the distance as if seeing his life shimmering somewhere out there.

She took his wrinkled hand. Many of his fingers were bent and swollen. No telling what he'd seen and lived through.

"Many moons ago I had land, family," he said

sadly. "All gone now. White men take. Force us to reservation."

"I'm sorry. I wish I could make it better." Rayna wondered how many people had lost everything they had because of hate and greed—the same hate that kept her and Brett apart. "Tell me what life was like when you were happy with your wife."

"Had big tepee, many horses. Land fed, buffalo gave us clothes, furs, bones."

Rayna jerked in surprise. "Bones?"

"Make tools, dishes, weapons from bone."

It shocked her to think of the total devastation Bob's people had suffered. The bones she and her family picked up had helped bring about the ruination of a total way of life. Though the guilt wasn't hers to bear, she felt it anyway. The lump in her throat choked her.

"Come from proud people. Just want our land. Battle-ax right. I am worthless."

"No, don't say that. Everyone has worth." Rayna watched the children playing quietly. Now that most were on the mend, they spent a good part of the day being children. Some would say they weren't worth much. She begged to differ.

"Comanche have custom. Old people go off alone to die away from village when no need to live. I will do soon."

"There is always, always a need to live," Rayna argued, laying her head on his shoulder. "Promise you won't do this. It would break my heart. I love you, Bob. You remind me of my grandfather, and he was a proud man too. I think you would've been friends."

Sister Bronwen trudged from the creek with a pail

of water. Rayna watched Bob's eyes narrow. The little nun's face seemed frozen in a permanent frown, as if she found no happiness anywhere. But the children loved her. As she came closer, they ran up to her, and all spoke at once. She laid a loving hand on top of Flower's head.

Maybe Rayna had been too hard on her. Maybe she too just needed a chance.

The sister told the children to run along, and drew near. She stopped in front of Bob and set down the pail. "Everyone is working around here but you, old man. Earn your keep. Besides, you stink. Wash yourself."

Bob recoiled as though she'd struck him. "Do not speak to me. I am Comanche warrior."

"In your dreams, perhaps." The sister stepped backward when Bob rose to his full height.

Shooting her a glare, he stalked into the tepee.

Rayna stood also, although her height wasn't near as impressive as Bob's. "Sister, please don't be so mean. Bob has feelings, you know. The things you say are very hurtful."

"I doubt the old coot... He can barely... He doesn't know..." Sister Bronwen's words faded as she glanced in the direction Bob had gone. She finally threw up her hands. "I've never been the holy sister I needed to be." She sighed. "When I first put on this sanctified habit, Mother Constance warned me that my sharp tongue would be my downfall. I realize how pitiful this sounds, but my knees hurt, my bones creak, and I can barely see. It's not that I don't like Bob. I do. I will pray for compassion and forgiveness."

"Begging your pardon, Sister, but you need to

apologize to him," Rayna said bluntly and was immediately ashamed.

In need of more cheerful company, she went to join Sarah and Adam, who were fishing for supper.

When she glanced up a short while later, she saw Bob inside the corral. He'd removed his shirt and had three black streaks of ash below each eye. In one hand he clutched a flaming torch. In the other he held a small burlap bag. She hollered and started toward him but was too late. With an agility she could hardly believe, he swung onto the back of a mustang and took off at a gallop toward Edgar Dowlen's ranch.

Just then, she heard the growing thunder of hooves coming from there as an army of men bore down on the playing children.

Bob gave a fierce war whoop and spurred his horse directly for the wall of horsemen.

Thirty

RAYNA'S SCREAMS GOT LOST SOMEWHERE IN HER chest. She was aware of Adam racing toward the nearest horse as the ranch hands scrambled for their mounts. All she could do was pray that they hurried.

Pray that they saved Bob and the children.

But in the passing moments, it became apparent that no one would reach them in time.

She lifted her skirts and began running as hard as she could. She had to at least try, even though Dowlen and his men might kill her.

As she ran, she kept her focus on Bob. He'd changed direction and now rode up the width of the line, leaving a trail of a black powder from the bag as he went. She'd noticed that Dowlen's men had slowed, as if they didn't know what to make of the Comanche.

When they unloosed a barrage of gunfire, she froze and put her hand to her mouth while her heart pounded like the mustang's hooves against the packed earth.

A red stain spread across the old Comanche's shoulder as one of the bullets found the mark.

"Bob!" she screamed.

If he heard her, he didn't look her way. Once he finished emptying everything out of the bag, he let it flutter to the ground. Leaning down, Bob touched the torch to the black substance, and it immediately flamed up, putting a wall of fire between Dowlen's men and the children.

The riders pulled hard on their reins to avoid riding into it. Horses shrieked. Rearing up on their back legs, they dumped their riders.

Men yelled as their mounts took off at a gallop.

The trail of black powder had done the trick. Without stopping to see what would happen next, Rayna and the others began snatching up the orphans and running for the protection of the trees.

Bob had bought them precious time. Safe in the woods, Rayna turned. The old Comanche paused high up on a hill and raised an arm to the heavens as though in good-bye. Through her tears, she watched him turn and disappear over the ridge.

He'd performed one last heroic act before he rode off to die. Maybe to prove to himself he wasn't worthless. Or maybe to regain a little dignity that he'd lost with age. A sob rose. She knew she would never see him again, and the pain nearly doubled her over.

Brett and Rand returned just then to join Adam and the ranch hands in chasing the renegade army of cutthroats off the Wild Horse.

Flower tugged on Rayna's skirt. "Where did Poechna Quahip go?"

"I don't know, honey. I wish I did though." If she did, she'd ride after him and sit with him while he waited to die. Without food or water, it wouldn't take long. "Never forget what he did here today, Flower. He was a very brave, powerful warrior." She would've said more, but the thickness in her breaking voice wouldn't allow her to continue.

"Will he come back?" Flower asked quietly with round eyes.

"No, honey. I don't think he will."

"I'm sad."

Rayna put her arms around the child and pulled her close. "You can cry, little one. It's all right."

When Brett galloped up a few minutes later, Rayna threw herself into his arms. As he held her and smoothed back her hair, she told him what Bob said to her, then his unselfish act that had saved them all.

"I'm sorry, darlin'. I wish I'd have been here."

"Me too. You might have stopped him."

Brett kissed her and wiped her tears. "It wouldn't have made any difference. I've heard of this belief among the Comanche. His time with us ended as he wanted—with dignity and great courage."

"He'd just come into our lives. I loved him. I wasn't ready to say good-bye."

"I know. We never are."

"Will you go after him?"

"No. Bob is following the sacred path of his ancestors. We have to respect that."

He held her while she pressed her face into his chest and sobbed. At last she raised her head, feeling spent. "I don't know where he got the black powder. Do you?"

"I had a bag of it in my tepee that was left over from

when I blew up a tree stump a few months ago. He must've found it."

"What do we do now?" Rayna felt so tired.

"Keep living and fighting for these orphans." He rested his chin on top of her head. "I thought we'd have time to get back. I didn't think they'd mount a raid so fast. Dowlen had called his followers to a meeting when we left. It took us some time making it back to the horses, only to find Rand's had wandered off after the branch it was tied to broke. We finally found the gelding in a patch of sweet clover. Dowlen must've had his men mount up shortly after we turned back."

Rayna heard the disbelief and remorse in his voice. Now it was her turn to comfort. "You couldn't have known what the man planned. He's evil."

"It's my job to know." His angry words were hard. He moved her aside and stalked toward his tepee, leading his horse.

Whatever he planned, he kept to himself. With an ache in her heart, she watched him disappear into his house made of buffalo hides. When he emerged a few minutes later, he carried rifles in both hands and had a gun belt strapped around his waist with a deadly Colt hanging from it. From where she was, she couldn't read his expression, but she imagined it was grim.

The sight made her chest hurt even worse. Dowlen was changing the gentle man who'd made love to her by the waterfall and called her his lady.

Yet, if she owned a Colt, she knew she'd strap it on as Brett had done. There came a time for standing up to bullies and hatemongers. This was such a time.

God help her, she'd stand by Brett's side and fight until the last breath.

Rand hollered that he was going after a wagon, and waved to her before galloping toward the road. Relief washed over her. To have a way to move the children would make her happy.

As Rayna stood riveted by her thoughts, a lone wagon pulled by mules rolled across the meadow's tall grass. Even from this distance, she could see bones piled high in the back.

Despite the effort to remain calm, she inhaled sharply. The sight of those bones swept her back to a time of misery and pain and loneliness.

But maybe it was the Clark family that she'd helped at the clinic. It would be nice to see Silas and Elizabeth and the children.

Shielding her eyes from the sun, she could make out two people. Whoever they were, she'd offer them a meal if they were hungry. She told Sarah to keep the children out of sight and moved away from the trees.

When the wagon drew to a stop, her breath made a hissing sound in the back of her throat. A fist gripped her heart and squeezed.

"What are you doing here?" she demanded.

Raymond Harper's vile grin showed his rotting yellow teeth. "Hello, Daughter. The good folk in Battle Creek told me where I could find you."

"How dare you! You're not welcome here." Rayna's gaze flicked to the woman beside him, recognizing Mrs. Vager. The woman had a black eye and split lip. One thing for sure, her father hadn't changed an iota. His handiwork was as familiar as the blue sky overhead.

Turning on her heel, she moved toward the protection of the men, who sat in a circle by the cold
campfire. Brett rose and hurried to meet her.

"What's the matter? Who are these people?" he
asked, putting his arm around her.

The bitter words spilled out. "Meet my dear father
and his *lady friend*. I told them they aren't welcome."

"Mayhap you'll change your tune, little girl,"
Raymond Harper snarled, "after I lay into you and slap
some respect into that uppity face."

Quickly, Brett tucked her behind him and rested
his hand on the Colt at his hip. "Touch her again, and
you'll die."

Peeking around him, she watched surprise widen
the old bone-picker's eyes.

"Me an' her got business. Snuck off while I was
sleepin'. You ain't got no right to interfere."

Though trembles shook her from her head to her
toes, Rayna felt safe behind Brett. Why had her father
come? Why couldn't he leave her alone? Standing
close to Brett with her hand on his back, she felt his
muscles grow taut beneath his skin. Gone was his
easy, quiet way. The man before her had become
hard and deadly.

Brett removed the small leather strap securing the
Colt to the holster. "Get off my land before I kill you."

"Figures that she'd take up with a breed. Guess
she ain't interested in her worthless ol' mama."
Raymond Harper flicked the reins. "Get on up there,
you fleabags."

Rayna shot from behind Brett. "What have you
done with Mama? Talk or I'll let him shoot you."

Her father grinned. "Thought that'd bring you off your high horse. Mayhap I might be of a mind to do a little swappin'. I'll tell you where your mama is in exchange for a few dollars."

"She won't pay you one cent." Brett widened his stance.

Laying a hand on his arm, Rayna spoke up. "I have two dollars. I reckon that'll buy some truth."

Though she didn't tell her father, she knew she'd pay far more for the location of Elna Harper. "Is she alive?"

Raymond wiped the spit from his mouth with the back of his hand. "Heard you've been workin'. Bet you've put back a lot more than two measly dollars."

"It's all you'll get," Rayna said firmly. "I asked if she's alive."

"Was last time I saw her."

Rayna reached into her pocket and drew out a plain knotted handkerchief. Loosening the knot, she held out two dollars. "Now speak, or I'm walking away and your name will never cross my lips again."

The old bone-picker stared at the money with a strange gleam in his eyes. "A little food first. Ain't had nothin' to eat for days. Some for my new wife too. Not above dickerin'."

"We'll feed you out here," Brett insisted. "Stay with your wagon. Only friends eat at my fire."

"Any chance you got a snort of whiskey? I could use some."

"Never touch the stuff."

"More's the pity." Raymond Harper gave a deep sigh.

Though Rayna couldn't be sure, she thought she saw a flicker of a smile cross Mrs. Vager's swollen lips.

Though she didn't like the woman, she couldn't help but feel sorry for her. "One question first," Rayna said. "Why have you really come? If you think for one second I'm leaving with you, you've been eating locoweed."

"Like I said, I happened to pass through Battle Creek. Heard a Rayna Harper's working for some doctor. Figured it might be you, and thought I'd see what it's worth to you to get rid of me." Harper's eyes glittered like cold stones.

"You'll get no more than what's been agreed on," Brett snapped.

Harper glared, rubbing his whiskered jaw. "Whatever you say, boy."

Rayna took Brett's arm, borrowing from his strength, and they walked toward the camp. "Thank you. I hate that my father found me. But if he can shed some light on my mother's whereabouts, I'll gladly pay him."

"Just don't be disappointed," Brett cautioned. "He never said if your mother is alive or dead."

"You don't have to worry. I learned the hard way what a son of a jack's word is worth. I didn't trust him then, and I don't trust him now."

He pulled her closer against him. "Remember, you're not alone, and I'm not going to let anything happen to you."

A tremble ran through her. "That's the only thing keeping me from getting a horse and riding away like Bob did. I don't have much courage where Raymond Harper is concerned."

Brett helped her prepare some food, and while they worked, she told him a little about her mother. "The last time I saw her, she took a beating for me, to keep him from striking me with a stick of firewood. She screamed for me to run and keep running. I took off into a cornfield and hid. I watched him hitch up the horses and throw Mama into the wagon bed. When he came back, he was alone."

He put some venison into the skillet and glanced up. "What do you think happened to her?"

"Raymond either sold or traded her, or else he killed her. I know my mother wouldn't have left me with him. Not in a million years." Hatred for the man who'd sired her sat on her tongue like the rancid meat he'd made her eat.

"You mentioned the town of Mobeetie to me before."

"That was his story. He said he'd taken her there, that she took up with a gambler and refused to come back. But then, the story always changed when he got a snootful. Once he said he traded her but never could remember what for. Another story was that he sold her into a brothel. I just wish I knew the truth, but the truth and Raymond Harper parted company a long time ago." She stirred the onions and winter squash.

"Look at me," Brett requested softly, taking her hand. "You may not ever learn what happened from your father, but it doesn't mean you have to stop searching. I'll help you. Together we can sort this out."

Tears lurked behind her eyes as she met his gaze, yet she refused to let them fall. "I don't deserve you, Brett Liberty. I've done a bad thing. I may not be any better than he is."

Brett brushed her cheek with his fingertips. "Don't ever say that. I wish I could kiss you. I'd give anything to take you to our spot and make love to you until you forget about evil and heartbreak and Raymond Harper."

"I wish you could too." She noticed that Rand had moved everyone away so they could have some privacy. How like Brett's brother. He seemed to sense when she and Brett needed some time alone. The men had a special kind of love for each other and truly an unbreakable bond.

She thought of Hershel and wished he was here. He'd send their father on his way.

At last the food was ready. She filled two plates, and Brett helped carry them to the wagon where the waiting couple sat.

"It's about time," Raymond Harper complained.

"Shut up, or I'll dump it out on the ground and you can eat it like a dog," Brett ordered, handing the first plate up to the woman, who hadn't uttered a word. Raymond tried to snatch it, but Brett was too fast.

Rayna wanted to laugh at her father's frustration but decided against it. She waited to give her plate to him until he'd settled down. When she did, he jerked it from her and began cramming food into his mouth with his dirty fingers.

After a few minutes, she held up the two dollars and said, "I've kept my end of the bargain. Now talk."

"Cain't a man eat his food first?"

From the corner of her eye, she saw Brett slide the Colt from his holster and heard the click of the hammer when he pulled it back. A muscle in his jaw worked. "Tell her what she wants to know."

The deadly steel underlying Brett's words and the

Colt pointed at her father's rotten heart got the right results. Rayna had no sympathy for the man who inflicted so much misery.

Raymond swallowed hard and put down his plate. "Reckon I ain't got much choice in the matter."

"That is correct," Brett snapped.

"Speak the truth," Rayna said firmly. "No more lies."

Raymond's shifty gaze focused on her. "It's all your fault, you know. Your ma didn't give me much choice. She thought the sun rose an' set in you, her precious little girl. Wouldn't listen to a damn word I said. The woman was gonna have me locked up for what she saw me do. I weren't about to let that happen. Elna jumped out of the back of the wagon an' took off walkin'. I chased her down."

He fell silent.

"The rest of it, you sorry rotten vermin," Brett ordered.

"The money, girl. Give me the money." Raymond started to get down from the wagon seat.

"Step one foot on the ground, and I'll kill you."

Rayna stared at Brett. She'd never heard such threatening words from him or witnessed such fury in his dark eyes. Evidently, he'd reached his limit with men like Raymond Harper, Edgar Dowlen, and Oldham.

Her father sank weakly onto the seat in the wagon box and pointed to Rayna. "It's all your fault, like I said. You ain't my kid. Never was. I stole you after I slit your ma's and pa's throats. Should'a drowned you in a river somewhere. Ain't never been nothin' but trouble."

The horror hit Rayna with the force of a bullet.

Brett's arms went around her as she buried her face in his chest, drawing from the security he offered. She wanted to put her fingers in her ears to block out the pain and the sound of Raymond's voice.

The growling rumble of Brett's voice vibrated his chest. "Why tell her this now?"

"She always thought she was better'n me. Better than a bone-picker. Goin' around with a secret smile like she knew somethin' I didn't. Whimperin' when I told her she had to pay for my liquor with her body, like she was too damn good. Guess I showed her."

"Tell 'em the rest," Mrs. Vager said through her swollen lips. "You tell 'em or I will."

"I went after Elna that night an' shot her between the eyes," Harper said. "Left her for the damn coyotes. There. You happy?"

Rayna raised her head and threw the money on the ground. "Rot in hell. You'd better run and find a hole to crawl into, because every lawman in Texas will be looking for you." She stood straight and tall. "I'm glad you're not my father. If I ever see you again, I won't need a gun. I'll kill you with my bare hands."

Thirty-one

IF BRETT DIDN'T HAVE MORE PROBLEMS THAN HE could handle with protecting the orphans, he'd hold Raymond Harper until Cooper could ride back in and cart him to jail. But they didn't have anywhere to put him and couldn't spare a man to guard him.

Weighing his options, he decided to send the man on his way and let Cooper hunt him down after this was over. "You've got two seconds to get the hell off my land." Brett shook with rage. Never had he wanted to take a life, but he could shoot Raymond Harper and not bat an eye. He wanted to comfort Rayna—who was walking back to camp—but he first had to make sure he rid them of this evil monster.

"Ain't done eatin'."

Upon Brett's signal, the ranch hands led by Rand rode out and encircled the wagon.

Mrs. Vager handed the plates down to Brett. "Thank you for the food. We'll be on our way."

Raymond Harper finally saw the wisdom in leaving. He slowly turned the wagon around.

"My brother's the sheriff in Battle Creek," Brett

said. "I'd hide if I were you. You ever come back here, you'll find a grave waiting."

He stood rooted to the spot under the noonday sun until Raymond Harper and his wagon of bones had faded from view. Then he turned to Rand, who had dismounted. "Thanks, Brother. How did you get back so fast?"

"Never got past the bend. Road's blocked again by armed gunmen. I hid in the brush and watched for a bit, but they never left. They're turning back everyone passing on the road. We're on our own."

"I wonder if you and the men can move the children deeper into the trees? I meant to do that right away but had my hands full here. I hate to ask, but I have something I need to do."

Rand grinned, slapping him on the back. "Be happy to. Go comfort Miss Rayna. She needs you."

"How did you know…?" Brett stopped then said, "Never mind."

He took off at a lope, his moccasins barely touching the ground. Within a few seconds, he stood beside Rayna, who sat outside his tepee, staring at the horizon with sightless eyes.

Tugging her to her feet, he said, "Come."

"Where are we going?"

"Need you ask?"

"Oh, Brett, thank you." She threw her arms around his neck and held tight. "You always know how to make me smile again."

Arm in arm, they walked to their hidden sanctuary. There was no need for words as he held her until her trembling stopped. He gently kissed her, letting soothing caresses of the soft lines of her back and waist speak for him.

Rayna glanced up at him and said simply, "I need you."

Silently, they undressed each other and lay down on the carpet of grass.

Brett smoothed back her hair and stared into her blue-green eyes that had seen so much sorrow. "Darlin', I'm sorry you had to learn all this."

Her bottom lip quivered. "I don't know what to do next. Everything I knew about myself was a lie, from my name to where I came from. My grandfather wasn't even mine. Who am I now?"

"I can't imagine how much you hurt. I wish I could take it all away. We'll figure this out together." Brett's lips brushed her brow. "In the Indian culture, they take their names from the wild creatures and birds. Maybe you can too."

"I'll have to think on that. Thank you."

Silence stretched for a long minute before Brett spoke. "I have no right to say these words, but I can't keep silent. Danger lies at every turn, and we never know how much time we have left. I love you. I have from the first moment I ever laid eyes on you in that jail in Steele's Hollow. I was out of my mind with pain, but I recognized an angel when I saw one."

Rayna cupped his jaw. "I love you, Brett. I never had anyone to stand up for me until you. No one to show me what love was really like. That it could be so wonderful."

Tenderly, he crushed her to him, breathing in her special scent that reminded him of ripe berries. With a cry, his lips found hers, and he drank his fill while his hands sought the contours of her body.

Touching.

Tasting.

Teasing.

A lazy, lingering kiss here, a burning touch there—he hungered for every inch of her as fire rose from his belly. His breath became ragged as he captured the tip of her breast in his mouth and was rewarded with her low moan. She arched her back, rising to meet his caresses while pulling him closer with fevered hands. She seemed to need him every bit as much as he needed her.

Though he didn't know how that was possible, seeing as how his hunger for her totally consumed him, mind, body, and soul.

Burying his hands in her hair, Brett moved on top of her, saying her name over and over. Knowing what awaited, his anticipation for the release that would come hurried him.

Brett eased into her in one gliding motion, feeling her warmth surround him, welcome him into her depths.

With the joining of their bodies, the world appeared to spin out of control around him into dizzying spirals of scorching heat and shuddering waves of passion.

As he settled into a smooth rhythm, he focused on her. He would not take his pleasure until she did.

To help her toward the moment of glorious release, he kissed her slightly parted mouth, the curve of her jaw, the pulsing hollow of her throat. His hand slid down the side of her breast to the swell of her hips, caressing, brushing, always stroking.

Rayna gave a cry and gripped him as she surrendered to the ecstasy. Vibrations of her body squeezed around him in the soaring climb toward rapture.

Panting, he took his pleasure and the much needed relief.

He didn't think he could ever grow tired of making love to Rayna. He'd heard of men in the different tribes turning to peyote for enlightenment and direction. None of that for him. All he needed was Rayna by his side. She was his medicine, his strength, his power.

Excitement never failed to ripple through him with the first glimpse of her each morning. Seeing her smile and those russet curls always made his heart race. To have to hide his feelings from those who would ridicule and speak ill of her tore at him. Such an unjust, criticizing world.

He rolled off and settled his body around her soft curves, draping an arm across her stomach. "I love you so much," he whispered into her hair.

"You don't know how desperately I've wanted to hear you say that. For so long I felt unworthy of having love." She snuggled against him, running her fingers lightly over his skin. "It seemed farfetched that anyone would ever soften their heart to me. And why should they? I'm no one's prize."

Brett lifted her palm and pressed a kiss to the sensitive flesh. "You're *my* prize. Lady, you *are* worthy of love and adoration and everything else I intend to shower on you as long as I'm able. I cherish everything about you—your past because it made you the kind, compassionate woman you are, and the present because of all you've overcome to get here."

Rayna swiveled in his arms and pressed a kiss into the hollow of his throat. He loved the feel of her warm lips on him.

Beautiful blue-green eyes stared into his. "Without you, I would be so lost and afraid right now. I don't even know my parents' names, and I have no way of finding out. What am I going to do?" A cry burst free, followed by a shuddering breath. "I wonder how my life would've turned out if Raymond Harper hadn't entered it. Do you think my parents loved me? At least a little bit?"

The misery in her voice sent a piercing ache into his chest. He'd never known a more helpless feeling. He couldn't do anything except hold her and brush away her tears. It was pitiful little against such agony.

"I'm positive of that," he said hoarsely.

"I don't want anything of Raymond Harper's, not even his name." She turned to face him. "But how do I go about changing it? And to what? It's not like I can post a notice in the newspaper asking for volunteers to give me theirs."

"I'll speak to Cooper. He'll know what to do."

From the way Rayna lightly drew circles on his arm, he knew she was deep in thought. He smoothed back her hair and brushed a kiss to her temple. "I know it's hard to believe, but there is a bright side. I would never have met you if you'd grown up some-place else and hadn't had to resort to picking pockets."

Rayna's eyes widened. "That's so true. I never thought of that. I feel better already."

"Glad I could help."

"You know, I truly loved Elna Harper, and I know

she loved me. She taught me to read, and she took the blows that Raymond meant for me. Until that rotten piece of trash ended her life. She was a victim as much as I was. I don't think she married him willingly. I always got the impression she came from a better class of people."

"It sounds like she made a good substitute mother."

"Brett, there's something I have to tell you, and it may change everything between us."

"Nothing can ever make me love you less."

"This might."

Rayna turned in his arms, her beautiful eyes staring into his. He wanted to silence her, to tell her to keep her secret, whatever it was. But he could see how much she needed to bare her soul, so he waited.

"I did a really bad, horrible thing." She took a deep breath. "I killed a man five years ago. I beat him with a shovel until the life went out of him." Rayna's hard voice became void of emotion. "And I didn't bat an eye."

"Please, you don't have to tell me any more." Brett touched her hair and let his hand slide down her throat. "I'm sure he deserved it, because I know how much you value life."

"He was a bone-picker too, and I never knew his name. He caught my...Raymond...liquored-up and attacked Elna. She'd spurned him, and that made him angry. I grabbed a shovel that Raymond kept beside the wagon and hit him as hard as I could. Blood went everywhere, but I kept on hitting him, because I knew if I let him up, we were dead. She helped me drag his body far away from the camp where the coyotes would find him, and I stole his shoes—the god-awful ones you hated."

The true picture of the horrors she'd endured became clear. It was a wonder she'd survived. His life, as bad as it sometimes was, paled in comparison. Love for her filled his heart.

"You didn't have a choice," Brett said softly. "You were protecting Elna. And yourself. The man deserved what he got."

"I'm no better than Raymond, though, don't you see? I'm dirty. I have blood on my hands that I can't get rid of. At odd moments of each day I see him lying there in my mind, so still with blood spilling onto the ground."

Her anguished cry pierced Brett. He gathered her into his arms and stood. Holding her close, he walked into the pool of crystal blue water.

"We're going to wash all that away, and when we leave this place today, what you told me will stay here. You need never speak of it again."

Brett sat her on a big rock at the base of the waterfall and kissed her. Then he cupped his hands, filling them with water again and again and pouring it over her beautiful body that glistened in the golden sun.

"Nothing will ever make me stop loving you, Rayna. I've been alone so long and was afraid I'd never find you. Now that I have, I'm not letting you go. Our lives are tied together for all eternity."

Rayna touched his face. "We have no more secrets between us. Thank you for understanding and loving me anyway."

"Lady, I don't have a choice, because we are one. You are the keeper of the flame that burns in my heart."

Pulling her off the rock into the deep water, Brett stood with the woman he loved. Their bodies touched as their lips met, and before long, Brett was making love to her again in the silent pool where there was no pain—only goodness and light.

He made a vow that their forbidden love would not always be so.

Rayna was his, and he'd grown tired of hiding it. Now more so than ever, for she had given him a great treasure.

She'd given him her trust.

Thirty-two

THOUGH DARK CLOUDS HAD FORMED OVERHEAD AND the afternoon air was heavy with the scent of rain, Rayna dressed with a lighter heart. Taking Brett's hand, she walked back to camp. Raymond Harper and the lies and pain he'd brought stayed behind in the deep, cleansing water of their secret oasis.

She was free of the nightmares.

A last name wasn't important. She was Rayna, and that was enough for now, because Brett loved her.

Rayna could relate to his last name: Liberty. That said everything for them both. Maybe someday the world would be bright enough that she could share it.

"Will you be all right while I go keep watch for intruders?" he asked.

"I'm happy and at peace for the first time that I can ever remember." She squeezed his hand. "Go do what you need to. I'll guard the children from here. It appears we may all get wet before morning."

"Within a few hours, unless I miss my guess."

"Be safe, my love."

"I will carry your love with me and think of you

during the long hours." He gathered her in his arms and kissed her, then strode toward his horse that was quietly grazing.

She joined Sarah and Sister Bronwen, who was stirring some kind of stew over the campfire. Rayna noticed tears on the old woman's face. She touched her shoulder. "What's wrong, Sister?"

The nun turned, wiping away the evidence. "I've disobeyed God and must pay for my sin. I'm a mean, spiteful old woman, and because of it, I ran Bob off."

"We all do and say things we shouldn't sometimes," Sarah said quietly. "The Great Spirit knows what's in your heart. You can ask for peace, and it will be granted."

"The children loved that old Comanche, and now he's gone. Went off to die by himself. I...I can't bear it."

Rayna put her arms around Bronwen's shoulders. At first the nun held herself as rigidly as she'd probably lived most of her life, but finally she relaxed.

"We all miss Bob, but this is what he chose. He got back his dignity and is now able to meet his end in peace. We should be glad for him and celebrate his life, not mourn his passing." Rayna stopped. That's exactly what they needed to do. "Tonight we'll gather the children, and each person can say a little about what Bob meant to them. It'll be a nice way to honor him."

"I'd like that." Bronwen stepped back and gave her a smile.

Rayna turned at the sound of a horse. She recognized Cooper. He rode up and dismounted. The big man's gaunt face and dark circles under his eyes told of sleepless nights filled with worry.

He nodded. "Miss Rayna. Miss Sarah. Sister."

"How did you get past the blocked road? Rand tried to go after a wagon earlier but had to turn around."

"I cut through the woods and went around them. Where is everyone?"

"The men have taken up guard positions, and the children are hiding in the trees." Rayna filled him in on the latest. "We have to stay on alert every second."

Cooper nodded. "Sounds like Dowlen's upped the ante. Sorry I wasn't here."

"You couldn't help it. How's Delta?"

"Much better. Doc Yates operated on her and removed her appendix in time. She's going to be all right. I have someone staying with her night and day."

Rayna laid a hand on his arm. "I'm glad she'll recover. We were all worried. Would you like some coffee?"

"I need to join the men. Maybe another time."

"It's always here. I know Brett, Rand, and the others will be happy to see you."

"Most likely." After touching the brim of his hat in polite good-bye, he climbed into the saddle and, with a wave, rode in the direction Brett had gone.

She watched for a minute then went back to helping the sister cook food for the children. But her thoughts were on a certain man with dark eyes and kissable lips.

A few minutes later, a sense of disquiet and fore-boding descended over her. She grabbed her chest and fumbled for the log she'd sat on with Bob. The horses were screaming and running to and fro, as if looking for shelter of some sort. Whatever they saw was invisible to her.

But she knew there would be no stopping this. Trouble marched toward them with guns that spat orange flame and death.

∽∾

In the midst of thunder and fierce lightning but little rain, Brett gave a sigh of relief when he saw Cooper riding toward him. Even one extra gun sometimes made a huge difference.

And when you put three committed brothers who didn't know the meaning of the word *quit* fighting side by side, nothing or no one could beat them.

Reining to a stop, Cooper dismounted and strode to him with his Winchester propped on his shoulder.

Brett allowed a smile. "You're a sight for sore eyes, Coop. How did you get through?"

After explaining how he took a grueling path through the woods, Cooper added, "This group is becoming organized. Those blocking the road were well armed and dangerous. One man alone trying to force them to reopen it would pretty much mean a death sentence. They'd shoot me on the spot."

"I'm glad you didn't try." To have to tell Delta she was a widow would rip his heart out. "I hate this waiting, never having any advance warning. When I post a man in one place, they pour in at another hole."

"And we don't have enough men to plug all of them." Cooper shifted his rifle to his chest.

"The only way we've survived so far is because of Dowlen's class of recruits."

"Drunks and unskilled fighters are no match. But with Oldham joining up, that's going to be a different story."

Unease crawled up Brett's neck. "We could sure use some more help. What are the people of Battle Creek saying?"

"They're trying to stay out of the ruckus. Many are caught in the middle and don't want to have to choose sides. Dowlen and his new friend have been trying like hell to stir them up though."

"I won't ask anyone to go against their principles."

"With us cut off from town, they couldn't get through anyway. They're not against you, Brett," Cooper said quietly. "You have a lot of friends in town. But showing loyalty is dangerous, and people are afraid."

With a heavy sigh, Brett changed the subject. "I take it your being here means Delta is all right?"

"Much better. Has a ways to go before she'll be up and around a lot, but she's out of the woods." Cooper pushed back his hat. "Miss Rayna filled me in on the latest and how the old Comanche saved the day."

"If Bob hadn't done what he had, Dowlen and his men would've unleashed fury on the orphans." The thought of how close they came still twisted Brett's stomach, especially since he hadn't been there to help. "After Bob bought us some time, he left."

Cooper stared into the distance. "I've heard of that custom among the tribes. But it's what he wanted."

"I would want that for me if I were in his shoes."

Brett knew nothing worse than being a burden and living a useless life.

"Let's hope that's far off, after I'm dead and gone. I don't want to think about such. Damn, you're depressing me, little brother."

"Sorry, but it's the truth." Brett's thoughts returned to the current situation. "I sure wish I had more of the gunpowder Bob used. We could rig some traps."

"It would be nice," Cooper agreed.

"What about the Texas Rangers? Will they come?"

Cooper shook his head. "Already contacted them. They've sent most of their men down to the border to handle a huge outlaw problem. Outlaw gangs are murdering and rustling and raising hell. The captain I telegraphed said they'll come this way whenever they can."

Brett's heart sank. "It's just us then. When Rand and I went over to scout, we saw probably fifty men."

"We can handle them, little brother."

"You sound pretty confident."

"I am. We didn't start this fight, but we sure know how to end it. The same way we took care of all the others."

But at what cost? Brett was smart enough to know that there were always casualties. Cold fear settled in his chest like a nagging cough he couldn't get rid of.

~~◆~~

The afternoon wore on with little to break the monotony. Brett rode down the line to where Adam was. He needed to make sure his nephew was up to the task. None of them had gotten much sleep in the last four days. Each grabbed what he could in spurts. A few hours here and there. All to a man were dead on their feet.

Adam glanced up as Brett dismounted. "Come to check on me, Uncle?"

"Promised your mama I would." Brett hunkered down next to his nephew. "You were laid up not that many days ago."

"I'm fine." Adam flicked a large black beetle off his pants leg. "I already proved I can handle myself."

"Yes, you have. I'm proud to have you beside me. Whatever happens, I want you to keep low. Don't take any big chances. I want you safe."

Adam swallowed hard, and Brett could see his struggle to keep his fear hidden. "You think this will be it?"

"I wish I could say no, but my gut tells me different."

"You be safe too, Uncle Brett. I need you."

Giving his nephew a brief clap on the back, Brett returned and settled down to wait. Twilight would come in a few hours. Brett's stomach rumbled, and he realized he hadn't eaten anything since breakfast. He'd been too intent on comforting Rayna and putting her in a better place.

He didn't know how much he'd helped, but at least she'd been able to smile again, even though it had wobbled and faded.

Minutes later, a bullet slammed into the tree he was leaning against. Ducking down, he quickly brought his rifle to his shoulder, looking for movement.

Another shot echoed in the stillness, but he had no idea where it landed. Some of the men returned fire, but though Brett tensed, he watched...waiting.

Finally, he decided to try a bluff. "Our reinforcements scaring you, Dowlen? You're about to wind up in a place you don't want to be. Got my crosshairs on you."

No mistaking Dowlen's gravelly voice. "Don't know who'd be fool enough to side with an Indian. Bet we can handle 'em though. An' about that other—I ain't afraid of you, Liberty. Ain't afraid of nothing."

"Except catching something from these poor children. You're mighty scared of that."

"That's why we gotta get rid of 'em once and for all."

"You're welcome to try," Rand yelled from his position.

Cooper joined in. "Texas Rangers are coming. You'll be laughing out the other side of your mouth when they tote your carcass to jail. The judge might throw the book at you, and those working for you as well."

"Let 'em come," Oldham hollered.

The sound of that voice still chilled Brett's bones. He'd never forget the man who wanted him dead so badly he'd do anything.

"Can't we talk about this?" Brett asked. "There's no need for bloodshed. Surely we can work something out."

"Nothing to say. Long as you're keeping those heathens over there, I see it as my duty to get rid of 'em," Dowlen answered.

Heathens? Brett's jaw clenched. Over his dead body.

The remainder of the night passed in brittle silence, each side waiting for the deadlock to shatter at any time.

⤸⤺

When he rode into camp long after dawn, Rayna came running. Her ashen face scared him.

"What's wrong?"

"Sarah left. I tried to stop her, but she went anyway."

"Where? Why?" Brett couldn't imagine his sister being a coward and running. Just not possible.

"Her plan is to sneak through the woods. If she can get through, she's going to try to rally the people of Battle Creek. I'm worried Dowlen's men will kill her."

"If anyone can do it, my sister can. I haven't known her long, but I've seen her with people. They trust her word. She's a born leader, and she's determined. She'll make it safely."

Rayna nodded, and the lines on her forehead vanished. "You need to eat. Get some coffee while I dish up a plate of what I cooked for the children."

When she turned, Brett's gaze followed her soft curves, wishing he had the power to freeze time so he could take the fear and worry from her for a day or two. He'd wrap her in his arms and block it all out.

It took everything he had to drag his eyes from her. With a sigh, he moved toward the coffee. This wasn't sustainable—there were too few of them. They were going at this all wrong. They had to change tactics.

Taking his coffee, he joined the tired group of men. "What we're doing isn't working. We've separated ourselves from the women and children, when we should be standing guard here, not out there with too large an area to patrol."

Rand nodded. "If we had more men, keeping the fight away from the children would be best, but you're right—it's getting clearer and clearer we just don't have that option. We can do a better job here and block any attempt to ride in between us."

"Makes sense," Cooper said to a round of agreement.

"Fill your bellies then, and we'll get started on our fort." Now that they had a better—if still risky—plan, Brett felt some of the tension leave his neck and shoulders.

After eating, they got busy. For the rest of the day, every man worked feverishly to make the camp more secure. They brought downed logs from the woods and piled them up to form a chest-high barrier for the men to hide behind. Brett got two of his horses and managed to drag the wagon that was damaged during the stampede into place as a buffer. They piled all their ammunition behind the barricade.

When they were finally done, twilight painted the sky dark purple. Brett and his brothers stood back to survey their work. Each agreed it was the best they could make in a short time.

"I think the children will be all right in the safety of the trees," Brett said. "Even if Dowlen or his men know where they are, they'll have to go through us to get to them."

And they'd face a hail of bullets if they tried.

Adam joined them, wearing streaks of dirt on his face, looking very similar to their ancestors when they geared up for a fight. He dusted off his hands. "I think we did good. We're ready for them."

"As much as we can be," Brett agreed, tossing him his rifle. Pride in his nephew burst anew in his chest. He worked as hard as any man and did everything

Brett asked. "Remember, don't take any chances. Your mother will kill me if anything happens to you."

"I'm not a kid anymore. Don't worry so much, Uncle Brett."

"It's my job to worry." He glanced toward the sheltering trees then back to Rayna, who had just finished tying off a bandage on a man who'd caught a bullet during last night's standoff. The light of the campfire caressed her face, doing things he wished his hands were doing. Everyone counted on him to keep them safe.

A muscle bunched in his jaw. That's what he'd do, no matter how he accomplished it. He'd walk barefoot through fire for her, the unwanted orphans, and his family.

She finished up and poured a cup of coffee, bringing it to him. They moved to one of logs and sat down. With her shoulder brushing his, she stared into the flames. "I'm worried. Something is coming."

"I know." Brett took a sip of the hot brew and added with an edge to his voice, "We'll defend this place with our lives."

In one of the conversations he'd had with Bob, he'd learned that the Comanche believed that the greatest glory wasn't in killing an enemy but in getting close enough to touch him and taking his power.

Maybe it was true. He knew Bob's spirit was still with them. Earlier this afternoon when he'd looked up on the ridge, he thought he saw the old Comanche standing up there. But then he decided it was the light bouncing off the limestone. One day he'd like to find his friend's bones and bury him.

The thought brought comfort.

Rayna rested her head on his shoulder. "I like having you close, not out in the darkness."

"How are the children, Rayna?"

"Safe as I can make them. They know to stay put and not make a sound. I pray we make it through this. I have a bad feeling."

When she reached for his hand, he squeezed her cold fingers. "We're going to survive this. Sure, Dowlen has amassed a lot on his side. But what does he really have? Drunks and fat, lazy old men with a grudge. That's why they haven't won, and why they'll never win." He touched her hair. "We'll be enjoying the privacy of our oasis before you know it."

"Yes, we will." Her smile quivered as she kissed his cheek.

Brett soaked up the quiet moment with the woman who filled his dreams. He didn't need her omens that prophesied death at every turn to know something bad was coming. He felt it in his bones. They were as ready as they'd ever be.

No matter what happened to him, he prayed Rayna, the orphans, and everyone else came to no harm.

Before he could tell her he loved her once more, sudden gunshots rang out, and the world plunged into turmoil and chaos.

Thirty-three

Hoofbeats pounded, men yelled, and a barrage of bullets exploded around the camp in a chaotic frenzy. Brett threw down his cup and grabbed his rifle, his senses instantly on high alert. He dove for safety behind the pile of logs, dragging Rayna with him.

"Stay down," he ordered.

"Give me a gun. I can shoot. You need me."

His brothers, Adam, and the ranch hands ran from everywhere, converging behind the security of the wall of timber and broken wagon.

The thickest, blackest night Brett had ever seen enveloped them with no hint a dawn would ever come again.

A handful of men to rebuff an attack three times their size. Brett's stomach clenched. Still, the defenders of the Alamo would've taken these odds in a heartbeat.

Brett cursed the fact that Dowlen and Oldham's army had caught their small and exhausted group off guard time and again. He cursed the overwhelming odds stacked against them by men eaten up with hate.

And he cursed the fact that somewhere deep in

the trees, orphans huddled in terror, asking only for a chance to grow up.

A muscle worked in Brett's jaw. God willing, he would give them that.

He would not give up, as his opponents counted on. Those who had killing on their minds would see and finally come to know the strength of his heart and the fiery purpose that beat inside each of them. They'd fight until life left their bodies. This cause was right and just.

Then there was Sarah. If she made it to town, she'd bring help. When she told the townspeople what had happened, they'd come. They were good, decent people. But if he was wrong and Sarah couldn't sway them, he'd put fourteen seasoned men up against anything Dowlen and Oldham threw at them.

With renewed determination, he fired at the nearest horseman, hitting him, but not knocking him from the saddle. Rayna spoke the truth. He reached for a second rifle at his feet, handing it to her. "Aim at the chest, and take your time with the shot."

Wave after wave of riders hit them. This would be a fight measured in so many heartbeats instead of minutes. If they made it to daylight…

Brett gripped the rifle, firing until he ran out of ammunition. Pulling his Colt from the holster, he kept shooting until he could reload the rifle.

From out of nowhere, a bullet slammed into the wood he crouched behind, splintering it.

He spared the hole a glance, grateful the hot metal had missed him. However, seconds later, the next bullet struck his chest below his collarbone. The impact spun him around as hot fire pierced, sending mind-numbing pain through his body.

The rifle fell from his hands as he battled to stay on his feet. Losing that fight a second later, he slid to the ground in a heap.

Rayna screamed and grabbed him. "Brett, keep breathing and look at me. I'm not going to let you die. Do you hear me? You will not die on me!"

While he tried to make sense of her words, she ripped off his shirt, pressed it tightly to the wound, and ordered him to hold on.

From the sound of her distant voice, she seemed in the grips of a heavy fog. He kept losing her. He wished he'd told her one more time that he loved her.

Kissed her once more.

Breathing hard, he tried to focus on her face, but he couldn't keep his eyes from drifting shut.

Where had she gone? She promised to wait for him.

No. He couldn't give up.

Inch by inch, he fought his way through the pain back to Rayna, back to the woman he loved. She needed him. The others needed him. He couldn't let them down. He had powerful medicine.

"Bandage me and let me up," he rasped, forcing his eyes open.

"You're hurt. You can't. The blood…"

A muscle worked in his jaw as he groped for the Colt that was somewhere around his hip. His trembling hand couldn't locate it. "Help me to my feet. I have to fight."

"I'll do what you want, but only after I bandage you," she said mulishly.

Silently, Rayna helped him sit. Brett could see anger and frustration in her eyes and body movements, but he knew it came out of concern for him and nothing more.

"See if you can tell if the bullet is still in there."

"I'll try." She slid her hand over his skin, both chest and back.

Brett gritted his teeth against the throbbing pain while she poked around in the wound and felt along his back before announcing, "I think it went through. I can feel a hole on the back side where the bullet came out."

"Good news." Sweat formed on his forehead.

As the battle raged around them, she wadded his shirt into a tighter ball and told him to hold it to the wound as hard as he could. His ragged breath hurt his chest as he watched her tear off a length of her petticoat and bind it tightly around his shoulder and chest. Giving the fabric an extra tug, she tied it off. Then putting her arm around his waist, she hoisted him to his feet.

The ground whirled with the effort, and he clenched his teeth against the searing agony. "Will you reload my rifle for me, please?"

"I already have." She handed the Winchester to him. "Don't pass out on me."

"Aw, Rayna darlin', I don't plan on it." He was tired of fighting. His soul was weary. He wanted only to take Rayna's hand and lead her to their special place, where peace and harmony lived, and never leave.

It wasn't possible though. The killing wouldn't stop.

Screams of terrified orphans suddenly burst through

the noise and chaos of the night. They must've crept from their hiding place. To them, they must think the world was coming to an end. Maybe it was. Maybe the next world would be more accepting.

Brett holstered his Colt and propped the rifle on the top log in the pile. Though his grip was shaky, he fired at the blur of movement. At times he had to close his eyes for a half second to enable a sharper focus.

His legs wobbled, threatening to collapse as his pain increased. He wasn't sure how long he'd be able to continue, but prayed he could last the distance.

The mounted army kept coming. When one rider plunged to the ground, another took his place. Brett lost count of the hours that seemed to bleed into days in his delirious mind. He kept thinking about the blood moon and Rayna's whispered statement that it meant death.

Brett had long since lost feeling in his body. His legs threatened to collapse under him, and his fingers were numb. Relentless pain was the only thing he was able to feel, and it was like a wild animal gnawing into him.

Finally, unable to stand, he sank to the ground in despair.

Just before black fog stole his vision, he heard a sound. A bugle? What the hell?

His first thought was that he'd gone crazy. The second was of Rayna and wishing he didn't have to leave her. Wetness trickled down his cheek. Sweat? A tear?

"Please forgive me," he whispered.

Hues of pink and gold marked the breaking daylight when Brett next managed to open his eyes. Cooper was leaning over him, trying his best to pry the rifle from Brett's hand.

"I think you've seen better days, little brother."

"Hurts like someone pressed a hot brand to me," he rasped. "How about you?"

"Just a few scratches," Cooper said, wiping blood from his face. "Weren't as lucky with the men. We lost another, two are missing, and several have gunshot wounds. One of the wounded is Fletcher. He's been with me a long time."

Rand strode forward with a cup of water and held it to Brett's mouth.

He took a long drink. "Sorry about Fletcher. Which one died?"

Deep sorrow and guilt pierced Brett's heart. He couldn't stand the thought of any of the men dying. Especially not on his behalf. He didn't need that on his conscience.

The lines in Cooper's face deepened. "Gabe Booker. He hired on at the start of the Long Odds Ranch and leaves a wife and kids." The tightness in Cooper's voice spoke of his grief.

"Damn. Gabe was a good man. What about the two missing?"

"Not sure. It's a battlefield out there." Cooper wearily rubbed his eyes. "Bodies lying everywhere. We're just beginning to check for survivors. You seen Rayna? We need her doctoring skills."

Brett glanced around. "She was beside me all night.

Fought as well as any of us. She bandaged me up after I got hit."

Rand held the water up to his mouth again. "I'm sure she's around here someplace."

Panic swept through Brett. He couldn't see her anywhere. With every bit of strength he had, he pushed away the cup and struggled to his feet. "I have to find her."

To lose the only thing that gave his life real meaning scared him worse than facing a hangman's noose. He didn't want to live in a world without her.

The ranch hand named Fletcher approached with a soldier wearing an army uniform. "Need a word, boss."

Cooper straightened and disappeared with them around the makeshift barricade.

"What's going on? Where did the soldier come from?"

"The cavalry rode in with guns blazing just when all seemed lost," Rand explained. "If it hadn't been for them, we wouldn't have survived."

Their miracle had happened.

"I hope they plan on staying awhile."

Rand put an arm around him and helped him to one of the seats outside the tepee. "Not sure how long they'll have. Rest here, little brother. You're in no shape to look for anyone. Coop and I will locate her for you."

"Thanks." Brett's harsh breath was loud in his ears. The short walk had winded him. "Find Rayna. Promise me."

"I promise." Rand raced toward the woods where the children were.

If Brett was prone to cussing, he'd let some fly.

He remembered back to the time after Cooper and Rand had helped him escape the jail in Steele's Hollow and how totally useless he'd felt when they made camp. Now everyone scurried around trying to help the wounded, and he just sat there like a doddering old man with one foot in the grave. Bob appeared to have had more life than Brett did at the moment.

His heartbeats were measured in minutes while he waited for his brothers to return, his searching gaze seeking a glimpse of the woman who filled his heart.

The longer time dragged by, the more his hopes dimmed.

He saw only one choice left—he had to go look for her himself. A downward glance at his soaked bandage revealed the extent of his blood loss. He had to call on every bit of bravery he had.

Finally, taking deep breaths, he staggered to the fire and laid his knife in the hot coals. Then he removed the crude bandage Rayna had wrapped around him.

Brett had heard of cauterizing a wound to stop the bleeding from an old mountain man he'd run across years ago, but he'd never done it. The tough frontiersman had told of the enormous pain, saying he'd done it as a last resort but wouldn't recommend it to anyone.

This was Brett's only option, and he'd gladly do it if it helped to find Rayna. He'd do anything.

Even crawl through the flames of hell on his belly.

By the time the knife glowed red, Brett had given himself a talking-to. Before he could lift the knife from the coals, Cooper and Rand strode toward him. He could tell by their faces they hadn't found her.

"Brett, let us help. You won't be able to hold that knife to the wound long enough to seal it off." Cooper knelt down, and Rand helped to lay Brett on the ground. "Are you sure you want to do this? We could try to get you to town to Doc."

"No time. Just do it. Rand, will you find me something to bite down on?"

"We'll need something to kill the infection once we're through." Cooper glanced toward his men. "See if any of our men have some whiskey."

Rand left and came back a few minutes later with half a bottle of whiskey and several pieces of soft leather, which he stuck into Brett's mouth. "Are you sure about this?"

Brett gave a furious nod.

"Okay, little brother, this is gonna hurt like hell." After drenching the wound good with the alcohol, Cooper lifted the knife from the fire. "Rand, hold him still. Sit on him if you have to."

The smell of searing flesh met Brett's nose the instant Cooper pressed the bowie knife to the wound. Brett screamed from the pain that gnawed down to the core of his body like a ferocious beast.

He cursed Edgar Dowlen and all his followers before blessed darkness slammed around him again.

❦

When Brett came to, Cooper and Rand were sitting beside him, and a bandage covered his wound. "How long was I out?"

"A while," Rand admitted, handing him a cup of water. "I'm really proud of you. I don't think I could've done that."

"You could if you had to." Brett's gaze swung to Cooper. "I take it you didn't find Rayna, or she'd be here."

Cooper shook his head. "Looked everywhere. No one's seen her, not even the children. No sign of the two missing men either. Only one thing could've happened. Somehow Dowlen took them. You said Rayna was beside you all night? You remember her leaving for something?"

"It was chaos, and I'd been shot. It took everything I had to stay on my feet and keep shooting. She could easily have slipped away, and I wouldn't have noticed." His brothers helped him to a sitting position. "Saddle some horses. We're paying the devil a visit, and we're taking the soldiers."

Cooper's voice was ragged when he spoke. "Soldiers left under orders to ride to Switchback where outlaws have taken over the town and are threatening to execute its citizens."

Crushing disappointment pierced Brett's chest. "But they'll be back?"

"The captain said they'd wire Fort Worth and ask for troops to come help us. Not sure when that'll be though."

Brett set his jaw and got back to the subject of rescuing Rayna. "Doesn't matter, I'm still going after Rayna and our men."

Rand held out his hands as though to stop him. "You're not able. Let us make sure the weasel-eyed bastard has them."

Brett's eyes narrowed, and his voice hardened to granite. "I'm going with or without you, but you're not keeping me from it unless you chain me up. Best make sure you use some of the strongest iron when you do."

"No one will ever chain you again as long as I'm alive." Steel layered Cooper's words. "I'd feel the same way if I wore your moccasins, but you won't help her by riding in and demanding her release." Cooper rested a hand on Brett's arm. "All that will do is get you and her both killed. Plus our men if they're there. You're not thinking with your head."

"I'm doing what I have to."

"I swear, you're a stubborn cuss." Rand shook his head.

"Look, Brett," Cooper reasoned. "Rest until dark. We'll go after her then. It's the only thing that makes sense."

"All right." Brett closed his eyes. "We'll do this your way."

Fury at his neighbor's newest low burned like the hot knife that had seared his flesh. Rayna had nothing to do with any of this.

The woman whose kisses could make his body sing had nothing but goodness and love for others in her heart. He wouldn't rest until he brought her home.

Not until he could wrap his arms around her and breathe in her sweet fragrance.

He had a great hunger for his Wish Book woman. The world would tilt at this crazy off-kilter angle until she was by his side once more.

"I love you," he whispered. "I didn't find you just to lose you this way."

Thirty-four

WITH RAYNA'S HEART POUNDING, SHE CURLED ON A thin bed of straw where Raymond Harper had thrown her.

She'd cried out when he grabbed her during the attack, but in the confusion and noise, no one heard her scream. Shock of seeing him coming through the thick rifle smoke had paralyzed her. He was the last person she'd expected to see on the Wild Horse. He'd reeked of whiskey, shoving his face into hers. His fingers dug into her arms, instantly hurling her back to the past to all those times when she'd been at his mercy.

Once again he had control over her fate. How many times before she would finally know freedom?

Something told her it would end in death, either his…or hers. It was the only way.

Rayna welcomed death if she could be rid of him and his kind.

A moan drew her attention to the ranch hand named Charles who lay a few feet away. The former sheriff of Steele's Hollow had beaten him, and though she didn't know the extent of his injuries, she knew Oldham had hurt him bad.

Tied to a post, she couldn't even check on him. In the dim shadows of the barn, she could barely make out the form of the second ranch hand. "Joe, can you see to Charles?"

"No, Miss Rayna. I'm staked to the ground like a dog. Did they hurt you?"

"I'm fine." Though she didn't know for how long. She knew Raymond Harper and his need to inflict pain and misery. It seemed his sole enjoyment. "Joe, when they come for me, will you say a prayer that it'll be over with quick?"

"I don't really know how to pray, but I'll do my best. Maybe they'll leave you alone."

"Raymond Harper will come."

A strange acceptance passed over her. Meeting her fate was better than waiting in the darkness. Ever since she could remember, she'd hated when night fell.

Bad stuff always happened in the dark.

Bugs and spiders could come out and crawl on her. Or rats. She hated rats.

But the things men did when they thought no one could see were the worst.

That's why she'd been so relieved when Oldham had brought Brett into the cell next to her that day. She knew Deputy Dingleby would take what he wanted before long. Men like him always did. Even with the iron bars separating her from Brett, she'd felt better just having company in that dark earthen dungeon.

Here she was again, only this time without Brett's strong arms.

Her jaw throbbed where Oldham hit her earlier as he called her a whore and squaw. At first she thought he'd broken it, but now that she could move it, she was pretty sure it wasn't.

That had been the extent of his vile anger...for now. Yes, darkness brought out the worst in some men. Raymond Harper for sure.

Thank goodness not everyone. The light and hope Brett gave her meant more than sacksful of money. His gentle love had scrubbed away years of tarnish on her soul.

Suppressing a groan, she moved to a sitting position and brought her legs up in order to rest her chin on her knees. Her stomach growled, and she realized she hadn't had anything to eat since yesterday about noon. Who was taking care of the children? With Sarah gone, maybe Sister Bronwen would do more than the pitiful little she had previously.

Thoughts of Flower and little Joseph and the others, who were unwanted and unloved, filled her head. They must be terrified. Her heart ached to hold them and whisper words of comfort. What would become of those orphans?

With nothing to do, Rayna turned her thoughts toward making a wonderful place for them in her head. She pictured a beautiful home surrounded by acres of grassy land for them to roam. Each child would have a bedroom of their own, and toys of all kinds would fill it.

They wouldn't have to worry about food, because they'd have more than enough.

When she closed her eyes, she pictured Brett and herself standing on a wide porch, watching the children playing. His arm would be around her, and she'd be smiling up at him with so much love.

In this imaginary world, they'd be married, and no one would speak ill of them.

Tears burned behind her eyes. If only this place existed. If only they could be husband and wife.

Oh, Brett, I love you so much.

She would wait as long as it took for attitudes to change. She'd promised herself and Brett.

And if they never lived to see the day, she'd continue to love him, even to her last breath on earth.

◆

The scent of the earth wrapped around Brett like the comforting arms of an old friend as he lay on his pallet in misery, trying to will away his crushing pain. He would rest and gain some strength so he could fight for the woman who protected the dream that beat inside them both.

Rand entered the tepee with a cup of water. "How are you feeling?"

"I'll be fine as soon as I get Rayna back. How long till dark?"

"Probably another four hours. Coop and I don't think you'll be able to go. You've been through hell."

"I'm going." Brett wished he could've put more steel behind the words. The pain made them come out far too weak.

Cooper pushed through the flap and stood to his imposing height. "You'll sit this out. Rand and I aren't as quiet as you, but at least we won't collapse in a heap at our enemy's feet. We *can* fight."

"It's the only choice, little brother," Rand said. "You're too weak. You've lost too much blood. Digging in your heels about this won't change the facts."

"Do you mind if I get a little sleep? You can chew on my butt some more when I wake up. It's a while until dark. I'll see how I feel once the sun goes down." Brett raised on an elbow though it sapped his strength. "Just know that I will not leave Rayna there another day. I'm bringing her home. And that's all I'm saying on the subject."

Faced with his defiance, they left. Brett lay back on the pallet.

Thoughts ran through his head. It would be no problem getting onto the land and to the house if he exercised patience and didn't get in a hurry. But then they had to find the three captives once they got there. What bothered him was the shape Rayna and the men were in and not knowing how far they'd be able to walk. With his injury, he might not be able to carry anyone. Still, if it came down to it, he'd manage somehow, no matter his own pain.

Maybe letting Coop and Rand come was the best answer.

The point that stuck in his brain was that they couldn't walk as softly as he could. They might give everything away. But if they made it, coming out would be a whole lot easier.

He lifted a cold palm to his pounding head. He couldn't afford to fail.

Lives depended on it.

The flap of the tepee opened, and Cooper stepped through. "You need to eat. I brought some venison from the smokehouse. And while you fill your belly, I'm going to take a look at that wound. I don't much care how I have to do it."

That his brother, who was six years older, ordered instead of asked him crawled up the back of Brett's neck. Still, he knew Cooper was right. Food would strengthen him, and the wound did need tending to.

Rayna would have a fit if she came back to an infected gunshot. He didn't want that. When she came back, he had things of a more pleasurable nature in mind.

Like making her purr.

"Well, make it snappy. A man needs his rest," Brett grumbled, eying the venison.

By the time Cooper announced the wound looked good and applied a clean bandage, Brett had eaten all of the meat. He felt much better, though he wouldn't be a hundred percent until he had Rayna where she belonged.

With him and in his arms. Forever and ever.

❧

Rayna froze when the barn door opened and Dowlen and Oldham marched inside, holding a lantern. Raymond Harper followed behind the arguing pair.

"Joe," she whispered, "when you get out, will you tell Brett that I love him—and that I wish I could've stuck around to wait longer?"

"Yes, and I'll add that you're the bravest woman I know," he whispered back.

"I only wanted to scare the Indian into leaving," Edgar Dowlen yelled. "I ain't gonna kill anyone, especially a bunch of little kids."

"You lily-livered pansy. I thought you had guts." Oldham stood in Dowlen's face, so close their noses touched. "I'm taking over. I'll lead these men into battle. They know what's at stake here. Liberty is gathering all his kind so they can rise up against us."

Fear for Brett and the children pierced Rayna's heart. Someone had to warn him.

Dowlen gave a snort. "They're just kids."

"Kids grow up," Oldham snapped. "Kill 'em now before they do."

Raymond Harper stepped forward. "I'll be happy to follow you and do what needs doin'."

Oldham thanked him and swung back to Dowlen. "Go on about your business. This is men's work."

"I'll take care of the girl for you," Raymond Harper said, licking his lips. "I know how to treat uppity women. 'Sides, I owe her for all those times of sassing me…among other things."

"Fine." Oldham waved his arm. "Glad to see a man for once."

Panic rose up so strong it blocked the ability to breathe. Rayna shrank into the shadows as Dowlen and the former sheriff set down the lantern and left. The man she'd once believed to be her rotten father came for her, wearing a twisted smirk. But it was the crazed, glittering eyes that struck terror.

"Time for your medicine, girlie." Harper bent down to untie her from the post.

The second she was free, she kicked him in the privates with both feet then ran for the door. She raced out into the night, searching for a place to hide until she could get her bearings. A stand of trees cloaked in darkness called. She lifted her skirts and headed there.

Sudden arms fastened around her, lifting her off the ground before she reached the thick brush she aimed for.

"Not so fast," a voice said in her ear.

When her feet touched the ground, she swiveled around to see one of the recruits, a man around Cooper's age. "If you let me go, I'll see that you're rewarded. Just give me five minutes before you sound the alarm. That's all I ask."

He gave a bark of laughter. "You must be crazy, lady. That would buy me a grave."

A desperate glance at the barn door told her she'd better talk fast. Raymond Harper would appear any minute. "No one would have to know. You're better than these cutthroats. I can tell you want to do the right thing."

A silent stare indicated he was thinking about it. The longer he hesitated, the more time it gave Harper to recover.

"Please."

The noise of the barn door slamming back against the wooden planks brought a sharp cry. She was too late. Everything was too late.

"Good, I see you caught her." Harper caught up with them and wrenched her arms behind her back. "Get some rope."

Without a word, the recruit went to do his bidding.

Harper put his mouth next to her ear. "I promise a very slow, very painful, very miserable death."

"You'll never hear me beg. I never begged you for

a crumb, and I won't start now. Brett was right. You are a rotten piece of cow dung."

If his hands hadn't been busy holding her, she knew he'd have drawn back a fist.

Seconds later, the recruit returned with rope and bound her hands tightly, after which Harper jerked her roughly away from the buildings. She stumbled along, trying to keep her footing, knowing if she lost it, he'd drag her.

Where was he taking her? She could see nothing but inky blackness.

Suddenly a wagon appeared. She sucked in a sharp breath.

It was piled high with sun-bleached bones.

Harper slammed her against the side, making the bones rattle. "Got a special place for you." He ripped off the medicine bag from around her neck. "You won't need that, squaw. This is your grave. You'll slowly starve until your bones will blend with the buffaloes'."

Rayna lifted her chin. "I'm not frightened of death or *you*."

Fury twisted his ugly face. A sweep of his arms sent the bones on top tumbling to the ground. Next he hit her, sending her backward. Reaching down the side of the wagon, he brought out a pistol. "I'll shoot you if you run. Not in the heart. I'll shoot your damn knees."

She watched in mounting horror as he removed enough bones to create a small hollow. Then, stuffing a gag into her mouth, he lifted her, struggling, into the grave and piled the heavy bones on top of her before she could break free. They jabbed into and around her, the weight making it difficult to breathe. Pinning her in place.

Trapped. She was trapped here, surrounded by a cage of bones, where she would surely die.

Bracing against the fear that chilled her through and through, Rayna closed her eyes and whispered, "We almost made it, Brett. We almost had our dream."

&

The evening shadows had grown long by the time Brett woke. Movement at his elbow startled him. His hand stole to his knife, and he had the weapon halfway out of its sheath before he recognized Cooper.

"Good, you're awake." Cooper leaned over him. "Rand and I are about to leave for your neighbor's ranch."

"Not without me." As Brett sat up, pain knifed his chest and shoulder, and he sucked in a breath. "I am dead serious about that, Brother."

"Figured as much. That's why I'm here. How do you feel?"

"Won't lie. Feels like a wild stallion stomped on me then turned around and invited his whole family to join him." Brett got to his feet, along with Cooper. "I can do the job though. Rayna is the most important person to me. I love her, Coop."

"I know. I'm happy for you, little brother. We're going to get her back. Tonight." The shadows didn't hide the hardness in Cooper's eyes.

"I won't come home without her again." Brett stepped through the opening, and Cooper followed.

Rand stood beside the fire, stirring something.

He glanced up. "Fixed you some supper, little brother. Not gonna argue about it. Eat and we'll ride. Don't eat, and we'll tie you up and leave without you."

"You know what, Rand? You have a sorry attitude," Brett said, taking a seat beside him. He would've said a lot more, but he saw his horse saddled and waiting with the others.

He filled a plate with beans and potatoes and sat down next to Adam. While the men ate, they formed a plan, leaving no margin for error. They'd tie up the horses in the deep shadows of the trees, and then all three would slip through the brush to the clearing. Brett and Cooper would make their way to the barn. Rand would stay near in case they needed him, either to help fight or lend a hand with Rayna and the men after they rescued them.

"It's good," Rand said. "We'll make it work. What do you think about a few of the ranch hands lighting a bonfire in the corner of the property to draw some of the riffraff from across the way?"

Cooper frowned. "That would make it easier for us, but wouldn't that just draw them over here? If they attacked, we wouldn't have anyone much here to defend the women and children. Do we really want to risk that?"

"One man could do it, then ride back here," Adam said quietly. "I will do it."

The fire crackled and popped as Brett weighed the pros and cons. Finally, he spoke. "No. It's too dangerous. I think it's better not to prod them. We'll manage."

"She's family," Adam said quietly. "Bring her home."

How true. She was from the first time he laid eyes on her and she'd snuck into his heart.

Brett took Adam aside and squeezed his shoulder. "I want you to watch over the children. I know you won't let me down."

His nephew's Adam's apple bobbed when he swallowed. "Yes, sir. I'll see to it, but I wish I was going with you."

"I know, but I need you here more." Brett's gaze scanned the land he loved. "In case I don't make it back, the Wild Horse is yours. I've seen how much this place means to you, and you'll cherish it as I do."

The tremble of Adam's bottom lip gave him away, as did the fact that he had to clear his throat before he could speak. "You're coming back, ain't you? I don't know enough yet."

"Neither did I at first. You'll learn. I'm proud of you, son. If I could have a boy, I'd want him to be just like you."

"Uncle Brett, I never told you how glad I am we came here and how much your patience meant. No one treated me like a man before or took time to show me things. I'm sure you wanted to wring my neck though." Adam gave a strangled laugh.

"True, but I saw that you were worth every second spent. I don't regret a thing."

"Me neither."

From the corner of his eye, Brett noticed Cooper and Rand moving toward six horses—one for each plus three for Rayna and the men. Grim-faced ranch hands gathered around. Each man carried a rifle in the crook of his elbow. Each one would give his all. They were as tough a bunch as Brett had seen.

He told them that he'd be ready in five minutes and strode a few yards toward the corral. Relying on some instinct that his proud ancestors had passed down in their blood, he raised both arms toward the sky, even though his right arm pulled his wound, causing him to suck in a breath against the blinding pain.

With his eyes closed and head tilted back, he called on the spirits to surround and protect. He asked for their wisdom, guidance, and help in freeing Rayna and the men.

He knew all eyes were on him and the ranch hands probably thought him strange, but it didn't matter. His heart told him this was important.

Before he moved back to them, he opened his eyes and drew his leather medicine pouch over his head, holding it out away from him. "Great Spirit, please see fit to let me return. If it's not to be, allow my spirit to remain here on this land where the horses roam free and the sky meets the earth."

Kissing the sacred bag that contained his power and courage, he returned it to his neck. He embraced the strong feeling of peace surrounding him as he joined the others.

His heart spoke the words that filled his head. *Rayna, I'm coming for you.*

◈

A black canopy had dropped over the countryside by the time Brett and his brothers crossed onto Dowlen's land from the road.

They tied their horses in a thick grove of oak and elm. Brett felt satisfied they'd hidden the animals well and far enough away in case they nickered. Giving the mounts one last look and issuing his brothers a warning not to make noise, Brett led his brothers' painstaking advance.

Each step meant carefully lifting their heels and placing them down no more than six inches ahead. Time passed slowly as they crept closer. Sweat rose on his forehead and covered his palms. He stood to lose so much.

An hour must've passed before they heard the first low murmur of voices. Flickering light from a campfire glimmered through the brush. Brett held up his arm, signaling for Cooper and Rand to stop.

He listened to the men complain that they didn't have any liquor. Seemed their employer had confiscated all their whiskey. Brett grinned. A sad state of affairs for sure.

They proceeded with even more caution and began a path around the disgruntled group.

Brett froze at the snapping of a twig that echoed in the darkness like the crack of a gunshot. One bead of sweat broke away from the others and trickled toward his eye. Barely moving a muscle, he brushed it away.

"What's that?" One of the men by the campfire jerked to his feet. "I heard something."

"For God's sake, George, sit down," another said. "You're awful jumpy. It was probably a fox creepin' around in the woods. Can't be anything else but a varmint out here. That Indian an' his brothers ain't gonna be messin' with the new boss man."

"Probably right. Be damn fools if they did." The man named George sat down. "He'll give 'em a taste of how it feels to lose everything—just like we did to the damn Comanche."

A third spoke up, "Where the hell did those damn soldiers come from? We had 'em whipped until they showed up. Thought I wouldn't get out alive. I ain't gonna fight a bunch of soldiers. How did the breed get 'em here?"

"Don't know. Maybe he used one of those magic chants or something," George said.

"Well, I ain't gonna mess with the U.S. Army. No way."

A grin curved Brett's lips. Sounded like Edgar Dowlen and Oldham had a mutiny on their hands. They waited until the grumblers settled back by the fire before resuming their mission. They couldn't afford to make another mistake.

Their inch by inch progress measured a slow passage of time. When they reached the edge of the clearing, the moon was high overhead.

In front of them was a large corral that had to hold at least fifty or sixty horses. Though definitely less than before, tents formed a circle around the enclosure.

It appeared the enemy forces had seen a slight shrinkage but still outnumbered them significantly.

Brett stared at that corral, his brain working. If only he could creep over to it and let the animals out. That would give them the advantage.

Only the open ground had no place to hide. Not so much as a bush or wagon. That, plus the dozens of men milling around the horse pen, made him scrap the plan. He lay in the tall grass on his stomach, his attention shifting to the dark barn. The guards in front of the structure seemed to indicate Rayna was probably inside. Her presence washed over him. His blood pounded in his ears, drowning out everything else. He needed to, or he'd make a fatal mistake.

Knowing she was somewhere nearby played havoc with his mental state.

Soon, he promised. Soon he'd free her.

But the lever of a rifle above him, ratcheting a bullet into the chamber, froze his blood.

Thirty-five

"GET UP SLOW AN' KEEP YOUR HANDS WHERE I CAN SEE 'em," a man barked.

Brett recognized that voice. This wasn't a drunk. He turned.

Oldham.

With slow movements, Brett and his brothers stood.

"Toss the rifles," the ex-lawman ordered.

Cooper laid his rifle on the ground beside Brett's and Rand's and drawled, "Our paths sure do seem to keep crossing."

Oldham glared. "You put a kink in my plans before, but this time I've got the upper hand, Thorne."

"I wouldn't be too sure of that."

"By rights I could shoot all three of you. You're trespassing."

A distraction would sure come in handy. Brett caught Rand's attention with a faint motion of his head.

A second later, Rand began coughing, lightly at first, then doubling over with the effort. With the show his brother put on, he needed to be onstage.

The minute Oldham focused on Rand, Brett slid

his knife from the sheath in one smooth sweep while the other hand grabbed the rotten sheriff around the neck. The sudden movement sent sharp waves of agony through Brett's shoulder and chest.

Fighting back a wave of nausea, Brett anchored Oldham tightly against him and pressed the knife to his throat. "One sound and you're dead."

"You won't get away with this. I reckon you came after your dirty squaw. You won't find her."

"We'll see." Brett increased the pressure of the knife, drawing blood. "I said no talking."

Cooper quickly took possession of the rifle and the Colt in the holster. "Nice work."

"Rand deserves a pat on the back. That was some performance. Anyone happen to bring some rope?" Brett whispered, forcing their prisoner into the dense brush.

Their middle brother pulled a good-sized length from inside his shirt. "I thought this might come in handy."

"Great." Cooper took it and bound Oldham's hands behind his back while Rand removed the bandanna from his neck and tied it around their captive's mouth.

Once they had him secured and hidden, Cooper delivered a blow to the back of his head with one of the Colts. The man slumped over. Brett returned his bowie knife to its sheath.

This was twice they'd escaped in one night. He knew they might not be so lucky again. Luck ran out eventually.

And when it did…

He tried to push that thought out of his mind as he slowed his breathing and settled back into the grass, watching, waiting. So far no one seemed to have heard them.

The two guards patrolling the dark barn walked back and forth in front of the entrance. One stopped to light a cigarette, and the pinpoint of light gave Brett hope that they were too busy seeing to their own cravings to pay attention.

"What do you think?" Cooper asked low, lying next to him.

"We can use the brush as cover, work our way around until we're dead even, then rush the two guards and knock them out." Brett prayed it would be as easy as it sounded.

"I agree."

Rand dropped down on his belly next to them. "I noticed some hounds over by the house in the shadows. Looks to be about three or four. How are you going to keep them from sounding the alarm?"

Brett mentally kicked himself. He should've seen those dogs. What was the matter with him, and what else had he missed? The pain and fear had dulled his brain.

"Wish we had a hunk of meat or a juicy bone." Cooper propped himself on his elbows. "But since we don't, we have to come up with something, or we'll be up a creek as soon as we move toward the barn."

One thing about it, Brett wasn't going to leave without Rayna. He didn't care how many obstacles stood in his way.

After carefully studying the situation for a good

five minutes, Brett spoke. "I'll draw them out and get them barking their fool heads off. Whoever checks on the pack won't find anything. Then as soon as they stop barking, I'll do it over and over until no one will pay them any mind, and the men will stop coming to find out the cause of the ruckus."

"Damn, Brett, you have quite a devious mind," Rand said.

"Thanks. But there is one flaw. What if they don't stay next to the house? What if they come sniffing around over here?"

"Maybe they're tied up," Rand said hopefully. "Only one way to find out."

Cooper frowned. "Little brother, any ideas about how to get the mutts to bark?"

"Might. Got some string?"

"Now do we look like we carry string around everyplace we go?" Rand whispered furiously.

"Guess that leaves rocks," Brett declared. "I'll move closer and pitch some in their direction. Coop, if it works, meet me by the barn."

"Might not hurt to check on Oldham." Rand rolled to a sitting position. "I'll tie him to a tree and conk him on the head again to make sure he stays out. Might knock some sense into him too."

"Be careful, Brett," Cooper said low.

Brett nodded and melted into the darkness. He silently moved from tree to tree, and it didn't take long to reach the hounds. He scoured the ground for pebbles and found some nice ones. Drawing back, he let one fly and it landed perfectly about a yard on the other side of the dogs.

They set up some furious barking, straining on their ropes. Brett grinned and shrank into the shadows.

A rifle-toting, whiskered man flew from the house, searching for the cause. He hollered to the guards in front of the barn, asking if they'd seen anything. When they said no, he shook his head and went back inside, muttering something about crazy, worthless hounds and the moon.

Again and again, Brett made them bark until finally, the rifle-toter got disgusted and moved them around to the back of the house.

The plan worked.

Brett met Cooper deep in the shadows of the barn and quietly advanced on the two guards. Striking them sharply on the back of the head, they dragged them into the brush.

Brett cautiously led the way into the barn in case Dowlen had posted more guards inside. But they encountered no problems.

…until he discovered Rayna wasn't with the ranch hands.

Fear of what might've happened to her left deep ruts inside. Removing the gag from Joe's mouth, Brett learned that a man had come and taken Rayna. Joe didn't know where though.

"She was real brave. Fought like a wildcat," Joe said and gave Brett her message.

A muscle quivered in Brett's jaw as he tried to control the flood of emotion. He'd tear the place up looking for her.

"There's something else," Joe said, telling them about the fight between Dowlen and Oldham and that Oldham was now in charge.

"Not anymore." Brett told him Oldham was tied up. "Maybe this will end now."

Cooper's care in helping his men up came as no surprise. Brett knew they meant much more to his brother than hired ranch hands. They were family, just like Rayna was his. The way Cooper's arm slid around Charles's badly injured body, gripping him tightly, said everything.

"Can you get them back to Rand and then to the horses by yourself?" Brett asked.

"I can walk under my own power, boss," Joe insisted.

"Good." Cooper turned to Brett. "You go find Rayna. We'll be fine. Wish I could stay to help, but all hell may break loose here in a minute. If you're not at the Wild Horse in a few hours, I'm coming back."

Brett gave a curt nod, then Cooper moved toward the door, half carrying Charles. Brett followed them into the inky blackness, his mind already working on finding Rayna.

Mindful of the dogs, he snuck to all the outbuildings and peered inside.

When he didn't find her, he glanced toward the two-story house, wondering if they could have her inside. His mind went to places that he'd rather not go, but one thing for sure, he wouldn't put anything past his enemy.

The minutes ticked loudly in Brett's head as he stood there, stumped. The longer he spent on the property, the riskier it was. He turned to retrace his steps when he spied a wagon.

The hair rose on the back of his neck.

Bones, piled high, glistened in the moonlight with

an unearthly glow. Some had spilled on the ground, and the sloppy pile stood higher on one side. A sixth sense urged him forward. As he approached, he heard a muffled moan.

Down at his feet lay Rayna's medicine bag. The long, narrow strap had been cut.

"Rayna, it's me," he whispered, picking up the soft pouch and sticking it inside his shirt. "I'll have you out in a minute."

One by one, Brett silently lifted the bones, placing them on the ground. At last he saw some blue fabric.

Removing a few more bones, he saw her—his Wish Book woman.

His hands shook as he placed his arms under her legs and freed her from her chilling prison. Cradling her against him, he held her for a long moment before setting her down and removing the gag from her mouth.

"You came," she said low. "Raymond Harper promised a slow, painful death by starvation."

"That's not going to happen." He couldn't resist her moist lips. Giving her a quick kiss, he asked, "How did Harper come to be here?"

Rayna clung tightly to him. "I'm not sure, but he's thrown in with them."

"Doesn't surprise me. Are you able to walk?"

"Yes. How far to the horses?"

"A ways. If you can't make it, I can carry you."

With an emphatic shake of her head, she said, "I don't know how you're standing. I'm sure you hurt something awful. I can make it."

He put his arm around her anyway, and they hurried toward the trees and safety.

Before they reached the cool, dark shadows of the woods, a voice behind said, "Not so fast, breed. You ain't goin' nowhere."

Raymond Harper.

Brett turned and stared into the glistening eyes that bore so much hatred. Harper pointed a pistol at his heart.

It had been a trap, and Brett had fallen into it. "I don't think you're going to stop me from taking back my woman."

"Your filthy squaw, you mean. She ain't nothing but a lazy, stinkin' whore." Harper held a jug of whiskey in his free hand.

The words Brett had tried to shield her from brought rage. "I'll cut your tongue out before this is over and feed it to you. I'm taking her far away from you."

"Try it an' you'll die."

"Reckon it's a good night for it. I'll happily risk my life, do anything, to set Rayna free." Anger so deep and bitter rose until he tasted it on his tongue. Brett had never felt such hatred for anyone, but this shook him all the way to his toes.

A distance of about three feet stood between them. He took a moment to inhale a calming breath against the pain that would surely come. Marshaling every bit of strength in his body, he leaped and delivered a powerful kick to the black-hearted bone-picker's midsection. The whiskey jug flew from his hand.

Harper went down to his knees but got up quickly, fumbling for the gun that had slipped from his grasp.

Having lost the weapon in the darkness, he dropped his head and charged.

Brett was ready, and when the man reached him, he sidestepped and gripped his opponent under his right armpit. Again, using all his remaining strength, Brett slung him over his shoulder.

The sharp cry when Harper slammed into the ground brought his men running.

Desperate for any leverage Brett could use, and knowing he was out of time, he grabbed his enemy's shirt, heaved him to his feet, and pressed his knife to his throat.

"Stay back or he dies," Brett ordered. "I won't hesitate to slice his gizzard out."

"Do as he says. He'll kill me." Harper's pleas stopped the group's advance.

For now anyway.

Rayna clutched Brett from behind, letting him know she was out of immediate danger. Slowly he backed into the woods, using the bone-picker as a shield. "You're coming with us, and then I'm turning you over to the law."

"We'll put you an' every one of your kind into the ground before the next nightfall," Harper vowed.

"When hell freezes over." The brittle hardness of Brett's reply must've gotten his hostage's attention, because he lapsed into silence.

Or it could've been the increased pressure of the keen edge of the knife blade.

Though Brett had always embraced peace and harmony, he'd once killed a man, Tolbert Early, to protect Cooper's life. The violent rage building inside him again threatened to explode.

It wouldn't be difficult at all to end Raymond Harper's miserable existence.

Rayna must've sensed that. She placed her hand over the one holding the knife. "Not this way, Brett. That's not who you are."

Thirty-six

THE EDGES OF DAWN, REMINDING BRETT OF A FRAYED pair of lacy curtains at Mabel's Boardinghouse, spread across the sky as he rode onto the Wild Horse. Looking ready to collapse, Raymond Harper staggered behind, tethered to him by a rope.

Alongside on her gray mare, Lady Pearl, Rayna maneuvered closer and laid her hand on Brett's. "I knew you'd come. I'm glad you brought me home."

Home. There was that word again. They were both home.

"Don't you know my heart isn't happy unless you're near? It beats only for you, my Wish Book woman."

"I'm not something out of reach now. You have me."

The streaks of dirt amid the bruises on her cheeks, and her ripped dress, told of what she'd endured, but she had never been more beautiful or desirable. He was about to lean over and whisper sweet nothings in her ear when Cooper and Rand galloped toward them.

"Got a present for you, Coop," Brett said, handing him the rope tied around Harper's chest.

Cooper grinned. "Don't know how you managed this, but glad you did. Oldham got away, the weasel. He'll be disoriented, so it'll take some time before he can find his way back to camp, but he'll sure be rallying his men when he gets there. We need to be ready."

Harper snarled and bragged, "Won't be here long. Those men are coming, an' we'll take pleasure in killin' all of you. We'll start with the snot-nosed brats first."

"Don't we have a good ant bed we can stake him out in?" Rand asked. "Be a pure shame not to."

In a sudden move, Cooper's buckskin leaped forward into a jog before he could settle him down, forcing the bone-picker to run to keep from being dragged. It appeared to take the bluster out of him.

Brett hurried to catch up to his brothers. They had more plans to make.

His neighbor and Oldham had taken people's fear of ones like him, like Adam, like the orphans, and whipped their jitters into a frenzy until Brett was certain the whole lot would stop at nothing to wipe them from the earth. At first glance, he couldn't see how to survive. He just knew it would take every bit of their strength and will to defeat the foe.

Somehow, someway they would, because they had to. The choice wasn't theirs.

❧

As soon as Cooper tied Harper to a stout tree and gagged him, each man filled their bellies. Afterward, Rayna checked Brett's wound and changed the bandage, her gentle touch seeping into his soul where his deep love for her dwelt.

He closed his eyes, loving the feel of her hands on his skin. He wished for time to make love to her, but there wasn't any—only a moment to bring her hand to his lips, where he pressed a kiss. Releasing her, he brushed his fingertips across her face and down her throat, wanting to prolong the sound of the wild beating of her heart.

Once she declared him in good shape, Brett called all the men around the campfire.

"They're coming," he said, "and it's not going to be easy."

Rand shook his head. "This is going to be a final, winner-take-all battle. How are we going to defend these orphans? I won't let anything happen to them, however we have to do it."

"We have to take them somewhere." Cooper's face had set in deep lines, giving evidence of the toll. "Any suggestions?"

"The box canyon." Brett stared toward the place that might provide a haven. A couple of men posted at the entrance that measured only four horses wide could hold off an army.

Adam spoke quietly. "If you don't mind, Uncle Brett, I'd like that job."

"It's yours. I know you'll guard them with your life." Brett stared at the boy who'd grown into a man in front of his eyes. He'd never felt such pride in anyone.

Cooper seemed in deep thought. "Since the wagon's busted, horseback is the only way of getting them there."

"With three kids on each horse, plus the two women, it'll take about ten or so." Brett stared toward the grazing mustangs and Thoroughbreds. Some had yet to be gentled; still, he felt confident he could pick out a dozen. "It's the only way."

"I agree." Cooper leaned forward on the log seat. "Once we have them to safety, how will we defend this place against a blistering attack? We lost Gabe Booker, and three more are wounded. We're down to ten. On the ground, they'll pick us off like sitting ducks."

Brett grinned. "Then we'll go up. Into the trees."

Rand slapped Brett on the back. "You should be a general. Are you sure you're not kin to one of the great Indian chiefs?"

"Maybe one." Sarah had told him their grandfather was a chief. Brett wished he'd asked his name. "Their numbers are large, and after they know to look up, they'll shoot us out of the trees."

Brett had always wondered what it would feel like when his time was up. He was about to find out. So were the others. He searched each face but found no wavering in the men staring back at him. Their grim features said more than words.

"We'll hold off firing until a big group rides in," Cooper said. "When they don't see anyone, they'll relax, thinking we've lit out of here. Brett can give us a birdcall when it's time to let loose. The element of surprise will give us the advantage. I like it." Cooper stood. "We'd best get the children heading toward the canyon."

Once Brett told Rayna the plan and asked her to get the little ones ready, he and Adam went to get enough bridles for a dozen horses. Adam's long gait matched him stride for stride, and when they began picking out the gentlest of the herd, Adam instinctively knew which ones would be easiest to ride.

His nephew was a natural. The Wild Horse was in his blood.

"What?" Adam asked when he glanced up and caught Brett staring.

"I never told you I love you. But I do."

"I feel the same, Uncle. But why now?"

Brett shrugged. "Seems a good time. May not get another chance, and I don't want to leave this world without saying it."

He took a piece of leather from inside his trouser pocket. "I've been meaning to give you this. You may need it."

Adam unwound the strip holding the pouch closed then grinned, slipping it over his dark head. "A medicine bag like yours."

"You're a man, and a man needs his power. I put some sage, a piece of flint, and a stone I once found that's in the shape of a half-moon inside. You can add to those."

"I'll never take it off. Thank you."

Before Adam turned away, Brett saw him blink hard to get rid of the tears in his eyes.

After that they worked silently, each focused on the task.

Once they had bridles on the horses, Rand led them to the edge of the tree line, where the frightened orphans waited. Brett noticed some were crying when he brought the last two horses.

Flower sobbed. "Why do people hate?"

He knelt down, wiped her tears, and put his arms around her. "I wish I knew. There's nothing to worry about, honey. In no time, we'll bring you back here, and everything will be all right. No more running or hiding, I promise. Try to be real brave." Picking her up, he sat her on the bare back of a sorrel mare behind an older child, and handed one of the cats up to her. "Can you take good care of your friend?"

"I will," she said, sniffling.

Soon all had mounted except Rayna. The dark bruise on her jaw added the only color to her pale face. She tried to still her quivering lips as she tilted her face for a kiss. He held her against his chest, feeling the frantic beating of her heart, and pressed his mouth firmly to hers. "You'll be fine. I won't let anything happen to you."

"But who's going to look after you?" she asked. "I should stay here and help fight. You can use the extra gun."

Brett brushed back her glorious hair. "The orphans' need is greater." Staring into her beautiful eyes, he moved on to something else he needed to wrap up. "This horse you're riding, Lady Pearl, is yours. She belongs to you now."

A little sob escaped. "This sounds like good-bye. I will die if I never see you again. Please tell me it's going to be all right."

If only he could.

He held her against him and spoke against her hair. "However this ends, just know that I love you with all that I am and all I will ever be. We are one heart, one body, one soul. You are as much my wife as if we saw a preacher. We said our vows in all the ways that matter." He wanted to say more, only his voice cracked. He cleared his throat, hoping the words he'd managed were enough. "Did you remember everything to take with you?"

Her blue-green eyes filled with tears. "Water, blankets, food, and my medicines." He cupped his hands to form a step, and she mounted. "Come get us the minute this is over."

"If I am able." And then if the light hadn't gone from his eyes, he'd take her to their special place and fill her with his love, so she would have no doubts about how much he cherished each second spent with her.

He moved to the horse Adam was riding with little Joseph. "Take good care of them. Let Cooper's man, Fletcher, lead, and you stay behind the children so you can help if they need it."

"I will. Don't worry about us," Adam said. "Take care of yourself and the Wild Horse."

"Now get going. I have lots to do."

The minute the line of horses began to move, Brett turned his attention to the rest of the plan, aware that Raymond Harper watched everything they did. Being gagged, he couldn't alert anyone, but to make sure, they moved him out of sight, deeper into the woods.

They had barely gathered all the ammunition and positioned themselves in the trees when thundering hooves shattered the silence. If Brett had been standing, he'd have felt the trembling ground.

Hidden by the green canopy, he took a deep breath, tightening his grip on the rifle.

Dust rose around the horses' feet in great billows with the first wave of probably two dozen whooping riders filled with bloodlust.

Brett and the others held their fire, watching and waiting.

When the riders didn't see anyone and weren't met with gunfire, they stopped, perplexed. The horses danced in circles while they yelled to one another.

The second wave brought another dozen or so, men they must've pulled from blockading the road.

Men and horses swarmed over his beloved land, trampling everything he'd built. The land that represented all his hopes and dreams was defiled by hate and prejudice.

It was time. Be it good or ill, it would end here today.

This was their chance to stand up for those who couldn't fend for themselves. Time to put evil men where they belonged.

Sweat coated Brett's palms as he cupped his hands and sounded the birdcall.

Firing began simultaneously, and bullets rained down on the army of attackers.

In the confusion below, a dozen riders plunged to the ground, their lifeless bodies lying like sticks of cordwood tossed by the wind.

But once they figured out the blasts came from above, they began shooting into the trees.

Bullets whizzed by Brett's body. Some found only air, while others split the branches.

Somehow in the midst of the chaos, Brett spotted

Raymond Harper running from the woods, yelling to the men. How he'd gotten free was beyond him. But then, rats always gnawed their way out.

Helpless terror gripped him as Harper jumped onto a horse, and with Oldham, raced toward the canyon with five of their fighters.

Brett's gut churned with the need to go after them, though he knew he'd be cut down the minute he climbed from the tree. All he could do was to keep firing and pray that Adam and Fletcher could hold off the onslaught riding their way.

Rayna's beautiful eyes brimming with tears as she'd said good-bye filled his mind.

He had to get to her. He was willing to risk anything.

Below, he made out the form of Edgar Dowlen, and watched him ride closer. So much for bowing out of the fight. It made what he had to do easier. No matter what, he had to have that horse.

When he had Dowlen clearly in his sights, he squeezed the trigger.

But instead of a rifle blast that would've sent the scum to the hereafter, nothing happened. No shot, no scream. Dowlen didn't fall, writhing on the ground. Nothing.

The rifle had no more bullets.

Pulling his Colt from the holster, he fired…and missed when the horse made a sudden move.

Dowlen glanced up and sent a ball of orange flame into the tree, the metal grazing Brett's leg.

Stinging pain tore through him, but he gritted his teeth and again drew a bead on the man who'd started all of this. But before he could press the trigger,

Dowlen fired a shot that struck the Colt, knocking it from his hand.

Perched on a branch, Brett did the only thing he could. He jumped. He landed on Dowlen, and the momentum carried both to the ground. He got to his feet first, dragging the man upright by the front of his shirt. Around them, rifles blasted as men yelled. Dragging smoke-filled air into his lungs, he slammed a fist into the man's pockmarked face with all the force he could muster.

Though Brett stood three inches taller, he discovered he'd underestimated his scrappy opponent. Edgar wasn't afraid to use his fists. He delivered a blow to Brett's jaw, followed by one to his gut, and the pain took his breath.

"Got you now, breed," Dowlen gloated. "Best stay down."

"I never give up," Brett shouted, shaking his head to clear it. A glance around gave him strength. His Winchester must've fallen from the tree and lay no more than two feet away.

With a rolling twist, he grabbed the rifle and stood. Drawing back, he swung and caught the man's midsection. Dowlen screamed and went down, but he didn't stay. With blood streaming from his mouth, he staggered to his feet, trying to reach a riderless mount. He managed to stick a foot in the stirrup.

In the midst of rearing, terrified horses, Brett lunged and caught his ankle, pulling him down. He crawled on top and tightened his hands around Dowlen's throat.

"You're done with this madness. I'm going to make

sure you don't strike fear in any more children if it's the last thing I do." The force driving him to end the man's life rose up so powerfully his arms shook.

While Brett fought the urge to make Dowlen pay for all he'd done, his attention swept to a new influx of riders.

Fresh despair and hopelessness washed over him as they swarmed onto the Wild Horse, followed by careening wagons and buggies.

To his surprise, the new bunch began shooting at Dowlen's men. A closer look revealed familiar faces— the people of Battle Creek.

Astride a roan, looking like an avenging queen, sat Sarah, sending a barrage of bullets at the invaders.

Rifle fire stopped as Dowlen's recruits turned, raising their hands in surrender.

He didn't have time to waste. Brett released his adversary and flung himself onto the nearest horse, spurring the animal into a gallop.

Though the Thoroughbred gobbled up ground, it seemed to take forever to reach the canyon. With each pounding hoof, the harder his heart beat in his chest. Desperate to save the ones he loved, he urged the animal faster until it had no more to give.

Gunfire sounded as he neared.

The lathered horse's sides heaved in and out like the bellows of a blacksmith by the time he dismounted a short distance from the canyon's opening. He had no weapons except his knife, clearly a disadvantage in that it required close contact. But he loved the familiar feel of it in his hand as he quickly took cover in the thick brush.

The bowie knife would not misfire or aim crooked.

For a long heartbeat, he assessed the situation, figuring out each of the enemy's location.

Finally, he began to move.

Within a few yards of the first shooter, he became aware of someone behind him.

He silently whirled with the knife raised, then relaxed when he stared into the hard lines of Cooper's face.

"If you'll take this man, I'll move to the next," Brett whispered.

"I brought rope."

"Good. We'll need it. Ready?"

At Cooper's nod, they crept forward on the balls of their feet. Cooper clamped his hand over the shooter's mouth and dragged him toward the horses.

Brett took the next man, striking the back of his head with the hilt of the knife, knocking him out. Knowing Cooper would tie him up, he left him where he lay and pressed ahead.

The firing continued around him as he took out the next two in similar fashion. Eaten up with hate and so focused on winning, the men never knew what hit them.

Only Oldham turned a second before Brett got into position. Fury raged in the former lawman's face and glowed in his dark eyes as if they were red-hot coals.

"What does it take to kill you, half-breed?"

"More than you and all your men together have. I promise you that." Brett readied for the fight, taking in the gun that Oldham leveled at his heart.

In a whirling motion, Brett knocked the weapon away and sent it flying into the vegetation. Then the kick of a moccasin met with the hard muscle of Oldham's chest. He grunted and staggered backward, but the rocky wall kept him from falling. He picked up a piece of wood and came at Brett again.

A searching glance located a similar weapon. Brett grabbed it and held it in front of him, looking for an opening. They sparred, slamming wood against wood, the sound echoing off the rocks. Finally, Brett struck Oldham's weapon with such force it splintered both pieces of wood.

Empty-handed, his adversary gave a guttural bellow and swung.

With a last burst of agility, Brett grabbed him under the arm and slung him against the rocks.

The man doubled over, struggling to breathe.

Confident the fight was over, Brett turned to pick up his knife that had fallen in the scuffle. In the next moment, he heard a loud grunt as Oldham's shoulder plowed into him and sent him facedown onto the rocky terrain.

Shards of pain ripped through him, and he felt a sticky warmth soaking his shirt. The fight must've started his wound bleeding. The taste of blood filled the inside of his mouth and covered his tongue.

He had to finish this soon, or he'd be too weak.

Jerking to his feet, Brett braced himself against the throbbing agony and drove a fist into Oldham's jaw. Even though his enemy's head snapped back, he wasn't done for.

Slamming Brett to the ground with his beefy hands, Oldham jumped on his stomach with his boots. The air left him with a whoosh.

Out of air. Depleted of strength. He had no more tricks.

"I got you now, savage," Oldham cried.

Using his last bit of energy, Brett managed to grab one of Oldham's legs. Gritting his teeth, he yanked it out from under him. When the man tumbled to the floor of the canyon, Brett crawled on top. Putting one arm under Oldham's leg, he drew it up to his chest, pinning him.

Stay down, he willed.

Suddenly, he realized the shooting had stopped.

In the silence, he heard a child's cries. Had one of the attackers shot Adam and Fletcher and gotten through?

"Adam, are you all right?" he called.

The deafening silence echoed inside his head.

Thirty-seven

THE SINISTER MAN WHO DESPISED AND HATED WITH A vengeance spat in Brett's face, then threw back his head and roared with laughter.

"You just thought you won, *boy*. You're gonna pay. If we didn't kill that Injun nephew, he's too busy to answer. All it took was my man's quick thinking and one match. We planned somethin' different, but this is a whole bunch better. You ain't got much time, breed. Every last one of them murderin' Comanche are gonna blast into a million pieces." The bearded, middle-aged has-been smirked.

Brett's eyes narrowed to slits. He couldn't breathe past the intense pain and thunder of his heart. Whatever the heinous man had planned was too late to stop. "You just sealed your fate, Oldham. Whatever happens to them, I'll deliver to you tenfold."

As he got off and hauled the child killer to his feet, Cooper emerged between the rock walls. With a vicious yank, he twisted Oldham's arms behind his back and turned to Brett. "Maybe it's not too late. Go. Find out what he's done. You can still save them, Brother."

Without bothering to nod, Brett wiped the spittle off his face and raced to try to cheat death, scanning the ground, looking and listening for anything that was out of place.

A sizzling noise reached his ears a second before his eyes detected flames rushing along the ground.

Dynamite.

The man meant to blow up the canyon.

A scared yell came from beyond the rock. "Uncle Brett, I don't know what to do."

"Run, Adam! Get everyone as far back as you can, and take cover behind the rocks. They've planted dynamite in the canyon opening!"

Brett charged forward, pushing back the thin edge of fear driving into him.

He had to get there in time.

They couldn't die.

Evil would not win. He wouldn't let it.

The terrified faces of the children and his beloved Rayna swam in front of him.

The roar in Brett's ears magnified the hammering of his heart as he dropped to his knees amid the low brush, straining to see the fuse and where it led, hoping to snuff it out before it reached the dynamite. But when he finally located the fire, he saw it was racing too fast.

Sweat trickled down his face and into his eyes, blinding him. The rate at which the fire gobbled up the fuse told him they must've packed gunpowder around the string. He desperately clawed the ground, but all he found was black, twisted remains.

The only way to stop the detonation was to get ahead of the fuse.

Scrambling to his feet, he planted himself in the box canyon's opening, his frantic gaze searching for the explosives that would destroy everyone he loved.

Then he saw the dynamite wedged into a crevice of the limestone wall about six feet up. The bundle looked to contain at least ten sticks of destruction and raw power. He froze, watching the flame eating up the fuse at the rate of one inch per second.

His throat went dry. He was too far away. He couldn't get to it in time.

Like Oldham said, he was going to make them pay. Though Brett was going to lose his life as sure as he stood there, he prayed his Wish Book woman, his family, and the little orphans would by some miracle live.

Still, until the force killed him, he had a fighting chance. Life had taught him that.

Rocks peeled back the skin on his fingers in one last frenzied gamble to claw his way toward the dynamite.

Then Adam appeared in Brett's line of vision, straining for the explosives that were above his head in a crevice, just beyond his fingertips. Jumping, he kept trying to reach it.

The burning fuse grew shorter and shorter.

"Get back, Adam. Try to save yourself!" Brett yelled.

"No," Adam insisted. "I can get it. I have to."

The fuse had only a few inches left.

The chilling sizzle of the flame of destruction drowned out everything. Consuming. Devouring. Marching to its destination.

Within a second another inch was gone. Two inches remained.

Brett braced himself for the deadly force of the explosion that would hurtle him into the hereafter. But his thoughts were not for himself. Cold fear for Adam clamped around his throat, strangling him.

The boy who became a man would never know how it felt to kiss a girl for the first time, fall in love… or discover pieces of himself in the eyes of a beautiful lady as Brett had done.

He couldn't see through the curtain of blinding anguish.

One more second ticked by. Now the flame was out of sight, too short to see next to the deadly bundle.

He kept moving forward as fast as he could, praying for a miracle.

A half second before the flame set off the explosion, Adam grabbed the fuse, ripping it away.

Giving a cry, he sank weakly to the canyon floor. The brave new warrior had managed the impossible.

Rushing forward, Brett lifted him up. Laughing in breathless relief, he clasped Adam to his chest. "You did it! I don't know how, but you saved everyone. I'm so proud of you, proud we have the same blood."

Adam grinned. "I had to. I couldn't let them kill these orphans. I didn't care if I died saving them. Uncle Brett, they killed Fletcher."

Pain of the loss pierced him. The ranch hand had given his life on account of him, loyal to the very end. "He was a good friend of Cooper's, and I'll miss him."

Adam suddenly gripped his arm. "I know there's one more attacker here somewhere. I lost him in the scramble for the dynamite. Miss Rayna, the children—"

"Rayna!" Brett's moccasins skimmed over the rocky terrain.

Rayna threw herself in front of the children, bracing for whatever came next, trying to shield their eyes from Fletcher's body that lay a few yards away, and the killer who stepped over him.

"This time you got no one to save you." Raymond Harper tossed his empty gun aside and advanced toward her, his deranged eyes glassy with bloodlust. "I wanted to make this last, to hear you beg for your life as it slowly drained from you. But this will have to satisfy. At least I'll enjoy my hands tightenin' around your pretty throat an' feel you slip away."

Chilling as the words were, concern for Adam swept through her. Maybe Raymond Harper killed him too. Grabbing a thick piece of wood, she tried to block out the sound of the crying little ones.

Inhaling a deep breath, she edged forward to meet him.

No more cowering.

No more trembling in fear.

No more looking over her shoulder.

Calm purpose rippled through her. This would be a fight to the death. One of them would not walk out.

Then, through the thick rock around her, came the blessed sound of voices—Adam and Brett. They would take care of the children if the crazed bone-picker won. With that worry gone, she steeled herself for what she must do.

Raising her club, she swung, barely catching the side of Harper's head when he swiveled. He grabbed for her weapon, but she was too quick.

A cruel, twisted smile formed on his lips. "You're draggin' this out just the way I dreamed, girl."

"Help is coming. They're going to cheat you out of your pleasure."

"They'll never get here in time."

Rayna tried to slow her pounding heart, to not miss even the slightest opportunity. "I don't need them. I will do the job. You're not going to win here. I'll make sure of it."

When he lunged for her, she struck him, this time landing a solid blow to the chest. He staggered back in disbelief.

"That's right. I'm not scared of you anymore. You have no hold over me. I'm already the victor." Rayna filled her lungs with air, shaking off the remaining bonds that had held her captive.

With an enraged roar, he flung himself at her. She tried to leap away but wasn't fast enough. He grabbed her, throwing her to the ground like a sack of meal. She landed hard, next to Fletcher's lifeless body. Dazed, with the breath knocked out of her, she couldn't move. Her stick of wood lay several feet away. Before she could tell her body to scramble for it, Harper was on top of her.

The grimy hands that had dealt so much death and misery closed around her throat. Rayna gasped for air as she struck him with her fists.

Screams of the orphans filled her ears. She hated they had to witness this violence. At least Brett was near and would stop Harper from doing them harm once he'd killed her.

In a flurry, two of the children crawled onto Harper's back and began pounding him with their fists.

He hollered and removed his hands from her neck for only a moment to toss them like rag dolls. Rayna's heart broke. They lay so still and quiet. But she couldn't help them, because Raymond's hands returned even as she lashed out, and this time with an even more vicious grip.

Stars filled her eyes as the edges of her vision turned black. Her lungs cried for air.

In one last desperate moment before death claimed her, she groped for whatever she could find that might aid her. Feeling along, her fingers encountered hard metal and realized it was Fletcher's gun.

Gripping it tightly, she jabbed the weapon under Raymond Harper's chin, forcing his head back. His eyes widened, and he suddenly found it hard to swallow. He removed his hands from her throat, and she gasped, gulping in huge amounts of air.

"This is for my mother and father. For Elna and all the others you probably killed."

"You won't pull that trigger," he gloated. "You don't have it in you."

Boots pounded the rocky ground then stopped. She didn't glance up. Her eyes remained locked on the cruel face before her.

Calm washed over Rayna as her finger tightened on the slender piece of metal.

❧

Brett stared transfixed at the scene, knowing Rayna needed this moment of victory to heal old wounds. No one needed killing more than Raymond Harper. But he thought of her words to him when he'd fought the overwhelming urge to do the same after he'd rescued her from the wagon of bones.

He stole forward on the balls of his feet and lightly placed his hand over hers. "This isn't who you are, who we are. I don't want you to add new scars to your soul."

Hardness dulled her eyes. "He deserves it."

"Yes, worse than anyone I've ever seen," he agreed, taking the gun from her. "But seeing him hang will bring immense satisfaction. Justice will prevail, and you won't have to live with the horror of dispensing it."

Bob had been right. The greatest glory wasn't in killing your opponent, but getting close enough to touch him and steal his power. With a gentle hand, Brett lifted her up and pulled her against him.

Adam, Cooper, and Rand rushed forward to take charge of the prisoner.

Brett held her near, feeling her heart beating next to his. The terror of almost losing her wouldn't go away.

When she tilted her head back, he cradled her face between his hands and claimed her mouth with a slow, drugging kiss that he could probably make last until the first frost.

He had no wish to hurry. They had plenty of time. The reign of terror was over.

It was only the slight jerk of a hand on his trousers that broke the kiss. He glanced down into Flower's small face.

"Thank you for saving us, Ahpu."

He didn't know what she'd just called him, but he knew it was something good. Kneeling, he pulled her onto his knee "You're welcome, but it took everyone, most of all Miss Rayna. You're free now. No more bad people. They're gone."

Picking her up, Brett put his arm around Rayna. "Let's go home."

"Wait!" Rayna tugged free and bent to pick up the feather that had dropped from his hat. "Not a barb out of place. A good omen," she said with her slow, sweet smile.

After all this, who was he to say that it wasn't?

❧

Brett hardly recognized the camp when they rode up. It more resembled an army fort, minus the barracks. People and horses were everywhere. He particularly noticed the groups of men who were tied up and guarded by some of Battle Creek's finest.

George Lexington, proprietor of the Lexington Arms Hotel, approached as Brett dismounted and helped Rayna down. "Might near took every bit of blamed rope in the state, but we got 'em all tied up and ready for Sheriff Thorne."

"You have my thanks." Brett put his arm around Rayna's waist and stared grief-stricken at the pile of dead who'd lost their lives fighting for the wrong side. Such a waste. They could've done so much good if they'd put their efforts into something worthwhile.

A second later, Potter Gray strode up as though he was a soldier reporting to a superior. "We'll take the dead into town for burial. You'll soon put this place back to rights."

"I'm very grateful for your help, but how and why did you men decide to jump into this fight now?"

Joining them, Doc Yates answered, "Your sister can take a lot of the credit for that. After she told everyone about the desperation out here and your neighbor's vow to eradicate the orphans, a plan came together. The next thing I knew, the whole town was riding out here with blood boiling and guns blazing, even the women."

Mabel King broke in, "What do you mean, Doc? We were leading the march."

"That's right," Jenny Barclay said. "We weren't going to stand by and let innocent children die, no matter what color they are. Some are about my son Ben's age."

"Our women's club, the Women of Vision, has decided to build an orphanage in Battle Creek for these kids, and we've asked your sister Sarah to run it," Mabel said.

Brett's chest tightened. This was the acceptance they needed. These generous people would welcome the Comanche orphans into their hearts. He had to clear his throat before speaking. "That's nice, ladies— real nice."

Rayna glanced up, her eyes glistening brightly. "Oh, Brett. This is what we've dreamed of, what we've waited for. Change is happening."

"Yes, it is." If there hadn't been so many children and people milling about, he'd have kissed those moist lips that beckoned him.

It appeared everything was going to work out just fine.

At the sound of a galloping horse, Brett turned, tightening his arm around Rayna. Seeing the Indian rider aroused curiosity. Flower gave a happy squeal and ran to him. The Comanche grinned, scooping up the little girl.

Striding forward, the man stuck out his hand. "Are you Brett Liberty?"

"I am. Flower seems very happy to see you. Are you from her tribe?"

"Her brother. I am John Little Hawk. We got separated after a fire, and I have been looking everywhere for her. I heard news of an orphan train this way. What has happened?" John glanced around at the bedlam.

"Just settled a dispute over the children, but they're safe. I assume you'll take Flower home with you?"

"Yes. We are all each other has now."

John Abercrombie, the mercantile owner, put his arm around Brett's shoulder. "We'd be pleased to throw you two a big shindig to show our appreciation for standing up for right and justice, even if you did have to do it mostly alone."

Rayna smiled and looked up at Brett, clutching his hand. "Maybe later. We have a ranch to put back together, and children to tend until the orphanage gets built. And of course, some quiet time will help heal the pain of what we endured."

Her blue-green eyes held a secret message, and Brett couldn't wait to get her alone, because he had secrets of his own that he yearned to tell.

ᴄ∕ᴏ

Rayna couldn't wait to find the peace in their private paradise, to lie in the circle of Brett's strong arms, but so much had to be done. First, though, she insisted he let Doc examine his wounds and treat the horrible burn left by cauterization. She'd almost fainted when she'd seen the blood soaking his shirt and realized how hard he'd fought to save them, despite his immense pain.

Relief had filled her after Doc Yates removed burnt, dead tissue from the wound and smeared it good with antiseptic, then asked her to put on a fresh bandage.

Still, the hideous burn left by the heated knife told of Brett's agony. She couldn't imagine enduring that. A lump formed in her throat. He'd done it for her. So he could come save her.

Lazy afternoon clouds drifted overhead by the time Rayna took Brett's hand and issued a silent invitation.

Hunger simmered in his dark eyes as his arm slid around her waist, allowing her to lead him to their sanctuary. Her heart burst with so much joy at how things had turned out.

Her skirts swished against his moccasins. "A thrilling moment happened when Cooper took Raymond Harper into town to stand trial."

"When I ran into that canyon and saw you sitting on him, threatening to shoot his head off, I froze. I just knew he'd wrench that gun away from you, so I stood ready to rush forward if he did. But then I saw you had firm control of the situation, and my heart burst with pride. You're a fighter, darlin'. It's one of the million and one reasons I fell in love with you." His hold on her tightened.

"You gave me strength to fight him. And then when I yearned to kill him so badly I could taste it, I let you have the gun. You're right. He's nothing—just a bug to be squashed. I'm free."

"You certainly are, although I can't take any credit. You're an amazing woman. I noticed that when I first saw you between the bars of that jail cell."

They went around the limestone rocks into their place of beauty and light. With the gentle splash of the waterfall behind them, Rayna slid her hand around his neck and leaned into him, pressing her lips to his.

Brett spoke when they broke for air. "You don't have to worry about whether or not you have his last name."

"But I do. I refuse to be Rayna Harper."

"Not gonna have to." His grin made his dark eyes twinkle. "Because, my darlin' Rayna, it'll be Liberty. Rayna Liberty, will you marry me?"

"Oh, Brett." Rayna swallowed a happy cry and threw her arms around him. "Are you sure it's time?"

"It is. There will always be people against me…us, but we're accepted by the ones who count, and that's enough. I won't be apart another second."

"My heart is going to explode. Yes, yes, I'll be your wife." Rayna chewed her bottom lip, wondering if it was too soon to ask for another piece of her dream. "Can we adopt one of the orphans?"

"However many your heart wants. The Wild Horse has plenty of room."

"Maybe Joseph. That little boy has pain in his eyes." She felt like climbing on a horse and riding through Battle Creek, screaming at the top of her lungs that she was marrying Brett. But first they had other pleasurable things to do.

Yanking his shirt over his head, she ran her hands across his broad chest, avoiding the fresh bandage. With a tug of the leather strip that held back his midnight hair, she buried her hands in the long strands and pressed her lips to his.

They parted only to remove bothersome clothes. Before long they stood bare, surrounded by the peaceful beauty of their private sanctuary, while little cheeps sounded from the nest beside the waterfall.

"Your poor body. It's taken much abuse." She kissed the wound on his back then pressed her lips gently to the gauze on his chest.

"I'll heal," he rasped. "You suffered just as much."

Rayna laughed. "I'll heal. I'm serious though about not wanting to cause you more pain. Just hold me in your arms for now."

"No way, lady." Passion glittered in Brett's dark eyes.

"Are you sure?" Rayna traced the lines of his kissable mouth. "We don't have to do more."

"I have to have you, and that's that."

Next to the banks of the pool of crystal blue water, Rayna lay down and pulled him beside her. "Make love to me, Brett. I need you."

He grinned. "Now there's a request I can't refuse."

His hands moved over her skin like gentle, soothing waves upon a shore, washing away everything except their love that would remain until the end of time.

Soon his lips replaced those magic fingers and left a trail of kisses over her flesh, hitching her breath and filling her with a prayer that this would last forever.

Brett nibbled, teased, and flicked his way slowly down her body until every nerve begged for release, and though he kept that cresting wave just out of reach, it only made her hunger for him more.

Lying next to him, she trailed her fingers across the contours of his lean body that could bring so much pleasure. The depth of her love made her tremble. She loved Brett Liberty with every ounce of her being. He was all she'd ever dreamed of during those dark, scary times when all seemed hopeless.

He no longer straddled two worlds. He was in the only one that mattered—hers.

"Thank you, Brett," she murmured. "Thank you for loving me."

In a sudden move, he wrapped his arms around her and pulled her on top of him. Staring down into his eyes that spoke of his love for her, she lowered her mouth and tasted his need.

Finally, raising her head, Rayna trembled with hunger as she ran her tongue across his brown nipples, watching his eyes darken with desire. She liked looking down and seeing all the emotions that crossed his face instead of simply sensing them.

That each one spoke of his pleasure at being with her made her the happiest woman alive.

They'd come close to never having this again. Maybe it was that fact that made Rayna feel deeper and love harder. Maybe it was the same for Brett too. Their breathing became ragged and loud as they took pleasure in giving and taking.

At last he shuddered with longing. Positioning her on him, she took him into her body. Wondrous heat consumed her, sweeping her up in a raging fire that made another second unbearable.

She sucked in a breath as he captured an aching breast and sent her soaring into the sky.

With Brett's uneven breath on her cheek, she found heaven and danced amongst the clouds as he joined her.

Later, Rayna lay facing him, slowing the beat of her racing heart. She didn't need diamonds or pearls or some great treasure. Simple things had the deepest value.

Just strong arms around her, bracing her, and feeling the steady beat of his heart, assuring her that he cherished his Wish Book woman.

He smoothed back the curls from her face and met her eyes. She saw happiness and pride in his gaze.

"I love you, Rayna Liberty," he murmured against her temple. "I will always wake beside you and hold you when happiness and sorrow come. We're one, and nothing or no one will ever separate us."

Rayna beamed through happy tears. "I love you, my darling Brett. I want to marry here on our beloved Wild Horse. Where the sky meets the earth is the perfect place to vow to forever be your Texas bride. And afterward, we can escape to our sanctuary."

A smile teased her lips as she reached for the feather on his hat.

Epilogue

Three months later

"BRETT, HONEY, DID YOU LOAD EVERYTHING IN THE wagon?" Rayna slipped her arms around his waist from behind and rested her face on his broad back. His earthy scent that reminded her of this wild Texas land swirled around her. "We don't want to be late for the dedication. I'm so excited that the orphans will finally have a permanent place to live, where they can run and play to their hearts' content."

He slowly turned in that deliberate way of his. His smile and the love shining in his eyes made her pulse race. He lifted a curl and gave her a kiss.

"With every single hand in Battle Creek that could hold a hammer, we built the orphanage in record time. I have everything you laid out already in the wagon, along with Joseph, and Adam is waiting to drive us."

Brett finally seemed at total peace, his smile coming easily. He knelt in front of her on the rug in their tepee and kissed her belly that was just beginning to round.

Rayna cherished the new life growing inside her, the product of their immeasurable love. She couldn't wait to hold the babe in her arms and touch the tiny face.

For some reason, she knew it would be a boy—a son who could learn the ways of his father and take over the Wild Horse one day along with Adam. They would shower their babe with love. Never would he know the heartbreak and sorrow they had.

She ran her fingers through Brett's long black hair that he hadn't yet pulled back with a leather strip. Her heart burst with happiness. "I love you, Brett."

"I never would've guessed." His eyes twinkled when he rose. "I think you kept the horses awake last night. You've gotten very vocal, my wife, when we make love."

"Me?" Rayna sputtered. "And whose fault is that, I wonder?"

He tugged her flush against him and kissed her so long she ran out of air. Finally, she stepped out of his arms.

"We'll have to continue this later. At our waterfall. Where the horses won't hear me."

"I can't wait. Our love does seem to be the noisy kind." Brett lifted her hand to his mouth. "You're all I ever wanted. My love for you is eternal and as broad as this Texas sky."

❧

It seemed everyone for miles had come to Battle Creek for the dedication and official opening of the Isaac Daffern Orphanage.

After everyone arrived, Cooper stepped on a raised

platform. "Thank you all for coming, and for your hard work in making this a reality."

"I'm sending you a bill for my broken thumb," a man yelled from the crowd.

"Send it on," Cooper said amid laughter. "It'll be the best money I ever spent. I know you're all wondering about the name we decided on. Without Isaac Daffern, Rand, Brett, and I wouldn't be here. We'd never have come to Battle Creek or made our home here. Isaac took us in after we escaped a nightmare, and molded us into the men we are today. I know he's smiling down, proud of what we accomplished. This is a great day for these children, who have lost everyone they loved. They don't have to worry about being mistreated." He paused, glaring into the sea of raised faces. "Anyone who lays a hand on them will answer to me, and I can guarantee my punishment will be swift and harsh."

"Three cheers for Sheriff Thorne and the Isaac Daffern Orphanage!" someone yelled.

Cooper waited until the hoopla had died down. "That's another thing. Two weeks from now, I'll no longer hold this office. You'll all get to welcome a new sheriff, and I'll get to devote my time to ranching."

"Who's the new sheriff?" John Abercrombie, the mercantile owner asked.

"Someone you all know and respect. He was Sheriff Strayhorn's deputy, Charlie Winters. He's moving back to Battle Creek and settling down. Wants to raise a family here. Now everyone get some refreshment and something from the table of goodies the women have brought." Cooper stepped off the platform to thunderous applause.

Delta handed him a cup of punch. "You make a good speech, my darling husband. Ever thought about being a politician?"

"Nope. I don't want to be anything except your husband and a father to our kids." Cooper took in her upswept golden hair that left the enticing curve of her neck bare. For two cents he'd scoop her up and carry her to a private place where he could nuzzle that neck and take the pins from her hair. He never tired of making love to her, even after two babies and countless nights in each other's arms. He glanced at the quilt under the shade of a tree where the twins lay sleeping, watched over by Ben Barclay—who took his job very seriously—and inhaled the breath of a satisfied man.

Around them, Comanche orphans ran and played with the sons and daughters of Battle Creek's families. Two colors with no separation between them.

His attention shifted to Brett's nephew, Adam, who sat with a pretty young girl, holding her hand. The kid was gone, and in his place stood a man. Cooper saw blossoming love written on his face. He suspected the two would someday tie the knot and start a new chapter in Battle Creek history.

Mabel King approached and spoke low to Delta about some slight problem. Delta gave her husband a kiss and went to fix whatever had put a fly in the ointment.

Cooper gulped down his punch and strode to where his brothers stood by the refreshment table. Rand had stuffed his mouth with a pastry of some kind. Cooper grinned. Typical. But he wouldn't change his brother for all the tea in China.

"Good speech," Brett said. "Truer words were never spoken. Glad to hear about the new sheriff."

"Yeah," Rand said. "Who's he marrying?"

Cooper's gaze found her talking to their wives. "Jenny Barclay."

"You don't say!" Rand grinned. "Good for her. She's earned some happiness after suffering through Hogue Barclay's beatings. But last I heard she's already married."

"A bounty hunter came through here a month ago with Hogue's body tied across his horse. Seems Hogue found his spot in hell when the bounty hunter caught up with the outlaw he was after." Cooper pushed back his hat. "Ben will have a good father in Charlie."

With her hand at the crook of Tom Mason's elbow, Abigail Sinclair sauntered over. "The town has thrown a nice party."

Rand wiped crumbs from his mouth and kissed his mother's cheek. After spending so many years apart and thinking she'd thrown him away, he'd finally made his peace with the woman who'd given him life. It was nice having her close and seeing her happy. "Hello, Mother. Is there a reason you're smiling so big?"

Abigail's eyes met Tom's. "We're going to be married in two weeks."

"You don't say!" Rand kissed her cheek again and shook Mason's hand. "A toast will be in order as soon as I find something to drink."

Once all three brothers gave the happy couple best wishes, they dodged excited children and sauntered to the wide porch of the two-story orphanage. They took a seat and propped up their feet, gazing out over the gathering.

Rand leaned back with a long sigh. "We didn't do too bad for three ragged boys who pricked our thumbs by the light of the moon and declared ourselves brothers. We each chose beautiful wives who love us and gave us families of our own. I don't know about you, but I couldn't fit another bit of happiness inside. Callie told me she's in the family way two days ago. My first created with our love."

Brett grinned. "Must be something in the water. Rayna and I too have happy news. Maybe your child and mine will grow up together."

"Congratulations to both of you." Cooper shook their hands. "We rode through hell, and at times I wouldn't have given you a plug nickel for our chances. But we came out the other side. A little bruised and battered, but in one piece."

"Problems aren't over because we whipped some evil men who wanted us dead," Brett said quietly. "Trouble will come again, because that's the nature of life. But so will plenty of happy times. Life is like a river—the current ebbs and flows as it goes along its path."

Cooper nodded. His eyes followed Delta as she took her new sister, Rayna, under her wing. Callie glowed and happily lent assistance. Though all three women were beautiful, he had eyes only for Delta as they weaved amongst the people of Battle Creek, laughing and talking and having a grand time. She was his world. His beginning and end and everything in between.

A glance at Rand and Brett found them equally occupied.

"You know," Cooper said, "we've done real fine and have more good fortune than any man has a right to."

Rand's eyes moved from Callie to his children. Toby and Mariah each held Wren's hand and were helping her walk. Cooper's heart swelled out of his chest, the way he knew his brother's was. Those children had been through so much.

Brett was quiet for a long while. Finally he spoke. "The influence of our journeys, along with our hopes and our dreams, will carry on in our children and to their children, for generations to come in ways we can't possibly know. We're giving them a rich legacy. They'll do us proud."

Cooper swallowed hard, touched by the words.

"Damn, Brett," Rand said with a grin. "Rayna must be rubbing off on you. You're getting downright poetic. And you finally remembered you have a tongue."

"Maybe someday you'll forget yours," Brett said.

Cooper laughed. "We can only hope."

They jostled together, as playful for a moment as boys: three blood brothers with a shared dream of family, who once boarded an orphan train…and against all odds, finally found a place to belong.

Read on for a sneak peek from
To Love a Texas Ranger, *the first book in*
the brand-new Men of Legend series by Linda Broday

Central Texas, Early Spring 1876

A MONTH AFTER SAM ALMOST DIED, AN EAR-SPLITTING crash of thunder rattled the windows and each unpainted board of the J.R. Simmons Mercantile. The ominous skies burst and rain pelted the ground in great sheets.

A handful of people scattered like buckshot along the Waco boardwalk in an effort to escape the thorough drenching of a spring gully-washer.

Texas Ranger Sam Legend paid the rain no mind. The storm barely registered, as few thing did these days. He could still feel the rope around his neck. The feeling was so overpowering, he reached to see if it was there, thankful not to find it.

More dead than alive, he moved toward his destination. When he reached the alley separating the two sections of boardwalk, he collided with a woman covered in a hooded cloak.

"Apologies, ma'am." Sam stared into startling blue eyes.

She nodded and opened her mouth to speak. Before she could, a man took her arm and jerked her into the alleyway.

"Hey there! Ma'am, do you need help?" Sam called, startled.

He received no answer as her companion towed her toward a horse where a group of riders waited.

Intent on stopping whatever was happening, Sam hurried to question her. Mere steps away from the woman, he came up short when the men threw her onto a horse and rode away.

Sam stood in the driving rain, staring.

It had all happened so fast. Hell, maybe he imagined the whole thing. Maybe she never existed. Maybe the heavy downpour and gray gloom had messed with his mind...again. In fact, the longer he stood there, the more convinced he became that he had dreamed it all up. There was no sign that anyone had been there at all—just him, the rain, and his uncontrolled thoughts.

Ever since the hanging, he'd been seeing things that weren't there. Twice, he'd yanked a man around, grabbing his hand, thinking he saw a black widow tattooed between his thumb and forefinger. The last time almost got Sam shot.

Folks claimed he was missing the top rung of his ladder. Now his captain was sending him home to find it.

Cold fear washing over him had nothing to do with the air temperature or rain. What if he never recovered?

Some never did.

His hand clenched. He'd fight like hell to be the vital man he once was. He had things to do—an outlaw to hunt down, a wrong to right…a promise to keep.

Squaring his jaw, Sam drew his coat tight against the wet chill, forcing himself to move on down the street toward the face-to-face with Captain O'Reilly. It stuck in his craw that they thought him too crazed to do his job.

Sam Legend had become a liability to the other rangers, and that one fact was what convinced him he needed a break. His heart couldn't hurt any worse than if someone had stomped on it with a pair of hobnail boots. He was imagining threats everywhere now.

But one thing he knew he hadn't imagined was the blurred figure of Luke Weston standing over him when he regained consciousness that fateful day. No mistaking those green eyes above the mask. They belonged to the outlaw he'd chased for over a year. He'd stake his life on it. And yet fellow rangers who'd ridden up told Sam he'd been alone, lying on the ground with the rope still around his neck.

So what the hell had happened? How did he get down? Why had they left his horse behind?

Those questions and others haunted him, and he wouldn't rest until he got answers. Somehow he knew Weston held the answers.

At ranger headquarters, he took a deep breath before opening the door. He pushed a mite too hard, banging the knob against the wall.

Captain O'Reilly jerked up from his desk. "What the hell, Legend? Trying to wake the dead?"

"Sorry, Cap'n. It got away from me." It seemed a good many things had.

The tall, slender captain waved him to the chair. "I haven't heard this much racket since the shoot-out inside that silo with the Arnie brothers down in Sweetwater."

"I hope I can talk you out of your decision." Sam sat down.

O'Reilly sauntered to the potbellied stove in the corner and lifted the coffeepot. "What's it been? A month?"

"An eternity," Sam said quietly.

"Want a snort of coffee? Might improve your outlook."

"I'll take you up on your offer, but doubt it'll improve anything. I need this job, sir. I need to work."

"What you *need* is some time off to get your head on straight. I can't have you seeing things that aren't there." O'Reilly sighed. "You're gonna get yourself or someone else killed. I'm ordering you to go home for a while, then come back ready to catch outlaws."

"Catching Luke Weston is my first priority."

"That wily outlaw has been taunting you for years." O'Reilly's eyes hardened as he handed him a tin cup. "It seems personal."

"Hell yes, it's personal!"

Weston had been there with the rustlers. For all Sam knew, he'd helped somehow with the hanging. Why else would Sam have seen those green eyes that were burned into his memory?

In addition to that, and though it sounded rather trivial, a year ago Weston had taken his pocket watch during a stagecoach holdup where Sam tried to protect a payroll shipment. Odd thing though. The outlaw had only taken exactly one hundred dollars, a paltry sum, and left the passengers' belongings untouched.

But he *had* seemed to take particular delight in pocketing Sam's prized timepiece. Memories of how Weston flipped it open and stared at the inscription before tucking it away drifted through Sam's mind.

"Makes me mad enough to chew nails, him calling himself Luke Legend half the time. Next thing I know, he'll lay claim to being my damn brother." The thought filled Sam's head with so many cusswords he feared it would burst open.

The captain leaned back in his chair and propped his boots on the scarred desk that Noah must've brought over on the ark. "Sometimes we all get cases that sink their teeth into us and won't let go."

"I just about had him the last time." And now the captain was forcing him to take time off. Sam would lose every bit of ground he'd gained.

Reaching for a poster that lay atop a pile on his desk, Captain O'Reilly passed it Sam. "Got this yesterday."

Bold lettering at the top screamed: *WANTED! Luke Weston a.k.a. Luke Legend: $1,000 reward for capture and conviction.*

Below stated the crimes of robbery and murder.

The murder charge was new since the last poster Sam had seen with its two-hundred-dollar reward.

"Who did he kill?"

O'Reilly's face darkened. "Federal judge. Edgar Percival."

A jolt of surprise went through Sam. "Stands to reason Weston would turn to outright murder eventually. Seems every month he's involved in a gunfight with someone, though folks say all were men who needed killing."

Yet the new charge did shock Sam. He'd come to know Weston pretty well. A period of four months separated all the robberies with only one hundred dollars taken. And in each instance, Weston had never shot anyone.

"A bad seed." The ranger captain's chair squeaked when he leaned forward. "Some men are born killers."

The line at the bottom of the poster, also in heavy bold print, read: *Armed and Extremely Dangerous*.

As with all the others, it didn't bear a likeness, not even a crude drawing.

No physical features to go on.

Frustration boiled. Weston was *his* outlaw to catch. Instead he'd been ordered to go home.

Hell! Spending one week on the huge Lone Star Ranch was barely tolerable. A month would either kill him or he'd kill his big brother, Houston.

The thought had no more than formed before guilt pricked his conscience. In the final moments before the outlaw had hit his horse and left Sam dangling by his neck, regrets had filled his thoughts. He'd begged God for a second chance so he could make things right.

Now it looked like he'd get it. He'd make the time count. One thing Sam had learned—each day was precious and once it was gone there was no getting it back.

Despite their better qualities, his father had caused problems for him. He'd had to work harder, be quicker and tougher to prove to everyone his father hadn't bought his job.

Overcoming the big ranch, the money, and the

power the Legend name evoked had been a continuing struggle.

Captain O'Reilly opened his desk drawer, uncorked a bottle of whiskey, and gave his coffee a generous dousing. "Want to doctor your coffee, Sam?"

"Don't think it'll help," he replied with a tight smile.

"Suit yourself." The hardened ranger who bore a white scar on his cheek from a skirmish with the Comanche put the bottle away.

Although Sam had intended to keep quiet about the woman he'd maybe or maybe not bumped into on the way over, he felt it his duty to say something. "Cap'n, I saw something that keeps nagging. I collided with a young woman a few minutes ago, but before I could question her, a man grabbed her arm and pushed her into the alley between the mercantile and telegraph office. When I followed, they got on horses and rode off. Can you send someone to check it out?"

Doubts filled O'Reilly's eyes and Sam knew he wondered if this was another instance of his break with reality.

O'Reilly twirled his empty cup. "After the bank robbery a few weeks ago, we don't need more trouble. I'll look into it."

"Thanks. I hope it was nothing, but you never know." Relieved, Sam took a sip of coffee, wishing it would warm the cold deep in his bones.

"When's the train due to arrive, Legend?"

"Within the hour." Sam would obey his orders, but the second the month was up, he'd hit the ground running. He'd dog Luke Weston's trail until there wouldn't be a safe place in all of Texas to even get a slug of whiskey. He'd heard the gunslinging outlaw spent time down around Galveston and San Antone. That would be a good starting point, Sam reckoned.

O'Reilly removed his boots from the desk and sat up. "I seem to recall your family ranch being northwest of here on the Red River."

"That's right."

"Ever hear of Lost Point?"

Sam nodded. "The town is west of us. Pretty lawless place by all accounts."

"It's become a no-man's land. Outlaws moved in, lock, stock, and barrel. Nothing north of it but Indian Territory. Jonathan Doan is requesting a ranger to the area. Seems he's struggling to get a trading post going on the Red River just west of Lost Point and outlaws are threatening."

"I'll take a ride over there while I'm home. Weston would fit right in."

"No hurry. Give yourself a few weeks."

"Sure thing, Cap'n." The clock on the town square chimed the half hour, reminding him he'd best get moving. Relieved that O'Reilly had softened and allowed him to still work, Sam set down his cup. "Appears I've got a train to catch."

O'Reilly shook his hand. "Get well, Sam. You're a good lawman. Come back stronger than ever."

"I will, sir."

At the livery, Sam hired a boy to fetch his bags from the hotel and take them to the station.

After settling with the owner and collecting his buckskin gelding, Sam rode to meet the train. He shivered in the cold, steady downpour. The gloomy day reflected his mood as he moved toward an uncertain future.

Amid plumes of hissing white steam, the Houston and Texas Central Railway train pulled up next to the loading platform on time.

Sam quickly loaded Trooper into the livestock car and paid the boy for bringing his bags. After making sure the kerchief around his neck hid the scar, he swung aboard. Passengers had just started to enter so he had his pick of seats. He chose one two strides from the door. Shrugging from his coat, he sat down and got comfortable.

A movement across the narrow aisle a few minutes later drew his attention. A tall passenger wearing a low-slung gun belt slid into the seat.

Sam studied the black leather vest and frock coat of the same color.

Gunslinger, bounty hunter, or maybe a gambler?

Bounty hunter seemed far-fetched. He'd never seen one dressed in anything as fine. Such men wasted no time with fancy clothing.

Definitely a gunslinger. Few others tied their holster down to their leg. No one else required speed when drawing.

Likely a gambler too. Usually the two went hand in hand.

His skin spoke of Mexican descent, though judging by the shade, he had one white parent.

Lines around the traveler's mouth and a gray hair or two in his dark hair put him somewhere around the near side of thirty. Though he wore his black Stetson low on his forehead, he tugged it even lower as he settled back against the cushion.

The fine hairs on Sam's arm twitched. He knew this man.

But from where? For the life of him, he couldn't recall. He leaned over. "Pardon me, but have we met?"

Without meeting Sam's gaze, the man allowed a tight smile. "Nope."

Darn the hat that kept his eyes in dusky shadows. "Guess I made a mistake. I'm Sam Legend."

"Appears so, Ranger."

How did he know Sam was a ranger? He wore no badge. Perhaps he'd seen Sam leave O'Reilly office.

"My apologies," Sam mumbled.

The train engineer blew the whistle and the mighty iron wheels began to slowly turn.

Sam swung his attention back to the gunslinger, determined to make him talk. "Would you have the time, Mr…?" Sam asked.

"Andrew. Andrew Evan." The man flipped open his timepiece. "It's 10:45."

"Obliged." Finally a name. Not that it proved helpful. Sam was sure he'd left his real one at the Texas border as men with something to hide tended to do.

The longer he sat near Evan, the stronger the feeling of familiarity became. And that was something Sam's brain had not conjured up. He glanced out the window at the passing scenery, trying to make sense of the thoughts clunking around in his head.

As Sam turned back to stare at Evan's hands, searching for the tattoo, a woman rushed down the aisle. When she got even, the train took a curve and she tumbled headlong into his lap. He found himself holding soft, warm curves encased in dark wool.

Stark fear darkened the blue eyes staring up at him and her bottom lip quivered.

A jolt went through him. For a moment, he mistook her for Lucinda Howard, a woman who'd betrayed him. She had the same dark hair and blue eyes framed by thick, sooty lashes. His body responded against his will as he struggled with the memory. Hell!

At last, he realized she was not the faithless lover he'd once known. But she *was* the woman he'd collided with on his way to the ranger headquarters—and she was very real.

"Are you all right, miss?"

"I…I'm so sorry," she murmured.

Through the fabric of his shirt, he felt her icy hand splayed against his chest where it landed in breaking her fall.

"Are you in trouble? I can help."

"They're…I've got to—" The mystery woman pushed away, extricating herself from his lap. Then with a strangled sob, ran toward the door leading into the next car.

Sam looked down. Prickles rose on the back of his neck.

A bloody handprint stained his shirt.

About the Author

Linda Broday resides in the Panhandle of Texas on the Llano Estacado. At a young age, she discovered a love for storytelling, history, and anything pertaining to the Old West. There's something about Stetsons, boots, and tall rugged cowboys that get her fired up! A *New York Times* and *USA Today* bestselling author, Linda has won many awards, including the prestigious National Readers' Choice Award and the Texas Gold Award. Visit her at www.LindaBroday.com.